Getting ME Back

Getting ME Back

MG VILLESCA

GRELI PUBLISHING COMPANY

Library of Congress Cataloging-in-Publication Date

Villesca, MG

   Getting ME Back/ MG Villesca — 1st Ed.

      p.   cm.

Summary: While becoming involved with Victor, a guy who is controlling and becoming more aggressive with his demands, Linda finds that she is losing herself and has no way to stop it, but when her friends try to help her, his actions become deadly.

      ISBN-13: 978-0-9827098-5-6

      [1. Dating Violence---Fiction. 2. Mexican Americans---Fiction.

      3. High Schools---Fiction. 4. Interpersonal Relationships---Fiction.

            5. Identity---Fiction.]

LCCN   2010917468

[Fic]---dc22   CIP

Book Design Copyright © 2010 Raul Villesca

Edited by Stacy Kinney

To my wonderful daughters, Victoria and Isabella

May you love with all your heart

Prologue

I'm sweating. My hands, my feet—even parts of me that haven't seen sweat for years are sweating. I've been trying to get to my destination for the better part of two days. Even my cotton shirt is sticking to me. Can this be possible? Can a person sweat to death?

I shift my carry-on to the other shoulder. It's getting heavier by the minute.

Sitting in the Heathrow London airport terminal and waiting in the packed lobby area is not making things better. People stretch out on the floor with blankets, all trying to get a few hours of sleep.

Creeping up on three in the morning, the terminal is full. The snow advisories and the future weather forecasts don't look promising. I kind of hope I'll be unable to make this meeting. Secretly hope that I'll be stuck here for another two days.

It's ridiculous to be so nervous. I work for a successful marketing company now. I'm a woman of the world, a woman who has taken her life and steered it in the direction I want. I'm not that dumb little girl they thought they knew so well. I can think of only one reason I have been summoned here after all these years . . . summoned.

Yes, summoned is a good word for what he said. I wish I hadn't answered my cell phone two weeks ago. That call made my world crash from the perfect life I force myself to lead and turned me into this person who has a sheen on her upper lip.

Forced to wait in the airport terminal yet again because of delays, I can't help but wonder what this meeting means.

I haven't seen or heard from Jack in over five years, not since the accident.

Sure, I've heard bits of information here and there from people I've inadvertently bumped into over the years, but never a face-to-face meeting.

I'm not completely surprised. We all knew it would come to this.

I watch as a young child with pigtails passes by me with her arm comfortably attached to her mother. She's skipping along with a teddy bear in her arms while her mother rushes to get back the coveted spot in the back corner that they had to abandon for the restroom. The young girl has a smile on her lips while she hums "Old McDonald."

To be that free again...

How would that feel, not to have a worry in the world, not to worry where your next meal will come from, to feel comforted and hugged by your parents? But I know better; even young, seemingly innocent girls have things to worry about, to even fear at night. I know some monsters are real.

Shaking my head to clear the thoughts that are rampant in my mind and the strange growing lump in my throat, I think about the others and what they're doing. My return, no doubt, may not matter as much to them as it does to me.

I'm dressed inconspicuously in my worn-out jeans and cotton pink shirt. My hair is thrown as an afterthought into a ponytail. My reading glasses hang heavily on my chest. My tennis shoes have seen better days.

I'm excited to be going back to Texas. It is home and comfort.

I had been on the hunt for a new marketing customer in Europe when the phone call came. I had just come off an exhausting twelve hours of interviews and meetings. It had taken me three days to convince my staff that I had to get back to Texas by the end of the week. Even on the ride to the airport my assistant, Liz, who has loyally been with me for the past year, had tried everything in her retinue to keep me there.

"Can you not stay just till the end of next week?"

"Can't this wait? What's going on?'

"Can we expect you back soon? Why won't you tell me?"

"No," had been my only reply to the barrage of questions Liz had flung at me in the last two days. Only after seeing me actually board the plane had she been convinced.

I take out the diary I've kept with me over the last five years. I haven't read it since I shut it for the last time all those years ago. The memories are too painful. I have to force myself to read it now on the plane—I have to remember all those horrible yet wonderful memories, feelings, and torments. It's essential for me to remember since I'm going back.

On the intercom, a whiney, raspy female voice breaks into my thoughts and announces the boarding of my plane, and, with anxiety suddenly at its peak, I reluctantly move forward.

Chapter 1

It was raining that Sunday over five years ago in Fort Stockton. My idea to wash the car was swept away by the torrents of water sweeping down the hot streets. From my bedroom window, I glanced longingly at my new car in the driveway.

Well, I called the car new but really it was about eight years old and in need of a new paint job, but it was new to me and that was what mattered most. It was a "sort of" sixteenth birthday present from my father. The car was a blue two-door Honda Accord that had certainly seen better days. I knew the realities of our situation and I knew that my father couldn't really afford that car, but he had worked very hard for so many nights trying to earn enough money to get it for me.

And there it was, sitting in the driveway and calling to me for just one trip down "the drag" (as all the young people called Main Street that stretched about a mile and a half—the length of our small town).

But I still could not get myself to drive it down the drag regardless of the weather. I knew all of my friends (and many enemies) would be out driving back and forth with nothing to do but go around another empty lot.

My car was a stick shift and for all the practicing I had been doing over the past two weeks, mostly on the old country roads that lined the small town, I still could not take off without it dying at every stop.

I knew one stall in that car on the drag would mean certain death to my already troubled social life. Which is why I was sitting there in my room, staring out the window, and watching the rain hit the roof of my new car when my older sister came in looking for her favorite shirt.

Stomping her foot and pointing at me with her black painted nail, Meg accused, "Okay, what have you done with my pink shirt?"

"What pink shirt?" I asked. I feigned stupidity, which was not hard for me to do.

"You know damn well what shirt. I saw you wearing it the other night on the drag. You didn't know I saw you—but I did!" Meg yelled.

"I didn't take it. I've got pink shirts too," I lied.

Meg walked calmly to the side of my bed and poked one finger into my chest. "You find that shirt or I'll kick your ass." She accented every word with a stab of her finger.

"I'll tell Dad!" I yelled. I didn't want the argument to escalate because I wasn't in the mood.

Meg shoved me one last time and stomped out.

With a heavy sigh, I turned back towards my window. I never understood how we could be sisters. Meg is so different than me in so many ways. I'm light in complexion with dark hair and blue eyes. Meg is completely dark in comparison with her dark oval face and hair and green eyes. Meg was always stubborn, wild, and crazy, and I felt I was always calmer and more collected. She always seemed confident while I tended to be insecure of myself. The difference in us is outstanding even to me sometimes.

I used to sit in my room for hours and pretend that my long lost rich family was out there somewhere looking for me and they would come rescue me and take me away from this little town. I knew it was just a fantasy because I can't deny the fact that every time I see my mother's blue eyes and brown hair it is as if I were looking at myself. People have always said I'm just like her, but I always thought I was just like my dad, even though no one believed me.

My father.

I knew we were going through some tough times, could see it written on his face. I felt it every time I walked into a room where my parents were talking and the conversation would suddenly stop. He was a tough man, my father. He had been working since he was eight years old (so he said all the time) and has never stopped. He lost his job when the oil refinery closed its doors, not because of a lack of oil but because of the downsizing in oil refineries in the nation. He was a foreman and was extremely good at his job. And it had closed its doors—just like that.

Jobs were hard to come by for a man who had dropped out of high school in the ninth grade. It had been six months since the shutdown and still my father had bought me that car, which I still didn't know how to drive.

That pink shirt was Meg's favorite and I had ruined it the night before during a fight. I sighed heavily and leaned my forehead against the cool glass again, took out my pink diary, and began remembering what happened the night before.

Dear Diary,

I totally got in a fight last night. It went down something like this:

We were at that large clearing everyone likes to call Knots Landing; I'm not sure why it's called that, it's just a patch of land with two perpendicular paved roads on the outskirts of town.

Knots Landing is a few miles south of the city limits. Very secluded and very much a part of the town where the cops (and especially parents) never come. The town lights could be seen clearly from where we stood.

Anyway, I was staring at those lights wondering how I had gotten myself into this situation. But after walking away twice on two separate occasions, I had to do something . . . it was getting out of hand.

She had called me a bitch again. She was laughing at me as she was surrounded by her friends.

Jack had tried talking me out of it and I should have listened. He told both of us to calm down several times as loud as he could and even offered to take me to another party.

We had no idea she was going to be out there; she just drove up with one of Jack's distant friends, Rodney. Jack kept telling me to just walk away.

She threw a beer bottle at me (which missed but I still got beer all over my hair and shirt).

I really had no choice — Jean and her big mouth.

So I squared my shoulders, turned around, and landed the first punch on her mouth. "It was a big mouth," I remember thinking as I swung away. I landed punches where I wanted them with only a small bit of resistance, or so I thought.

I could hear some chants and screams in the distance, but wasn't paying much attention. When Jack and two others finally stopped us, I couldn't quite get a grip on my shaking hands and racing heart.

Jack just grabbed my shoulders and told me he would take me home.

I glanced back at Jean and saw a huge clump of hair in her hands. I didn't feel that.

I sighed louder this time and looked out at the relentless rain coming down. How I got myself into those kinds of situations, I still wasn't sure. I knew Jean really hated me and knew that the guys were laughing at me—just another catfight, another story to talk about and exaggerate in this small town for at least a week until something better comes along.

I was slightly embarrassed; I knew this would get back to my father. Things always got back to him. He would just shake his head or put his head down, meaning I had disappointed him again.

But at that moment, it had just seemed like the right thing to do. I had taken a good look at Jean as her friends led her away and knew that she would have at least one good black-eye. I walked away with my sister's shirt torn at the sleeve.

I looked away from the window to take a quick glance at the secret wall compartment I had inside of my closet. That poor pink shirt was in there. I'd have to find a way to throw it away without Meg finding out.

I took another quick glance around my room. It was definitely a girl's room: pink, with all the trimmings and beads on the lamps and doorways, and everything pastel and frilly.

My track and cheerleading trophies littered the walls, collecting dust.

Again, a complete contrast to the black and purple Megadeath collection in Meg's room.

Fighting and skipping school was something my sister did on a regular basis and our parents would never bat an eye; however, if I got into a fight—there would be hell to pay when Dad found out.

But I knew that if anything good came out of yesterday, it was the four friends I had acquired through Jack Santiago. All of them were guys. I was okay with that; I seemed to get along better with guys anyway.

They were part of the crowd in high school that is easily overlooked; that is to say none were the school jocks and none of them were in the nerd group. And I was surprised I had so much fun with them.

Jack had invited me to a party in the outskirts of town about two weeks before. Surprisingly to both of us, I said yes and the camaraderie between us was easy and platonic. So after he saved me from making more of a fool of myself in the situation with Jean, we all went to Omar's house and met up with the others.

In Omar's small house near the city swimming pool, I met Lucas Casadena, the complete drama-king and loud jokester of the bunch, Omar Martinez, the smart philosophical one, and David Jallos, the infamous liar.

I was able to size them up quickly. They were all so loud and eager to be heard. They saw me, I think, as a welcome addition.

All in all, it was quite an interesting group of guys that saved me from becoming too depressed. I was totally looking forward to seeing them again on the weekend.

I knew hiding out in my room was not going to solve any of my problems. So with another quick sigh, I opened the secret door and slid the torn pink shirt into my jacket. I was going out to try and conquer my car and dispose of Meg's shirt in the process. Hoping no one would be out in the rain, I headed for the door.

Chapter 2

Somehow I had made it to the country roads outside of town. It had taken me ten minutes which was horrible because we only lived a quarter mile from where I was idled.

"Okay Linda, you can do this," I whispered to myself.

I was attempting to use the stick shift for the hundredth time. I lifted my foot off the break and slowly released the clutch while pushing the gas. The car sputtered twice, jolted me back and forth, and with a final whine died.

I had been at this for over an hour with no improvement. I was so frustrated that I hardly noticed the beautiful landscape with its sharp plateaus and mesquite bushes lining the road.

The rain had made small pockets of water on the dirt and the smell of wet rock permeated the air. I loved that smell after the rain. "Dammit!" I yelled at the top of my lungs.

I just couldn't get it right. I was never going to be able to drive this car in town. Once again I had used the country roads for just this purpose.

How could someone create a car that is so hard to drive? Maybe it was intended to be like this, maybe the car manufacturers were conspiring against me to make my already difficult life hell. Maybe it was the damn heat that was making me crazy.

A loud honk startled me from my thoughts and I was relieved to see Jack getting out of his green Chevy truck. He looked like a typical Texas cowboy. He had on his tight worn-out Wranglers and shiny boots. His light brown hair, square chin, and light green eyes fit him perfectly.

About a foot taller than average, he was muscular and

had a typical jock body but refused to play anything athletic even though he stayed in perfect shape.

For some reason he refused to wear a cowboy hat, something that would probably have come in handy with the drizzle that was once again coming down.

I think someone once told me that his real name was Juaquin, but anyone who wanted to keep their limbs intact wouldn't call him by his given name. I don't know how Jack came out of Juaquin, but I wasn't about to ask, not yet anyway.

"Hey! I knew I could find you here," Jack said as he approached the car. "Still trying to learn to drive that thing?"

"Yes, and I can't seem to get the hang of it. I've tried for two weeks and still it dies on me when I take off. I know it's gonna die on me on the drag—in front of everybody."

"You worry too much about what others think. You're trying too hard."

"Well, I just don't want anything else to embarrass me. I had enough of that last night," I complained. I put my head down on the steering wheel.

"Which reminds me," Jack said. "How are you today? Still depressed?"

"What do you think? I know it's just a matter of time before my dad finds out. Not to mention my sister. She's just gonna be mad that I didn't include her in the fight."

"Yeah I can see that about her," Jack laughed.

"So what brings you out to the middle of nowhere? Rescuing a damsel in distress?"

"Just came by to tell you we're getting together at my house. It's just the guys; we're gonna watch a movie."

"What movie?" I asked.

"Does it matter?" He smiled, "I think a funny one. I haven't gone to get one yet. So, I'll pick you up later?"

"What, you don't think I can get there on my own?"

Jack laughed walking back to his truck. "Not in one piece." The deep sounds of the motor made me think of a monster truck rally. He drove up to my window and shouted, "Don't stay out here too late. It's not safe."

Remembering Meg's pink torn shirt, I handed it to Jack.

"Can you get rid of this for me? It's Meg's and well . . ."

Jack threw his head back laughing. "You want me to do your dirty work?"

I nodded. He took the shirt, and drove off.

I looked around at the desolate roads and realized just how alone I was. I wasn't scared. Roads here are seldom traveled and I knew all the back roads in the area—that was, if I could just take off in the car when I needed to.

I sat in my car for awhile giving myself a good pep talk. I could do this. The only one holding me to these country roads was me. I started the car and tried again.

* * *

Jack's house is like a historical monument. It has three levels and is made of stone. His parents began building it twenty years ago and kept adding rooms that make the house seem strange and unorganized. The inside of the house, however, is a different story. His mother loves to shop at antique stores in Mexico City. Every room attests to this with every hardwood and ornate furniture piece in the rooms. The house is five miles outside of the city limits and sits on a small hill with a steep incline in the backyard. His family owns a Mexican restaurant in town and it seems to do quite well.

Entering the house and walking through it is like going into a maze. There's no conventional flow to the place. The kitchen is located in the middle of the house and is completely open to the rest of the house. In all of my visits, I have never seen the entire house.

I was sitting in the living area that we used all the time and had my mouth full of popcorn when David and Omar came strolling in.

"Hey," I said.

Omar smiled, "So, you have come to bless our humble companionship. I hope we will not bore you needlessly."

Omar loved to speak as if he were in the ancient Renaissance period. It was one of the things I liked the most about him. Behind him, Jack and David rolled their eyes, causing me to try hard not to laugh out.

Instead I said, "Why of course. My presence will liven things up and keep you civilized."

With all of them laughing now, Lucas entered the room. "Okay, what the hell did I miss? Hey Linda, great left-hook! Saw Jean's eye today. I'm surprised she came out at all."

And with those few words, he thoroughly crushed my spirits.

But Jack, who could not bear to see me so suddenly crushed, began throwing popcorn at Lucas. He yelled, "You can be such an ass sometimes, Lucas!"

Lucas gave an impish shrug and smiled with popcorn stuck in his teeth.

Comfy oversized green sofas surrounded the huge flat-screen television where we watched the movie. I relaxed on the larger sofa.

After the first ten minutes of the very boring film, I couldn't help but notice the quiet stares and awkward energy in the room. The guys hadn't said much of anything and they were talking to each other so that I couldn't hear what they were saying. This was not good.

"Okay what's wrong with you guys? Do you want me to leave?"

"NO!" they all cried in unison.

Suddenly worried, I asked, "What's wrong? You've been acting crazy."

"It's just that we're not used to having you around and don't know what to say that won't offend," Omar admitted.

I got up and started to walk out toward the door. "Well if you guys are gonna act like this, then I just won't come back!"

I was starting toward the door to grab my purse off of one of the mahogany tables when Lucas blocked my exit. "The hell with it. Did you see Rachel today? She had on a pink dress and I ain't shittin' you when I say that she had no bra on! They hung about to here." He said this as he raised his arms palm up on his stomach.

Rachel was an athletic sophomore on the swim team who loved teasing guys with her breasts. She loved them and wasn't afraid to show them off.

A still silence filled the room as they waited for my reaction. I turned to Lucas with a mischievous grin and said, "Lucas, Rachel never wears a bra after going swimming. Where have you been?"

They smiled to each other realizing that having a "girl friend" was going to have its advantages. They had gotten so used to each other that they treated each other like brothers, but having me around was definitely something different. They thought I was just going to hang out awhile and then go back to my stuck-up friends and forget about them (or so Jack told me later).

Omar rose from the floor and put his arm around me. "Let us venture out onto the drag. We can go park at the car wash and see who will grace us with their presence."

We piled into Jack's truck while Lucas followed in his little Pinto and met us in front of a furniture store. One great thing about this town is the drag where we can park in the empty lots.

Some other people began pulling up and before too long we had a pretty large group.

I loved it. I traveled from group to group to see what they were up to and what was going on and what the latest gossip was.

After I made my rounds and made my way back to Jack's truck, I got close to Omar and stopped. I heard my name several times, so I got close enough to hear what he was saying without being noticed.

I wasn't sure if I wanted to hear what they were saying. What had I done?

"I watched and weigh the fact that unknown to the others, we just let a girl be a part of our tight-knit group," Omar was saying to Jack in hushed tones.

"I knew it was inevitable for some girl to come in, but I honestly thought it would be a girl that one of us was dating. Linda is completely different than most other girls. She seems cool in our company and, best of all, I saw her the other day at the Town and Country and she said hi."

"So, she said hi to you, dude. Why's that important?" Jack asked.

"She treated me the same no matter who she was with." With a sigh, Omar said shrugging, "Maybe it's just a phase."

I walked behind him and pushed him with my hip. What they said was okay. Nothing too harsh but I couldn't understand why they thought I was just a phase. What did that mean?

* * *

We spent the next couple of weekends at the car wash. Not that we washed our cars all the time; we just liked to hang out there and watch the traffic go by.

I was on the track team and tried running every day after school and my school life was going great because of my newfound friends who always seemed to be around.

On Fridays, we would get together for a little while after the football games at the Pizza Parlor. I had to hurry home for curfew, but it was fun to see them.

The guys hardly ever attended any football games. They said it was because they were boring, but I think it was because they had to work most nights.

Yna, my very best friend, and I, of course, had to cheer at the football games. I enjoyed it because Yna and I could talk and I could watch Victor Balentez, totally the guy of my dreams, at my leisure. He and I would make eye contact throughout the game; it was seriously cool.

I tried spending time with Vic as much as possible, but things never really seemed to go our way and my dad didn't help either. Consequently, I hadn't had a chance to be alone with him except for maybe a handful of times. I couldn't find the nerve to tell Dad about Vic.

Victor has a strong square jaw and piercing dark eyes. He was certainly sought after by the girls in town, both old and young. He was a receiver on the high school football team, which meant he was fast and lean. We had known each other my whole life (like you can ever meet someone new in a small town) and it seemed we had only recently become interested in each other in a more romantic way.

I was at one of my track races last school year when I first really "noticed" him. He was there to watch his younger sister, Lilah, run. It had been a good run for me; I had won gold medals in two different races.

After my runs, Vic stayed in the stands to watch the relay team. I walked to the stands, sat near him, and spoke to his sister for most of the race. Why I sat there I'll never know, but it was a good thing because when the track meet was over, he offered to give me a ride home. I, of course, said yes and we ended-up taking a drive before he dropped me off at my house.

Our first few get-togethers were only friendly. That was what I called them—get-togethers—because technically he had never asked me out on a formal date, but he did seem to get more and more intense. At first we talked that summer a few times whenever we happened to be at the same place. Then he began stopping on purpose when he saw me just to talk. He'd held my hand a few times, but it was a slow relationship and kept me on my toes most of the time because I never knew if we were seeing each other or not.

He just happened to be at the same places I was.

Vic's parents had loads of money. His dad owned several car dealerships in the area so he was always super busy and since Vic was his only son, Vic pretty much got whatever he wanted. His fancy car, nice clothes, and the easy way he spent money all attested to the fact that his mom and dad pretty much gave him whatever he wanted.

It would be my unfortunate luck that my dad wouldn't approve of him and I didn't want to have to *really* do anything behind his back, so I ignored any subject of Vic, even though Meg had brought him up several times.

Vic and I ended up talking as much as possible online, which I felt made our relationship grow, but the anxiety of being alone with him was building. He was older and I knew expectations of sex would be there, especially since he was known as the "love 'em and leave 'em" type.

Anyway, Vic and I were sort of going together but sort

of not. He hadn't really asked me out on an official date yet and we hardly talked at school. We'd look at each other and he'd smile. Every now and then he'd walk me to my class or wait for me after athletics.

That was until Vic invited me to his house party Labor Day weekend.

That's when my life changed forever.

Chapter 3

A few days before Labor Day, Vic approached me at my locker. He took my breath away. That green long-sleeved shirt and those relaxed jeans that hugged his butt made my heart skip a beat.

My back was to my locker and I couldn't move. I watched his long easy strides as he sauntered over to me. How could he be so comfortable with being himself while I was just a total mess?

He put his hand just above the side of my head and leaned into me like he was going to kiss me. "You wanna come to a party?"

Chills ran up my spine. I tried to control my nervous giggle. "What?"

Of course, I would say something stupid like that. I heard him, the girl standing next to me staring at him heard him, and Jack heard him because he turned his head to give us privacy. And still I said what?

Of course.

His smile grew and he leaned closer to my ear and whispered, "You want to come to a party?"

He was so close to my ear, that I could smell his breath. It smelled like fruit.

I closed my eyes, enjoying the feel of him so close to me. "Sure."

When I opened my eyes, he was staring into my face. I felt hot suddenly and could feel my cheeks burning.

"Do you wanna know where it's at?"

I felt totally stupid at this point. I had to collect myself. I straightened my back and forced myself to look at him with a bored, nonchalant look. "Well, where is it? I'm assuming it's at your house."

His smile only made me feel worse. He had the ability to make me feel uncomfortable in my own skin. Like I was inadequate or something. "Yeah, it's at my house on Saturday. You'll be there?"

With a personal invite from the man of my dreams—of course I was going. "Yeah, I guess I can make it."

He grabbed a lock of my hair with his fingers and rubbed. He stole a quick glance at Jack, gave me a lopsided grin, and rubbed my arm. "Find me when you get there. I'll be waiting."

My skin burned where he'd just touched me. My heart had accelerated and I could feel my chest rising up and down rapidly.

It all happened in an instant, but it felt like time had stopped. He walked away and gave Jack a punch in the arm.

Jack didn't even acknowledge him. "You going to his party?"

"I really want to. I'm stoked that he personally asked me. Yna will go with me. You wanna go too?"

I opened my locker and grabbed the books for my next class. The tension coming from Jack was palpable. I could see him grinding his teeth and his knuckles had turned white as he gripped his books. I chose to ignore it. "I'll see you after class."

I walked away hoping he wouldn't stop me. I seriously didn't understand why people hated Vic so much.

Yna, my best friend, was in my next class, so I hurried to sit next to her and share my wonderful news.

People, as usual, surrounded Yna. Her personality was magnetic and it seemed like she was never alone.

Yna is the kind of girl that likes to hug—everyone. She isn't particular. She has a kind heart and an honest soul.

Her name was a source of contention. Whenever we had a new teacher or substitute at school, the teacher would always mispronounce her name and call her Yani or Yinaah or something ridiculous like that, but she'd just roll her eyes and say it correctly by making the Y sound like a long E. "Eeeennnnaa," she would say.

I could be myself with her and knew Yna wouldn't ever judge me. Her curly long black hair and dancer's body made her every guy's wet dream. She, however, was in love with Randy, the high school superstar jock, which was a complete mystery since he treated her like shit. The guys had told me over and over again that it was typical. I still didn't believe it.

I had to squeeze between her and some of her other friends. "You'll never guess who just asked me to his party."

She rolled her eyes. "Of course, Vic asked you. I told you he would."

"You gonna go with me? I can't show up by myself."

"Randy and I are going. We'll go together and I'll meet him there."

"You're the best."

With exaggeration, Yna brushed back her hair and smiled. "But of course."

Yna was great. Next to the guys, she was my only true friend. When I showed up in the morning sometimes there was no one for me to talk to. I generally sat by myself and looked around uncomfortably waiting for the guys or Yna to show up.

Yna, on the other hand, never had that problem. She was always surrounded by friends. She was the type of girl who knew what to say to guys, who wouldn't stutter, who always knew what to do, who everyone liked.

And then there was me.

The loner.

And not because I wanted to be, but because I wasn't given a choice.

If someone said something funny, I wasn't the type that had a quick response.

If I were to think for a few minutes or a few days, then yeah, I'd always know what to say, but by then no one would remember what the conversation was about. Yna was quick on her toes. She always had something funny, charming, and witty to say.

I saw Vic in the hallways for the next few days and he'd give me a warm knowing smile. It always gave me enough warmth to last the day. Some of his friends started nudging him when I passed by which was even better because it meant that they knew he had his eyes on me.

Every now and then he'd walk me to class but it seemed like every time he did, one of the guys was at my locker. Purely coincidental, I know, but the guys would mention it every now and then.

Friday night there were no football games so I took the opportunity to help out around the house and do everything I could to make sure I was able to go out with Yna.

Luckily, my dad went out of town and I got to ask my mom for permission. It was always easier to ask her than it was to ask my dad.

Yna picked me up at seven but I was ready at five. I couldn't keep the excitement down so I ended up trying on almost everything in my closet, another department I was lacking in. My family didn't have any money which meant that my clothes weren't the best looking and most were hand-me-downs from a distant cousin. Yna and Vic always dressed at the top of fashion. They always had something new on. It was a little depressing, especially when I looked at my closet for the hundredth time.

I settled on some haggard jeans I'd worn more than I care to admit and a purple top that fit me a little too tight but was the only thing that I could find that was acceptable.

Dressed in a black skirt and frilly white shirt, Yna walked into my bedroom. "You ready?"

I looked at her then looked at myself in the mirror. Jeez, we were not in the same league and neither was Vic.

I almost decided to stay home.

Almost.

I was too excited and a personal invite couldn't be ignored.

* * *

Vic's house is a two-story Spanish style home with a veranda in the back. The party was already going strong by the time Yna and I got there. Cars lined the road, stragglers talked outside, and couples were already making out in cars.

I told Yna not to leave me and warned her over and over again not to walk away from me, but as soon as we stepped into the house she went one way and I stayed there standing awkwardly in the middle of the entry room with my tight shirt and my worn out jeans.

Great.

A hand circled my waist, startling me out of my self-pity. "Hey, beautiful. Here with anyone?"

I giggled. "Not yet."

Vic grabbed my arm and led me to the kitchen. "Not unless it's me."

His words spiked my euphoria. It was great to feel that someone like him was so interested.

He handed me a beer and I took it. Not because I'd drink it, but because I didn't want to refuse it and sound like a complete bonehead.

"Drink up beautiful."

I smiled, took a small sip, and tried unsuccessfully to hide the look of distaste which made him laugh. "Come on, let's walk around."

He walked around with me and I met some of his friends who looked at me up and down and then didn't really bother talking to me again, but that didn't seem to faze Vic.

Julie Rivas was there with some of her friends. She was nice and tried every now and then to be my friend but she was considered somewhat of a loser so I stayed clear of her even though I knew since grade school.

We eventually made it back to Yna who by then was already standing beside Randy. They stood in the corner while she talked to her horde of groupies and he watched the girls pass by. He was such a jerk.

Yna smiled when Vic and I walked up to them. Vic and Randy shook hands and talked for awhile about the party, football, and other guy stuff while Yna and I smiled at each other with stupid crazy grins.

I slipped my hand boldly into Vic's and he comfortably squeezed my hand and held it. He didn't even skip a beat in his conversation and my heart soared.

After a few minutes of bliss, he slowly let go of my hand and, before I could wonder why, he slipped his arm around my waist.

I didn't think my smile could get any bigger but it did.

"Hey, Son. What do we have here?" Vic's father walked up behind us and fear shot through my body.

His father had peppered hair, the same square chin, dark eyes, and slim build. He exuded money and confidence in his slacks and sweater.

I, along with many many others around me, had a beer in my hand but it didn't seem to click with Vic because he took a long drink before introducing me to his dad. "This is Linda, Dad."

"Hey, Linda. So, you're the one he's talked about several times."

He shook my hand and I happily blushed. If he'd talked about me to his dad, then obviously there was something there. "Hello, Mr. Balentez."

"Hey Vic, don't forget to tell the Key Master not to forget about James. He's already pretty gone so I don't want him driving home."

"Alright Dad." Vic gave me a peck on the cheek, squeezed my hand and whispered intimately in my ear. "Be right back. Wait for me."

I beamed at him and nodded. He walked away with his dad and I stayed behind with Yna.

The music was pumping and the urge to dance was getting stronger and stronger. Just then I heard Yna and Randy arguing. This was nothing new. When they were on they were great together but when they were off, well, Randy sucked.

"I don't want you leaving yet. Stay with me." Yna pleaded.

"Sweetie, you know I like hanging out with the guys and it's a holiday. We're gonna spend all day tomorrow and the next at your family's house. I need my own time too."

Even though I tried not to look, I could see Yna's facial expressions as she started to cave in. She always did no matter what. He'd get a hold of her and make his excuses sound perfectly normal and sound and she'd agree to everything he said.

"Okay, but I want you to stay here with me for another thirty minutes before you leave to have fun with your friends." Of course, she was giving in.

Randy put his arms around her and kissed her. "You're the best."

I could only shake my head at her. Yna was blind to everything he did.

Can love really be that blind? How in love do you have to be for everything the other person says to make sense?

I believed that love can be wrong sometimes. It had to be because what Yna and Randy had was wrong. Plain and simple.

Love couldn't be lies, and betrayal, and pain. Randy went out on her all the time—but let Yna talk to one guy and there'd be hell to pay.

Completely unfair.

"Miss me?"

Vic always seemed to sneak up on me. I think he liked it. I had to admit that I liked it, too: his embrace, the touch of his hand, the smell of his neck. It was so sensual.

"Of course."

I was getting more and more comfortable with him. It was so much easier to talk to him here with all the noise. We were the only ones that seemed to matter. "Want to go outside and talk?"

Just when I thought I'd survive, he throws me for a loop. "Sure."

He guided me through the dancers, the football guys in the kitchen playing games and the crowd surrounding the keg. We found a small secluded spot near a bench toward the back of the perfectly landscaped yard.

Before we sat down, I tugged at his arm. I heard giggling.

"Stop it. Don't." The sound emanated from behind the wooden gate.

Whoever it was didn't really mean for the other person to stop because the giggling continued. I looked to Vic wondering if he'd recognized the giggling. He clenched his jaw. "Lilah, get out here."

Lilah, his sister, was nothing like Vic. She didn't play any sports, wasn't a good student, looks skipped her, and she was mean. Very mean.

She only giggled louder but after a few tense moments, she stepped out from behind a bush with some older guy I think I had once in one of my classes.

Needless to say, he wasn't the sharpest tool in the shed. I'd heard he'd taken the math class more than several times and here he was, with Lilah. Their clothes were disheveled and Lilah's lips were swollen.

Vic's steel stare would have scared me, but it did nothing to Lilah. "You need to go inside."

"Why? So you can use this place for *her*?"

She looked at me with such disdain that I couldn't even look back. I grabbed Vic's arm to calm him down. It was obvious he was getting angrier. I could feel his muscles flexing beneath the soft cotton of his shirt.

Lilah laughed a shrill, ugly laugh and walked away. Last year, she talked to me just fine but then again she did have an ulterior motive: my uncle.

She had liked him for a long time and last year he talked to her a few times, but since then hadn't given her the time of day. Thus, she had no reason to talk to me now.

"Sorry." Vic brushed his hands through his hair and looked at me. I smiled and so did he and the moment passed and was easily forgotten.

"Sit down."

I sat and suddenly I had nothing to say. I could think of nothing. It was all so quiet and it was just him and me. Usually someone was around. I wanted to ask him what he found in me, why he was interested, why he would take time away from his party to be with me. I was a nobody.

A runner, a nerd (sort of), innocent (I thought), passably pretty, cheerleader (barely) girl like me. I had nothing else to offer him.

Nothing.

And he wanted me instead of all those pretty girls like Yna in his house.

One of those girls would have known exactly what to say to him at this moment to make him laugh or make him smile or somehow start some intelligent conversation. I, on the other hand, had nothing.

"You having fun tonight?" He asked after several minutes of silence.

"Yes. You?"

He put his arms around me. "I'm with you tonight. What could be better?"

I smiled up at him and it was like our bodies fit just right. He towered over me, his broad arms comforting. It was an amazing feeling being held by him.

I thought he was going to kiss me but he didn't. He asked me all sorts of questions about myself and my friends. He wanted to know everything and my wariness and unease melted away.

"So, it's just you and your sister? Does your dad let you out much?"

I chuckled. "Yes, it's just the two of us. No, my dad watches me like a hawk. He doesn't let me do much; he's very protective and has never let me have a boyfriend."

He brushed a loose strand of hair from my face. "Until now, right?"

"He knows nothing about my life. He doesn't know what I do. Part of me thinks he doesn't want to know. So, he just makes life difficult. I can't talk to him like you talk to your parents. What's your mom like?"

Up until then, our conversation had centered around me.

"My parents are great. I do whatever I want, I get what I want, all the time."

He gave me a pointed intense look and a shiver went up my spine.

I cleared my throat and looked down at my hands. "In other words, no one ever tells you no?"

He threw me an easy grin. "Not yet. You gonna try to be

the first or something?"

I laughed. There was nothing I wouldn't give him at that moment. He looked so cute as he gazed at me with a lopsided grin. "I don't intend to be that person."

"You really are pretty innocent."

Quizzically, I turned my head to the side. "What does that mean?"

"Some of my friends said you were too innocent to mess with. Too pure. But I like it. It's refreshing. It's new. Like you've never done any of it before and I'm the first. Exploring new things with you. It's kinda cool."

"You make me sound like I'm some child."

Before he answered he looked at my tight shirt and his eyes dipped down to my breasts. "Nope. You are definitely not a child."

I didn't know how to take that so I just ignored it, but my cheeks got hot anyway and I thanked God for the darkness of our surroundings.

I knew it was getting late and I was going to have to leave. I had a curfew and I knew he didn't, which was frustrating but I had to tell him.

"I'm gonna have to leave soon. I have a curfew."

"See, you're innocent. Most girls here at the party don't have a curfew; they'll be here till the sun comes up."

A pang of jealousy shot through me. If only I could be like those girls and stay as late as I wanted to. Vic and I could really get to know each other and he wouldn't look at me like I was some child.

Having a curfew really sucked. "Sorry, I have to leave or I'll get grounded."

I wanted to say so much but I didn't know how. I wanted to bare my soul and tell him how much I liked him and how he was the man of my dreams and I wanted to beg him not to talk to any of those girls.

His cute grin soothed my fears and thankfully kept my mouth shut. "Can I take you home?"

It was so sweet. He was offering to leave his party just for me. "No, I can't let you leave your party. It's not fair."

His smile was warm. "Linda, I'd do it for you."

My heart hammered against my chest and again, I thought he'd kiss me but he didn't. I wanted him to crush me against him, to make me forget all my awkwardness, to reassure myself that I wasn't crazy.

But he didn't.

He simply held my hand then brought it to his lips slowly and kissed it. He held my gaze and the electricity in the air made goosebumps penetrate my skin.

"I'd love to take you home. Come on."

Vic led me through his beautiful house full of people, said a few things to the Key Master (he had a white bag full of keys) and walked me to his car.

Jean was leaning against a truck next to his car talking to one of her friends. She said nothing to me, barely gave me a cursory glance. Her eyes were only on Vic. I was just glad that she didn't cause a scene in front of him, but the look she gave him made me shudder. It only lasted a moment because Vic put his arm around me and I felt an elation of smugness course through my body.

Vic guided me to the passenger seat and even put my seatbelt on for me. I loved his car. It was a small little sports car that smelled like leather and Vic. It was sleek and fast and fit him perfectly. His stereo system thrummed through my veins and it didn't matter what song he put on, everything sounded great.

After a few moments, Vic slipped in a CD. When he pushed play, I was dumbfounded by his selection.

He listened to old music. "Faithfully" by Journey (I think that's the group) permeated the air. Vic chuckled at my questioning look and held my hand. Every now and then he'd kiss my hand.

After two kisses, I threw caution to the wind and kissed his hand.

His broad smile vanished and was replaced by a fiery look. I wondered whether or not it was the wrong thing to do but then he cupped my chin tenderly. "You're awesome. You're a breath of fresh air."

Tenderly, I put his hand to my face. We reached my house and he parked across the street. He knew without my telling him that he shouldn't be bringing me home.

"I'll see you on Monday at school."

I wanted him to kiss me but still he didn't. Maybe my breath smelled bad or maybe he was saving himself for someone else. I preferred to think that he was taking his time with me and respected me.

I silently got out of his car and ran across the dark street.

Before I entered my house, I looked back. Vic was still there waiting for me to enter my house safely.

When I got to my room and turned out the light, I went straight to my window. It was then that Vic put his car in gear and quietly drove away.

Chapter 4

In the weeks after the party, Vic would sometimes wait for me after my runs and we'd talk.

He was always so sweet and courteous with me. He seemed to hang on every word I said. He was always telling me how different I was from all the other girls he dated because I was so smart and clever.

Once we were sitting outside of the athletic building after practice. He had just showered and his hair smelled delicious and clean. I, on the other hand, stunk to high heaven because I had just left the track. He took a lock of my hair that had escaped from my ponytail and gently put it behind my ear.

He said he always wanted to see my pretty face. Then some senior girls came and said hi to him. I looked away and he gently pulled my chin back to him so he could assure me that those others girls didn't have anything on me and that I was different.

Small stolen moments like those had me wanting to see him more and more every day.

I saw Lilah more and more, it seemed, after the party. It was like she had it out for me or something. At first, Lilah and I pretty much ignored each other, but now that Vic was showing me more attention she seemed to get ugly. She'd make ugly comments here and there about Vic being with someone else or him not really caring about me. It seemed like the more attention Vic showed me the shittier she got.

All these thoughts rambled through my mind as I scrubbed the tires on my car at the carwash on Saturday, a week before October break.

Washing my car always gave me a chance to get in some deep thinking in.

The car wash has five brick carports at the front to wash cars and behind those are five steel covered carports to vacuum and dry them. Lucas, Jack, and I were in the last row of carports drying my car. I was wearing some purple shorts and a little white tank top. The air was a little brisk, but it was still warm enough for summer wear. Living in a desert has its advantages: hot days and cool nights.

I bent down to scrub the tires and remembered last weekend when Yna and I stopped by Vic's house.

Vic and I had made a bet on the football game and he lost.

I didn't want to think about what would've happened if he'd have won. He was very discreet about his side of the bet, but luckily I didn't have to worry about that.

I won lunch at his house. I took Yna with me because I didn't feel comfortable going by myself. I kind of had to take Yna anyway, since I told my dad I was going over to her house.

When we got to his house, Vic already had lunch ready, or better yet, his mother had lunch ready for us.

She's a beautiful woman. She has dark hair and is a little exotic looking the way her dark eyes slant just a bit on the edges.

She loves her son. It was evident because she would bustle about frantically to get him anything he asked for. Her warm smile and inviting sense of humor was easy to like.

By the end of our lunch, I couldn't help but be a little jealous of Vic. My mother would have made lunch, sure, but Vic's mom went over and beyond.

When Vic walked us out after lunch, I felt even more inadequate because I had hardly said a word. Yna and Vic had talked almost the entire time while I sat like an idiot in the corner.

"I don't mind losing a bet if it means you come to my house," Vic had said.

I had looked down at the floor and smiled when he said that, still utterly dumbfounded as to what to reply.

"You want to go out tonight?"

Startled, I looked up at him, but I knew right away I couldn't pull off getting out of my grandmother's birthday celebration. "No, I can't."

His eyes narrowed and gave me a peculiar look. "I don't like to be told no."

"I can't get out of what I have to do tonight. Sorry."

I didn't share why I couldn't go because he really didn't give me a chance to, but then Yna told him and his smile returned. I really wanted to go out with him.

I just couldn't find the nerve to tell him that.

Jack came up to me and kicked the bucket of water at my feet, bringing me back to the present moment. "Hey, beautiful," Jack said, pulling me out of my reverie.

I liked to joke that it wasn't just me in tank tops; he liked all girls that had a passably good body in tank tops.

Omar drove up to the carwash. "Hey what are ya'll doing?" Omar asked as he parked his little Pinto behind my car.

I turned and placed the vacuum hose on Jack's head. "I was waiting for you. Thought maybe you wanted to cool down a bit. Seeing as how you seem to think you're sooo cool now that you're seeing Brenda."

"Ouch, Linda I just did my hair. I have a date tonight."

I helped Omar get a date with Brenda by bringing her along to some of our get-togethers at Jack's house.

Before, Omar wouldn't have even dreamed about it.

I knew he wasn't an unattractive guy: his bronze hair and slim, tall stature is appealing to most girls, but I knew that without me he wouldn't have gotten the chance with Brenda.

He isn't a jock and not the smartest guy in the school, but he has his sense of humor.

He was known to be very compassionate, especially at the veterinary office where he worked part-time.

He loved that job and talked all the time about seeing himself in that profession in the future, and for some reason, chicks dug that.

It was evident, though, that right now girls and getting laid were his life.

"Like I said—too cool . . . .. Can you believe it! I finally got the hang of this damn car!" I said.

I swung one arm around Lucas. "Lucas here, pain in the ass that he is, finally taught me to drive it. It hasn't died on me all day."

"It was like shitting bricks trying to teach her. She had to learn how to handle a hard stick," Lucas joked with a smile on his face.

"Get your mind out of the gutter, Lucas. I swear he'd jack-off all day if he didn't have us to keep him busy." I was washing my beat up car and taking great pains to get every detail clean and shiny on one tire.

"Tell you what, Lucas. If you wax my car, I'll let you sit next to me at the Pizza Parlor. I might even let you rub my leg once."

Lucas laughed and, after a while, said with a smirk, "Okay." He was off to his car to get the wax from his backseat while Jack and Omar laughed and told me that I was taking advantage of him.

I just shrugged and watched Lucas with a smile on my lips.

"I was looking to see if you would double date tonight," Omar said to Jack.

"Why? I thought you had a date with Brenda," Jack said.

"I do."

"Well?"

"She can't go without her little sister," Omar said in a small whisper.

"Ooooh, hell no . . . .. You're not doing that again. I get stuck playing babysitter. You remember last year with Jackie? Her sister turned out to be seven years old and wanted every snack at the theater while you sat in the back with Jackie." Jack started to walk away shaking his head, "No. Absolutely not."

"Come on, her sister is fifteen, I think. I promise she's pretty."

"Why can't you go alone?" Jack asked.

Jack was shaking his head at the thought of a fifteen year-old. "Because I might go all the way with Brenda," Omar mumbled.

"And you're gonna do that where?" Jack laughed.

After thinking a minute and watching his best friend's pleading eyes, Jack finally conceded. "You owe me big. I mean really big and promise you won't leave me totally alone with this little girl."

Omar smiled, said his good-byes to me and Lucas, walked to his truck, and left.

Jack came back saying proudly, "Guess I'm not going out with you guys later. I have a date."

"Yeah, some date," I laughed. "Poor Lily, she has to go with Brenda every time she has a second date with a guy."

"Why didn't you tell me this before Omar drove up? You could have warned me."

"You agreed to go," Lucas said laughing. "So Linda, my love, what are we doing tonight? Poor Jack here will be in date hell so you, me, and that pain-in-the-ass liar David will have to make do."

"Well we could do the usual ride around or ride around or we could just ride around. Jeez, what choice do we have? What do you have in mind?"

"Well there is a party at the Rat Hole," Jack said.

The Rat Hole is a beat-up two-story house two miles out of the city limits. No one seemed to know who it belonged to or who threw the parties, only that they happened there about three times a year. The parties always seemed to be packed with people and the cops usually showed up around midnight to throw everyone out and arrest the minors who were stupid enough to get caught.

Its name came from some oil drilling area called the Rat Hole, but I never thought about oil when I saw it. Rather, I thought about the smell of beer and wet dog and kids throwing up around their cars.

"Well Lucas, we can hit the Hole tonight. Sounds like a plan," I said as I got into my car ready to leave. "Maybe I'll see Victor there."

Rolling their eyes, Jack and Lucas looked at each other with understanding. They thought Victor was obsessed with me. I knew he liked me a little, but I always got this strange vibe from them when I mentioned Vic.

Again, I was stuck with the reality of our relationship. Who would have thought someone like him would want someone like me? Seriously.

"Maybe he won't be," Lucas mumbled.

"I know you don't like him, but we have history," I said.

It had become my usual response when Victor's name became the topic of conversation. We had all become so close and it seemed like the guys pretty much understood all about me, but for some unknown reason they just didn't get Victor.

"Well, are we eating at the Pizza Parlor or what?" I called over my shoulder.

I put the towels and soap in the trunk of my car. I needed to somehow change the subject.

"No, I have to help my dad at the restaurant for a couple of hours," Jack said with a sigh. If there was one thing that he hated the most in life, it was working at the restaurant with his folks. Jack would rather be immersed in a good book or working on his poetry, a pastime that he still hadn't told the guys about but had shared with me last week.

"I wasn't talking to you Jack. I know where you'll be tonight." I throw him one of my lopsided grins.

Lucas went to hug me. "We'll go eat before we go out. Pick you up at seven and don't forget that leg rub you promised me."

"You'll never stop will you?" I asked with a feigned sigh.

"Nope."

I pushed him away and stepped into my car. I put the keys into the ignition, slid the gear into first, and took off down the road waving with a holler of triumph when the car didn't die.

I Wish I Had Known

While standing next to Jack, Lucas laughed at Linda's display of unmasked enthusiasm. "I taught her how to take off. She still has trouble—damn it was hard to teach her. I didn't think she would ever learn. I think it was just nerves."

"Nerves about what?" Jack asked over his shoulder while he climbed into his old truck.

"Who knows the female mind?"

"She's not your usual female," Jack said with a smile as they watched her take a curb with a back tire.

"Noticed that, too, did you?"

Lucas was picking up all the discarded towels, soaps, and wax that were scattered on the pavement near his silver Pinto.

With his usual grunt of acknowledgment, Jack asked, "Who wouldn't? You know it's just a matter of time till she finds a steady boyfriend and stops hanging with us."

"No, I don't think so, but we'll see. That is unless idiot psycho Vic gets a hold of her. So what about that hot date you have tonight?" Lucas asked taking his keys in his hands and twirling them on his little finger, a habit that he had developed when he started driving a few years back.

"Shoot, don't remind me. I've one week before Fall Break of our Junior year, and yet here I am wasting it away on a kid."

"Like I said, you agreed. Besides, I knew you couldn't say no to Omar; he thinks he's gonna get lucky tonight."

Grinning with understanding, Jack knew that Omar was looking for his first and knew that Omar didn't particularly care who it was as long as it happened before he graduated.

"I'll see you later. Oh yeah, don't forget to pick up David. He should be finished with his shift by nine."

"I get Linda all to myself at the Pizza Parlor, and she promised to let me rub her leg," Lucas said with a wink and a smile.

"Be careful, you know how stupid Victor gets when she's alone with one of us," Jack warned.

Lucas smiled again, got into his vehicle, started it and left while revving the engine causing rock and dirt to fly out behind his tires.

"Luckily, no one was behind him this time," Jack thought to himself as he quietly started his own vehicle and slowly moved out of the car wash.

Chapter 5

Iquietly opened the sliding door and slipped inside. My parents were in their bedroom with the door shut, no doubt having a discussion about their finances. Seeing that the coast was clear, I happily went to the kitchen and opened the fridge. I wanted something to drink while I got ready to go out.

Our kitchen had a typical L-shaped design. The dark wood cabinets and cream colored Formica countertops made a comfortable contrast with the interesting design of the carpet. I realized that most kitchens don't have carpet covering their entire floor, but the look it gave our kitchen was one of warmth and comfort. I walked to the fridge and peered in wondering what happened to all the sodas.

With my head stuck inside the fridge door, I suddenly felt that I wasn't alone. "I know you're there. What do you want?"

"I heard," was Meg's only reply.

With a loud sigh, I grabbed a water bottle and lifted my head to find Meg with her hands on her hips. I knew it was just a matter of time. I was just surprised it had taken as long as it had. "Found out what?"

"You know you're not supposed to fight without me there. What were you thinking? I know . . . you just don't want me to have any fun."

"I couldn't stand it anymore. Jean kept accusing me of sleeping with guys that I don't even talk to. I couldn't let her." I hated that kind of attention from people.

Jean hated me because of a guy. When two girls fight or argue, it's usually—no always—about a guy.

For me, though, it was a matter of defending myself

from the nasty mouth of my enemy. Jean and I had a long standing feud that had started three years ago when a guy that she liked asked me for my phone number. It didn't matter that I thought the guy was a dweeb or that I wasn't even interested in boys yet.

That was all. A damn phone number—a damn phone number had caused all of this. I knew I was somewhat to blame. I didn't have to listen to Jean's insulting remarks or even give them enough thought to say things back, but the old concept of *just walk away* does not work in any high school.

Parents think that is THE master, omnipotent advice, but it never works. You walk away and it gives the other person the okay to do it again with the full knowledge that they can say and do whatever they want with no consequences.

And that—I could not have.

"What if one of her sisters had been there? What would you have done then? Certainly not rely on your sissy friends," Meg said.

Meg hated all of my friends and thought they were nothing but fluff with no substance. She was always insulting them when they came around and she felt like they thought of nothing but themselves.

"None were there . . .. Besides there were a few other people there that didn't like her. I was fine," I said.

I headed through the dark hallway to my room.

Following on my heels, Meg did not let the subject drop. "You know she's doing this because of that loser Victor," she said and threw herself on my bed.

"I know," was my only reply.

We had gone over this dozens of times. The fact remained that Jean still hated me because of another guy, this time Victor. I felt it certainly wasn't my fault that Vic chose me. I didn't understand it.

Jean was very pretty and exotic looking. The one ugly quality that she seemed to have, in my mind, was that she was a vindictive bitch and couldn't seem to get over things.

She seemed to take pleasure in other people's pain. Vic had been seeing Jean for one month when he seemed to take notice of me. Come on, what can happen in a month that would make you so obsessed with a guy?

I hated causing fights and I was deathly afraid of my dad, so if he found out I got into a fight, there'd be hell to pay. I think this was probably the reason I was so easy on Jean and didn't defend myself all the time—it was fear, plain and simple. That is what I chose to tell myself anyway.

Besides, I thought as I sat to apply my make-up, it wasn't like Vic and I were an item yet. A few smiles and coincidental meetings didn't constitute a couple.

"I think you should stay away from Victor," Meg said for the hundredth time. She didn't particularly like him.

"I think it's none of your business. I don't say anything to you about your little boyfriends that show up at *my* window all the time," I said.

I threw her a little smirk knowing it would raise her ire.

Meg's windows had been nailed shut by our dad a few weeks ago when he found out that his precious, innocent daughter was seen out way past two in the morning.

How dad ever found these things out was still a mystery, but now, instead of using her own window to sneak out, she used mine.

"You better not say anything."

"Or what?" I asked innocently.

"I'll tell Dad how his precious little daughter went out and got into a fight. In front of a hell of a lot of people, I might add."

I turned back to the mirror with a sigh, "You're just upset that I didn't let you in on it."

"You're right . . ." she admitted.

Meg was always trying to protect me. We may not have gotten along, but only she could yell and scream at me. When I first started running track in middle school, there were many girls who were jealous and spiteful.

One girl in particular was cruel with the things she said about me.

Meg met that girl in the parking lot and quickly had her singing my praises. Meg wasn't mean or a bully; she just felt it was her duty to take care of her own.

"Just be careful. I don't trust Jean or her sisters. And I don't trust Victor either. He's mean and he's obsessed with you."

I laughed at that. People just didn't understand Vic like I did.

"I like Victor. He makes me feel special and he looks real good in his football uniform. Great butt," I said with a grin. I was definitely a butt girl.

"Oh man! Please tell me you haven't really fallen for him… have you?"

"Only a little," I said.

I got up and changed into jeans and a white printed cotton shirt. "Just don't worry. I'm fine. What's up with Mom and Dad?"

With a frown on her face Meg took a few minutes before she answered. "I think we're going to be moving soon. I think they're trying to postpone it, but it's inevitable. Dad can't find a good job in this town, but he wants to stick it out until you graduate."

"How do you know all that?" I asked, starting to feel anxious.

"Well I overheard them talking. I think a lot of people are moving. There just isn't a future here anymore for them. I graduate this year and I'm not sure how to pay for college."

"Wow, I thought I had problems. Are you alright?" I asked.

"Yeah where there's a will there's a way." Meg, with all her rebellious attitudes and low grades, was really a responsible teenager. She knew she wasn't staying in this town forever and she didn't care what people thought of her.

She dressed mostly in black and her makeup was usually done in black. But despite her "devil may care" attitude, she knew she wanted to go to college and move to a large city and build a career. Not too many people in this small town could boast about ambitions such as hers.

She dressed Goth but she wasn't into trouble like her friends and she had loads of boyfriends and went through them like she went through underwear.

Her sneaking out at night was just something that she enjoyed doing. She usually spent that time alone in a secluded part in the outskirts of town because she said, and I quote, "Guys are immature wastes of time." She would go there to think and sleep. She didn't feel like our dad could tell her when to come and go anymore.

But with all the confusion and turmoil Meg felt in her life, there was always a positive side to her that no one could shake.

After talking over our family situation for a while longer, I was ready for my get-together with Lucas and David.

I went in search of my dad to ask permission to go out. I found him in the kitchen reading some papers.

"Dad, I'm going out to eat with some friends. I'll be back later . . . " I told him. I tried hard to walk to the door without being called back.

"Is that a question or are you telling me?" he asked quietly, never taking his eyes from what he was reading.

As always, my father made such a huge deal out of my going out. It was never simple when I wanted to go out. He always made me feel like I was going out to do something wrong.

He was really good at getting everything out of me without so much as saying a word. Just a look from him was enough for me to spill the beans, regardless of what those beans were. "I'm going out with Lucas and David. They're taking me out to eat at the Pizza Parlor."

His answer, as usual, was to lift one eyebrow.

"I'll be home right after that."

With that he put his papers down and just stared at me.

"Well, we may go to a party after, but I won't get into any trouble. Like I said, I won't be late."

I never got into any trouble, but I always added that for effect. I wished I could just once keep my mouth shut. He never asked any direct questions about my friends, but I always felt like I had to defend them and I always tried to justify my actions. "So, can I go?"

His only reply was a swift nod and without waiting for

anything further, I sped toward the front door before he could change his mind, and hopped into David's truck.

* * *

Fort Stockton has a downtown area that is mostly kept alive by a furniture store and a bank. The main action—where everyone rides around at night—is on Dickinson Boulevard. The town does have its history, like the Paisano Pete statue of a roadrunner that is displayed lovingly on the drag headed toward the downtown area. And it does boast a great museum and an old fort that attracts many vacationers. It is also the only stop for hours between El Paso and Sonora. The closest large town is two hours away. The town itself is very isolated, quiet and peaceful—in other words, to the youngsters, extremely boring.

As anyone from a small hometown knows, you have to find some way of occupying your time. Tonight, luckily for me, I didn't have that problem. I had the guys.

David picked me up alone, explaining that Lucas had something to do and would meet us there.

The pizza joint is located on the drag next to a burger dive.

As we drove, David explained his last run-in with some nameless girl he was going to get lucky with tonight.

He was so full of shit I had to make fun of him when we got to the restaurant. "The door is stuck. You have a shovel?"

David didn't get my joke and went around to open my door. "It's not stuck Ms. Balle."

I threw him a lopsided grin, got out, and found Lucas waiting by the door.

"About time you got here, love. Thought you found someone else," Lucas said as he opened the restaurant door for me and shut it on David.

I smiled, kissed him on the cheek, and whispered, "Never," in his ear.

"You just gave me a hard-on. I'm not gonna be able to sit down," Lucas said shaking his body. "By the way, we won't be able to make out in the corner tonight. You brought the loser."

"I'm sure you won't have a problem . . . big guy," said David from behind us.

Laughing, we made our way to our favorite spot in the back booth overlooking the drag. It was important to sit in this spot because it gave us a view of the people driving back and forth. And, more importantly, we could be seen.

After ordering our drinks, we relaxed in comfortable conversation mostly about girls and their big boobs. It seemed to me that it was a major part of a guy's life—boobs. Not only how big they were, but also the color, the shape, and how they hung in a tight shirt all seemed to play an equally important role. The latest topic of boob conversation was Jenny. Jenny had some of the largest boobs in the school (even larger than Rachel's) and she wasn't too hard to look at, thus she was afforded a large amount of conversation almost nightly. They had done everything but actually massage them. Every chance they got to rub against, peek at, or just plain cop a feel—they took.

"Yeah, she bent over to pick up some dishes and I got the full Monty. I thought she was going to spill over; I could feel my mouth water," David said.

David, unfortunately, could be believed less than half the time.

If it was coming out of his mouth, it was probably a lie. In his own words he had gone out with and left more than half the high school girls and was starting in on the poor middle school girls.

To this day, however, none of them could verify even one of his alleged affairs. But we enjoyed his company, he always had money to spend, and he did pretty much whatever anyone told him to do.

"You mean you would actually put one in your mouth?" I asked puckering up my face.

"Hey, I would give anything a chance, you know me. Besides a guy like me can just love 'em and leave 'em."

"I think she does it on purpose. It's the only way she gets attention."

I took a sip of my water. "I know another way she gets

attention; she's not very picky. I've heard she's been around the block."

"Don't believe everything you hear. For instance, I heard Vic and you have become pretty close, if you know what I mean," Lucas said. He knew his statement would definitely get a full blown rise out of me.

"What? Da—"

I wasn't able to finish my cuss words because our waitress came to get the rest of our order.

That was one thing I would not ever do in public—cuss. But get me by myself and I could make even a sailor blush.

Lucas could tell I was fuming and itching to know where he had heard such a thing. As soon as the waitress walked away he blurted,"Just kidding." And smiled.

"That was not funny, you ass. I'm not letting you rub my leg anymore. Just forget it."

"I knew she would find an excuse," he said to David. Lucas and I played around more than I did with the others, but for some reason Lucas always made sure he kept his distance.

"So have you guys seen Omar and Jack out tonight?" I asked, trying to change the subject.

I didn't like talking about Vic. It was easier for me to enjoy him if I just kept him to myself.

"No, I wonder how Jack is making out with Lily," David said.

"More like how Jack is babysitting Lily," Lucas corrected.

"Well, I think it was sweet of him to go along. Jack's always doing things like that. He's like a big teddy bear," I said.

Lucas and David looked at each other and rolled their eyes then started yawning. "What? You guys always do that when I say anything about Jack."

David got up to go to the restroom and over his shoulder nodded his head. "When you talk about Jack, its always—Jack is great, Jack is so nice, and Jack is sweet. Makes me wanna barf."

With a mischievous grin, Lucas scooted over to sit next to me. "He's just jealous. You know we're all a little jealous."

"I told you I wasn't going to let you rub my leg," I laughed.

"Who said I wanted to rub your leg?"

"What are you doing?" I laughed at him as he tried to scoot closer.

I didn't move. Lucas didn't scare me.

Lucas leaned in towards my ear and whispered "There's Victor."

"What?"

I turned and found Vic walking towards our booth. I thought he looked very handsome with those tight jeans and a loose fitting green shirt.

He was definitely the tall, dark, and handsome type. He always had a smile on his face lately when I saw him. But today, the look he shot at us made me anxious for Lucas.

I stood up and smiled. "Hi, what are you doing here?"

"I should ask you the same thing."

With a smile I said, "Eating of course. This is Lucas."

"We've met," he said, giving Lucas what could only be described as a glare.

Lucas only smiled.

"Will you come outside for awhile? I need to speak to you?" he whispered in my ear. I got a soft hint of liquor coming from his breath.

I was surprised at his request, but with the look on his face I decided that it was probably for the best. "I'll be right back, Lucas."

Outside, Vic leaned on his truck. "I was passing by and saw you through the window. I recognized Lucas' car and figured it was you. I just have one question. What is going on between you two?"

I laughed, "I thought you knew they are all my friends. I spend a lot of time with them. I've been doing it all summer, why is now any different? I've told you about them."

"Because now you're with me. Or am I wrong about that?"

"If I'm with you, you'll still have to put up with them. They're my friends."

I guess Vic saw the look on my face and decided to go about it another way. "What are you doing later? There's a party at the Rat Hole."

"I know. I was going there in a little while. Are you going?"

"Yes. Why don't you go with me?"

I thought about it for a while, but decided against it.

It would upset the guys and I didn't want to do that. "No, but I'll meet you there. My dad knows I'm with them. It's better that way."

Victor nodded, "Alright, but promise me I'll see you there."

"Okay."

Vic gave me a peck on the cheek and again I got a whiff of alcohol that was not overbearing, but definitely present. As he drove away in his car, I realized that having an older boyfriend could have its advantages: he always seemed to be put together, confident, and just looked so much more mature and worldly.

I looked towards the Pizza Parlor and couldn't control my sigh. I knew they were in there talking shit about me, and I knew they didn't like Victor. I just couldn't understand why.

I Wish I Had Known

They *had* been talking about her. Lucas couldn't control his anger. "Why aren't we telling her about him?"

Taking a bite of his pepperoni pizza, David took a few minutes to answer because he had debated on this situation himself. "She has to see it herself. You tell her now and she'll turn on us and go to him. Eventually, she'll see him for what he is. You'll see."

"No, I don't see. We could save her this stupidity. You know what that piece of shit did to me the other day?" Lucas wanted to run outside and tear her away from his grasp.

David chewed slowly letting Lucas vent out his frustrations. "I told you that she'll have to see it for herself. What happened? Another run in with Mr. Wonderful?"

Ever since Linda had started talking to Victor, Victor had taken it upon himself to be shitty to them. He found little opportunities everywhere: a cut-off with his car here, a little revving of his engine next to them on the drag there. Little things that couldn't be told to Linda; it wasn't worth it yet.

"I was parked at Sonic getting a drink when he came through. He and his loser friends stopped and got out to sit in the small little patio area in the middle of Sonic." Lucas looked out the window to see Victor whispering in her ear. "They started acting stupid, saying things out loud about her. Before he left, he threw his drink at my car. I got so pissed off, but he got in his truck and drove away."

David took another bite and chewed slowly. The

problem with all this was that Victor had pegged Lucas as the main problem. He couldn't understand why. If anything, it was Jack that was the main problem for someone like Vic. Jack held Linda in his hands. She looked up to him and listened to everything he said. As far as David was concerned, he didn't think Victor had done anything to Jack. Maybe he was afraid of him or maybe he knew who he could mess with and who he couldn't.

"Just ignore him. You won't have to worry about him longer. You'll see. She'll see him for what he really is. You just need to let her see it on her own."

Linda was on her way back smiling. Which David thought infuriated Lucas more.

She sat down at the booth. "Alright, go ahead and let me have it," she said.

David smiled and Lucas looked away.

Chapter 6

L ucas hadn't said much on the way to the party and it was starting to piss me off. He had no right to get so angry. David, on the other hand, didn't care much about anything it seemed. "Ahhh, the great, old, wonderful Rat Hole at its finest."

"Yeah, isn't it great!" I loved it all. Every time I was out with the guys was wonderful. We could be at a funeral and I'd still enjoy myself.

I took a deep breath and turned when I heard a familiar voice yelling at me.

Yna had shown up as soon as I stepped out of the car. "Hey woman!"

"You look hot!" David said as he took Yna off her feet with a hug. Yna loved David and gave him a peck on the cheek. Well, to be fair, she loved everybody.

Yna grabbed me by the arm and pulled me off to the side. "Vic's been looking for you. You must've made some impression."

My heart soared. "You think he really likes me? He stopped when we were eating pizza to talk to me. I don't think he was very happy with me."

I told her everything that happened and we spent the next few minutes hashing over the details of what it all meant in the greater scheme of things.

"You girls gonna talk all night? Or are we going in?" Lucas asked giving me the first smile in the last half hour.

"Let's dance!" I yelled.

I was relieved that his angry bout was over. I knew it

was just a matter of time.

That was Lucas.

We entered the Rat Hole and the smell of wet dog and beer mingled with another distinct smell: sweat.

Huge speakers were positioned in the back of the club and a guy wearing oversized blue jeans flipped through CD's trying to figure out what to play next.

People were bumping in to each other dancing. Some were drunk, some were acting, and some looked bored with it all. It was a typical party at the Rat Hole. Lots of booze, dancing, and craziness and I loved it all. I loved how people seemed to always find something to do in this small town. It was amazing to see people that weren't from this town actually here. How did they even find out about this place?

Lucas seized my hand. "Come on Linda, come make out with me on the dance floor."

"Hey Lucas, isn't' that your cousin?" David asked pointing to a group of guys in a corner.

"Yeah, I didn't know they were coming." Lucas squeezed my hand and then walked over to them, but I wasn't able to follow since Yna had grabbed my shirt and whispered, "Who is that?"

"Which one?" I asked looking at the new guys.

"The one with the purple shirt," she said, trying to point without really pointing.

I tried looking at them a little closer but couldn't tell which one was wearing purple. The dark lighting in the room concealed a lot of things especially color. "The blue shirt you mean?"

"Does it matter what color? The cute one," Yna said exasperated.

"Of course it matters. Your idea of cute is definitely not mine." I couldn't quite see their faces, but as Lucas brought them over, I got a good look at one of them and Yna was right for once.

He was super cute with dark eyes, long shaggy hair, a tall, slim stature, and he looked totally edible and very single.

"Hey, guys this is my first cousin Jason," Lucas said introducing the others too. I caught only Jason's name. The others no longer mattered.

"I told you he was cute. Look at your face," Yna whispered into my ear.

"Stop it. Victor will be looking for me," I said.

"Victor? Who cares about Victor. Here's a guy from out of town that is super hot. What more do you want?" Yna asked. "He's looking at you, too. Perfect."

"He is not," I said, pushing Yna away just a little bit.

"This is our good friend, Linda, that I was telling you about the other day," Lucas said.

"You talking about me?" I asked smiling. It made me feel good to know he talked about me. "Was it good or bad?"

"What? You know my mind's always in the gutter," Lucas said smiling and putting a hand around my shoulders.

"Yeah, it is in the gutter about 90 percent of the time and the other 10 is spent figuring out how to get back into the gutter," I laughed.

The others joined the conversation, but I tuned them out. Lucas asked me a question, but I didn't even acknowledge him and it looked like Jason didn't either. He was looking at me and no one else.

Sticking out his hands, I stupidly looked down at them. "You wanna dance?" Jason asked.

Lucas' forehead crinkled and David and Yna laughed out loud.

"Sure," I answered after a few moments.

The crowds of people fighting for space made it difficult to even get through to dance, but Jason grabbed my hand and guided me to a corner with fewer people. I smiled at him and started to move to the music.

Dancing was my escape. I loved it and secretly thought I was pretty good at it. This was where I felt like I kept my shape for the most part. I loved dancing on the weekends. Going to weddings and quinceañeras are a must in my eyes. It's too bad some guys I had talked to couldn't dance, but Jack seemed to be pretty good at it so I'd always made sure to invite him when I wanted to dance.

Luckily, Jason seemed to know what he was doing. He looked cool and collected when he was dancing and he wouldn't stop looking into my eyes. They were burning a hole into me.

I was a little embarrassed. When I looked at them, most guys would turn away from me as if they were shy or were embarrassed at how they danced. Jason was not that type of guy. He seemed to have too much confidence. I finally looked away; I couldn't maintain eye contact.

Some of the girls around me were dancing while others were staring at us. Some looked at me with a smile and others weren't looking at me at all, only at him. He was cute and girls were honing in on him, especially since he was from out of town.

"Where are you from?" The least I could do was talk to him and ask him questions. It seemed like I always felt a little odd when it came to guys. What to ask that won't make me sound stupid or like an idiot? Would my questions be too boring or inappropriate? Sometimes I hated the vomit that came out of my mouth when I was alone with a guy I liked. It never seemed to happen when I was around the guys or even around Vic, but with others I felt like I had to pretend to be sophisticated or smart or something else equally stupid.

"We're from Iraan," he answered.

He was smiling with a strange look in his eyes. Maybe it was a stupid question or something I should have known.

That was it.

I couldn't think of what else to ask him; I was done. I thought about the weather, but that was definitely too stupid and I wouldn't dare. Maybe I could ask him if he comes around here often but that was stupid too because I would've noticed him long ago.

Iraan? Yes, my dad had gone over to the town two hours away a few times for work and mentioned they had a Dairy Queen and that was it. No stop light, three major roads, and lots of farm houses.

I got the impression from my dad that the town was super small—even smaller than this one—and that there were only fifteen or twenty kids in each grade.

No wonder he was here.

"You have a boyfriend?" Jason asked, making me jerk me head back. I wondered if I heard him right. Had he just asked me if I had a boyfriend?

Wait.

Was Vic my boyfriend? Not really. We weren't dating or anything. He kissed me on the forehead once and today on the cheek. He just talked to me when we happened to be at the same place, but no not really a boyfriend.

"That's not a trick question," he said after a few minutes.

I smiled at him, "No. No boyfriend. Just friends and acquaintances."

"Acquaintances?" His smile grew. He had a dimple. My heart shifted.

"Yeah, you know relationships that are less intimate than friends," I answered proud of myself.

He laughed out loud, "Okay, Webster, any of those friends and acquaintances important?"

"Of course, all my friends are important." This was good I thought. Be mysterious. Guys liked that.

"I'll take that like I want to then," he said.

I wasn't sure what that meant, but he got a little closer to me as we were dancing. I smiled at him. He smelled good like expensive cologne.

"You smell good too," he smiled at me.

I must have inhaled a little too loudly, or God forbid, said it out loud, but I didn't even care at that point.

He was a good dancer, the music was good with a great beat, and he smelled really, really good, so I closed my eyes and enjoyed the dance. I could dance with him all night if he'd let me and I'd be happy.

Suddenly someone clutched the back of my shirt and yanked me back. I was too shocked to respond but was ready to start punching if Jean was here with her sisters.

It wasn't Jean.

Vic stood in between Jason and me. He was saying something to him. This wasn't good.

"You need to leave her the hell alone. She's mine," Vic demanded, gritting his teeth.

"You have her marked or something? She got a sticker tag?" Jason asked, not backing down.

What had I done? I didn't want Vic hurting him although it looked to me like Jason could hold his own.

But I didn't want to be responsible for anything—especially not a fight. It would be my fault if a fight ensued.

I wasn't totally honest with Jason about Vic. I had encouraged him by smiling and flirting. This was all my fault and what was worse was that I had actually liked flirting with him. I started to feel horrible and my face turned red with embarrassment.

"You will leave her alone," Vic commanded.

He snatched me by the arm and guided me toward the door. I didn't fight him. I knew that resisting him now would be like setting off a cannon and I didn't want that fight to happen. It would hopefully end here.

I wouldn't be that lucky. Lucas stood blocking the door with all his cousins and friends from Iraan. Vic nodded to his friends, mostly all of whom were on the football team. They all walked toward Jason ready to fight. This was getting worse.

Approximately ten to fifteen guys were now itching for a fight.

The Rat Hole was notorious for fights; they always seemed to happen when the guys had a little too much to drink and got bored. They called it action but I called it stupidity because when the fights started, the party ended and the cops showed up.

"You really want to do this, Lucas?" Victor asked, refusing to let me go.

"You're making decisions here, asshole, not me. Maybe she doesn't want to go with you," Lucas said through gritted teeth.

All eyes turned to me. I glared at Lucas then glanced at Victor. His gaze told me what I needed to know.

I put my head down. If I said something about wanting to stay—what would Victor do or say? It was much easier to go with Vic and defuse the situation instead of making things worse. I looked at Lucas and stepped over to Vic.

"Get out of the way Lucas," Vic demanded and smiled triumphantly.

This only infuriated Lucas more. Throwing a last pleading gaze in my direction, he stepped aside.

I tried to give him an apologetic smile as we strolled past him, but Vic pushed him aside with his shoulder as we passed.

Shit.

I thought it would end with my agreement, but Vic was intentionally making things worse.

At that point, I couldn't do it anymore. I yanked my arm away from his grasp and yelled, "Stop it Vic! You don't have to do that."

I turned to walk away. I was done. I would find a ride home with someone. We had caused a scene, something I hated more than anything, so I put my head down and walked out of the party. I didn't care anymore if they got into a fight. I wouldn't talk to any of them. They treated me like some kind of property and it wasn't fair for Lucas to make me choose like that. He had intentionally put me on the spot. How dare he do that? Before I could get to where the cars were parked, Vic caught up to me.

"Linda, wait!" he called.

"No, leave me alone. I was just dancing. I wasn't doing anything wrong," I said.

I scanned the street to see if someone would give me a ride. I didn't see anyone I could trust to take me home, so I just kept looking.

"I just saw you two and it made me crazy. I know that sounds stupid, but I really like you and I thought you and I had some kind of understanding." He grabbed my shoulder again and tried to turn me towards him.

I shrugged his hands off. "Don't touch me."

"Look, I'm sorry. I didn't mean to make you mad. I just wanted to see you. I've been looking forward to this all week. We could finally spend some time together. You didn't want to come with me, so my first thought was that you wanted to be with him the whole time. What was I supposed to think?" Vic explained.

I sighed, looking at him. He was so cute and dressed so nice and smelled even better. "I don't even know him. I just met him and you know . . . you know I like to dance."

He stepped closer to me. He smelled so good. "I know, I'm sorry."

"Don't do that to me again," I pleaded.

"I'm sorry," Vic said again.

He tried to clutch my arm again. I shrugged it off.

"I need to go home. I don't want to be here anymore."

I couldn't see myself going back inside to the party with Jason and Lucas there. I didn't want to face them and then have Vic do something else to them to start the events going all over again.

No, going back inside was out of the question.

Yna walked up to us and asked me if I wanted a ride home. I glanced at Vic and walked away without saying good-bye. Vic let me leave knowing he wasn't going to convince me to stay.

"That was embarrassing," I told Yna as soon as we were in her black Jetta.

"Jason told me to tell you that he would catch you later. Maybe you could talk sometime."

"After all that?" I asked.

"I don't think it bothered him enough to stay away from you. He was ready to go after you, but Lucas wouldn't let him," Yna said speeding away.

One thing about Yna was that she was a horrible driver. She'd wrecked this little car at least three times. She drove like a bat out of hell. All those tickets didn't seem to trouble her or make her slow her butt down.

"Lucas is pretty mad at me, huh?" I asked.

"He'll get over it. He always does when it comes to you."

I rolled my eyes. Yna thought he had a crush on me, but she just didn't understand our relationship.

He just liked being around girls or anything with boobs.

"Vic's got some problems. I really like Jason. He was

cute but Victor is here all the time. You know long distance re-lationships don't work."

"You don't want to be tied down junior and senior year. We've talked about this remember?"

"Yeah," I said looking out the window. I couldn't stop thinking about Jason. He had dimples.

Dimples.

Those were the biggest turn-on for girls. He probably would never talk to me again.

So much for the flirty mysterious Linda.

"He's from Iraan," I told Yna.

"I know. Lucas said that a few times when he intro-duced them. You weren't listening." Yna laughed.

Chapter 7

"You need to stay away from him!" Meg yelled at me Sunday morning.

Meg and I had begun this discussion shortly after my breakfast and not once did she think she had gotten through to me. Meg heard about the incident from one of her friends earlier that morning. It had been a hard topic for me. I didn't like having to justify or stick up for Victor all the time.

"He's no good for you. Why can everyone see it but you?" Meg sighed exhausted.

"He's my problem if that's what you wanna call him. Just leave me alone. I don't tell you about your idiots that come to my window. Just stay out of it," I said.

I twirled my hair with my fingers and tried to pretend I didn't care what my sister said about him. In truth, I did care. I looked up to Meg more than I would ever let her know, but sometimes she was too much like our dad. Meg would shoot herself in the head if I ever told her that about Dad though.

I loved Sundays. They were awesome and lazy and wonderful. Every Sunday I washed my car for a few hours after lunch. Living in a small town had its perks because I could wash my car outside in the front yard and eventually someone would stop and talk. It happened whenever I spent time outside. Most of the time, it was one of the guys. They'd pass by and, if I was outside, it was always an invitation to stop.

Today it was Jack. He passed by on average about five times a day at different times. It was part of his drag he always liked to say.

Jack didn't say anything when he stopped. He picked up a wash rag and scrubbed my tires with too much gusto. Anger made his scrubbing more effective. His new boots were getting drenched as he scrubbed and sloshed the water around. It didn't look like he cared either. I worked quietly, somewhat afraid of why he might be mad or what he was going to say about the night before. I knew it wasn't going to be good so I didn't push him.

After twenty whole minutes of silence he mumbled, "Heard about last night."

I sighed. Here it came—the lectures, the talks, insults, finger pointing, and exaggerations all directed towards me. It happened all the time. Anything I did would be blown out of proportion. People would add what they wanted to make the story more interesting, and, finally, the story would get back to Dad.

Shit.

I didn't say anything. I didn't want to hear it.

"Who does Victor think he is, anyway?" Jack asked standing up and throwing the rag into the pail. "He just grabbed you. And Lucas didn't do anything about it. We all know you went with him so he wouldn't fight. Lucas shouldn't have let you leave with him. Did he hurt you?"

Confusion masked my face. "What do you mean?"

"I was told that you took off with him. Why didn't you just look for me? I was two minutes away. You could've walked to my cousin's house," he said, looking at me for the first time.

I had forgotten his cousins lived near the Rat Hole. I doubted it was merely two blocks away, probably more like a quarter of a mile but I had a feeling that wasn't something I should bring up at this time. "I didn't leave with him. Yna brought me home," I corrected.

If Jack thought I left with Vic, then others would be thinking the same thing. I hated how things always got screwed up. No one knew how to tell a story without adding shit to it.

"You didn't leave with him?" Jack asked.

"No, we talked outside for a few minutes then I left... with Yna. Lucas mad?"

"He's mad but I'm not sure about what yet. He's been mumbling about you, Victor, and for some reason his cousin

Jason. Know what that's about?"

"No."

I wasn't going to confide in Jack. Jack was cool to talk to about ordinary crazy stuff but not about feelings and emotions about guys. All the guys were different. I could joke all day with Lucas and even flirt with him. David would probably tell everyone he saw anything I said. Omar I could talk to, but he wasn't very nice and usually told me things I didn't want to hear. He believed in brutal truth and sometimes that truth was *too* brutal.

Yna.

Yna was my lifeline. I could tell her anything and she would never judge me, but sometimes she had so much going on that it was hard to get her alone. Sometimes Yna was too popular. Being a cheerleader and a dancer was enough to keep her gone most nights and weekends. Sure we spent time together on the squad and at games, but it wasn't the same. We never had alone time because of the other girls on the team.

The other girls never really took to me like Yna did and they'd frequently give me the cold shoulder. I never quite understood why. I tried to be nice and offered to do things for them, but outwardly they were aloof and slightly nice and I could tell they were holding something back from me.

More than a few times they'd stop talking when I walked up. They'd smile at me and make small talk, but the coolness in the air was suffocating. That suffocation caused me to close up which didn't allow them to see me like I really was.

That was another reason I loved being around the guys. I could be myself and they wanted me around.

He ripped me from my thoughts. "There's something you're not telling me. I can tell," Jack accused.

I rolled my eyes at him. "No, I'm not. I just get frustrated because everything gets turned around."

"What do you expect? Popularity has its price."

"Shut up weirdo," I said pushing him.

I laughed feeling better already. Amazing how these guys always made me feel better. They made me feel better about myself, my confidence soared, and I always felt pretty and witty around them. It was an awesome feeling. They made me feel like I was really liked for *me* and not because people *thought* I was popular or a cheerleader.

It sucked.

So when the guys took me in and really showed interest in me by wanting to be around *me*—it was an awesome feeling.

"Thanks for coming by Jack," I said.

I shot him my meanest smile.

"Of course, crazy. I wouldn't miss being able to spend time with you without Lucas slobbering all over you."

Jack helped me finish drying the car. He didn't say much for awhile, but it was a more calming silence and in no way awkward.

"Look, it's the beginning of October. Fall Break is around the corner. We need to treasure it and enjoy the hell out of it because it goes by too quickly. How about going out tonight? We can go to my house and watch a movie," he said. Sometimes he seemed older than he really was.

He had started to walk towards his truck. His boots and lower pants were completely soaked. His agitation in the beginning was pretty evident but the nice thing was that my rims had never looked better.

"I wanted to go out to eat with Yna and her parents. My dad already said I could go. Maybe we can come by after that. They're fast eaters."

He smiled at me, "Fast eaters, huh?"

"Yeah, Yna's parents are a lot cooler than mine. They'll let us out quick."

I said goodbye and went back into the house to take a shower and get ready for dinner.

I loved taking my time getting ready. I'd sit in the tub for an hour and read my latest Steven King novel. Then I'd take another hour to find something to wear. Maybe even talk on the phone with Yna for another hour and then get on the internet.

My dad was such a stickler that he wouldn't let me have a cell phone. I was lucky just to have a computer in my room. It had taken me three months to convince him to get the internet. Most times not having a cell phone didn't bother me because everyone else had one and if I needed one someone would volunteer theirs. Most of the time, this fell on Yna.

In my opinion, I didn't need a phone as much as I desperately needed the computer. My social page and my email were invaluable, although I didn't think my dad would approve of either one. He didn't like it when he couldn't check up on me and he couldn't check my page which was even better.

I logged on to my page to update my profile when suddenly a little box popped up at the bottom of my screen.

It was Vic.

Did I really want to talk to him? No, not at the moment, so I read through my posts and surfed the web for a while. I ignored his requests two more times. I had to show him that he wasn't in control of me and that I wasn't about to jump through hoops for him just because he wanted me. Anger at what he had done kept me from answering.

Secretly though, if I were really honest with myself, I was flattered. Cute, tall, dark, handsome, and the best looking butt around—that was Vic. He was popular and part of the "IN" crowd. People seemed to gravitate to him because of his humor and personality. Best of all, he was athletic and active in every sport he participated in.

His parents pretty much gave him everything he wanted and never said no to him. By the looks of things even his friends did everything he wanted. I'd heard his friends make little comments about what would happen if someone ever dared tell him no.

Mostly though, he was known for being a pretty fun guy to be around; he was funny, he had money, and he was hot. All of these attributes made for a great chick magnet.

And he wanted me.

It seemed unreal to me that someone like him was attracted to me. I didn't think I'd ever be so lucky. Up until junior high, I had been a gawky overweight nerd. My face had blown up like it had been soaked in formaldehyde and the ever increasing pimples on my face looked more like a pizza than a firm teenage face. I had been ignored by most of my male classmates until I made the cheerleading squad.

Sure, my popularity increased somewhat but it wasn't because of something I did or because of *me*—it was because I was now associating with some of the "IN" girls.

And he wanted me.

He tried again to chat and I decided that I better not push him too much. I'd better talk to him, give him a hard time but keep him interested. Maybe that mysterious Linda that came out with Jason could reappear.

Vic:	We need to talk
Linda:	Fine. What do you want
V:	when can I see you
L:	?
V:	you knw y
L:	you made me mad
V:	cuz you talked to him. What did you expect
L:	I didnt think youd try to fight someone. I hate fights
V:	jean
L:	that wasn't my fault and you know that. More like yours
V:	broke ip with her
L:	sure
V:	I want you
L:	why
V:	you know why
L:	I don't want a serious relationship
V:	k
L:	you going out tonight
V:	maybe
L:	going with yna to eat, maybe we'll see you out
V:	maybe

I hated how he could change things around on me. The conversation started by going my way with him apologizing and trying to talk. By the end of it, however, I wasn't so sure if he even wanted to see me again,

Had I gone too far? Why did things have to get so complicated? I wasn't good at relationships.

It was totally frustrating too because if anyone knows anything about a small town, it is that people talk. People talk a lot.

I was an expert at both manipulation and sex if the gossip could be believed. I'd be able to charge more money than the pros that walk the streets.

Really I had absolutely no experience whatsoever.

None.

Never even allowed anyone to cop a feel or anything much more than the short sloppy kiss Matt Lomas had been graciously kind enough to give me in 8th grade.

The 8th grade dance: that "dreamy" night had been wonderful. I danced my little butt off and I walked out of the school cafeteria with Matt. I had thought he was so very suave in a troublemaker sort of way, but when he kissed me and tried sliding his slimy tongue down my throat—I couldn't take it anymore. I threw up near the brick Fort Stockton Middle School sign. I was pathetic. Living through all the laughs and talking was an experience. It was horrible. Just when I thought I was fixing my rep as much as I possibly could by staying out of trouble, Jean and I fight, Vic causes a scene, and I don't want to lose him.

My computer chimed again. I had another message.

When I read it, my heart skipped a beat. My face turned as red and hot as Mom's chili peppers. It was a good thing no one was there to see me.

The message was from Vic.

Vic: bought you something. Give it to you tonight

I didn't bother to respond. What do you say to something so wonderful? Ask him what he got? That would be too corny and wrong.

One thing was certain, though: I was going to see Vic.

Life was good.

Chapter 8

Yna's parents are great. They're both pediatricians and way cooler than my parents.

Most days, they worked really hard so Yna was left to spend most of her time by herself. Her older brother had graduated two years earlier and was now in his second year at college in Lubbock.

They were pretty close and talked on the phone all the time but this essentially left Yna as an only child. This was pretty apparent when you looked at her wardrobe or the oversights when she wrecked her car. She wasn't the type to take advantage of it though; somehow she had continued to be a great person.

"So, what are you two up to tonight?" Mrs. Vallejo asked. She was stuffing her face with chips and salsa. Her thick glasses and long wavy hair kept getting in her eyes causing her to spill a chip or tomato on her blouse. Mr. Vallejo casually wiped her blouse every few minutes not skipping a beat.

"We're going to buy a case of beer and some weed and go crazy," Yna said, casually licking her greasy fingers.

I could never have told my parents something like that. I'd be picking up my face from off the floor. My dad was not a joking kind of person and he was far from fun.

"Just be home by midnight, young lady," Mr. Vallejo said.

He then passed her a twenty.

Amazing.

Not only did they NOT give her a hard time about who she'd be with and where she was going, but they also didn't lecture her about the what to do and what not to do on a night out.

"Where we going?" Yna later asked.

She buckled her seatbelt, put the car in reverse, and off we went.

I didn't bother to tell her that she hadn't even looked behind her. We didn't have a wreck so I let it go for now certain that I would have another opportunity to tell her.

"I don't care what we do, but I wanna see Vic," I said.

Yna rolled her eyes. "Why? Try seeing that Jason guy again, Linda. Stop wasting your time."

I sighed. I didn't feel like defending myself again, especially with Yna. "Why does everyone hate him? It's not like we're getting married or like he's really done anything bad."

"Yeah, but he's . . . well . . . you know. Look, he's not very loyal. History, you know."

"You're one to talk. Randy goes out with other girls all the time and you do nothing," I argued.

I'd had enough and I was just getting more and more frustrated with it all. Yna's boyfriend was a notorious player. He'd hook up with anything with legs and the girls were crazy for him which only made things worse. His buddies were losers too. They were always bullying kids in the restrooms at school or at the park. They seemed to think it was cool to humiliate the little guys. I thought it was sick and I was glad I didn't have anything to do with them. Yna, on the other hand, had a soft spot for them all, especially her on and off boyfriend, Randy, who'd managed to keep her hooked for the last few years.

Yna hadn't said anything. She glared at the road and her grip on the steering wheel tightened. Yna seemed to take any talk about Randy personally and she hated it, so I wanted to prove a point. How could she talk about Vic when she had Randy?

"Look, I'll make you a deal. You don't talk about Vic and I won't say a word about Randy," I offered.

"For one, Randy and I have been together for a long time and we've been through a lot. He's not controlling and we have history," Yna argued.

"You sound like me. I always tell the guys we have history when they say anything crappy about Vic. I just get tired and I was hoping I didn't have to defend him to you."

Yna ground her lips together. She did this whenever she didn't like something but was taking it into consideration. I knew she was thinking about what she would do if the roles were reversed. She was good at that. I didn't know anyone else who could do it better than her.

"Okay, it's a deal," Yna said smiling. "So where are we going?"

"Let's go down to the drag for a little bit and see who's out. There any parties tonight?"

"I think there's one at Donnie's house; you wanna go there?" Yna asked.

Donnie was one of Yna's other friends, which meant that he was not my friend. The crowd Yna hung out with sometimes wasn't really my crowd. I always felt a little intimidated by her friends because they were the hot senior guys everyone wanted to be around and they had loads of money. That alone was enough to separate me from them. You add in senior stuck-up girls that thought their shit didn't stink and forget it. Definitely not my type of crowd. Vic belonged to this group.

"I don't really feel like going over there," I said.

I looked out the window and hoped she wouldn't ask why.

"You're looking out the window which means you don't want to be around them but you do want to go to a party. I told you they weren't bad."

"I know what you told me, but I still don't want to go there. Let's do something fun. I don't get out too often with just me and you," I said.

After a few minutes of driving around the drag Yna pointed to a car. "Look, there's Randy. Let me just talk to him for a few minutes."

Yna flashed her lights to make Randy pull over. He was always in his sister's car. She was a much better person than her two-timing brother.

We pulled over at the car wash and parked next to Randy. No one really washed their car at night, but people parked in front and walked over to the Sonic that was next door to get drinks and hang out. It was a cool set up.

Randy stayed in his car which meant Yna had to get out. The scum.

I wasn't about to miss an opportunity to be seen by Vic, so I got out of the car and leaned against it while waiting for Yna to finish with her loser boyfriend.

Randy was with Daniel Vesta, the school jerk, and Junior, the idiot of the school. Daniel was really cute and I would've considered him if it weren't for his annoying habit of shaving off kids' eyebrows at school. I could tolerate many things, but sadistic habits like that I couldn't. Junior Finkle, on the other hand, stunk most times and was uglier than a monkey's armpit.

Mike was there too. I didn't know him that well. I heard things, but in this small town that wasn't saying much and I'm sure half the stuff wasn't true anyway. Victor hung out with Daniel every now and then. I hated that, but Victor was part of the "IN" crowd along with Randy and Yna, so I guess it was inevitable.

Once Victor and Daniel were together when Daniel thought it would be funny to take a picture of a guy after football practice in the locker room. He really humiliated that poor guy and I don't think he ever really got over it. Victor, of course, blamed it all on Daniel when I asked him about it, but, well, with Daniel you never knew.

I was getting tired of waiting, so I walked casually to the car and overheard their conversation. Randy was trying to justify wanting to be out with the guys tonight.

Sure, out with the guys. I heard through the grapevine that he had a hot date tonight with some new freshman girl. How he got her to go out with him when her father strictly forbade it was beyond me.

"Yna, you ready?" I asked.

Yna glanced in my direction and made a face. Meaning that this was going to take a while. Randy stepped out of the car and hugged her. I could only roll my eyes.

Just then, Jack passed by and honked his horn. He was a welcoming sight, so I called him over. He made a quick U-turn and jumped the curb getting over to me. Leave it to Jack, he was crazy sometimes and it was why I loved being around him.

"Hey, beautiful. You on your way over tonight? Lucas is coming too, so be ready," Jack said.

I really didn't want to deal with him tonight and I really wanted to see Victor, so I had to lay it out without really laying it out. "I'm with Yna tonight so we'll see."

"We'll see almost always means no."

"Yeah, but with Yna you never know."

I looked over toward Yna and noticed Randy quietly but determinedly ambling toward the car. He was so horrible to her.

Jack must have read my thoughts because he shook his head.

"Yeah, I know. Shoot me if I'm ever that stupid," I told him.

"Well, I better go. The guys will be over in a little while," he said.

Jack started his truck, sped over the curb again, and honked at Yna. I smiled. The guys were great.

After another five minutes, Yna got back in the car. I waited a few minutes more to ask her the obvious question, "He not meeting up with you?"

Her only reply was a shake of her head. She didn't even bother to look at me, probably because she'd just burst into tears which would prompt me to say something that she didn't want to hear.

"Hey, there's Vic," I said, pointing to his car.

Yna's only reply was to turn the Jetta around and follow him.

It didn't take much light flashing to get him to pull over into the empty parking lot.

I jumped out of the car and practically ran to him. His smile was warm and reassuring. "Hey, gorgeous."

I was giddy. Things were going to be okay even if the only thing I could think of to say was, "Hey."

So corny.

"What are ya'll doing tonight?" he asked still smiling.

I shrugged. We had nothing really to do and I wasn't about to bring up going to Jack's house.

Vic looked over at his buddy, James, before he turned back to me.

James Tundalle was one of those typical guys that always seems to be a sidekick. I don't think I'd ever seen him alone.

Vic took a swig of beer and winked at me. "You wanna take a ride with us?"

I wasn't sure whether or not Yna would want to go with them or go somewhere else. "I don't know. Let me ask Yna."

I went back to the car and found Yna crying quietly. This was not good and it wouldn't help to ask her about going with Vic. I really wanted to, but I had to stick with Yna. She didn't deserve to be left alone, even though she should know what Randy was capable of.

I didn't even bother to ask her. I opened the car door and smiled at her. "I'll be right back and we'll go get a drink from Sonic."

Her only reply was to give me a wavering smile.

I glanced at Vic before approaching him. He was going to be disappointed and I couldn't say I wasn't either. I was so looking forward to spending time with him. It was perfect tonight, too.

I sighed, shook my head and headed for the disappointment. "I'll have to take a rain check. Yna needs me."

I was right: his disappointment was definitely there. "Why? Leave her there. She's a big girl and she can go with her boyfriend. It's a good deal."

"I can't. She needs me."

"Like I said. She's a big girl and doesn't need you. Just tell her—for me?" His eyes pleaded, his head tilted, and then he nudged me toward the car.

I looked at him kind of strange, but then he added, "I really want to spend time with you. Besides if you don't come with me I won't be able to give you the gift I got you."

I had forgotten all about that.

I didn't want to leave Yna now that she was crying, but I really wanted to go and I have to admit that I contemplated it for more than a few seconds.

A quick glance toward her car was enough to convince me that I couldn't do that to Yna. I just couldn't.

"No I can't. Look, let me talk to her for a bit and then I'll pull you over in a little while. Okay?" Now it was my turn to plead.

"Maybe she just doesn't want you to have fun." He looked over at James and James nodded at him. Victor then turned to me and smiled. "Okay, but promise you'll look for me later."

I smiled at him. "I will."

He grabbed my arm, pulled me to him, and gave me a long kiss. I was floored.

He smiled and drove away. I walked slowly to the car and said nothing to Yna. She must have sensed something was going on because she didn't say anything and we drove around in silence for the next fifteen minutes.

Jack passed by and honked and honked, then Lucas passed by and did the same thing. The guys were great. We decided to pull over at an abandoned gas station at the end of the drag.

Yna finally smiled and so did I. Lucas went over two curbs and Jack almost wrecked into Yna's car he was driving so fast. Yna screamed and I laughed.

"Whoa! Did you see that? Inches, dude. Inches! Next time think centimeters!" Lucas said.

He had jumped out of the car and was screaming at Jack.

"Wow, Lucas I didn't know you knew math or anything else for that matter," I laughed.

"I'll show you what I know." Lucas smiled and put an arm around me.

I shook my head, shrugged off his arm and walked over to Jack. "Did you do that on purpose? I thought, for sure, you were gonna smack right into us!"

"It's cuz I'm cool like that," Jack smiled. "So what are you doing? Thought you were gonna be at the house?"

I shrugged and ignored it. Had I had my way, I'd have been in Vic's car right now.

"You guys wanna go to Knots Landing? There are some

people out there already," Lucas said.

He was already getting into the car. He obviously thought we wouldn't say no. He was right, of course. Yna was already smiling and laughing at something Jack said.

I followed everyone else to Yna's car and hopped in the back with Jack because Lucas had taken it upon himself to sit up front with Yna. "Where's David and Omar?"

Jack looked over at me and rolled his eyes, "You know Omar. He thinks he's getting lucky with a girl. You know that's not the case. We all know it, but well, he doesn't yet so . . . poor David's along for the ride."

"What, he's along to give pointers?" I laughed.

"Yeah, with a notepad and a pen. Now, let's see Omar, you need to put your hand here, and you need to put your hand there," Jack mimicked.

"Omar! You're doing it all wrong! Here, let me show you!" I laughed.

What the hell are you guys talkin' about?" Lucas and Yna had stopped talking and looked at us through the rearview mirror with questioning looks.

I smiled, "Nothing."

Lucas rolled his eyes then yelled, "You're missing the turn!"

Yna swerved, hit the brakes and just barely made the turn. The jerk of the car caused Jack to slide into me. "Ouch, Yna. Pay attention."

I was still rubbing my head when we drove up to Knots Landing. The last time I was here, I'd gotten into a fight. Hopefully, this trip would be more successful and chick-fight free.

The first person I noticed there was Steve because he had a huge Band-Aid above his eyes. "Hey, Steve. What happened to your eye?"

Sometimes I don't think before I say things (or that's what Jack says anyway). Jack nudged me with his shoulder and shook his head. Even then I didn't get it. "What?"

Touching the Band-Aid delicately and glancing toward Yna, Steve said, "It's okay, it was an accident."

He turned on his heels and swiftly stalked to his car.

I noticed that Julie was there too and tried to stop him but he ignored her.

"See, you don't think, Linda," Jack admonished.

"What are ya'll talking about? Something I don't know? I just asked about his Band-Aid. I didn't say anything wrong." I was getting angry. I hated when everyone else knew things that I didn't. I felt completely out of the loop.

In a whisper so no one would hear, Jack said, "Randy and Daniel happened."

I rolled my eyes. Why wasn't I surprised? It wasn't the first time they'd done something to Steve.

"What did they do now? They do that to Steve? Just a few weeks ago it was that poor dude and that picture. Which by the way, I didn't appreciate Lucas showing me." I hated those guys more now. Not just because of Randy and how horrible he was to Yna, but because things happened all the time around Daniel and nothing was ever done.

After what seemed like forever, I repeated myself, "So tell me. What did they do now?"

"I'll tell you later," Lucas said. He nodded towards Yna who was trying hard not to be a part of the conversation because of Randy.

"Fine." Sometimes I think she needs to hear things. So she'll know what she has. I don't know why she stays with him.

The party was going full blast. There were about twenty people there, all drinking with the music thumping. Some were smiling and starting to dance. When you're from a small town you learn to take the fun when you can because it may not be there again for a while.

I walked over to Julie to try to make up for what I had done to Steve. She was ultimately nice and really really funny so people seemed to migrate to her but I just couldn't see me being friends with her. "Hey Julie, whatcha doing?"

"Making my butt cheeks dance!" She turned around and started dancing. That was Julie. She made fun of herself all the time, but at least she didn't make fun of others like Daniel.

I laughed and joined her. I always loved to dance.

Yna nudged me with her hip and I thought it was because she wanted to join in too but it wasn't.

Vic had driven up as I was dancing. He must've seen me because his scowl was pretty evident.

I tried to shrug it off and playfully danced my way over to him. When I got close to him, he grabbed my arm and pulled me to his car.

"What the hell do you think you're doing? Don't you notice all those guys watching you?"

I pulled my arm free and started to walk away from him but he grabbed me again. "Look, don't you notice those guys? They were ogling you like you were their next meal. I know you don't mean that so I just grabbed you to get them to stop looking at you like that."

He really did care about me. He was everything to me and I hadn't really noticed it before.

"I just don't like you grabbing me like that," I said to him.

The others had watched from a distance, and no one dared come over to us because he was angry.

"I don't want others looking at you. Especially with that little bitty tank top. It doesn't cover anything, Linda. Are you trying to drive me crazy?"

He curled one finger through my spaghetti strap to prove his point. I smiled at him. "Are you a little jealous?"

He didn't smile back. "Yes."

I kept my smile. He was so possessive of me and I kind of liked it. It made me feel like he really, really liked me.

Him. He liked me. It was all so amazing.

"RUN!"

Suddenly people were dashing toward cars and running all over the place. Julie bumped into me as she ran past.

Only one thing could make people run and scramble like that.

The cops.

My heart leapt into my throat. There was no way I could ever get out of being grounded if I got caught. My dad would kill me.

Vic grabbed my arm again and this time I didn't shrug

it off. I welcomed it because I knew he'd take care of me and get me out of there.

Cops in our area seemed to have nothing better to do than to catch young people drinking. I hadn't seen any dope or hard drugs, but by the looks of some of the people, it was evident that they were throwing stuff from their vehicles. I wasn't about to stop and ask what all the stuff flying was. I just wanted to get out of there.

We ran to Vic's car and I jumped in. Vic didn't wait for James and the beating of my heart and fear of my father were so overwhelming that I didn't bother to ask for him.

Vic sped out of there and passed people left and right. One of the great things about Knots Landing was that there were many entrances to it. It had been easy to get away. I glanced back and saw Yna's car and immediately felt better. We had all gotten away.

"So, where you wanna go?"

Vic's question startled me and when I looked at him he smiled.

Being alone with Vic made me nervous.

We rode around in silence for awhile because I couldn't think of anything clever to say and anytime he asked me a question to get conversation going, I'd answer him with short one word answers.

He offered me a beer from the cooler in the back seat and when I shook my head he laughed at me knowingly, which only made me feel more inept and incompetent.

"So what do you like to do for fun?" he asked.

We had been on the drag for the last fifteen minutes, but instead of turning into the Sonic to turn around again, he kept going towards the outskirts of town.

That made me even more nervous, but excited too. "Well, you know I like to dance and of course run."

I couldn't think of anything fascinating to say. I was all in all, pretty boring, so I kept my eyes glued to the landscape.

It was beautiful here. The clear skies, fresh air, and mesas in the distance made the area so very nice. I loved the cool nights in Fort Stockton. Even deep into the summer when the rains come, the cool fresh smell of rock permeates the air. It's wonderful.

I realized something: I had not asked Vic any questions about himself. "So, what do you like to do for fun?"

He threw me a crooked smile, tilted his head, grabbed my hand and said, "You want me to show you?"

I felt the need to clear my throat and I sat up a little straighter in my seat. He was only holding my hand, yet he had me even more nervous.

"So where are we going?" I asked.

We made several turns in the outskirts of town and we were headed down a dirt road I didn't recognize right away.

"Am I making you nervous?" he asked.

"A little."

"Why?"

"Where are we going?"

He obviously hadn't heard me the first time, but even after the third time I asked, he still said nothing, so I assumed that he didn't want to tell me. I wasn't sure if I even wanted to be there.

Dear Diary,

October, was my first real kiss plus a little more.

Well, I went for a ride with Vic and he took me to this place I didn't really know until it opened up and we were suddenly at Beer Can Hill. I think he was trying to scare me into thinking he was gonna do something bad. He wouldn't answer any of my questions but I finally figured it out on my own. When I did he smiled at me like he knew exactly what he was doing. We got out of the car and sat on his hood. We talked a little bit but then he started to kiss me and not just on the mouth. He kissed me on my neck and shoulder and it was really nice. He told me that he really liked me and that it drove him crazy to see me talking to someone else because he wanted me only for himself.

That made me smile and I tried talking about the guys a little but he shook his head and said he wanted this to be just us without everyone else who'll try to break us up. He warned me that it would happen and it wasn't a question of if but of when. That's how he put it. He said we were perfect for each other and then kissed me again and said I smelled good.

He tried to touch other parts of me but I didn't let him because that really made me uncomfortable and a little scared. He said there was going to come a time when I could trust him and I would let him touch me because I would want to make him happy.

I think that means that we'll be seeing more of each other. And guess what?

The gift he got me was his class ring. He brought his ring and he is letting me use it. It's really very cool and I can't wait to show it off tomorrow at school. Everything is kind of happening fast with him but not really since we've been talking since the end of the summer but we haven't had a chance to spend some time together.

He thinks now will be different because now he can really call me his which is really cool and exciting.

I didn't want to leave and after ten minutes of convincing him that my dad would really get mad if I was late, he brought me home. Only I asked him to drop me off around the corner so Dad wouldn't see who dropped me off since I was supposed to be with Yna, but I'm still stoked about it because now I'm in bed and gonna dream of him.

I Wish I Had Known

"Did she make it out of there?" Jack asked.

Yna, Lucas, and Jack had taken off running toward Yna's car as soon as they heard the sirens. Lucas had seen Victor roughly grab Linda and steer her towards his car, but Yna's tugging had stopped Lucas from going after them. Victor would get her out; Lucas was sure of it.

"She got out. I saw her leave with the idiot."

Lucas called Vic "the idiot" whenever Linda wasn't around. After all the things he had heard about Victor, he hated that Linda wasted her time with him. It was a wonder that she hadn't heard all the rumors herself. Then again, maybe she had and didn't care. That possibility was the reason he stayed out of it.

"Do we follow her or what? Let's pull her over and ask her," Jack said.

"No. Let's let her pull us over *if* she wants to come with us. I have a feeling she wants to spend time with him," Yna replied.

"I don't want to leave her alone with that idiot. She's not safe with him. He's too cocky," Lucas said.

Yna laughed at him. The guys were so overprotective of Linda and they just didn't understand that Linda was really falling in love with Victor. They'd understand in the long run when she started spending more time with Victor than with them. They weren't going to like it though. Yna was certain of that. "You guys are in for a rude awakening. She is really falling for him and he seems to really like her. I am excited for her. You should be too."

"You don't know what he does Yna. You just don't know

all the—"

"Lucas, stop it. Yna doesn't need to know about all of the stupidity this town comes up with," Jack interrupted.

"What are you all talking about?" Yna asked.

"Nothing," Lucas conceded.

"Oh, that's a bold-faced lie and you know it. There's something you're not telling me and it's juicy. What is it?" Yna prodded. "Come on, I'll just drive you crazy until you tell me. Come on."

After several minutes of pleading, Lucas finally began the story.

"We were at the Circle K the other night getting gas and drinks. By the way, Karla was there. Hot mama, and she had this little blue dress on. Wow. And she—"

"Lucas stop it!" Yna yelled at him.

"Okay. Okay, anyway, we walked in and we were in there for a few minutes but when we walked out Victor was pulled over and talking to Jean. She was practically in his car she was leaning so far into it. I stopped Jack and David from going outside so Vic wouldn't see us, but I don't think he cared. Jean got into the car with him and I saw them kiss and drive away. It was like two in the morning so I guess he didn't care if anyone saw him, but we saw him, right Jack?"

Jack's only response was to nod his head.

"So he's cheating on her already? What scum . . . there's more isn't there? What are you guys not telling me?" Yna asked after several looks had gone back and forth between Jack and Lucas.

"Tell me. I want the rest of it," Yna pleaded.

"Look, if we tell you the rest you have to promise not to tell Linda. I think it's better if she learns of all this on her own. If we tell her it might look like we're trying to keep them away from each other," Jack said.

"I won't tell her," Yna promised.

Yna just kept driving around the drag. She was in no way letting them out of the car until they told her what they knew.

"Last week David was on his way to work when he got

pulled over by Victor. Victor was in one of his father's dealer-ship trucks, you know, those white utility trucks, and I think David thought it was someone else. It was dark, instead of get-ting out to talk, the truck kept coming at him. It rammed his truck twice before going around. David had to leap out of the way and didn't see it clearly, but Victor's dad has trucks like that and I think it was him, but we're not sure so we can't tell anyone. I tried to look at some of the trucks, but what excuse do we have? Shit, they all look the same and more than one has a scuffed bumper. Anyway, it's just speculation at this point, but it's clearly a warning to stay away from her."

"I don't believe it. Victor is bad but not that bad," Yna said.

"That's exactly why we haven't told Linda. She won't believe us either," Lucas said.

Chapter 9

School that Thursday was an early release day and I was so looking forward to the weekend. Victor told me he would be taking me out to eat at a nice restaurant.

I still hadn't figured out a way to ask my dad if I could go. I thought long and hard about what excuse I'd use, but nothing, so far, had come up.

I parked my car in the outskirts of the school parking lot and I could see Daniel and Randy had already parked and were leaning against the hood of the car calling people names.

They were such jerks.

I decided to park a little further down the parking lot when I noticed Lucas' silver Pinto. I parked next to his vehicle and he popped out from under the car.

"What are you doing over there?" I asked him as I got out of my car.

"Looking at my tires. Looks like one of them has been slashed or something's in it. Looks like the tip of a knife or something," Lucas said to me.

"Wow. Who could have done that? Are you sure? Maybe you ran over something," I asked.

Suddenly, a screech of tires and the crackle of pavement sent me looking for cover while an explosive sound pulsated through my veins.

I peeked out from behind Lucas to find Jack stepping out of his truck.

"Shit Jack, what did you do?" I yelled at him. There was no mistaking the crunch of metal I'd just heard.

"No, no, no. Jack what were you doing? Are you serious?" Lucas yelled at him.

Lucas had his hands on his head and Jack had a smile on his face. This wasn't good.

Jack's truck didn't have a scratch on it, but Lucas' car now sported a large dent. "Don't worry Lu, I'll get Mike to pound out the dent. No big deal."

While Lucas kept ranting his displeasure, I walked, calmly now, up to Jack. "Dude, what were you doing? Did you mean to do that?"

Jack shrugged his shoulders. "I was just trying to scare you but I think I hit some loose pavement and when the truck skidded it wouldn't stop."

I smiled at him but my smile didn't stay. "You know, Lucas just got one of his tires slashed, or so he thinks. I think he ran over something. Today probably wasn't such a good idea to ram his car."

"Shit, he know who did it?" Jack asked.

"No, he didn't say. Like I said, I think he ran over something sharp. If it was slashed, maybe it was over a girl. Isn't it always? Maybe Lucas is seeing some hot babe we don't know anything about."

"Lucas? No, he's probably pissed off some customer at the hotel where he works. Maybe some sheets he didn't change or slept in or farted on or whatever," Jack said, finally getting Lucas to smile.

"Well, I thought the car kept veering to the side but I didn't notice the tire was going low until after I took off from the house," Lucas said as he twirled his keys on his finger.

The guys stayed behind to inspect the tires, but I didn't. I didn't want to be late.

My first period class was with Mr. Farks (or Mr. Farts if you listened to some of the guys). I was headed that way when I was grabbed by the shoulder.

I was ready to start swinging away because I thought it was Jean. When I turned, I realized it was Vic. "You have to stop grabbing me like that."

"Who did you come to school with?"

There was no "hello" or "good morning" or anything. "Is that all I get?" I asked him.

"I'll kiss you if you can stop coming to school with your loser friends," he said, drawing me close with his arm.

"They are not losers and I didn't come to school with them. I parked next to them," I explained. I backed away from him just a little.

"I park in the back. Next time, park there. I'll meet you there. I'll walk you to your class," he said.

Walking through the halls with Vic was exhilarating. Lots of people looked at us, shocked that we were showing others that we were now an item. Usually he would just keep his distance when he walked me to class, but today he had his arm around my waist.

I wanted as many people as possible to see us together. I could finally show everyone that I could get someone like Victor to like me. It was a great feeling.

At the door of Mr. Farks' class, he drew close and whispered into my ear, "Remember that I don't like those guys. I want you all to myself."

With him so close to my ear and the strong scent of his cologne, all I could do was nod my head. I would have agreed to anything as long as he'd stay with me and make me feel like that over and over.

He grabbed a lock of my hair that had escaped from my barrette and gently put it behind my ear. "I don't like you wearing that skimpy shirt. I don't want anyone looking at you."

I gazed into his eyes, saw tenderness and caring, and slowly nodded my head. Of course, whatever he wanted I would gladly give.

The rest of the day passed in a haze. I couldn't even think about my work or the lessons from my teachers because I was so anxious for the bell to ring so I could see him again.

He even sat with me during lunch and introduced me to some of the other senior guys who'd never even considered paying attention to me. They smiled at me and all the girls were nice to me. Even those girls who never spoke to me before or usually just gave me the cold shoulder. It was nice to feel so welcome.

Early release days at school meant that we could leave at noon, so my shortened classes, Vic, and the excitement of Fall Break all combined to frazzle my already muddled senses.

Vic came to me after my last class to invite me to go eat at a steakhouse with some of the other seniors. I was ecstatic and of course I said yes.

I followed him in my car to the restaurant and couldn't keep my hands from shaking. I had to tell myself over and over not to think too much, to speak more, to smile, to be warm, to be attentive, and a whole bunch of other things. I knew if I froze, it would be the end of Vic and me.

He was waiting for me by the entrance with a smile on his face. It made some of my unease slip away.

"Hi," I said stupidly.

He smiled wider, if that were possible, and opened the door for me.

Dear Diary,

I finally had dinner with Vic and I didn't spit anything out or snort or do anything stupid or embarrassing. I ordered a salad because I didn't want him to see me pig out. Everyone was really nice. Even Jaclyn, one of the most popular girls at school. She talked to me for a long time and she said that it looked like he really liked me which was great because if she saw it, then maybe others did too and that would make it more real. Amazingly, Vic picked up the entire bill for all of us at the table. I was shocked but no one else seemed to be because they seemed like they were used to it. I even tried to steal a glance at the total cuz I knew it had to be in the triple digits. He was great and such a sweetheart.

After we ate, he asked me to go for a ride and took me back to Beer Can Hill (where we went last time) but there was another car I didn't recognize already parked there and the windows were fogged up, so Vic laughed and said we'd have to find somewhere else to go.

I didn't see why we couldn't just take a drive so other people could see us together, but he said he wanted me all to himself.

We got to this little clearing down 70 road and pulled

over. We talked for a little while but he kept trying to kiss me and then it felt like he had eight arms because I couldn't seem to stop them from grabbing me in places I wasn't sure I wanted him to touch. At times, I felt like I could just let him because it felt real good, but then I'd get uncomfortable with it and all kinds of sirens would go off in my head so I'd make him stop.

After a while I started getting mad because I kept telling him to stop and he wouldn't. He told me something that really got me thinking.

He said that he could have any girl he wanted but he chose to be with me so I need to think about that. He said he was falling for me and that other couples were already doing it after a few dates and we'd been together really since summer and that he wanted to take our relationship to the next level. It all sounded so sweet when he said it that I kind of let him do some things to me that I don't want to write about. I don't want to go all the way though, because that still scares me but I don't want to lose him either.

* * *

Friday passed quickly, not because I didn't have anything to do, but because there was too much to do. I had to run a few miles to stay in shape and I managed to do that before noon. My father was building a carport so we had to help. I was hoping to do as much as possible so that when I finally asked him if I could go out, he would be so impressed with all the work I had done that he would say yes automatically. It was a dream of mine but not very realistic because my father never let me go anywhere without finding out where, when, and with whom I was going.

I even helped my mother with dinner. She was surprised but didn't ask any questions because she welcomed the help.

As she stretched out the tortillas with a roller, she glanced at me. "I heard you were seeing a boy."

It wasn't really a question and I didn't want her to know

anything about Vic. I could handle others hating him, but not my mom.

She and I had a wonderful relationship. I used to tell her about everything: arguments with friends, my fears, wants, and dreams. That was until I entered high school and everything changed, especially now with Vic.

She glanced at me again and then stopped making the tortillas. "Okay, you are seeing this boy. Is he nice, good-looking, smart? How are his parents? I know who they are, of course, who doesn't, but how are they with you?"

I continued to slowly wash the dishes. "Gosh, Mom. You know all about him. You and Dad always do."

She smiled, resumed making tortillas, and said, "I just want to make sure you're not doing anything you don't want to do. I love you and you're a smart girl. Just don't let those boys trick you."

I had heard this lecture many times, ever since I started my period. "I know. I know, Mom. You've told me like a million times."

She sighed quietly, put down her roller, and then gently grabbed my shoulders. "Look, baby. I just want better for you. I don't want you to be like me."

This was another thing my mother continuously lectured me about. The don't-be-like-me bit. My mother is a sweet woman, but I couldn't see myself talking to her about Vic. That wasn't something I want a lecture about.

My mom's set in the old ways of Mexico where you listen to your husband and never ask any questions.

For example, her idea of the "sex talk" was to take me to my aunt's house so that she could explain what getting my period was all about. That talk still is way up there on my "Most Embarrassing Moments" list because my uncle, three older kids, and a cute cousin were all in the kitchen when we had it. Talk about uncomfortable.

I got out of the kitchen as soon as I could and went to get ready for the football game.

We were playing the Monahans Lobos.

They were a great team with my favorite colors and

their band always knocked our socks off.

Vic and I made eye contact throughout the game. It was a cold and crisp night, perfect football weather. My spirits soared and life was good. I didn't get a chance to talk to him after the game, but he emailed later that night.

All in all, I thought Friday night was a success—that was, until Saturday morning when I went to the kitchen to scrounge around for some breakfast. I had just sat down to eat my cereal when my dad walked in. I knew right away he was in a bad mood.

He threw the paper down on the kitchen table, grumbled something about classifieds and wasted space, and then slammed his bedroom door.

Unless something drastic came up, it was going to be hell trying to get out of there. I definitely had my work cut out.

I decided to stay out of the way as much as possible and not rattle any cages. When Meg came into my room looking for a shirt, I didn't even bat an eye. She glanced back at me as she rummaged through my closet. "Well, aren't you gonna say something? I'm taking this black shirt. I have a date tonight."

"Dad know that?"

I knew she had to get through to Dad in order to go out. It wasn't like with me, though. She always *told* Dad she was going out while I had to *ask* him. It sucked and it was completely unfair.

"Dad doesn't need to know what he doesn't need to know."

"Which tells me that you haven't asked yet. Let me ask first. I have a date tonight too."

I was pretty proud of the fact that Vic and I were finally going out on a real date.

Frowning, she asked, "Who are you going out with?"

"You don't know him," I lied.

"There's no one in this po-dunk town that I don't know. I haven't heard of you going out with anyone except that loser—wait, you're not seriously going out with that loser are you? If you say yes, I *will* tell Dad what kind of a loser he is because he is, you know. He talks about all the girls he's 'done' and all the things he does with them."

"He won't talk about me. I think he really likes me, and Meg, I think I'm really really starting to like him."

"Linda. Can I tell you a few things without you getting angry?"

"If this is about Victor and me, then no."

"It's about you and the wonderful catch you are."

I rolled my eyes at her. I knew she didn't want to see me with Vic, but was the buttering-up completely necessary? I get it, she didn't want me to see Vic. It seemed no one did.

I guess this is how Yna felt when people talked to her about Randy. I made a mental note to not say anything but positive stuff to her.

"You're not listening. What I'm saying is that you are very pretty and young and untouched and vulnerable. You can have anyone you want—"

"I am not vulnerable and I can't have anyone I want. I want him. I don't know why you don't see it."

"I know he's cute, I know you think he's a catch, and I know you think you'll be the one to change him, but the fact is that he's a hoe."

I had heard this argument many, many times and it was really getting old. I no longer wanted to hear it from anyone, least of all my sister who didn't understand anything about me anyway.

"You can leave now. I don't need any lectures and I don't need you to tell me not to see him when that's exactly what I'm doing tonight."

I shut the door in her face and didn't wait for her to say anything.

I was going to have to go ask Dad if I could go out. Did I really really want to tell him where and with whom though?

If I did tell him, then I'd have to ask Vic to come meet my dad.

I didn't want to run the risk of having Vic come out and my dad cause a scene that would really embarrass me. Besides, no one else liked Vic it seemed. What were the chances of my dad liking him? Probably slim to none.

I couldn't tell him. I ached to go out on a date with Vic. If he didn't like Vic and then didn't let me go, I'd be really embarrassed and angry.

I thought I'd just tell him that I was going out with Yna again. He liked her.

I found my Dad welding the last few parts of the carport he was making. A friend of his was there, something that gave me hope because my father was always a lot nicer in front of others.

I stood there for a few moments and chit-chatted with his buddy hoping to score some brownie points.

"Uhmmm . . . Dad? Can I go out with Yna tonight?"

"I knew something was coming."

I stood there determined not to start adding any details like where I was going, when I'd be back, or anything else (all lies). Like I said, it was like verbal vomit when I started asking for permission to go somewhere.

After several gut-wrenching moments of silence, I started it all started with, "We won't be late."

And, after he said nothing, "We're just going to go riding around. Nothing special; maybe go get something to eat." Then I really overdid it: "She said she'd pay."

That must've really gotten his attention because he turned to me, took off the welding helmet that made him look like an alien astronaut, and said, "Why can't you pay for yourself?"

I had to think fast. My father did not like to take something for nothing and he didn't believe in taking advantage of people just because we were struggling.

"I paid last time, so she owes me." Lies just kept spewing out of my mouth.

My dad's friend, whose name I can never remember because it's like weird like Beto or Vato or something like that, finally spoke up. "Man, we're gonna be out here forever if you don't hurry."

He threw me a wink when my dad said, "Don't be late."

I turned and practically ran to the house. All I had to do now was avoid him at all costs just in case he changed his mind.

In my room, I heard my computer chime. I had gotten a message and I knew instinctively that it was from Vic. I couldn't wait to tell him I'd gotten the green light from my dad.

Vic: Hey gorgus u there?
Linda: Hi

My stomach did a somersault when I read his message but all I could reply was "hi." How cheesy and unoriginal could I be?

Vic: we on for 2nite?
Linda: Yup!
Vic: Pick you up in front of your house?
Linda: I'll meet you somewhere
Vic: cool
Linda: How about the carwash?
Vic: No meet me at my house. U can leave ur car there and no one will see it
Linda: cool see you then

I read his message over and over again. He thought I was beautiful and he must've known that I'd lied to my dad because he offered to hide my car.

I was so excited and took extra care with what I was going to wear. I decided on a skirt and tank top. Casual and sexy. I wanted him to really think I was beautiful and mysterious.

I was applying mascara when Meg came into my room. "What do you want?" I asked her.

I didn't want to hear another long lecture about Vic.

"You're going out with him aren't you? Just be smart with him. He's a jerk and stupid and a loser and—"

"Okay. I get it. Get out of my room!"

I slammed the door in her face again. It was getting easier to do especially since this time, like last time, she actually left me alone. Usually she'd bug me and force the door open, but this time she didn't.

Thirty minutes before I was supposed to meet Vic, I left

the house. I rode around the drag for a little while but, well, riding around by yourself sucks because everyone sees you do it. Socially, you don't want to be caught all by yourself. The only people I'd ever seen alone were the older deadbeat guys who had nothing to do but scam on young girls. Every town has those "glory day" guys.

I parked in front of Vic's house and immediately started panicking, sweating, and getting those huge butterflies that seemed to want to jump out from my mouth.

Breathe, breathe, I whispered to myself. I got out of my car (grateful that I had parked right and my car hadn't died) and went to knock on the door.

I didn't get the chance to knock. The door just opened as I lifted my arm and I stupidly almost hit him in the face.

Vic smiled at me and some of those butterflies evaporated. He smelled clean, crisp, and sexy. As I followed him into his house, I caught a glimpse of jeans that hugged his butt and how his tight collared green shirt accentuated his abs. He definitely spent lots of time in the gym.

Lucky me.

He was all mine.

Vic's parents were sitting in the living room watching television. They looked so unlike my parents. Vic's mom seemed to dress regally all the time. Hardly a hair was out of place and she had on a white dress that made her look like she was ready to go to work rather than to sit at home on a Saturday. His father had loosened his tie a little but that was it.

"Hello, Mr. and Mrs. Bentave."

I went to shake their hands but Vic's mother got up and graced me with a hug. I was too surprised to hug her back which made me feel bad.

"So what are you young people doing tonight?" Vic's father asked.

"We're just going to eat something and hang out," Vic replied.

Vic's father pointed a finger at him. "Mind your manners, young man."

"Do you have enough money, dear? I've got plenty in

my purse. Take what you need, sweetheart," his mother said as she walked us to the door.

My parents would never tell me that. Take what you need? Is she kidding? I'd take it all (well, not all but a lot).

"Ready?" he asked.

I only nodded. I didn't want to say anything stupid because I couldn't think.

"When I move my car, you put yours into the garage."

I smiled at him. He was really trying to take care of me.

I moved my car quickly and walked to his car.

He opened the door for me and buckled my seatbelt. As he leaned to fasten the clasp, he turned his head slightly and gave me a long languorous kiss.

My nerves shot up again and I had to make sure I kept my wits about me. I thought about the last time we went out when his octopus hands had gone where they weren't supposed to. I'd just have to make sure not to let it get to that point.

"You hungry?"

I really wasn't, but eating and ordering seemed like the right thing to do on a date so I nodded.

He smiled and patted me on the knee. I felt like the family pet you stroke when it's minding. I had to snap out of it.

"Where do you wanna go?" I asked. I was excited to let people see us together so that other girls would know he was mine. "How about Pizza Parlor?"

"That what you want? I was thinking Rico's Mexican Restaurant."

I felt really stupid now. I mentioned pizza but he had other, fancier things on his mind. Rico's wasn't somewhere my family went because it was too pricey, not to mention the fact that Jack's family owned the restaurant. They would know me and talk to me. It wasn't a good idea to take me there. I could already see Vic causing a scene. Especially if Jack was there or any of the guys and they tried talking to me.

I was stuck. He was waiting for me to reply. I knew, instinctively that he was testing me. If I said no, I had something to hide. If I said yes, he'd make sure to cause some kind of a scene. It was a lose-lose situation for me.

I decided to give in and act nonchalant about it all. "Okay, we can go there if you want. It doesn't matter."

But as I said the words, a chill went through my body. I suddenly wanted to think of an excuse not to go. No matter how much I tried (and I did) I couldn't think of one.

Once we arrived, he opened my car door and then held the restaurant door for me to step in. People said *hello* to him. It was quite obvious that he was a frequent visitor and I was way out of my element.

We sat in a booth and I recognized several people I knew and others my dad knew, which wasn't a good thing because eventually he'd find out. I just hoped they wouldn't tell him for awhile and I'd be saved by playing ignorant.

People kept stealing glances at us. Probably because Vic was so popular and I was not the type to be out on a date. Whatever the reason, the constant stares were unnerving but I had to try and focus only on him and not worry so much about others. When they brought out our Cokes, chips, and salsa, Vic took out a small silver flask from his pocket. He smiled at me and I looked at the flask dumbfounded.

"You want some?" he asked. He poured a hefty portion into his drink.

"Aren't you driving?" I asked.

The way he smiled at me gave me the impression that he was smiling at a naïve little girl. I suddenly felt really stupid for asking.

"No, I think I'll pass."

"You afraid of me or something?" he asked.

"No, of course not. I'm just not a drinker."

"Okay, so you're not a drinker. Do you want some? Come on, just a little won't hurt you. It might even loosen you up."

His words stung. I knew I was uptight and I knew I was nervous, but he didn't have to point that out. A pretty young waitress walked up and asked Vic if he wanted a refill on his full drink. She didn't glance once in my direction. Vic smiled innocently at her them threw me a wink. My heart swelled and I spent the next ten minutes convincing myself that a swig of whatever was in that flask was harmless.

My family doesn't drink. I often went over to Yna's house or other friends' houses and beer, wine, and mixed drinks came hand-in-hand with parties and get-togethers. Cousins and uncles walking around slurring their words or falling over was something I was not used to.

At our parties, we had more Coke and lemonade than you could imagine. Alcoholic drinks were rare.

"You're staring at my drink. Change your mind? Your mouth watering?"

I nodded and his smile widened.

He poured a little into my drink, but not enough to make me gasp. The taste was sweet and felt warm in my throat. I could drink this all night.

Just then Jack, Lucas, and David walked in the door. I wanted to melt into my seat. I hoped and prayed that they wouldn't see me, but I knew it was no use. They were headed right toward us.

I took a deep breath and waited for the inevitable fight.

Lucas nudged Jack and I was really glad that Vic couldn't see them.

Jack was the first to pass us. "Hey, Victor. How's it going?"

Victor turned, I guess expecting someone else because when he saw who it was the smile left his face. He didn't even look at Jack, but right at Lucas. Vic nodded but didn't even answer Jack.

"Hey guys! What are ya'll doing?" I asked trying desperately to keep my voice happy and neutral.

"Hey pretty girl. Call me later," Lucas said.

Lucas went to hug me but Vic was up in a flash. Vic said nothing and there was a palpable silence emanating from both of them. My heart skipped, my hands started to sweat, and anger coursed through my veins. Guys suck sometimes.

Jack stepped in between them and smiled. "Hey, I'll tell your waitress to send you a dessert on the house."

Jack grabbed Lucas' arm. "We'll see you later."

Jack had saved me from the embarrassing moment.

Their anger at each other was annoying. They just couldn't get along.

Vic and I sat in silence for a few moments. I could see him grinding his teeth and gripping his drink.

I had to try to alleviate some of the discomfort. "So, what are we ordering?"

At first Vic said nothing. He looked away from me and I thought for sure he was going to take me home or, worse, ignore me for the rest of the night, but he didn't. He sighed, "I think I'll have some fajitas, maybe chicken. You?"

Relief soared through my soul. He wasn't going to take me home and he wasn't going to ignore me.

We ordered and started to talk about school, sports, and food. I finally felt a little more comfortable, but I couldn't get the guys out of my mind. Part of me wanted to get up and walk out that door and just take off with Jack, but I really wanted to be with Vic. He was my dream. I would do anything for him. I knew sometimes he was super intense with me, but that was just him. It was one of the things I loved so much about him.

I excused myself and headed toward the restroom to check out how I looked and to make sure there wasn't anything stuck in my teeth. I looked in the mirror and saw a scared shy little girl looking back at me. I hated that look. Meg was right; I did look like I was vulnerable and frightened of my own shadow. I was pathetic.

You will not mess this up, I whispered to myself as I took a deep, calming breath and headed back to our table determined to be more outgoing and to loosen up a little.

"Missed you."

I smiled at him, "Yeah, how much?"

"I'll show you later," he answered.

A flush crawled from my stomach straight to my cheeks.

With my pale complexion, I was sure he saw it. I took a drink of my Coke and gasped. It was really strong. My cough made him laugh. I didn't dare say anything though. I was determined to loosen up. Plus, I felt I owed him something because of what had happened with the guys.

By the time our food came, I was laughing at practically

everything he said, whether it was funny or not.

We talked about Yna and my friends and he listened intently and said he hadn't known how much I liked them. I told him how they made me feel, like I was special and like they wanted to be with me for me and not for some ulterior motive. But somehow all the conversations ended up coming right back to him. He would say little comments about what he was going to do to me or how beautiful I was that would make my stomach somersault.

We left after I convinced him that I wasn't very hungry. I had barely touched anything on my plate and I hadn't eaten anything all day because of my nerves.

"So, you wanna ride around a little?"

"Sure, I'd like that," I answered.

We got on the drag and right away I noticed ambulances and cars speeding out of town. Something had happened, but I thought nothing of it. Accidents happened all the time on the highways.

"Something's happened on the highway again," I said.

He leaned over and put his hand behind my neck, caressing it. "Looks like it. Wanna go see? I can become an ambulance chaser for you."

I laughed, "No. We can just ride around. I'm sure it's nothing."

We rode around for another twenty minutes. He honked several times at people and some others would pass by him and scream out the window. After a while, instead of turning out of Sonic, he stopped, ordered us drinks, poured more "drink" into both cups, and continued out of town.

By then, I was pretty tipsy. I'm pretty sure I was more than a little drunk.

I didn't care where we went. I was having too much fun. I continuously sipped on my drink. When he parked on the other side of Beer Can Hill, I hopped out of the car. He turned up the music and I started to dance. He watched as he leaned against the hood of car. He had his hands in his pockets and a huge grin on his face.

After two songs, he joined me and he smelled so very

good. We swayed to the music and he kissed me on the neck. The music changed several times but we continued to dance close to each other. I'd take a sip, dance, take another sip, and dance some more. He had a great stereo system. My heart thumped to the sound of the bass.

He kissed me holding onto my face. He was so tender, "Let's get in the car."

I couldn't seem to focus on his face; I saw his hand grab mine, but I couldn't walk straight when he led me to his car.

He grabbed my arm a little rougher and guided me to the backseat.

Alarm bells went off inside my skull like bouncing tennis balls. "I don't want to do anything."

He shook his head and kissed me long and hard. My lips felt swollen and he felt so good and I couldn't think straight. He cupped me under my skirt and whispered in my ear. "Why not? Everyone's doing it. My friends make fun of me because we aren't. You want them to make fun of me?"

"No."Of course I didn't want them to make fun of him. I let him grab my breast under my shirt and he squeezed. Then he squeezed again. Hard.

I was getting dizzy and it hurt, so I started to push him away. "Shhhh . . . shhhh." he coaxed.

He moved his hand away from my breast and kissed me again and it felt good so I made myself relax. I didn't want him to be made fun of did I? I wanted to be part of his life and if I didn't do this, what would he do? Break up with me? Ignore me? That's not what I wanted. I wanted him to really like me and I couldn't seem to think about anything specific. I shook my head several times trying to clear my thoughts, but that didn't work and it just made me feel dizzier.

Is this what I wanted? I couldn't seem to keep my thoughts straight.

But we were in the backseat of a car. My first time wasn't supposed to be in the backseat of a car. Candles, nice hotel room, wine, chocolate covered strawberries, all laid out for a romantic ambiance sort of thing.

His gym bag was close to my head and the smell of dirty

socks and sweat invaded my senses.

His hands were everywhere. My thoughts were jumbled, scrambled, and all mixed up in my head. My responses were slow so his hands went everywhere and I was too slow to stop him. I felt myself losing control. I felt him doing things that I wanted to stop, but the only thing I could think about was his dirty socks. I stared at them and noticed the red hint of dirt on the soles and the smell. The horrifyingly awful smell of them.

He grabbed at my shirt and was under my bra in what felt like seconds.

Before I knew what was happening, he had my skirt up above my waist. My bra was off and hanging on one arm. The gym bag closed in on me until I felt like I was inside of it and the pungent smell started me in a panic.

I shook my head but was unable to make a sound. I pushed at his shoulders but I couldn't get him to stop or to even slow down. I heard his zipper and I heard his grunts.

Pain suddenly shot through my insides. I clawed at him and tried pushing away roughly, desperately pushing him. I heard myself say "no" over and over again, but he wasn't listening anymore, only grunting into me.

My chest felt crushed, I couldn't breathe, and the more I struggled, the heavier he was. It hurt and it was sticky and my head banged on the side of his car with every push and with every grunt I felt like I was going to die.

I wanted to die.

I was bleeding.

I could smell it.

I could feel it.

I was ashamed.

I Wish I Had Known

Yna was at Donnie's house party when Jaclyn came storming through the door with tears in her eyes. From that point on it was all a blur.

Less than an hour later, Yna leaned her head against the cold hospital cinderblock walls. She couldn't believe this was happening.

No one would tell her the truth.

She saw Daniel's beat-up mangled feet and her stomach started to ache. Her mascara had bled down her face and she didn't even care.

Nothing from tonight would be okay. Nothing would ever be the same.

Junior and Mike, Randy's friends, walked in quietly with blood all over their clothes. They looked scared, gaunt, and lost.Kenneth was there too.

Yna didn't even know they knew someone like him. He looked just as bewildered as everyone else.

Yna turned her head just in time to let the vomit escape on the ground a foot away from the trash can.

She didn't care.

"Where is he? Why won't they let me see him?" Yna cried.

Donnie, Yna's good friend, held her tight and whispered reassurances in her ear. He turned to Jaclyn and said, "Call Linda. She'll need her here tonight."

"Okay, I'll call her at home," Jacyln said, running to the phonebook at the nurse's station.

"I need Linda here. She'll make things right. She'll set things straight and she'll get some answers." Yna was crying uncontrollably.

It took only seconds for Jaclyn to come back, but her answer only made Yna cry harder. "She's not there. Her dad said she was supposed to be with you."

Chapter 10

Dear Diary,

I'm grounded for a month. Probably more. I don't even want to leave my room. Thank God October break is a full week. I'd be completely embarrassed to leave my room and be seen with this huge red mark on my face.

Yeah, you don't know what happened.

After I came home from my horrible date with Vic, I must have looked bad with my hair a mess and some blood on my skirt. My dad took one look at me and slapped me—hard. I hit the ground and a lamp. My dad hasn't talked to me since. I didn't even go to Randy's funeral.

Yeah, you don't know about that either.

Randy died on that stupid camping trip they went on. He was climbing a wall and Daniel wasn't able to run fast enough to save him. Yna was at the hospital and I'm sure Jaclyn knew I was out with Vic, so she called my dad to supposedly call me to be with Yna. I'm sure Jaclyn feels real bad about that. I think she wants Vic for herself.

I guess I should feel bad about Randy, but I don't. I don't feel bad about anything, not even Yna because I've closed myself off to feeling anything. So now I'm lying here, not feeling anything, and making myself forget about it all.

It's hard though. I don't know if I want to talk to Vic. I don't know if I want to talk to anyone. What I thought was my dream-come-true date ended up turning into a nightmare.

The ride back to Vic's house was filled with a silence you could taste. The smell of sex still lingered in the air and it was making my stomach clench.

I threw up twice on the way home and almost wrecked my car. That would've been the cherry on top of an outrageously horrid night.

Then Meg comes in and yells at me about being stupid and says she can guess what I'd been up to and so could Dad. It was horrible and then, to top it off, they told me about Randy and I should have felt bad for Yna, but I don't. Yna doesn't know what pain is.

I finished writing the entry in my diary and then closed the book and hid it in the secret compartment in my closet. If anyone ever found it, they'd think I was a terrible person, full of hate and anger.

My dad hadn't thought of taking away my computer. The chime that let me know when I had a message was barely audible (I had turned the volume way down so that no one would pay attention to it and I could, hopefully, keep it).

I wasn't sure I even wanted to read the message.

It was probably from Vic. How could I even face him? Even if I didn't have to see him, I still felt like he could see my red face. How would I explain being grounded for a month? I'd have to make excuses because there was no way that I'd be able to tell him the truth.

Or maybe it was from Yna. She'd give me a guilt trip about not being there for her and how could I ever tell her about what really happened myself with Vic when I'm not even sure what happened. I mean, yeah, I know what happened, but what REALLY happened?

Did he take advantage of me? Did I tell him no? I think I did, but I didn't fight him and it wasn't really rape because I sort of let him. I walked into the backseat of that car of my own free will and I let him kiss me. I felt my panties crawling down my legs and did nothing to stop it. Or did I?

My thoughts were still knotted and twisted in my foggy head—which was a clear indication that I should not be conversing with anyone, in person *or* via computer.

Chiming again, the computer sat glaring at me. I stole a

glance at it from my bed; the accusations that were coming from the computer were too much to take. The pillow didn't block out the third chime as I'd hoped.

Chime.

Someone really wanted to get a hold of me. I slowly approached the computer as if the other person could see me.

It was Jack.

He hardly ever chatted with me on the computer. He probably wanted to know why I hadn't been there for Yna. Not only had I just become a slut, but also a horrible friend. Jack chimed another three times looking for me, but I refused to respond.

Finally, he gave up. How would I face the guys again? I wasn't worthy of anyone's company anymore. I'd become a liar, a fake, a hypocrite, a slut, a shitty friend, and a nasty daughter all in one final swoop.

* * *

After three days of solitary confinement, Meg came in to grace me with her presence.

"You ready to listen to reason?" Meg asked, sitting at the edge of my bed.

"Please get out. I'm not letting you tell me what to do."

"Okay. Fair enough, but know that everyone's gonna know what you did the other night. He will not keep his mouth shut, so I'm gonna try to make it like it's a rumor and nothing else. Be prepared for Monday morning."

She quietly exited the room and shut the door.

Ten minutes later, my mother opened the door and informed me that part of my sentence would be washing dishes for the next three weeks.

Great.

I always hated washing dishes more than anything in the world. I'd rather scrub toilets than wash dishes. Especially after Meg cooks. She always used a separate dish for everything. Then, when people ate just a little, she'd transfer that dish into a smaller one. I never understood it, but that's what she does. It makes for a lot of dirty dishes.

I guess my staying in my room had ended and soon I was going to have to face my dad. I just had to make sure I looked him in the eye and didn't start with the vomit of the mouth.

Vic hadn't even bothered to try to contact me. I wasn't sure yet how I felt about that. It could've meant that he knew I was in trouble. I was sure he knew about Randy by then. Maybe he went to the funeral. They knew each other.

Maybe he found out I was supposed to be with Yna.

Maybe, just maybe, he simply hadn't called because he already got what he wanted. I had to face that brutal truth head-on and I'd have to face that truth coming from the worst person it could come from: Meg.

Meg would not let this go and she wouldn't let Vic off the hook without saying something to him. It would all end up being so embarrassing. The guys would find out and they wouldn't talk to me anymore.

What had I done?

I tossed and turned on my bed willing myself to go back to sleep. I didn't have much to look forward to at night, so sleep could at least block out everything, but it wouldn't come. Sleep eluded me like everyone else eventually would.

Chime.

I slowly crawled to the computer and willed the name on that chime to be Vic's.

It was.

He hadn't contacted me in three days, what would his excuse be?

Vic: U there?

I didn't answer him. What for?

I lay back down on the soft shag carpet. I didn't know whether to feel excited or sad or even angry.

Was I angry at him? Or was I just angry at myself for putting myself in that situation? Was it my fault or his?

I thought it could be my fault.

How could I be mad at him for something that I failed to do? We never really talked about doing that and I had never really told him that I wanted to wait or that I was afraid. He insinuated things all the time and never once had I told him to stop.

Nothing.

I had never said anything, so, in his eyes, I wasn't even new to the whole thing.

But I was and by now he had to know that, which was embarrassing. I probably bled all over his back seat and I moved so much trying to get away . . .

I did try to get away and I did tell him no.

I remember.

Now he was trying to talk to me after three days.

I decided not to answer. I would not talk to him until I felt better about all this.

My mom called me to the kitchen and I got up to go wash the dishes. I hoped Dad wasn't there.

He wasn't. I asked my mom where he was to prepare myself, and she said he was out working in the garage with his friends. That was good news. That could keep him outside until late at night and by then I'd be finished with the dishes and back in my room. I could face him tomorrow.

His friends like to drink. I could see my dad already holding his one can of beer for the entire night while the others threw back dozens.

I was right.

My dad and his buddies laughed outside through the entire night. My bedroom was close by and I could hear their muffled laughter.

Early the next morning, my mom sent me to the store for some eggs. Generally, when I'm grounded, my mom wouldn't ask me, but when I crawled out of bed I found out that my dad had gone to Odessa for some garage parts he couldn't find in town.

Odessa is about an hour and a half away which meant that he'd be gone, at the very least, most of the morning.

I dressed casually in jeans and a t-shirt and went out the

door. The fresh cool air brushed against my face invitingly. I decided to take a ride. Surely no one was out this early.

I got all the way past the Town and Country convenience store a quarter of a mile down the road when Jack pulled up next to me. I didn't want to stop, but shy of blatantly ignoring him, which I didn't want to do, I had to pull over and stop.

"Hey, stranger? Where have you been? I've been trying to call and IM you, and everything else. You haven't answered anything." Jack hadn't even stepped completely out of his Chevy before he started his accusations.

I didn't even bother to get out of my car. My old chipper self was absent and I silently wondered if that person would ever present itself again. What had I really done to myself?

I didn't look him in the face. I couldn't.

"I've gotten grounded. I was only out because my mom needs some eggs."

I knew the moment, the second, he saw my face.

"That a gift from your dad?" he asked moving my chin gently with his fingers.

My face flushed. I couldn't tell him the real reason why my dad had hit me. Jack would be disappointed in me or, worse, hate me.

"My dad is so unfair sometimes," I said.

"How long you grounded for?"

"Three weeks, maybe longer."

"Ouch. Well, he take your computer? I tried sending you a message and you didn't answer."

I couldn't very well tell him that I knew about his messages without giving away the fact I had ignored them. "No, but I turned down the alerts, so I haven't bothered to check them. Besides I want the dust to settle before I get on the computer in case he comes in."

"Well, will you send me a message when you can talk?"

"Sure. I better go."

We said our goodbyes with smiles but I could feel the tension in the air. It was thick and suffocating and it made me feel bad.

Luckily, I didn't meet or see anyone else at the store so I

got what I needed quickly and returned home. I was still scared that maybe my dad would come home early and find me out. That would not be good even though Mom had sent me. She'd probably get in trouble too.

I spent the rest of the day in my room and only came out to wash the dinner dishes and put in a load of laundry, another chore my mother had added to my list.

The next few days were the same dull nonsense. My dad went out of his way to stay away from me, which was fine, and it only made me feel worse than I already did.

I didn't know if anyone called for me. The first day I was grounded my dad must've answered the phone because it was suddenly off the wall, only a cord was left hanging in the kitchen.

On Saturday I went outside to wash my car. Somewhere in the back of my mind, I thought someone would see me and stop, but a bigger part of me hoped no one would. I didn't want to have to deal with my dad just yet, and I didn't want to have to answer all the questions I knew were inevitable.

Jack passed by twice, Lucas and David once, and Omar broke all kinds of records by passing by more than I could count. As usual they made me feel good but as I took out my chamois to dry the car, I started to cry.

I couldn't contain myself. I felt like such a loser and a slut and they were trying so hard to make me smile and feel better. I just didn't deserve it.

As I was going inside, someone honked. I turned just in time to see Vic passing by. The door slammed behind me and I didn't dare go back outside.

* * *

Sunday was dreadful. I went to church and sat in the back by myself. Luckily, my mom decided to go to the Baptist church. Most of my friends were Catholics and that church would be full of them.

My family is a strange mixture so we frequented both religions. Maybe it was a convenience thing, but it worked for us, especially that day. I only knew a few people at the Baptist church and most weren't below the age of fifty so I was safe.

Four messages from Vic were on the computer when I got home but I still didn't answer him. I just wasn't ready.

I stayed up late dreading the next morning when I'd have to go back to school and what it all implied.

After about three in the morning, I finally fell into a restless sleep.

My dreams were full of demons in fire and brimstone where the boulders, rocks, and stones sizzled with the blazing heat of an erratic volcano. People screamed in anguish as demons chased them.

Near a myriad of mirrors, the demons stopped to leer at their reflections.

I was astonished by the reflection. Horror filled my veins.

Those demons looked like me.

Chapter 11

School Monday morning sucked. I drove up fashion-ably late, but the guys were waiting for me anyway. They asked a whole boat-load of questions that I didn't want to answer. The only ones I did answer were the ones about Yna. My excuse for everything was that I was grounded. I was going to stick to that one.

We all walked in together and right away Lucas told me Yna hadn't shown up to school. I guess she was really messed up, but I just couldn't bring myself to face her yet.

Her absence gave me a little bit of relief; that was, until I saw Vic waiting by my locker. He leaned on it casually, but the unhappy and accusing look on his face was unmistakable. He obviously didn't know about my being grounded.

I pasted a strained smile on my face and said my fare-wells to the others.

"I told you I wanted you to start parking behind the school."

He hadn't even let me get close enough to him so that others wouldn't hear. I nervously looked around hoping the guys hadn't heard him. That's all I needed on the home front—someone calling my dad about me causing a fight with Vic.

I chose not to answer him. I opened my locker and didn't bother to look at him.

I couldn't. I was so ashamed.

"I thought you and I had an understanding now. I thought you were mine."

He grabbed my arm roughly, probably shocked that someone had deliberately not given in to him. "You're mine now."

"I'm not anyone's. I'm me." I couldn't stand it anymore. I felt like I had to defend myself.

I shrugged away from him and headed to my class.

"Linda, please don't walk away from me. You are mine now."

He didn't follow me though. I was glad because I probably would have cried. I made it to my desk while breathing heavily, trying desperately to get control of my erratic emotions.

I had to figure out what I was going to say to Vic after class. I was sure he'd be there waiting for me. I didn't like that he thought of me as some kind of possession, but in the same breath, it was comforting and made me feel good.

Was there something wrong with me to feel like that? Did I like him treating me like that?

Somehow I felt honored that he—the popular, good-looking, senior, money-out-the-wazoo guy—would like me. Me—the nobody, the loser, the minion.

He looked so attractive today too with his perfect fitting jeans and collared polo shirt. It had taken everything I had to walk away when all I wanted to do was throw my arms around him and sob like a baby.

I completely missed the math lesson and didn't even bother to answer when I was called on. Luckily, my geeky over-eager classmate, Steve, answered the question.

I didn't even feel bad when I looked at him and saw the Band-Aid above his eye. I just rolled my eyes at him. His problems were minute compared to mine. Eyebrows grow back.

When I shook my head in an effort to come back to reality, I was sorely mistaken. I should have kept my head in the clouds. I could hear some whispers behind me.

I turned in that direction and saw Jaclyn and Jean whispering to each other. When I looked at them they laughed.

Loud.

I felt my face burn to a crimson red. Was Meg right? Had Vic gone out and told others what we had done?

I don't think I could take others knowing. Not yet.

I put my head down for the rest of the class period hoping just to survive the next twenty minutes.

It never failed.

When you start to watch the clock, that's when it daw-
dles, slows down, and creeps to a near halt. It stalls and it takes
forever.

Finally, after what felt like an eternity, the bell rang.

I went straight to my locker determined to get to my
next class. Vic wasn't there. I guess he was mad at me too now.
Join the crowd.

I made it through the rest of the school day without seeing Vic and I managed to eat lunch by myself, standing in a
corner behind a big group of people so no one would see me.

I had to stay behind after school to get some last minute
handouts the cheer coach was giving out, so the halls were vir-
tually empty when I walked out to the parking lot.

"We need to talk," Vic said, startling me out of my daze.

He had obviously been waiting for me by my vehicle.
I noticed the guys hadn't waited, but I couldn't blame them.
Some of them worked part of the day as a class. It was a sweet
deal for them because they got out of school, which they hated
anyway, and were able to go to work at noon and earn money,
which they were all about.

I thought for a split second that I'd just ignore him, but
then decided against it. I really did want to be with him and it
wasn't his fault I had acted like a fool and drank too much.

I guess he could tell when I gave in, maybe it was the
look on my face. Whatever it was gave him the green light to get
close to me. He held me in his arms and stroked my hair, "You
haven't answered any of my phone calls, you ignore me, and
then you act so mean to me. What's going on?

I thought about his point of view and the fact that in his
eyes we were perfectly fine and nothing I had done with him
was out of the ordinary. To him, it was business as usual. To me
it was so much more.

"Look, you just really hurt me. That's all. I got grounded, too, because I was supposed to be out with Yna." I finally
allowed myself to hug him back.

He hugged me harder. "Is that why you haven't returned my e-mails? You sure looked like you'd been talking to your friends."

"Today was the first time I've talked to any of them. I hadn't seen them all week."

"Well, we're okay now, right? I want us to go out again this weekend. I'll show you that it won't hurt again. The last thing I want to do is hurt you. You should know that by now."

Every fiber of my being wanted to scream and run as fast and as far away from him as I could, but I didn't because my being grounded was going to help me here too. "I'm grounded for a month, at least."

His disappointment was clear, but the look on my face was enough for him to say, "It's okay, we'll get through this. I can wait."

I wasn't sure what he could wait for, but I had a pretty good idea and for the first time in my life I was so glad that I was grounded.

He held me for a long time stroking my hair, and the anxiety that had filled my body since the backseat of his car finally released its evil grip and I began to relax.

I looked into his eyes and he smiled. "Don't worry. We are together now. You and I are going to make it. You're mine now. You've proven that to me."

Before I left for home after some comforting words and sweet stolen kisses, he made me promise to park in the back so he could walk me to my classes and then he really showed me he cared: "I want to know where you are at all times. I care about you and I want to make sure you're okay,"

* * *

For the next month, we were inseparable. I parked in the back just like he wanted me to and we'd meet ten minutes early so we could talk. We really got to know each other, but in the same sense, I felt my relationship with the guys getting more and more distant.

Vic took up all of my time at school and since I was grounded I didn't have any time to do anything else because I was expected at home.

I was even able to share my feelings about Yna with Vic. He kept telling me that she was just jealous of our relationship and wanted for me to be as miserable as she was now that Randy was dead.

He was a great sounding board and saved me when Yna would approach me in school. He was always there so I never had the chance to talk to her in private, which in a way was a great thing because I didn't want to face her alone anymore.

He was even there for my cheer practices and sometimes he'd follow me in his car when I ran. He really took care of me.

I felt like a coward and a shitty friend, but Vic said it had to be that way so we could be together like we wanted.

Several times, the guys, mainly Jack, came by my locker to talk to me before Vic showed up. (Sometimes Vic was late and I had to wait for him, even if it meant my being late to class.)

Jack would try to ask me to go to his house or Lucas' house, but Vic and I were doing so well, and well, I was still grounded, so I continued to say no.

Jack would stand there looking at me and I'd glance around nervously hoping Vic wouldn't see us talking. After a while, Jack gave up and hadn't been near my locker for a couple of weeks.

It wasn't long before Jack stopped coming by my locker and stopped talking to me all together.

I lost all my friends, but Vic said he was the only friend I needed and, in a way, he was right.

I was happy, comforted and reassured when we were together. He was absolutely wonderful.

At night, we would talk on the computer as soon as he got home from football practice. I would get off only when I had to wash dishes and get right back on when I was done. He would time me and make fun of me if I took too long so, for the most part, I would wash them as quickly as I could. Then we would stay on until I had to get into bed at ten. I always felt stupid when bedtime came around because it seemed so childish. Every night, I'd think of the other girls he could be going out with that could see and talk to him anytime he wanted. It sucked, but Vic seemed to take it in stride.

My dad still hadn't talked to me. He continued to go out of his way to avoid me. I was beginning to think that he didn't know what to say to me. Still, Vic helped me out there too because I wanted to approach my dad about what happened and explain some things, but Vic said he thought I should just stay away from him.

I did the same thing with Meg.

She was always harping on and on about what a horrible guy Vic was. I mistakenly told Vic about Meg's feelings, and they'd had some words at school, but Vic was my champion. He was always there for me.

Vic and I got to where we could talk about most things, but I still felt like I had to watch what I said about the guys and Yna.

One day, I wore a mini-skirt and a fitted yellow shirt to school and he about flipped a wig. He was so cute when he asked me never to wear that again. He said I was his and he didn't like to think of the other guys looking at me.

After that, there wasn't a day that went by that he didn't complain about something I wore. I seemed to look too pretty or I had on too much make-up or something along those lines.

He would take me into his arms and kiss me and tell me that I was killing him. He'd smile, roll his eyes, and hug me hard.

I found myself being real conscious of what I wore and what make-up, if any, I put on. I only wanted to please him.

By the fourth week, I felt like I didn't have any friends. The guys ignored me completely and Jack had long since stopped sending me messages on the computer. Even Yna stopped trying to talk to me and male classmates seemed to avoid me like the plague.

I felt just a little twinge of guilt, but then I thought about the fact that for the first time I was really happy with a guy who took so much interest in me. I'd never had a relationship like this. I felt so adult and special.

I got my period too, thank God, because I don't know what I would have done if I hadn't. I only sweated it for a little bit because it was my first time, but still. It was a close call and one I didn't want to repeat.

Vic told me most relationships weren't like ours. I'd seen Yna with Randy plenty of times and had to agree with him. I loved our relationship and I didn't want anyone messing that up. Vic felt the same way because he went out of his way to be so nice to me by giving me gifts, love letters, opening doors for me, and so many other wonderful things.

One of his gifts was a beautiful white gold and onyx journey pendant on a dainty silver chain. I was floored when he bought it and when he put it on me himself—I was in heaven.

On Saturday morning, the fourth week of my grounding, God threw me a wicked screwball.

I had gone outside to wash my car when my mom called me inside to answer a phone call.

Little by little, my independence had been given back to me. I had been able to use the phone for the last two days, but since Vic and I talked on the computer and none of my "friends" called me, I hadn't received any phone call.

I ran inside hoping it was Vic surprising me.

It wasn't.

Jean was on the phone laughing and giggling. I could recognize her whiney, annoying voice anywhere.

I thought she was calling to argue with me about the fight we had a few weeks ago or maybe she wanted to gloat about the math test we took the week before when she got a better grade than I did. I knew, though, that the phone call was not going to be a good one.

I took a deep breath and answered, "Hello."

The laughter was annoying and I could hear someone in the background.

I was about to start in on her when she answered, "Linda?"

"Yes. What do you want?"

Laughter. "I just wanted to ask you if you knew where your boyfriend was last night."

I rolled my eyes. Of course she was calling about Vic. The jealousy in her eyes was evident every time I saw her in the hallways. "Don't call me anymore. You're just jealous. You need to grow up."

I don't know why I stayed on the line. *Curiosity killed the cat* or so Meg liked to say, but a little minute part of me wanted to know what sort of information she thought she had.

So I waited, through all the laughter and giggles and the girl in the background whispering loud enough for me to hear her say, "Just tell her."

"I was with Vic last night."

Chapter 12

A nd she hung up on me. She didn't give me a chance to respond, yell, or question. I guess that was her intention from the beginning.

I went to my room in a daze, forgetting about washing the car. My hand automatically flew to the pendant.

I had begun rubbing it with my thumb as soon as I heard the laughter.

I sat at my computer and contemplated asking Vic about it. Was this just something Jean was making up because we were so happy? Jean hated me—that was nothing new, so her phone call didn't surprise me in the least.

However, there was a small part of me that questioned why she would call when she knew I'd ask Vic. I thought about asking him online, but I wanted to see his face. That would tell me if he was lying or not. I decided to ignore it until Monday.

No.

I couldn't do that.

It was going to kill me to have to wait that long. I had to find a way to ask him in person. My mom had to be out of something in the kitchen. Something she needed from the store that I could conveniently go get. I could slip by Vic's house and ask him in person.

Excitement, anticipation, and a twinge of nervousness attacked me as soon as I stepped out of my bedroom.

I found my mom sitting at the table peeling potatoes. From the looks of things she was making beef, potatoes, rice and beans. She had a fresh batch of tortillas on the stove. Suddenly I knew exactly what to ask for. "Hey, do we have avocados?"

My mom glanced at the table then got up and looked in

the fridge. My dad was an avocado freak. He loved them with this meal and I knew we didn't have any more. I had finished off the last one a few days ago.

"Can you go to the store?"

I made a face like it was a huge inconvenience, sighed, and shrugged my shoulders. "I guess."

It had been too easy. I had to force myself to walk slowly and breathe. I practically threw myself into my car and sped out of there as fast as I could without going over the speed limit.

Vic's house came into view in a flash. I found him outside with some of his friends playing basketball. A few of them had their shirts off, including Vic. His hard and smooth abs flexed as he walked toward me. His long fingers wrapped around the basketball and his strong arms reeked of masculinity.

"Hey, gorgeous! What a great surprise. Did you come over to watch me beat these losers?"

He bent over to give me a quick hug and I couldn't believe he smelled good. When I worked out I smelled like a wet dog.

"I just got sent out to buy some stuff, so I can't stay long. Can I talk to you for a sec?"

He looked at me closely trying to read my thoughts. "Sure."

He walked with me toward my car and then kissed me deeply. I almost lost my train of thought.

Almost.

The image of him with Jean flashed through my mind. I pictured them laughing, snuggling, and kissing in his car. I began to get angry again.

I would say what I had to say and watch his reaction closely.

"Jean called me," I said, a little too briskly.

A flicker of something passed through his eyes. I wasn't sure if I had really seen it because it passed so quickly, but something had definitely sputtered across his eyes.

"What did she want? I thought you guys hated each other."

"She called to tell me she was with you last night."

He didn't look at me for a few seconds but seemed to focus on a oil stain on the road. My heart dropped like a ton of rocks and then started to beat hard against my shirt and pound in my ears and I thought I was going to be sick. I wanted to grab him and yell at him so that he would tell me that it was all a lie and he'd do anything to prove it to me.

Instead he simply asked me, "Do you believe her?"

I took a minute to respond. This time it was he who looked just a little panicked which made me feel good. Did I really believe her or not? I wasn't sure, but this conversation wasn't going as I had planned.

"That's why I'm here." I chose not to answer his question. "I wanted to hear what you had to say."

"She's lying. I told you other people would try to do anything just to keep us apart. Don't you love me? I thought we were past all this bullshit."

He started to walk away like all this was my fault. I walked after him and I found myself apologizing. "Look, I'm sorry but I had to ask. Wouldn't you do the same?"

He kept on walking towards his friends and my heart broke just a little more. He was walking away from me. He had never done that.

I quietly walked back towards my car, got in, and took off. I cried all the way to the store and I didn't even pay attention to the still green and hard avocados I purchased. How could our conversation have ended so badly?

I got home and realized I had no one to talk to. I couldn't call Yna because I still hadn't talked to her about Randy and the guys had already given up on me. They'd say that I only called them when I needed them. How selfish could I be?

So I just sat in my room listening to music and surfing the web for the rest of the afternoon. No one sent me a message, I didn't get an e-mail, and I didn't get one phone call. I was pathetic.

Sunday came and went just as Saturday had. More times than I could count, I picked up the phone, dialed Yna's number and hung up before anyone could answer. I even typed a long message to Jack, but I couldn't bring myself to send it. I had completely lost my friends.

Meg came in that night to talk. She was not Vic's number one fan, so we stayed away from talking about him. She seemed to sense something had gone wrong so she didn't press me. We talked for a little while about nothing and then she offered to do my nails. I knew right then that she was feeling sorry for me. She never offered things like that.

Before she left to her room, she finally ventured to ask, "Something happen?"

I couldn't tell her about the phone call because she would automatically believe Jean and throw Vic to the wolves. I knew she'd jump at the chance to bash Vic. I couldn't even tell her about my friendship problems because they all stemmed from Vic too. She hated him already and I didn't want to make it worse. People just couldn't seem to understand our relationship, so it was questioned and bashed all the time.

And I had gone over and messed it up. It was all my fault for questioning him and not putting my trust in him like I should have.

I wondered what would happen in the morning.

* * *

Monday morning I thought long and hard about whether or not to park in back with Vic or to park where I used to. I still couldn't face the guys and I couldn't face Vic, so I parked completely by myself in the north end of the parking lot where all the Beaners parked.

No one bothered me and I was able to slip inside and into my classroom without being seen.

First period with Mr. Farks was a breeze. We were watching a movie that I'd seen already, so I didn't have to pay attention. I kind of wanted the lesson to be hard and interesting so that I wouldn't be able to think about anything else.

When the bell rang I walked swiftly to my locker hoping to get to my next class as inconspicuously as I had before.

Luck wasn't on my side.

My steps faltered. Jean and Vic were waiting for me at

my locker. I couldn't believe it. Why would they both be at my locker waiting for me? Did they want to flaunt their relationship in front of me? Was it not enough that they'd embarrassed me already?

Everyone knew Jean and I hated each other and the fact that she was waiting at my locker with Vic had everyone staring, itching for a fight. Some people smiled and made it quite obvious that they wanted to see some action.

I decided to play it cool. "What do you want?"

I directed my attention completely to Jean. She was still smiling and giggling. The situation was ridiculous and an urge to throw a few punches at her again began to get overwhelming.

"Vic *said* I had to come over here and tell you that I wasn't telling the truth," Jean said smiling.

I stared at her closer and could tell she wasn't taking any of this seriously. She couldn't care less what I thought and she emphasized the word *said*.

Why?

"Why did you call me?" I wanted some answers.

She glanced questioningly at Vic before answering, "I was just playing. No sense getting your panties in a wad."

That made me angry and I took one step toward her. If she did this only because she wanted to get a rise out of me then she was doing a really good job.

Still. I didn't see the point. Why call me?

Vic whispered something to her, and, when he turned to face me, she winked at me.

Which made me question all this even more.

She sauntered away and joined her friends who all had a good laugh.

He smiled at me, grabbed me by the arm, and walked me the few feet to my locker. "See, I told you she was lying."

Somehow all this didn't make me feel better or reassure me.

I glanced around to see if people were still gawking at us when I caught a glimpse of Yna circled by friends with pity in her eyes.

I wanted to cry.

After all I had done to her, she could still find it in her-self to pity me.

What had I done?

I let him walk me to my next class but didn't say much of anything. He seemed content to let it stay that way.

"I'll meet you at your locker and we'll have lunch just like always."

I didn't even bother to look at him or reply.

Jean was in my class. She sat four rows behind me with her friends, Gina and Kaley.

Gina was the gossip girl of the town. You probably know the type: pretty, short, and thin with silver little glasses that made her look smart even though she wasn't. If you ever wanted to find out about something, all you had to do was ask her and she would never hesitate to answer, especially if it was something that would hurt you.

Kaley, on the other hand, was the tag-along. She was a short and gawky, long-haired girl that looked like she was scared all the time. She was always tagging along with what others were doing or thinking. She never had an original thought.

They were both girls that enjoyed making up or spreading horrible rumors about poor unsuspecting people. They always knew everything about everyone, and if they didn't, they'd just make something up. They dressed in what they thought was the highest fashion and laughed at everyone who didn't, or worse, couldn't and they made fun of people when they were already down.

Hypocrites.

I knew the class was going to be a long one when I heard Jean's strangled-something's-dying laugh. Then someone else I didn't recognize snickered and a spitwad grazed my temple. I turned and looked at Jean but I couldn't tell who had thrown it. Gina and Kaley glared at me as Jean looked away seemingly innocent.

"Don't let them bother you," Julie said.

My reply was wedged in my throat. I knew Julie was try-ing to help. She was always making jokes and always seemed so happy. She didn't know what real problems were.

That class was one of the longest I'd ever had. It only got worse when they started whispering to each other and I knew I was intended to hear some of it. I caught bits and pieces: *she'll find out sooner or later; now tell her what you did with him; he uses her.*

All these comments hurt like a dagger through my heart. My stomach rumbled in torment and a headache pounded my veins.

Finally, I had had enough. I asked to go to the nurse. I was going home. One way or another I was going to go.

As I practically ran out of the room, the laughter of Jean and her friends rang in my ears. I couldn't face this alone but I had to. I had no one to turn to.

When I got to the nurse's office, I had to wait in line. It seemed that I wasn't the only one itching to go home. The line was long and the students would moan every now and then to see if they could grab her attention. None of it worked.

The nurse's features were hard and looked like she continuously sucked on lemons. Old age lines covered her face and she slouched when she walked, as if her body were too heavy for her. She couldn't weigh more than a buck ten on a wet, soggy day.

When I finally got to her, she explained that she wouldn't let me go home unless someone witnessed me throwing up and that someone had to be a teacher.

So I walked calmly to her restroom, left the door open, and threw up all of my breakfast.

Easy.

She called my mom and I was sent home. I didn't even bother to go back and get my books. There wasn't anything there that anyone would find interesting or valuable.

Before I went home, I drove around town for a few minutes in peace and just cried. I let it all out because I knew I wouldn't be able to do it at home without arousing suspicion.

Once at home, I took a long hot shower and then pretended to be sick for the next two days.

That's how long I was able to go without seeing a doctor. My mom threatened to take me if I didn't get out of bed by Wednesday morning.

I had long since stopped worrying about my dad making a surprise entrance demanding that I go to school. I realized I couldn't care less about what he thought. Ignoring me didn't solve anything. It just made me more miserable.

I hadn't answered the messages on my computer and I hadn't even answered the phone. I didn't care who was calling and I didn't want to talk to anyone.

Meg came in several times during the two days but I would really milk my sickness when she came in. Finally, on the night before I was set to go back to school, she came in with some serious questions.

She sat down at the edge of my bed and looked at me the same way Yna had after that horrible scene with Vic. I wasn't about to prod her into asking the questions I knew were coming.

I grabbed the nearest pillow and put it over my head.

"You're not gonna stop me from asking questions and the pillow ain't helping you either," Meg said.

"Yeah, I can't stop you from asking and you can't force me to answer." My voice was muffled against the pillow but I knew she could still hear and understand with perfect clarity that I didn't want her in my room.

"Are you pregnant?" Meg asked.

Startled and embarrassed I jerked the pillow off my head. "No!"

I couldn't believe she would dare ask me that. What did she think I was doing? Leaving school to meet up with him? I'd been grounded for the last four weeks. I looked into her eyes to see if maybe, just maybe, she was pulling my leg or playing with me or trying to startle me into talking to her. Anything other than the fact that she really wanted to know because she believed that I was sexually active.

"You mope around the house, you're always sleeping or crying, and now you're sick and you threw up at school. What do you expect me to think?"

"I expect you to mind your own business."

"I've been hearing a lot of things and I'm tired of not knowing what's going on. The guys have called you several times and so has Yna. You aren't answering any of their phone calls. Something's going on."

The guys called me? And Yna?

I couldn't believe it. They were really asking about me and I hadn't done anything *so* bad that they had completely turned their back on me. Even Yna was trying to contact me.

I didn't pay any attention to anything else Meg was saying until she hit me with the pillow.

"Hello. Aren't you listening to what I said?"

"Yes, now will you get out of my room?" I asked.

She only nodded her head.

The thought of doing my old throw-up-of-the-mouth bit I usually reserved for my dad crossed my mind—then it quickly faded into apprehension.

I couldn't tell her.

I still wasn't sure what I was going to do about Vic and if I told her and then Vic and I turned out okay after this, then she'd really hate him. I decided just to sulk through her questions. "No, I'm not pregnant. I'm absolutely sure."

"Well at least there's that. Did you and Vic cause a scene the other day? Since I actually listen to the teachers, I wasn't around your neck of the woods at school, but I heard plenty."

"What did you hear?" I asked.

Curiosity ate me up. The need to know other people's thoughts about me haunted me, but sometimes, most of the time, I hated what I found out. The gossip was never good. I knew that so I steeled myself for whatever it was she was going to say.

"Oh, not much, just that Vic's been seeing Jean behind your back and he's making her lie to you so he doesn't get caught so he can continue to use you for sex."

Chapter 13

Thursday morning I began to feel sick like I was going to pass out. My head thrummed, my neck ached, butterflies were taking pot shots at my insides, and suddenly the room became hazy and I lost my peripheral vision.

My heart ached.

I knew that some people regard a heartache as if it's nothing, but I don't think they've ever had it happen to them. My heart truly thumped against my chest with a steady ache. This was physical pain as if I were being stabbed. This was not just sadness. They should call them heartstabs.

I was a coward.

What was the worst that could happen?

I thought about the situation with Vic all through the night. What was I supposed to do?

After several attempts at talking myself into breaking up with Vic, I just couldn't do it.

I wasn't sure if he was seeing Jean. She was just a horrible person and she wouldn't hesitate to ruin my life. I had to believe what Vic said until I had something substantial that could prove he was with her.

Rumors. They sucked.

Lives have been destroyed by rumors.

I had to give Vic the benefit of the doubt. What if Jean were making it all up? Vic and I had something together that was potentially the best thing that would ever happened to me. And here I was throwing it all away.

I set my mind to put everything behind me and start a new day.

I went to school early and parked where the guys parked. As I walked toward the school, I caught a glimpse of

Daniel going in early. I hadn't thought of him since Randy died.

I wondered how he was taking it all.

Judging from his lowered head, beaten stance, and down-trodden expression, he was lonely, upset, and lost.

I probably mirrored him completely.

My brisk walk quickened once I got inside the school. I had so much to do. My homework for Mr. Farks' class was due in fifteen minutes and I hadn't even started it. I had cheer practice that afternoon and I hadn't run in weeks.

The track season started full swing in two short months and already I was behind. I had to get back on track, but being grounded sure put a mammoth of a dent in my plans.

My homework was finished a few seconds before the tardy bell rang. I breathed a sigh of relief and started to arrange my notebook. It, too, was a mess.

After class I walked slowly to my locker, not knowing who or what I'd find there.

Lucas leaned against my locker, smiling at all the big-breasted girls that passed by. When he looked at me, his smile vanished like a ghost. Was he here to yell at me for what I'd done to Yna or to Jack?

"You okay? I've been worried about you."

That was not something I was expecting him to say. After all I had done, he was actually worried about me. I was so shitty.

"Yeah, I'm fine. I just got sick. I think it was a virus or something. I still feel a little queasy."

He looked down and I could tell right away that he didn't believe a word I said.

He was such a nice guy. His hair fell over his left eye and his casual jeans and canary yellow shirt complimented his skin. He was cute and clean. He wasn't muscular or tall or overly good-looking, but there was something about him that made people look twice. Maybe it was the confidence he exuded.

"Really, I'm okay. I'll be fine."

He smiled at me for the first time in a very long time. It was so comforting. I smiled back and I felt hope for myself.

"What the hell are you doing here?" Vic asked suddenly

very close to my ear.

I jumped and started to push away when Vic put his arm around me to hold me still.

One glance at Lucas and I could tell he was ready to fight. For what seemed like a million tense moments there was an eerie kind of quiet. No one moved or said a word. Other students began to stop and stare, sensing that something bad was about to happen.

I had to stop this before it escalated into something more. "I'm fine, Lucas. I'll talk to you later."

I couldn't bear Vic doing something to Lucas just because of me. It always seemed to be Vic and Lucas fighting. I shook my head at him and pleaded with my eyes not to do anything.

"I'll call you later," Lucas said giving Vic one last withering look of contempt before he walked away. Lucas had done that for me. I know he had.

I turned to face Vic. "Why would you do that? You know we're just friends."

He narrowed his eyes as if he couldn't see me clearly. "You're always with other guys. Every time I turn the corner there's a different guy. What am I supposed to think?"

I remembered Jason: dimples, manly smells, and mysterious Linda. I had forgotten about him.

"Am I not allowed to talk to guys now? Am I supposed to stay at home every night while you're out with Jean?"

Enraged, he pushed me against the locker—hard.

Time froze for a moment. I couldn't believe he hit me. I couldn't believe he'd actually do that.

"Stay away from me," I whispered. I turned to walk away but he grabbed my arm and forcibly pushed me against the locker again.

"You will not walk away from me. You are mine. That was decided a few nights ago."

My face turned beet red, the crowd was getting bigger, and, no matter how much I tugged and tugged, he would not let go of my arm.

His eyes were dark and unfocused.

"You make me do this. I love you," he pleaded.

My heart turned to mush. He did these things to me because he loved me. He loved me so much it was violent, passionate, and fierce.

"Please," I whispered again.

I hated all those horrible stares from people. Luckily Meg, Jean, and even Yna weren't there to see my embarrassment.

He took a few slow breaths, looked around, and said, "I will be here to walk you to your next class. I promise." He quietly walked away, nudging a few students in the process.

Shaking, I turned to my locker, grabbed my books for my next class, slammed it shut, and started to make a break for my next class when Mrs. Hinho cut off my getaway with her enormously large body.

"Ms. Balle? Can I see you in my office for a few minutes?"

Fear shot through my veins. What if she called my dad?

"Yes ma'am." I had no other choice.

Mrs. Hinho was the school counselor. She and her assistant thought they ran the school. She could be sweet and insightful to the female students from what I heard, but to the guys—she was just plain shitty.

I followed her from a safe distance, hoping she'd see someone more important and forget all about me.

"Please take a seat in my office, Ms. Balli. I'll be right with you," she said. She walked briskly toward the attendance clerk.

No such luck that she'd forget about me. Now I had to wait in her stinky office full of cat pictures and think about what had just happened.

The morning that I had resigned myself to have was lost forever. I thought Vic and I would be okay if I just put Jean and all those rumors behind me, but now it seemed like we had more problems.

I felt loved and lucky that he loved me like he did. Who could ask for anything more? And what would I do if I continually found him talking to other girls? I'd be pissed off just like he was. I knew I'd throw a huge sarcastic fit. So how could I blame him? And if he walked away from me when I was feeling betrayed, well, I'd probably do the same and force him to listen to me.

The problem was that my left side hurt and my arm felt sore. He was fervently trying to make me understand how much he loved me.

"Okay, Ms. Balle. I'd like to ask you a few questions."

"Do I have to answer them?"

As soon as I said that I wanted to take it back.

Lucky for me, she ignored my response and started scribbling on a notepad."Do you have a relationship with Vic?"

"What do you mean?"

"Is he your boyfriend?"

"Yes."

At this point, she looked up at me, took her reading glasses off, and crossed her hands under her chin. "Can you tell me what just happened?"

I knew immediately that she'd just witnessed the entire episode. Why hadn't she intervened?

"We were just playing." I had to play it off.

"It didn't look like you were playing. It looked like you were in pain."

I shook my head and looked at the carpet. "No, he likes to play around and see how many people we can attract. We get a good laugh about it."

"Are your parents still married?"

Why would she want to know about my parents? Was she going to call home? "Yes, they are."

"If you walked up and saw your dad push your mom against a wall and keep her against her will, would you think that was okay?"

Shifting my eyes away from her uncomfortable stare, I said, "My parents play like that sometimes."

Her eyes narrowed. "Do you know what an abusive relationship is?"

"I think so."

She looked around as if summoning some memory.

"Well, at first the guy is very receptive and will be like Romeo, then he'll get pushy wanting you to do things that make you uncomfortable. Finally he'll start isolating you. This isolation will make you feel completely dependent on him. He will seem like your only friend, the only one who really, truly cares about you. Then he'll become violent. He'll begin to hit you. Does this sound familiar?"

All I could respond with was, "No."

Vic wasn't cold-blooded. He really loved me. I could tell. He was always on my side.

"Sooner or later he'll really get violent and then you'll try to get out and it will be too late."

She smiled at me on this point as if she had just recited a grocery list. She was talking about my life and she thought it was inconsequential. I was nothing to her.

"Can I go now?" I asked. I wanted to put as much distance between us as possible and I was already late to class.

"Look Linda, you seem like a nice girl. If something happens, will you promise to come talk to me? I can make a world of difference in your life. In the past, I've helped many girls. They love me."

I had no idea who loved her and no one ever said anything nice about her, but, well, who knew?

"Better yet, I'll call you back in a few weeks to see how things are going. I can't do anything unless you own up to what's going on. Like I said, I can help anyone. I am really good at what I do." She tapped the nameplate on her desk as she said the last sentence.

"Yes ma'am." I was so ready to get out of there.

"I'll write you a note. Please tell Mike to come in," she said, scribbling on a small purple notepad.

As I left I caught a glimpse of Mike, a guy who spoke to no one and worked all the time with his dad.

I had seen him several times around Daniel and Randy but since he seemed to melt into the wallpaper, or was a wallflower as they say, I never noticed him much.

The only thought I had when I saw him was that I felt sorry for him. Mrs. Hinho was not a guy-lover.

"Sorry, but it's your turn."

***

Walking into class after causing a huge scene is pretty embarrassing. Conversation stopped completely when I stepped inside. I put my head down lower, if that were possible, and walked quickly to my seat.

I didn't want to talk to anyone and it seemed that others felt the same way about me because no one bothered to ask me what happened or even if I was okay.

Vic was waiting for me at my locker after class. His smile made my stomach take a somersault. After all this, he still wanted me.

"Linda, look, I'm sorry. I don't want you to leave me. All these people want us apart. I won't do that again. I just get crazy when it comes to you. I just want it to be me and you like it was," Vic said.

My heart swelled and all the events that had led up to this melted away. He just wanted to be with me.

Me—the loser, the shitty friend, and the worst girlfriend in the world.

I shot him a smile and looked down. I felt so ashamed that I couldn't even look him in the eye. All of this was my fault.

"I'm sorry. I was just talking to Lucas. There is nothing going on, but I've put myself in your shoes and I understand it, but you have to learn to trust me," I said just above a whisper.

"Trust is earned, Linda," he said touching my cheek.

"I know and I'll earn it back. I promise." I was going to make it work. He loved me and he'd made that clear by sticking with me through all this craziness.

He smiled. "Come on, we'll walk to athletics together."

The two athletics buildings were located across the parking lot away from the school. The facility on the west side was connected to the football stadium and housed the boy's locker room as well as a large weight room.

The south building housed dressing rooms for tennis players and an indoor gym. I used the dressing room to change for track practice. Since I was one of the few marathon runners on the team, I didn't practice with the others.

We walked together in silence. Other people looked our way but I refused to look down. When he was by my side, I felt like I could take on the world.

He squeezed my arm and when I looked up at him he smiled. "We're going to make it. You'll see."

Dear Diary,

It has been a horrible couple of weeks. Jean says she and Vic are seeing each other and that he's using me for sex. What am I supposed to do about that?

I don't believe it. How can I when Vic is so kind to me? We spent an hour chatting online. He says he'll take good care of me and that he'll never hurt me. He's so sweet and has apologized lots of times for grabbing me so roughly and said he'd never do that again. He says that we're meant to be together and that his parents met when they were in high school and that they are happy together.

Can you imagine our life together? I'll be a nurse and he'll be something important.

We'll have two awesome kids and a dog. It'll be great and I get giddy just thinking about our future. He treats me like a queen and he's so confident in everything and I'm so stupid sometimes when I can't think of what to say.

I've thought about sending Jack a message but I just can't do it yet. I will though because the guys mean so much to me but it's hard because I know they don't like Vic and it kinda puts me in the middle and I don't want to be in the middle anymore. I just want them to see what I see.

I can make things better between us if I watch what I do and who I talk to. I don't want to make him angry. A few weeks ago at school when he was walking me to class he put his arms around my waist. I thought he was going to hug me but he just grabbed my fat on my waist. He said something like I was gaining weight and it was a sign of being in love.

Yeah, I was in love but his comment about my waist made me feel kind of bad like if I was fat or something. I thought I was pretty skinny but since I hadn't been running I probably was gaining a little. I've stopped eating so much and I've made a promise to myself to start working out again. I don't want him playing around with my fat because that's just plain embarrassing.

I've decided to start over again tomorrow. I want things to be okay just like he said and if I try real hard to do the things he wants, then he won't leave me and he'll stay with me.

Chapter 14

Friday morning I dressed in my blue and white cheerleading uniform. Our school mascot and my name were plastered across my chest. I always felt that the little cheerleading skirt was a bit too revealing, but judging from the other skimpy uniforms we had seen at summer cheer camp, ours was pretty modest.

I focused on the wonderful day I was determined to have. I parked in the back where Vic was already waiting. His smile lifted my spirits. It was going to be a great weekend. My mom had given me a message from my dad.

I was no longer grounded. I guess Dad still wasn't talking to me. Home life was awkward at best. I refused to go and talk to him. He was supposed to be the adult. He should be approaching me. That's what Vic said anyway last night when I brought it up again.

It had been a long month of boredom and loneliness. I thought long and hard about telling Vic that I was no longer grounded, but I wanted to surprise him.

"Hi, baby," Vic said gathering me in his arm for a warm embrace.

I happily kissed him back.

He was right, things were going to okay with us.

"Having a cheerleader for a girlfriend has its perks, but I hate that you have to wear that short little thing. No talking to boys today alright? I don't think I can handle it."

I smiled up at him and kissed him on the side of his lips. I joked with him online about that lip. I told him it was my own special place.

"Yes, I remember," he said. He touched that same corner of his lip with his two forefingers and then put his fingers to my lips.

It was a gesture he'd reenact several times throughout the day. It was as if he were telling me he loved me every time he did it.

The day floated by as if in a dream. He wore his football jersey, as was customary for the football players on the team, and I had my uniform on with his ring around my neck on a chain. I was so proud of being with him, and I held my head up for the first time in a long time.

Even Jean and her friends, Gina and Kaley, couldn't dampen my spirits. They sat behind me again in class and laughed at whatever it was they thought was so funny, but I had Vic.

I was the one he was walking to class, not Jean. I was the one he was talking to online late at night. I was the one he loved.

I smiled back at them a few times just to let them know they didn't faze me, but for some reason that made them laugh even more. It seemed like they knew something I didn't.

I refused to let them play with my mind or cause any more doubts in our relationship, so I staunchly ignored them.

I caught a glimpse of Lucas and Jack in the hallway after first period, but Vic grabbed my arm and steered me toward the opposite end of the hallway. They didn't seem to even notice me. They had been in deep conversation about something and hadn't even bothered to look up.

Their blatant disregard stung.

They were now ignoring me.

As if reading my thoughts, Vic squeezed my arm and held me tight.

My spirits were lifted.

The rest of the day flew by without incident. We laughed and hugged before he left for the game.

It was an out of town game in Pecos, a short hour away, and we weren't going to ride the bus there together, which would have been great, but we would see each other again in Pecos.

During our cheers I'd catch a glimpse of him running

through the line of tackle or see him block someone with his wonderfully taut body. His butt tightened with every step he took and I found myself staring at him instead of keeping up with the cheers.

Yna still hadn't come back to the squad. I heard from other girls that she still wasn't up to doing much of anything and had chosen to seclude herself from anything that would remind her of Randy.

In my eyes, that was practically everything. How could you get away from something like memories?

Having Yna absent from the game, however, was a relief.

I really was a coward.

I couldn't face her just yet. I would make it a point to go visit her on Sunday. Now that I wasn't grounded maybe I could stop being a coward. Maybe I could wait till next week or next weekend.

She wasn't trying to get in touch with me either, so I didn't think I was the only one to be blamed for all this.

"Linda, pay attention," someone said behind me.

I turned away from the field and tried to focus on the cheer we were doing.

The end of the game signaled the start of my wonderful weekend. I ran onto the field and found Vic right away.

Jumping on him, he spun me around. They had won and students were celebrating on the field. The band was playing in the background. He kissed me deeply in the middle of the football field with the drums beating, the crowd screaming, and my heart thumping out of my chest.

It was a wonderful night and after a short thirty minutes, we loaded the buses and headed for home.

* * *

Saturday morning I decided to wash my car.

The day was clear, crisp, and bright. I could almost smell the air. It was just like it was months before when all was right with my world—except no one passed by my house, or honked, or stopped to help me with my tires.

Every time I heard a car coming I'd stop what I was doing and hope that it was one of the guys. Numerous cars passed by, but none of them were the guys. The radio was my only companion.

I missed the guys more now that I was no longer grounded. Maybe it was because I was now free to do and go wherever I wanted, but things were going so well with Vic that I didn't want to mess that up.

Instead of fretting over things I couldn't control, I washed dishes quickly because Mom said I still had a few weeks left on that one and spent the afternoon getting ready to go out with Vic.

I must have typed a million times a message online that I'd be over at his house, but I didn't send any of them. I really wanted it to be a surprise when I drove up. He thought I was still grounded, and it would be great to see his face when I surprised him tonight by showing up at his house.

Meg had already gone out with some friends, so, luckily, I didn't have to listen to her lectures or answer any of her questions.

I had to ask my mom for permission to go out. I found her sitting in the kitchen in a flowered dress with her hair tied up in a tight bun.

Asking her for permission was just a formality because she'd already mentioned my going out, but I wanted to stay in her good graces so I had to make it official.

The stack of papers weighed heavily on the counter and the tack-tack of the calculator keys signaled the desperate situation we were in, but my mom turned to me and smiled, "Hey. What's up?"

"I wanted to go out. Is that okay?" Part of me still worried about whether she would say yes or not.

Maybe my dad had changed his mind. My heart thrummed with anticipation.

"Yes, but don't be late. You know how your dad is."

I smiled and hugged her before I turned to rush to my room, but she stopped me. "Linda, sit down. We need to talk."

Dread filled me. Another lecture was rearing its ugly head.

She made me sit down next to her. "I wanted to talk to you about your attitude lately. I'm a little worried about you. You've been walking around like some zombie-nutcase. You're hardly eating, you're crying a lot, and don't shake your head, I can tell. I just want to make sure you're okay."

I made myself smile at her even though I just wanted to burst into tears and lose myself on her lap like I was a child again. "I'm fine Mom. Really. I've just been a little sick that's all."

She sighed. "Meg told me it was some guy that's been upsetting you. Is he not treating you right? What is it?"

That wasn't it. Vic treated me like a queen, we'd just been on shaky ground lately. "I'm fine, Mom. It's just normal stuff. No big deal."

She gave me a long measured look. "I just want you to know that you don't have to do anything you don't want to do and the boy should always treat you with respect. No exceptions."

"Like Dad?"

I couldn't help my response. It just came out before I had a chance to stop it. My dad was known for his quick temper, especially when it was aimed at Mom. It was no secret, but I'd never really pointed it out. It was just a silent disease that ate everything up on the inside. I regretted it the moment I said it

She looked hurt but continued. "Look, I just don't want you to think it's okay for a guy to treat you cruelly or unfairly. If you want to use me as an example and this will save you heartache in the long run, then do it."

Ashamed at what I'd said, I kept my mouth shut and after a few tense moments, she let me go to my room. I let what she said go in one ear and out the other because Vic wasn't like that. He loved me.

I ended up waiting as long as I could to go out, which put me at his house at around eight.

We had just chatted online so I knew he was home. His mom had called him to dinner, so he had to go but said he'd send me a message in a few hours.

I drove as slowly as I could to his house trying to savor the anticipation. It had killed me not to tell him but the wait was going to be worth it.

I also went through a dozen scenarios that would transpire when I got there: he'd be so excited that I wasn't grounded that he'd jump up and down and swing me around, or maybe he'd walk slowly to me, cup my face in his hands, and kiss me deeply. The scenarios went on and on.

I wasn't prepared for what I saw.

Jean.

Vic was in front of his house along with some of his friends and Jean and her friends were there as well.

The hood of his car sank slightly under the weight of Vic and Jean's bodies.

Jean leaned up against him—kissing him on the ear, neck, and lips . . . right on the spot that I had called my own just last night.

Because I had driven up so slowly and because the music was blaring, they hadn't noticed me.

I was able to watch as Vic put his hand on Jean's ass and patted it. She smiled up at him and grabbed his hair roughly and brought him to her so she could kiss him. This didn't look like something they hadn't done before.

I couldn't remember getting out of the car or walking to them, but I must have because I was standing right behind Vic.

Jean saw me first and threw me a long languorous smile.

She kissed him slowly sticking her tongue into his ear for my benefit. She grabbed a chunk of his hair and brought his face to her breasts. Such a bold move and all to give me a show.

"Hey, Vic. You got company," Mark Magallon said.

Vic turned toward me and his smile disappeared.

I couldn't believe what I was seeing.

I was so stupid. How could I be so stupid? All those rumors weren't rumors. They were truths.

All of them.

I shook my head slowly. I couldn't even trust myself to speak. Gina and Kaley stopped playing basketball and glared at me. They looked at each other and broke out laughing.

Of course.

Now I knew why they were laughing—because I was stupid.

I was stupid.

I turned and started to walk slowly to my car. I didn't run or scream or cause a scene. I very quietly walked to my car. I could feel him running toward me, but I would not give any of them the satisfaction of running away or letting him talk.

"She doesn't mean anything, Linda," Vic said, trying to stop me from getting in the car.

I couldn't even cry, or scream, or even look at him. I couldn't seem to think. Everything was happening in slow motion: my turning the ignition, the car's engine revving, gears releasing, the car sputtering along the road, the door shutting on its own when I turned the corner.

I registered enough to know that I had almost hit him with the car. He had jumped out of the way just in time.

I hadn't even slowed down.

I was done.

Chapter 15

I veered the car toward home. There wasn't anywhere else to go.

Jean had kissed him, grabbed him, and stuck his face in her shirt.

Disgusting.

And I had kissed him, probably on the same day she had.

I was sure they'd had had sex. It was evident.

I was stupid.

How could I have been so stupid?

What had I done to make him go to her and why *her*? What was so special about her and what could she give him that I couldn't?

Was it because I was grounded and he found someone else?

It was all my fault.

If I hadn't lied to my dad about being with Yna that night, none of this would've happened. I wouldn't be grounded and he wouldn't have had to find someone else.

I rode around on the back feeder roads of town. I rode towards the freeway, turned a sad song up higher on the radio and wallowed in self-pity.

This is the time of our lives.

The chorus of the melancholy song seemed like such a contradiction and it only made me feel worse. I stopped on the side of the road and bawled.

I had no one to call for advice or to tell me that things were going to be all right. I didn't even have anyone to vent with. I couldn't even confide in my sister. She already hated him and the words *I told you so* were something I didn't want to hear.

I had done this to myself. I had done this.

I couldn't go to the guys now or to Yna. I would look like I only came when I needed something.

I sat in desolation for an hour watching the cars go by and wondering what would happen if I just hopped on the freeway and kept going. I could make it to California on this highway.

I could get lost and leave my dad, the guys, Yna, Vic, and Jean all behind.

Hiding in a small cave, wrapped up in a tight ball seemed like a great idea. How could I even lift my head up in the hallways?

Everyone would know what had happened and how stupid I had been. They would see me in the hallways and then look at each other and a knowing smile would cross their faces. It would happen over and over again.

Gina and Kaley's laughter echoed in my ears. They had known all along. They had probably seen more than I ever wanted to know.

Those two girls had probably already begun to spread the vicious accounts of what had just happened. I could see them already hopping from car to car, like in that *Grease* movie from years ago when everyone finds out about Rizzo's pregnancy before she can even cross the parking lot. The guys and Yna will soon find out what's happened.

They'll probably laugh amongst each other and say, "That's what she gets for choosing Vic over us."

That's really what I had done. I had stupidly chosen Vic because I thought he was in love with me.

It was all a lie.

All of it. Just to get into my pants and I had let him. I gave him what he wanted and he left. Meg had told me he was like that, but I didn't believe it, not with me. I thought I was different, and that our love and relationship was different, but it wasn't. He had moved on to someone else. People would find out about that, too.

Maybe even my father who finds out everything. Would

he find out what really happened that night? How his precious little daughter had lost her virginity in the backseat of a sports car? So classy.

He was so ashamed of me that he'd stopped talking to me and couldn't even look at me. I hadn't done anything about that either because Vic had convinced me otherwise. I still thought he was right on that one, though.

The lump in my throat grew and the tide of grief overcame me once again and I started to cry.

I was so ashamed, mortified, humiliated, and disgraced. Shame.

Shame was an emotion I had become familiar with since I had started to see Vic.

Shame was such an ugly word.

Headlights illuminated the inside of my car causing me to look up and realize exactly where I was.

I hadn't parked on the side of the road like I thought. I had parked right smack in the middle of the street.

I turned my car onto the embankment hoping to get a little more time to myself before I had to go back home, but the oncoming car began to slow and I didn't want anyone else to see me crying, so I slowly moved my car onto the road and headed for home.

My house appeared faster than I was ready for so I sat in the driveway for awhile hoping to time my parent's absence from the kitchen or living room. Tear stains and red eyes were apparent when I glanced in the rear-view mirror.

I couldn't do explanations tonight. I didn't think I could handle it.

I crept slowly to the living room window hoping that it was empty.

Luck was finally on my side. There was no one there, the television was on, and the Cokes and potato chips were on the coffee table.

It was a restroom break, and as it turned out, my break too. I was able to get to my room without anyone seeing me.

I changed into my pajamas and sat at my computer. The black screen glared back at me accusingly. I hadn't done anything on it but talk to Vic. I had ignored everyone else.

I checked my e-mails and my pages, even my social page, but no one had commented on my files or posted anything in the last month.

I was pathetic.

I looked toward my closet.

I once read an article in the local newspaper about a young girl who committed suicide. She had gotten into a fight with her father, her friends had abandoned her, and her life was seemingly over. Her mother had found her.

She had hung herself in her closet. I remember her father was the most upset about her death. He blamed himself. I saw pictures of her friends crying out of guilt.

I could easily walk in there and finish all this. I could grab my sheets, wrap them around my neck, and throw myself off my computer chair. It would be easy.

Or would it?

Could I do that?

I had done everything else. I had lost my virginity, my friends, my best friend and my boyfriend.

What did I have left?

Dear Diary,

Today started out so wonderful. I thought things were going to be great between Vic and me.

I had even decided to give him what he wanted, again. But this time I had promised to relax and try to enjoy it as much as others seemed to. I figured that was the price I had to pay to be with him and I really wanted to be with him.

But I got a shock instead. I found Vic with Jean. I don't know who to turn to or what to do. I cried for a long time. I even cried myself to sleep but woke up in the middle of the night.

The closet glares at me accusingly. He tells me I can come in and everything will be okay.

Is that what I want? I even walked to him and tested the rod where my clothes hang. It seems sturdy enough. I must have watched him for an hour before I decided to go back to bed. He will be there if things get worse.

No one cares about me. Maybe they'd be sorry if they came in and found me hanging inside him. My dad would regret this past month. Vic would cry for me or so I hope and the guys will wish they had been there for me.

I'm not sure this is what I want though, but I know he will be there if I need him.

Chapter 16

Sunday morning I woke up to the smell of fresh torit-
illas, bacon, and eggs. I loved my mom's breakfast.
My stomach growled and I got out of bed and started to head to
the kitchen when the events of last night came crashing down
on me.

Last night had been so cold and desolate. Images of Jean
and Vic returned to haunt my thoughts again and it all returned
in a flood of emotions.

I sat back down on my bed and looked at my closet.

I had to make today different. What was it that Scarlett
O'Hara says in that old movie my dad forced me to watch? *Tomorrow is another day* or *tomorrow is a brand new day*, something
like that.

Either way, she was right. I had to make things better for
myself. I had to make it seem like I wasn't completely shattered
by last night's events.

Even though I was.

It would be worse on Monday when I had to face everyone alone. In class I'd have to keep my head up and try to be in
a good mood even if it killed me. I had to pretend because the
alternative would be to accept defeat. I wasn't ready to do that.

But how could I do it alone? I didn't think I could, but
today I would make myself face the new day.

The sun streaming in through the curtains, the smell of
breakfast, and the chill of the morning encouraged me to face
the new day.

Today had to get better. How could it get any worse?

I found my mother and sister eating at the bar. My dad,
as usual, was nowhere to be seen.

"You want some breakfast?" Mom asked.

-153-

"I'll take some eggs." I was determined to make today better even though I didn't feel like eating.

I sat down on the stool my mom had occupied and glanced at Meg. Her look of pity brought about a lump in my throat. She must know what happened. I just hoped she would keep it to herself in front of Mom.

I knew I couldn't hope that she'd keep it to herself completely; this was only going to add fuel to the fire of hate she had towards Vic.

I ate quickly and told my mom I was going for a run.

The day was perfect for a run. It would give me a chance to think.

I stretched my legs, my arms, and my neck. It felt good to be out in the open air. It was still early morning so the air was slightly brisk. Today the cold wasn't so bad. I had on my black running tights, long black tight shirt, and a bandana for my sweat.

I'm not the type of person who can run and still look like a goddess. Not that I look like a goddess at any other time, but when I run, I sweat like a stuck pig and I smell even worse.

I ran toward the east side of town and the highway. My goal was to get to the transfer prison unit on the east side of town, make a right, and head northwest.

After several minutes my adrenaline kicked in and I began to feel good and strong.

Cars passed by and honked their horns. I didn't once look up to acknowledge anyone.

After having neglected my running for months, I started to struggle at the two-mile mark, which wasn't a good sign.

I was hoping to be a real competitor this spring in the 3,200 meter. I had also tried the 1,600 meter, but I found that my stamina was better for the thirty-two.

Last year, I had placed second in every track meet we went to. Stacy Barber from Monahans always seemed to beat me.

No matter how much I trained and pushed myself, she would always end up right in front of me and out of my reach. She was pretty, popular, and exceptionally sweet, so I couldn't even hate her for being so good.

Yna would come out to support me; she'd run beside me the last legs of the race and scream at me to push harder. She hated to run, but she'd do it for me.

Once she even tripped on someone's red bag as she ran next to me; I started to laugh because she said "shit" in front of our coach. It didn't slow me down but I was still unable to catch up to Stacy.

And that image in my head of Yna tripping over that bag brought the first smile all day to my lips.

I rounded my halfway point on the north side of town just past the railroad tracks. My trek back home would total ten miles.

Our coach always preached that we had to run harder, longer, and faster than our competitors, so my goal for the next few months would be to run ten miles.

I checked my watch. I had to record my time in my book so that I could make sure to decrease it. I had to win this spring.

That would make up for all the stupidness that was going on in my life.

I breathed in deeply as I remembered exactly why I had come out in the first place.

That familiar ache in my chest I was getting to know so well tightened.

I loved Vic still. Even after all this, all I wanted was to erase the past and get back to what we had.

But what did we have? Was it all a lie? Had he been seeing her all along and just toying with me?

I wondered what he was thinking now. Was this something about which he casually said, "*Oh well, I'll just find another gullible girl to screw around with.*"

My hope was that he was aching inside just as much as I was and that he was regretting all that he had done.

I was so lost in my thoughts that I didn't hear the truck creep up behind me until it honked.

I must've jumped a mile and my scream must have been one of sheer terror because Jack came out of the truck.

"Sorry, it was too easy to resist. Especially since you

didn't turn around when I drove up."

I couldn't even look at him in the eye. What was I supposed to say to that?

I put my head down and that stupid little lump that had been haunting me all day veered its ugly head back into my throat. He was talking to me like we had never stopped talking or like I had never ignored him in the hallway.

"Linda? Hey, Linda?" Jack asked.

He came toward me and placed a comforting hand on my slumped shoulder.

"Are you okay? Shit Linda, say something."

I couldn't clear the lump in my throat enough to answer him. I just shook my head and looked away.

The railroad tracks were deserted and a slow procession of cars climbed over the hill. Everyone had gone on with their daily lives as if nothing had happened the night before. Maybe he didn't know what happened. Maybe those stupid girls hadn't told anyone.

"I heard about last night."

I jerked my head back to look at him. My sight became blurred and I couldn't stop the tears from streaming down my face. I hadn't even blinked and they were still falling freely.

He put his other hand on my shoulder and brought me to him. He held me for a long time.

He didn't seem to care that I looked like I had just woke up or that I smelled like the boy's locker room.

After a few minutes, I hugged him back.

I let the tears fall and let him stroke my back as he whispered words of comfort.

I couldn't trust myself to speak and he didn't pressure me with questions or accusations. He seemed to know that what I needed was comfort.

I don't know how long we stayed like that, but I do know that I was the one to step back.

I reached deep and gave him a smile. "How have you been?"

"Fine, we're all fine," he said. "You want a ride back home?"

I shook my head. "No, I have to get back into shape. I've let myself go. I have to get ready for spring."

"You want to go out tonight? We're just hanging out, but you're welcome to come."

I looked to the railroad tracks again and thought about saying no. I felt like such a loser to go back to the guys only because I had no one.

It wasn't fair to them and I didn't know how they'd take me coming back. Maybe I was a phase like they thought.

"No, I think I'll stay home."

"Okay, pick you up at 6 o'clock at your house. Dress comfortably."

He didn't give me a chance to stop him or respond. After he drove away, I was kind of happy that he hadn't. It would be nice to get back to them and laugh and joke and kid around.

I picked up my pace and made it home quickly. I showered and changed into some comfy clothes. I lay down on my pink-covered bed and tried to read a book.

"Can I shoot him now?" Meg asked as she came in to lay on top of me.

"Get off me. I don't care what you do to him," I answered.

I pushed her off me and she landed on the floor. She didn't move, just lay there as if daydreaming.

"Cool, well, I was thinking death by stones, or castration, maybe a sprinkle of mutilation. Castration is my choice if you don't have a preference."

I could actually picture her doing all of those and smiling while she did it.

"No, just leave him alone and don't talk to him. It's better that way."

"You're no fun," she said and smiled at me. "You okay?"

"Yeah, and please don't rub it in right now. I don't need you bashing him."

"Still stuck on him, huh? Even after all this?"

I didn't answer. I pretended to read my book. Hopefully this would make her go away.

"I heard about it from Kaley's big sister. There was a

few of them talking at the Town and Country and I was buying a drink. I know they knew I was there, but when I went up to the front they left pretty quickly. Bitches."

I smiled at her. She always was a character.

"That's cause they thought you'd smash them into the chocolate bars."

"Wouldn't that have been great? I'll have to try that sometime."

"Go away. I'm trying to read," I said kicking her.

As she walked out the computer chimed to signal that I had a message.

Before I could stop her, Meg grabbed the mouse and the screen lit up.

"It's Mister Wonderful. Would you like me to answer?"

My heart skipped a beat. "No, I'll handle this."

"Sure you will."

Meg left but not before giving me a small lecture on how to handle boys. Her idea of a relationship was totalitarian. She said what to do and the guy would do it, no questions asked.

With a heavy heart, I sat at my computer.

Vic: Are you there? Please answer me

I contemplated answering him. Wouldn't it be best if I just left him alone and didn't respond? Or would that be the coward in me again?

Vic: I know you're there. I love you. This is all a
       misunderstanding.

A misunderstanding? How was that possible?

What could he possibly say?

Oh excuse me, that wasn't me you saw with my face in her breasts. That wasn't me she stuck her tongue into. That was some other guy.

I couldn't resist.

Linda: A misunderstanding? I know what I saw.

V: Look its not what you think she was upset and her
    and her friends showd up at my house I didn't know
    you were coming. You didn't tell me and you should
    have
L: you weren't sorry last night
V: come one linda what was I suposed to do u were
    grounded 4 ever

I didn't bother to answer. He would somehow make me apologize. Somehow it would be my fault and I would be stupid enough to agree with him.

I focused my attention on the book. I heard the computer chime several times before it stopped.

I was going to focus on the guys tonight.

* * *

Jack picked me up at six o'clock sharp. My dad and my mom for some unknown reason liked Jack and his parents, so they never gave me much grief when I said I was going with him. I guess they thought he was harmless.

Jack was alone.

I kind of figured that a lecture and questions would come, but they didn't. Instead he asked me about what I had been doing and how my school life was.

All those mundane things no one ever talks about. I half expected him to ask me about the weather, but he didn't.

Finally I got enough courage to ask him about the guys. "How are the guys doing? Do they know I'm coming?"

It took him a few minutes to answer me which made me nervous. I knew whatever he said next was going to upset me, so I took a deep breath and held it.

"Omar's Omar. He doesn't care and neither does David. They'll be glad to see you," he said.

He hadn't mentioned Lucas. I couldn't figure out why or maybe I could.

Lucas would be the one I should have worried about

all along. He'd be the most critical and if he heard about what I'd done with Vic in the backseat of his car, then he'd really be pissed off.

I took the plunge. I wanted to know what to expect. "How's Lucas? Is he mad?"

Again, he didn't answer me. I sort of expected that would be the case, but it stung just the same.

"Lucas refuses to talk to you. He won't be there tonight so you don't have to worry. I think he feels . . . I don't know how that dumbass feels. Just enjoy the night okay?"

I smiled at him and nodded.

It was easy with Jack; he was the one that would pull me through this mess. He was strong, in personality, build, and mind.

We rode around for about an hour talking about mundane school things like who was dating whom, who had dumped whom and who was arguing. All those important small town things.

"You ready to go by the house? I'm sure the guys are there," Jack said.

He smiled and squeezed my shoulder.

"Yes, I think it will be fun," I answered him.

I was ready and relaxed and he would take care of me. He would make sure that Omar and David would not say anything he didn't approve of. I felt certain that they'd talked about it at length.

That's what they did when things were going on. They'd sit in Jack's living room, he'd pass out some drinks, and they'd hash it out.

Most times they'd argue, something would get thrown, and, in the end, they would walk out in complete agreement.

They did this once when Lucas and David liked the same girl. I told them it was a small town and it was inevitable, so they should just flip a coin. They thought it was an insane idea because each one of them felt like she liked them more. Cassandra was her name.

She was a small little wisp of a thing, sweet, and overly nice to everyone. I honestly thought she didn't like either of them and that she was just being nice.

They argued for a good hour and I had been completely enthralled with it all.

In the end, David won out because he had a class with her and had probably talked to her more than Lucas. I didn't understand how that made sense, but it did for them. The only problem was that little Cassandra said no to David and then to Lucas. She ended up dating some football jock which surprised the hell out of all of us.

We arrived to a house full of lights. Several cars were parked in the driveway. Jack's mom, it seemed, had added a huge shiny wooden bench with a Texas star stamped on the seat. Maybe she was running out of room inside. "Nice bench."

"Yeah, my Mom found it in Austin when she went last week. It didn't fit in the entryway," he said.

When we walked into the living room Omar and David got up from their perches on the couch. David gave me a hug, but Omar didn't.

"Hey, Linda. Delighted to see that you have graced us with your presence again," Omar said.

He sauntered over to me and punched me lightly on the shoulder.

Typical Omar.

He wasn't the kind that would hug—talk like he was intelligent yes, hug you and show emotion, nope.

David, on the other hand, stayed back and scrutinized me. "You okay?"

It was so nice and I knew I didn't deserve them.

I almost lost it right then but suddenly Lucas appeared behind David. My breath caught and I froze.

Lucas did what he did best: pretended I wasn't there.

Tense moments ensued.

Omar looked down at the floor, David pretended to be real interested in whatever was showing on television, and Jack glared at Lucas.

Before Jack could come to my defense, I decided to try to stand up for myself. "I thought you didn't want to see me."

I stared at him daring him to be shitty to me.

He picked up his drink and took a long swig, perhaps contemplating what he'd say to me. "Are we ready to go?"

He didn't even bother to acknowledge me so I turned my attention to Jack. "Where are we going, or am I not allowed to go?"

Jack threw Lucas a searing look then smiled at me. "Yeah, Omar found some legend in one of his books and he wants to check it out."

"Omar? You can read?" I asked.

He smiled, put his hand on my arm, and led me to the door. "Sweetheart, you would be surprised what is in this wonderfully superior mind."

It was nice to know that some things didn't change. I decided to ignore Lucas until he could get his head out of his ass long enough to get over it.

Although, if I really thought about it, I knew he had every right to be angry at me.

But in the same sense, I wasn't about to beg him for forgiveness.

Turning to Omar once we were on the road, I asked, "So what kind of legend did you read about?"

I was in the front seat in the middle between Jack and David; Lucas and Omar sat in the back. I had no idea where we were going.

Fort Stockton was a military fort a long time ago so there are countless testimonies of ghost stories, legends, and even a few UFO sightings.

During the summer we'd go out to the park late at night to see if we saw anything or someone would dare someone else to walk through the cemetery late at night.

The Alamo Elementary is said to be haunted by a young boy who's come out in pictures. One only needs to look on the internet to find a plethora of information on ghost stories in Fort Stockton.

So when Omar wanted to go see another alleged ghost site, I wasn't even impressed, but I was really glad to be back with them instead of at home alone.

"There's a mausoleum in the old cemetery. If you knock three times, then something knocks back. I read it on the internet. Some guy tried it and he set up a site where he explains his experience."

Great, we were going to the cemetery. This was crazy— and typical of the guys.

"So why wait until its dark-thirty? Are we really going out there?"

I felt like such a loser and a dweeb, but I hated to be scared.

Yna and I were the same in that respect; we hated watching scary movies or going into haunted houses during Halloween. We just stayed away from them and mutually agreed that they were ridiculous and a waste of time.

The guys, on the other hand, were all about doing scary things.

When I first started hanging out with the guys, we decided to go to The Moon, a huge cleared area that used to be an old rock quarry.

Once we got out there, we were sitting on the back of Daniel's truck and drinking some beers supplied by his uncle (who profited from our desperation). Omar and Lucas walked away from the group, explaining that they were on a hunt for exploratory purposes. The rest of us were just drinking and watching the clear midnight sky.

After about ten minutes, Omar and Lucas rounded a curve while screaming at the top of their lungs. Omar got in the driver's seat, revved the engine, and put the truck in gear while screaming at us to hold on.

Lucas had jumped into the back of the truck and, in a frantic rush, recanted what they'd just seen.

Lucas said they had stumbled onto a drug deal that had gone bad. Two guys had bashed the third guy's head in with a baseball bat. Lucas had made a noise and they had run away with the drug dealers in hot pursuit.

We were all freaking out because we didn't know whether to believe them and, with Lucas acting crazy and screaming, it was hard not to. They even went so far as to drive to the police station.

Omar got out and walked right in and we were really getting scared because it sounded like it was for real. But when Omar returned he was eating a donut and had a huge smile on his face. I realized they were full of shit at that point, but they had played it off so well that I had to hand it to them.

After that fiasco, I couldn't imagine what would happen at the cemetery.

We drove through the wrought iron entrance gate into the heart of the cemetery.

I didn't want to get out, but as soon as the truck stopped, everyone filed out.

"I guess some people got chicken while they chose to stay away," said Lucas.

It infuriated me that he could be so ugly. He was trying to get a rise out of me and I was determined not to let him.

I slid out of the truck and looked around. It was one of those perfectly cool, clear nights where you can see every star in the sky. The moon was shining and illuminating everything in sight.

It was spooky, too, and I didn't want to be there.

"Why are we here? I don't want to be here. Let's go back into town. We can park at the car wash," I offered.

"Chicken, fowl, rooster, hen—how pathetic," Lucas said glaring at me.

I had had enough. "Why don't you just say what you really think instead of saying 'some people?' That's pathetic," I screamed at him.

The others stopped what they were doing and stared at us. I guess they knew this was inevitable.

"What's pathetic is what he did to you. That's pathetic," Lucas said through gritted teeth.

"No what's pathetic is that you have no one and you're jealous because I do."

"You call what you and Vic have a relationship? You're stupider than I thought." Lucas had walked right up to me.

I refused to back down even though it hurt. "It's better than what you have which is nothing."

"I'd rather have nothing than a piece of shit that got what he wanted in the back seat of a stupid car and then went off and found some other slut!"

It literally felt like a slap in the face. My face grew hot, my eyesight blurred, and I couldn't speak.

"You are an asshole Lucas," Jack said standing between us. He got eye to eye with Lucas. "What are you trying to do? I told you to stay away if you couldn't control yourself."

"No leave him. He's only telling the truth. Can you please take me home?" I asked to Jack.

No one said anything for a few minutes. Omar took a deep breath and walked away.

"I'll be back," Omar said as he was leaving.

"I'll come with you," I said.

There was no way I was going to stay behind with Lucas and if Jack wasn't going to take me home yet, I might as well go with Omar.

We went to several mausoleums, knocked three times, and waited. Each time I was scared out of my mind that something would knock back. On the other hand, I wanted to leave so bad that maybe a knock back would get us out of there faster.

Suddenly, Lucas screamed.

We ran back scared that something had happened. Lucas was frantically running from the opposite direction yelling for us to get in the truck.

This time I didn't even bother. I wasn't going to run but I was happy that we were leaving this haunted place. It gave me some horribly bad vibes.

I sauntered slowly to the truck.

"Hurry up, Linda. What are you doing?" Omar asked.

"I'm not falling for this one again. You know how that loser is with his drama," I said as loud as I could.

Headlights illuminated the pathway in front of me. I jerked to glance in that direction and saw the very distinct lights of a cop car.

I took off.

We ran to the truck, threw ourselves in, and sped out of there.

"Hurry Jack," I squeezed his leg. "Take me home please."

When it became clear that we weren't being followed, Jack headed toward the drag. "We'll ride around for a few minutes and then I'll take you home."

"Okay."

At this point, it couldn't hurt but I didn't want to be out anymore. I just wanted to be home, especially when Jack pulled into the carwash ten minutes later.

There were about five cars there in the parking lot. I knew most of the people there and they were all really nice.

"I'll take you home in a few minutes. I promise," Jack said, climbing out of the truck.

I wasn't sure what he was trying to accomplish by taking me out there, but I knew he'd keep his promise and take me home soon.

Lucas walked away from me without looking back. Omar put his arm around me and David started talking about some girl he'd had sex with last week.

Of course, he never said her name or anything that would lead to the idea that he was actually telling the truth, so I halfheartedly listened but said nothing.

Cars passed by and some honked. After several minutes Lucas came over to me. "You want something to drink?"

I glared at him wondering what he was up to and what his angle was. "No, I don't."

He put his head down and leaned against someone's car. "Look Linda. I'm sorry for what I said I—"

"You don't have to explain. I'm the one that should be sorry. "

He didn't say anything for a little while. He quietly moved to me and gave me a reassuring hug. It was nice to be back with them again.

I let him hold me for a long while until I felt the backs of my hairs stand on end. I felt his body tense and I looked up to see what he was glaring at.

It was Vic.

He was with his friends, James and Mark, in his car. He had slowed down to a very deliberate crawl. His glare sent a shiver through my body. I could see his anger etched in every line on his face but with the guys suddenly surrounding me, he didn't bother to stop.

"I want to go home, Jack," I pleaded.

I Wish I Had Known

"Did you see how Vic looked when he passed by?" Lucas asked Jack after they dropped off Linda.

"Yeah, he looked like he could commit murder and enjoy it. He didn't look at any of us. He had eyes only for you," Omar said to Lucas.

"Well, bring it on. I don't care what that son of a bitch says or does. He's a damn idiot. What's he gonna do? Shoot me? Run over me? Beat me up? He's an ass," Lucas said.

They drove the rest of the way to Jack's house in silence. Each one contemplating the night they'd had.

Omar and David left as soon as they got to the house. Lucas went inside to watch the remainder of a movie with Jack because he wasn't in the mood for sleep.

It was a stupid movie about vampires and demons and the end of the world, so they turned it off at the half-way point at about two in the morning.

Lucas refused to stay the night and headed for home.

Since Jack lived outside of town, the night was quiet and the crickets were singing their songs. Clouds had covered the moon making it difficult to see very far ahead.

Lucas got in his car, turned up the radio, and headed home.

He didn't notice the car that left right after him until it rammed him in the back bumper.

Stunned and confused, he was about to pull over to exchange information or at least see the damage when the car deliberately rammed into him again.

Chills went up and down his spine. He swerved and

tried to move away. He made a sharp left turn and accelerated. The car stayed on his tail and rammed him two more times.

It was all Lucas could do to keep his car on the road.

The last hit did him in and he was unable to swerve away from the embankment.

The jarring crash hurt him more than the car. He hit the ditch, just barely missing a cement drainage ditch.

He thought that whoever drove the car behind him would come after him, so he frantically looked for some kind of weapon but the car sped away with tires screeching.

He hopped out of the car and took out his cell phone. Jack came quickly in his truck and together they pulled Lucas' car out of the ditch.

"Who do you think it was? Was it an accident?" Jack asked.

"No. No accident. I think it was Vic," Lucas said, shaking his head in disbelief.

"We'll tell Linda tomorrow," Jack said.

Lucas was silent for a moment contemplating the situation and flipping his keys with his fingers. "No, she won't believe it because he hit me exactly where you did the other day at school."

"Yeah, but the front dents and the fact that he did it is enough."

Lucas shook his head. "No, she won't believe me and I didn't see the car. Vic could've used another car from his dad's work or something. She won't believe us."

"Shit, maybe you're right," Jack said. "This all sucks."

Chapter 17

Monday morning I woke up to the sound of rain tapping on my window. I knew it was going to be a tough day.

With the guys there for a little bit of support, maybe I could face it. I hoped that Vic would stay away. Facing him was something I didn't want to have to do for a long while. I didn't think I was strong enough yet.

Meg and I rode to school together which was a nice change because her little Nissan truck was broke again.

I parked with the guys and we talked for awhile before we walked into the school.

Being happy and joking with them again set a nice tone for the day.

Jean and her friends didn't help with their laughter and snide little remarks, but I didn't let it phase me.

Lucas walked me to my first few classes because we had classes close to each other.

Our lockers weren't nearby, but by the time I got out of my class, he was waiting for me at my locker. I don't think he ever carried anything except a pencil to his classes. I don't know how he got away with it.

He always seemed to have more homework than everyone else, though. I told him once that since I was in the Gifted and Talented classes my teachers gave us more breaks. He said that was totally unfair, and I told him that if he did his work like he was supposed to, Mr. Nelson would probably let him in the class and then he could be with me. When it came to doing anything extra however, Lucas was not game.

Jack came by for third period, but my class was only

across the hall. He promised that he'd call me that evening because he had to work and then he was gone.

After lunch with the rest of the guys, I started to let my guard down. I hadn't seen Vic; he hadn't been at my locker and I wasn't even sure he was at school.

That was until last period.

I was getting my reading books and dirty athletic clothes out of my locker to take home to wash, tugging at the bag that was jammed in, when someone came up behind me and helped me tug at the bag. When we were finally able to get it free, I turned around with a smile, ready to thank whoever it was that had helped me.

It was Vic.

My heart skipped a beat, my eyes grew to giant orbs, my hands started to sweat, and I dropped the bag.

I couldn't even talk.

"Linda, I need to talk to you," he said.

Words stuck in my throat and I tried to swallow the lump that had continued to veer its ugly head throughout the last month.

"Linda, I'm sorry. What else do you want me to do?"

He grabbed my arm. I looked down at his hand on my arm and tried to register the fact that he had touched me.

His hand—the same one that had probably touched Jean in all sorts of places I didn't want to think about—grabbed my arm.

I yanked my arm free and pushed him away from me. "Don't touch me."

With the same force he probably used in football, Vic pushed me against the lockers. A large ball lock punched me in my back and my breath vanished.

Bent over and trying to catch my breath, I whispered, "Don't touch me."

Vic grabbed me by the throat, pushed me up against the lockers, and squeezed. "Linda, I'm trying to talk to you, that's it. You will listen to me."

Tears began to flow steadily down my face. We were at school, people were watching, and no one was doing anything to help me.

"I love you Linda, you know that. Talk to me after school. I'll be waiting."

And with that, he slowly walked away from the crowds, the gawkers, and me.

With tears blurring my vision, I clumsily picked up my bags and books.

No one helped me. No one asked me if I was okay or if I needed something.

I walked to my last class in a daze.

When I sat down at my desk, a pain shot through me starting at my lower back and traveling all the way up to my neck. Something was seriously wrong because I couldn't seem catch my breath.

Dear Diary,

I don't know why no one came to my rescue. I was alone when he shoved me into the lockers, alone after school when he drove up, and so alone when he shoved me into his car. I didn't think he'd actually go that far but he did.

Now I really hurt. My insides hurt real bad. I thought that at first the guys or Meg would be outside waiting for me, but they weren't. David stayed late in tutorials, Jack and Lucas left school early to work, and I have no idea where Omar was. Meg must have gotten a ride with someone because I walked out of school expecting to have lots of people around.

I didn't have practice today, so I didn't think I'd have a problem not being alone.

He drove up suddenly when I was getting in my car and he made me get in. To tell you the truth, I did want to see him.

I love him so I was okay getting in his car but when he started apologizing and I started arguing with him he got real angry. He had taken me to 7D road so we could be alone.

He pushed me into the backseat again and said that I was going to be his no matter what and that we'd grow old together and have lots of babies and everything would be alright.

He hurt me again. I thought at first that it wouldn't hurt again since it would be my second time but he was so rough and it hurt so bad. I still bled and this time all over his seat. I was so embarrassed but he said it was necessary so we could be together.

He even apologized again for Jean and for what I had just forced him to do to me. He said it was my fault because he loved me so much.

He said he couldn't live without me. What does that mean?

I hate him and I love him. How can that be possible? I'm completely stupid and ignorant and I don't even feel like I fought him that hard. What is wrong with me?

He said I should be pregnant now so that will solve all our problems but it won't. I don't want to be alone with him but I want so much for him to like me. He loves me with such passion. How can I be angry at someone who loves me like that?

My dad's pretty harsh with my mom most times, so isn't that the way men are supposed to be? I don't know what I'm doing anymore.

I've got to find a way to stay away from him.

"What happened today?" Meg asked from the doorway of my room.

I'm sure I looked like shit.

I had been crying ever since I slowly walked from his car to mine.

My eyes and nose were puffy and red.

"Nothing," I answered, covering my face and stuffing my diary under my pillow.

Meg was the last person I wanted to talk to or read my diary, so I rolled over to move away from her.

"Holy shit, Linda! What happened to you? You have bruises all over your back." Meg lifted my shirt and I swatted her hand away.

"Leave me alone. Nothing happened. I just tripped into my locker today," I said.

"Yeah and what tripped you? Victor? Just say the word and I'll go kick his ass. You can't keep hiding from this Linda. He's got problems and you know it. You just keep defending him."

"How do you know he pushed me? One of your friends? Did any of your low-life friends help me? No, they watched—just like everyone else. And we were having an argument. It's what couples do. We argue, we get over it, and it's done."

"No Linda. Not like everyone else. I don't have boy-friends pushing me against my locker and neither do the other girls in school. Just you."

This didn't make me feel any better. Victor and I had a different relationship and it was hard for people to understand it because they didn't have what we had.

I honestly believed he loved me and would not inten-tionally hurt me. He loved me, that I was sure of. When things were good, he was so sweet and courteous and did all those wonderful little things boyfriends are supposed to do.

Meg started to walk to her room but stopped suddenly. I thought we were in for another argument but she said the words I'd hoped for but never thought I'd hear again: "Yna's here."

Jumping off of my bed, I ran out of my bedroom. As I got closer to the living room door, my steps faltered. Was she here to make my life worse or better? Would she throw some-thing in my face or hug me? I so wished that she'd throw her arms around me and hug me.

I opened the door and got a shock.

Tears were streaming down her face, her hair was a mess, and she stood looking at me and pleading for me to hug *her*.

I did.

For a long time we stood there on the front steps em-bracing each other. It felt so good and it was such a comfort.

"You alright?" I asked, guiding her to my room.

"Yes, I just talked to Daniel. He told me about Randy and made me feel better," she said.

She walked into my room and threw herself on my bed like we had never stopped talking.

I tried really hard to focus on what she was saying. I hadn't been there for her when she needed me. How could I expect her to be there for me?

I hadn't called or gone by and I was completely selfish. Maybe that's why no one came to my rescue. Maybe I was so selfish for thinking that people would help me when I couldn't even help my friends or be there for them.

"Do you feel better?" I asked for the utter lack of anything to say.

"I do." She graced me with one of her brilliant smiles.

I loved her. I didn't deserve her.

So I took the plunge. "Look, I'm sorry for the total shit I've been the last few weeks. I wasn't there for you when Randy died and I know it's no excuse, but I've had some horrible things happen to me."

I didn't feel like today was the day to divulge all that had happened, so I asked her about her last few weeks and kept the conversation based solely on her. I had lots to make up for, so I didn't tell her what had happened to me.

I think she knew some of it because she asked me about my back, but I was sure she didn't know about the events in Vic's car.

She said she'd become a pretty big homebody because everywhere she went she thought of Randy. She thought of the life she was going to have with him, the life she'd been cheated out of. She mentioned the funeral and that she'd tried talking to Daniel, Randy's best friend, several times but each time he either ignored her or simply walked away.

She had been over to see Lizzie, Randy's sister, and Mr. and Mrs. Cuellar several times, but Randy's mother couldn't bear the sight of her, so her visits were always brief.

Lizzie was struggling with every aspect of her life even going so far as contemplating quitting school and just leaving town. Yna tried every day to convince her to stay.

Yna said she struggled to get out of bed every morning and was just now able to come see me. She went to school and stopped talking to people, she stopped showing up at football games and practices, which I already knew, and she had given up on having fun all together.

Considering all we'd been through, it was a wonder we hadn't fallen into some deep depression. Although, I'm sure by some clinical standards and according to our school counselor, I was institutional ready.

"I know I should be angry with you about not being there, but, well, I missed you and I have so much to tell you so you're just gonna have to spend the next two years showing me how sorry you are. And you have to promise you'll never do that to me again. Okay?"

"Deal." I was so relieved.

"Before we talk about you, I have to show you something. I don't know what's going on, but, well, I didn't want to show you this, but you have to know what's really going on . . ."

"Yna, just spit it out. What are you talking about?" I asked.

She didn't say anything.

For the few moments she looked at me, my guess was that she was contemplating whether or not to tell me or to just show me or whatever she intended to do.

"Just spit it out," I prodded.

She flipped open her phone, scrolled through her pictures, and turned the phone over so I could see it.

The picture was of me. It was clear that it was me even though I couldn't see my face. The backseat was Victor's, those were my breasts, and those were Vic's hands.

Stunned, I couldn't believe what I was seeing. How did she get a picture of me and Vic?

I grabbed her phone to look closer, "What is this Yna? How did you get this?" I whispered.

The image was seared into my brain. I closed my eyes but I could still see my naked breasts in Vic's hands and my arms looked like they were embracing him. I knew they were pushing him away but how could I prove that without really admitting what I had done?

My hands shook, and my temper flared, but the bottom of my stomach fell.

Humiliation.

My life was getting worse.

"I got it from my friend, Donnie, who got it from one of the guys on the football team. Vic sent this out to some of the guys warning them that you were his now and not to talk to you."

Surely it was a mistake. What would Vic get out of sending this? He said he loved me yet, this is what he would do to me?

"Why would he do this Yna?" I asked.

I gave her back the phone and sat with my head in my hands on my bed.

Again, I wanted to climb into a bottomless pit of isolation and never come out.

How could he think this was okay? What had I done to deserve this?

Yna put her arm around my shoulder just as Jack and Omar and even Lucas had done.

It was a pity-party and I was the hostess.

Chapter 18

I made up my mind to stay away from Vic. I did a pretty good job of it for the most part. He pretty much left me alone too which really surprised me.

Maybe he could tell by the look on my face when I saw him in the morning. Whatever the reason, I was glad I didn't have to deal with him.

Facing the guys in the morning was the hardest thing I had to do.

I saw myself in that graphic picture every time I closed my eyes and the humiliation of knowing others had seen it was even worse.

Lucas didn't say anything about the picture or about anything else, although I knew for a fact he knew about it. He was really the only one I was worried about because he'd be the one to tell it to me straight. Luckily, he just ignored me.

Yna and I had practice after school for the remainder of the week and then we'd drive home together.

She stayed over with me several nights and we talked into the wee hours of the night, but I never told her anything about Vic and me. It was easier to keep all the embarrassing information to myself. I had enough to deal with.

Vic came by my locker once every day and I'd ignore him. He'd smile and kiss me on the cheek and tell me I was his no matter what. I didn't answer any of his emails or posts or anything else. It seemed like every time I told him to leave me alone it didn't faze him. He acted like whatever I said was inconsequential. It was frustrating.

Jean and her demon friends stopped messing with me so much that the occasional remark or paper thrown didn't deter me from my determination to ignore them.

Other students ignored me as well. No one said a word about the cell phone pictures. For that I was totally surprised because if there were ever a chance to be ugly to me or embarrass me, this was the time.

But no one did.

I had to attribute that to Yna and the guys. They probably stood up for me and again, I didn't feel like I deserved them.

By Friday, I thought Vic had finally gotten the message because he didn't approach me the entire day, nor did he send out anymore pictures.

I was too chicken to approach him about the picture too; I kind of felt that maybe if I ignored it, then it would disappear.

I was surprised Meg hadn't found out about it, but I knew it was only a matter of time.

Yna and I had a wonderful Friday night at the football game. We were together again after the game for pizza and I had a blast because the guys (minus Lucas) showed up and we laughed until it was time for me to go home.

My life was getting better and I was finally starting to get me back again.

Yna had to be in her cousin's quinceañera Saturday night and there would be a dance.

I was totally excited. Finally, I could let loose and dance. Lucas and Jack had to work late, but David and Omar said they'd go with us. Omar wanted to take Brenda to the dance but he was having a difficult time convincing her dad.

Having David to myself was nice because he was a decent dancer.

I promised Yna I'd spend the entire day with her doing whatever she needed done from the church to the dance hall.

I still hadn't talked to Vic, but every time I saw him he'd give me a knowing look that gave me goosebumps.

* * *

Saturday morning Yna picked me up at eight-thirty. It was an ungodly hour. I had stayed up late the night before watching a scary movie with Meg and I ended up scared out of my mind the entire night.

I had a bag packed for the night because I had permission to spend the night at her house. I was really excited that I didn't have a curfew since Yna's parents would be attending the dance too.

They always stayed until the end of the dance (unlike my parents who never went anywhere).

I ended up helping Yna throughout the church service, helping people find seats, and being an all around gopher for whatever they needed.

The ancient church looked like someone found a bargain basement sale on pink decorations. White and pink streamers lined the pews, old ladies arrived sporting mauve and pink hats and dresses, and big bows lined the doors draped with pink hydrangeas.

Peonies and lilies draped the curtains, all pink of course.

It was more than a little sickening.

Yna attempted to dress me in some pink concoction, but I was adamant not to blend in with the peonies or add to the pink insanity.

I chose instead to wear a soft blue sleeveless dress. It wasn't the kind of dress I'd ever owned. Yna had such a large family that dances, weddings, and quinceañeras were commonplace. A closet full of dresses attested to that fact and this dress was one of those. It was beautiful and made me feel unsoiled.

"Mrs. Centrillo told me to ask you to please go buy some more white ribbon and pins for the decorations for the *comida*," an old lady said to me.

I wasn't sure who she was, but she didn't give me a chance to respond. She just handed me a ten dollar bill and walked away.

I couldn't find Yna so I took her keys, jumped in her car, swore that I'd be better to it than Yna ever was, and sped away.

I had to go all the way to Wal-Mart on the other side of town.

After I arrived, I realized that I honestly wasn't looking forward to making it back in time for the ceremony. This was a perfect excuse, so I started to look around. I browsed the music and movie section.

"I'll buy you whatever you want," Vic said, behind me.

I couldn't believe my luck. Was he following me or was this just a chance coincidence?

It was always hard to tell with him.

"I don't want to talk to you," I said.

I turned to walk away and I braced myself. I thought for sure he'd push me against the wall or the movie displays.

He didn't. Instead he simply said, "I just love you, Linda, that's all. I don't mean to hurt you."

I stopped to look at him stunned. He reached out and twirled his finger through a loose lock of my hair. "You look beautiful. I would never hurt something so gorgeous."

"Hurt? You don't know the first thing about hurt. That's all you've ever done to me. You lie, you cheat, and you send people a dirty picture of us. What was that?" I pleaded.

I had to know why he had done such a horrible thing.

He ran his strong hands through his shaggy hair. He always looked so cool and collected.

His dark hair and eyes seemed to see right through me and clouded over as if contemplating what to do about me.

Suddenly his gaze softened. "I just want guys to stay away from you. You don't know what guys say in the locker room. I overheard some idiot talk about you. He said you were ripe and he was ready. I sent the message to him and he's the one that sent it to everyone else. I wouldn't hurt you."

He always had a way of explaining things so rationally. It would be so easy to just step into his arms and start over again, but I couldn't. "Look, whatever your reason, you hurt me. What am I supposed to do after that? I've been so humiliated."

"I know what you do. You stay with me. I'll protect you."

I shook my head, "I can't trust you. You said you have to earn trust."

"I'll do whatever you want Linda. Just say the word."

He was coming towards me again. I took a step back from him.

"Look, just give me some space okay? I need it and you owe me," I pleaded.

Maybe I was grasping at straws. Maybe if he would give me time this would all blow over and things would get better with us. Don't people say that time heals all wounds?

"If you want time, I'll give it to you. I love you, Linda. You have to know that by now. You are mine," he smiled.

Relief flooded my veins and I was even able give a hint of a smile. I told him goodbye and walked away. That had been one of the best conversations we'd had in weeks. I wasn't sure if what I'd done was the right thing, but at least it gave me some time to think about things.

I felt a little bad about it all because I knew that everyone would be highly disappointed if I went back to him. It would have to be months before I caved in and I'd have to be strong until then.

I hurried back to the church to find the ceremony in full swing. I was a little bummed that I hadn't missed it because the hour and half mass felt like ten.

I dozed several times (quite loudly) through it and Yna had to keep pinching me on the side to keep me awake.

She did throw me a smile every time my head jerked down.

The *comida*, or dinner reception, was awesome. Here it also looked like the young girl had gone way overboard with the pink, but the food made up for it.

They served fajitas, brisket, ribs, and about ten different kinds of rice and beans. Aunts and uncles must have contributed because homemade tortillas were abundant and Mexican wedding cookies littered the tables.

The church service, the dinner, and the dance were held in three separate locations.

To me, that was a waste. Why decorate three places

when you only really need to decorate two?

Crazy, but that's what she wanted.

Yna and I went back to her house after we finished stuffing ourselves to take a well deserved nap.

I didn't tell Yna about my encounter with Vic but I did dream of him, of course. He always haunted my dreams. One moment, I was fighting him in the backseat of his car and the next I'd be walking in the hallway at school with him proudly by my side. The images became distorted and intertwined and I'd be fighting Vic in the hallway and smiling at him in the back of his car. Jean would enter my dream and the images would spiral out of control.

"Wake up loser," Yna said.

I opened one eye and looked at her. "I don't want to. Just leave me here and promise to never ask me to one of these damn things again."

She smiled at me and pushed me off her bed. Yna's room was a complete pigsty. She wasn't much for cleaning and when she tried something on, it was way too much trouble to put the discarded clothes back on the hanger.

My mother would've killed me if I left my room like she did, but, as always, Yna had her wonderful parents.

Sometimes things were so unfair.

I reluctantly got up to put my dress back on. I had hung it from a hanger on her closet door in order to keep it from getting wrinkled.

Yna was fully clad in a different dress. She had worn a different dress to all of the ceremonies. This time, she had on a light purple sequined dress that would have looked completely tacky on anyone else, but it just made her look more beautiful. Her long, shapely legs and flowing black hair complemented the dress.

As David liked to say, she was a real fine piece of art. Well sometimes he said art and other times he said ass.

"You gonna do my hair?" I asked her.

She had three curling irons, a flat iron and rollers all plugged in her large bathroom.

As I sat in her chair, I looked around and tried to wake

up and get my bearings.

Yna's bedroom was twice as big as mine. She had this Cinderella bed that must have been there since she was a little girl. I teased her about it all the time, but she's added her own spice to it with purple, black, and hot pink curtains and a black twined rope that encircled the top bedposts.

In spite of Randy's death, Yna was persevering. She was going to keep on going. She was determined. Her smiles were contagious and her positive attitude made me feel like life wasn't so bad. Because of her, I hadn't looked into my closet for answers nor had I been swallowed up by self-pity all week.

"I'll do your hair," she answered, "but only if you do mine."

Her smile made me laugh. Yna's hair was something else. I told her all the time it was a work of art with a mind of its own. I could curl, straighten, or comb her hair till my hand fell off, but her damn hair would never look different.

"How about I put it up somehow? It'll look pretty with the low neckline of your dress."

She didn't answer me but simply sat in front of the mirror and waited.

I worked on her hair for an hour before I called it quits. I hadn't done too badly; she looked very pretty with her hair up and little ringlets of curls framing her face.

I probably could've put her hair in a ponytail and she still would have looked better than Miss America.

She then set to work on my wavy hair. Together we decided to straighten it and tie a few locks in the back with a silver pin.

Working on my hair was much easier since it was shoulder length and, most of the time, seemed to listen to me.

When I looked in the mirror I was stunned. Gone was the scared mouse of a girl who ran from her own shadow; she had been replaced with a pretty, sophisticated woman.

Amazed, I stared in awe at my reflection. Remarkable what a little hair spray and make-up could do.

"Linda, you look great," Yna said, tearing up.

"Are you gonna cry? I'm not getting married you dope. We're going to a dance," I laughed.

"It's just that we've had such a hard time these last few months and I know we deserve tonight," she answered with tears slowly streaming down her face.

I gave her a quick hug and handed over her dress. I hadn't told her everything about what had happened between Vic and me. I was still so embarrassed because I'd have to admit that a lot of the stuff was my fault.

I wasn't ready to let her in yet and I didn't know if I ever would. All she knew was that I had had sex with Vic.

The more I thought about it the more I felt convinced that it had been a consensual thing and I was just as much at fault for what had happened as Vic was.

We dressed quickly and ran out of the house. Yna was notorious for being late and tonight was no exception.

Chapter 19

The Civic Center is a large building used for banquets, dances, weddings, and anything else that requires lots of space. The coliseum, which is used for graduations and such, lies directly behind it and the city golf course is located to the right. Across the highway to the left is another venue that is open to the elements. All in all, the small area just outside of town was always jumping with crowds on the weekends and tonight was no exception.

There was a wedding across the street and already cars were squeezing into the parking lots.

"We're gonna have so much fun, girl. You just wait. I have some cousins too that are down from out of town and just got in; they are really cute and really nice," Yna said, rounding the curb a little too tight and forcing her small Jetta to jump the steep curb. She didn't skip a beat, "One of them is real cute and has green eyes, although I don't remember how old he is and he may be in college or something like that but I think you'll like him."

"Okay, stop right there. Don't start. You're always try-ing to pawn me off on someone; don't do it tonight. Let me just enjoy the dance with no pressure. I need to have fun," I pleaded.

I knew she would agree with me to shut me up, but she would never stop trying to hook me up with someone.

"Come on, I think we're late."

"Imagine that," I laughed.

People were already dancing when we got there. We had missed the *marcha*, or ceremony, at the beginning of the dance.

I can't say that I was disappointed though.

Lights were strung around the perimeter of the hall, the tables were draped in white soft linen, the centerpieces were decorated with peonies and hydrangeas, and the band playing was actually really good.

We found seats with Yna's parents and said our hellos to everyone we knew. I stayed with Mrs. Centrillo for about an hour while Yna made the rounds with her family.

I didn't mind.

My location gave me a chance to look around and people-watch.

Some of our friends had begun to arrive and I caught a glimpse of David coming my way.

I was happy to see him because it meant that I could now dance the night away.

"Hey, you look very pretty," David smiled.

"Thanks, you wanna dance?"

I didn't even give him a chance to respond. Grabbing his arm and pulling him through the crowds, I led him to the dance floor.

We stayed out there for five songs and I could've stayed for more, but he said he was tired because he had worked all day and was thirsty.

Reluctantly, we left the dance floor.

"Hey, losers. I thought you'd never get off the dance floor.

I turned to see Lucas walking toward us. Lucas still hadn't really spoken to me and I didn't want to deal with him tonight.

I was about to turn to find Yna when suddenly, behind Lucas, I caught a glimpse of a light blue shirt and a familiar (and very good-looking) face.

Dimples.

Jason had come and suddenly I was embarrassed. What had Lucas told him? Had he shown him the picture on the phone? Had he told him about me?

Part of me wanted to run and hide under a large

boulder, but another part, a much larger part, of me wanted to guide him to the dance floor and never let him go.

What should I say to him?

I was at a loss, so I did what any sane person would do.

I walked away.

I had every intention of heading straight to the restroom.

Jason caught up to me, but he didn't yank my arm or push me against the wall. He simply stood in front of me.

My stomach did a dozen somersaults and suddenly I couldn't breathe.

He looked so adorable with his easy stance, completely masculine physique, and dimples.

"Where are you going? You owe me a dance."

I couldn't even answer him and again, just as before, I stared stupidly at his hand.

Gently he took my hand and guided me to the dance floor. It was just my luck that the song had a slow and easy beat.

Tenderly, he put his strong arm around my waist and we started to move.

His eyes met mine and captivated me. I couldn't look away.

We didn't say one word but if felt like I knew him. I wondered what would have happened between us had I not gone with Vic that night at the Rat Hole.

What if I had chosen differently?

None of the horrible things that had transpired would have happened.

My father would still be talking to me, I wouldn't be jumping every time I heard a bang, I wouldn't be dressing like a frumpy old maid all the time, and I wouldn't be battered with guilt and shame and humiliation.

If only.

For now, though, I decided to enjoy the moment. I lay my head on his well-built shoulders and closed my eyes.

After the song ended, he did not let me go. I stood

there in the middle of the dance floor waiting to see what he was going to do. A lively beat came on, he smiled, my heart melted, and off we went.

We danced through five songs when the mother of the quinceañera girl, Yna's aunt, announced that the cake was ready. Most of the time, the younger people would stand around the front entrances as the older people occupied the tables. If you were single, you stood. If you were taken and came with a date, you sat.

It was simple. So for obvious reasons, we joined David, Lucas, and Yna standing near the double entrances.

"You want some cake?" Jason asked Yna.

Yna, who was always quick with some savvy reply, only smiled. I was secretly glad I wasn't the only one who got tongue-tied with Jason.

Jason nudged Lucas with his shoulder. "Wanna join me Lucas?"

Lucas turned to me and smiled. It comforted my heart because I hated the disappointment I saw in his face. "Linda, you want some cake?"

I shot him a lop-sided grin. "Sure."

Watching Jason and Lucas walk away felt good. They were both so handsome, tall, and sweet.

"Wow, Ms. Balle. You certainly look like you're having fun." Yna grabbed my hand and put it around her shoulder. "Good for you. You deserve it."

"She deserves what?"

A chill vibrated through my body. I knew that voice.

Vic coming to this dance had never even entered my mind, but here he was putting his arm around my waist just as he had many times at school.

I grabbed his hand and stepped swiftly away from his embrace.

I faced him. Even though I still felt my heart breaking, it didn't make me want to be with him.

Still the desire to please, to be accepted, to be loved by him was almost overwhelming. I wanted him to be the sweet, gentle, strong boyfriend that he was before all this mess. His eyes seemed to know what I was thinking when they shrank and sneered. That was the Vic I had come to know and fear.

Yes, fear.

I did fear him. I feared what he would do to me again if we were alone in the car. I was terrified what he'd do to me if I really made him angry. Would he push me so hard next time that I'd hit something sharp or would he really hurt me? He'd been pushing me, but he'd never actually struck me. Looking at him glaring at me, I realized that it was only a matter of time.

I suddenly wanted to run away and I realized, at that moment, that I didn't need time to think about our relationship.

I was done.

Vic grabbed my hand. "Linda, you wanna dance?"

I gently but firmly removed it. "No."

He stood next to me, smiled, and refused to move.

Yna took two steps toward him and tried to stand in between us. "She said no, Vic. Didn't you hear her?"

Vic glared angrily at Yna from top to bottom. "Randy's dead. Maybe you should go find another idiot to put up with you."

Yna's face went completely white and her mouth gaped open. "You son-of—"

"Yna, it's okay. I'll stay here with him. I want to talk to him."

Out of the corner of my eye, I had seen Jason and Lucas making their way back to us. Here I was again in the same damn situation I was in two months ago. I still didn't want to cause any fights and I didn't want to cause a scene at Yna's family dance.

I was stuck, again. I had to stand here with him or leave and I couldn't leave because I had come with Yna.

Vic tried putting his arm around me again but I cleverly stepped aside and pretended to look down at something. "I told you to give me time Vic."

He frowned at me. "I am. But I'm not standing around to watch you with other guys."

I glanced behind me to see Yna arguing with Lucas and then looked to see if Vic had seen me. He was looking straight ahead, so I chanced another look behind me.

Jason caught my gaze and held it. I wanted to go back out on the dance floor or just go stand with him.

His frown was evident as was the grim determination I saw in his eyes.

All I had to do was say the word and they'd come to my rescue. I couldn't do that.

I had to find a way to get away from Vic, but I still didn't want to hurt him. It was crazy, but I still cared for him and part of me was in awe and astounded by how much he loved me. He was here.

With me.

He could be with anyone else. Girls would certainly line up to be with him, but he didn't care about them. He cared only about me.

But what about Jean? What had happened with her? Was he still seeing her?

I had asked myself so many questions about Vic that I was half expecting someone to answer them. So I took the plunge. "Why aren't you with Jean?"

Running a hand through his hair, he sighed. "I thought we'd been through this. I told you, Jean means nothing to me. It was a stupid mistake and I'm sorry. What else do you want me to do?"

Vic put a hand on the small of my back but I shook my head at him. "I told you I need time. I'm going to the restroom."

I didn't wait for an answer. I just turned and walked away while swiftly giving Yna a meaningful glance.

I wanted to take a right towards the exit, but I didn't. I turned left and entered the stuffy and very full restroom.

In the women's restroom there's always a long line of women leaning on one foot then the other, toilet paper littering the floor, and that one person who's hogging the mirror putting on more make-up than I wear in a year.

This restroom was no different.

Yna stormed in and stopped in front of me with her hands on her hips. "What are you doing? I thought you were having fun with Jason."

I rolled my eyes. "I was Yna, but I don't want any fights and I don't want any scenes and I really don't want to hurt Vic."

Sulking in disbelief Yna shook her head. "Are you serious? You don't want to hurt him? Linda, all he's done is hurt *you*."

I grabbed her shoulders to get her attention. "I have an idea. Can you get Jason and Lucas to meet me outside? I don't mind going home."

Lost in thought, Yna put her head down for a moment. "Look, I'll go with you. We can get something to eat. I'm starving."

Relieved, I said, "Okay, thanks."

I waited by the door while several older women, all dressed in black (because they thought black was slimming but it's not always), talked about someone who had on too much make-up and was hitting on their husbands. Every now and then, they shot me a vicious look as if I were next on their hate list.

Not wanting any more shit, I smiled knowingly at them and even nodded my head every few minutes to agree with whatever theory they were creating.

After ten minutes of waiting, I figured Yna and the guys had more than enough time to grab the car. The plan was for me to sneak out and get outside where they'd be waiting for me out front.

It would be a clean get-away.

I stepped out of the restroom and took a quick glance around to see if Vic was watching the entrance to the restroom.

He wasn't.

I could see his back in silhouette as he talked to his friend, Jerry.

The Civic Center has two glass double-door entrances that are separated by a small area that is used to collect money, invitations, or take pictures.

I made it through the first door and I was just about to open the second door where I could see Lucas's car waiting out front.

I was smiling—until Vic yanked my hair causing me to jerk back toward him. My spine convulsed awkwardly and pain shot down my leg.

Tears of pain blurred my vision, but I was unwilling to give up, so I yanked back at my hair and practically ran towards freedom.

Vic was stronger. He grabbed my arm and roughly pulled me to the side of the building.

By then I was sobbing and asked him to let me go.

He pushed me toward the white brick wall. "Why would you sneak away from me like that, Linda?"

He ran his fingers through his hair and I took a step to try to leave.

The impact of him throwing me against the wall again jarred through my body.

"Just let me go. What are you doing?"

"You gave yourself to me and now you're mine. I will not step aside while you hoe around with other people."

He put his hands on my shoulders and shook me. His voice was cruel and malicious. "Don't you see what you make me do? Every time I turn around you're with someone else, dancing, flirting, and hoeing around. Do you honestly think I believe you when you tell me you and those loser guys are just friends? How many of them have you slept with? How many, Linda?"

Stunned, I couldn't find my voice. I had never heard him talk like that.

Ever.

I shook my head. His rage was almost palpable.

Even when he had gotten angry before, he never treated me like this. "Is this what you think of me? Vic, is this what you think I am? Then why don't you let me go?"

Vic cupped my chin and squeezed harder with every word. I stared at this person who I didn't really know. "Because you're mine. Do you want to go fuck someone else? Is that what you want?"

I hesitated to answer. Maybe if I disgusted him he'd let me go. Maybe this was my window to get him to understand that I wasn't into him anymore. I tried slapping his cold hand away from my face. "Yes, I do."

Anger seemed to resonate through his body. He tensed up and a glassy vacant look pierced his eyes.

It was as if he were no longer there.

Soulless.

The hit was hard. As if in slow motion, I saw his fist ball up and the swing of his arm.

His closed fist hit me squarely in the left eye. I saw red and I must have blanked out for a few seconds because I couldn't remember hitting the pavement. Lifting my head caused a sharp pain in my temple and my vision cleared enough to see that I had hit a concrete parking block with my hip.

Vic wasn't through with me. He stooped down and grabbed my shoulders roughly and shook. "You're a liar and a bitch. You said to give you time and I did. The next thing I see is you with—" I saw his arm rise again and I knew he was going to hit me again. I braced myself.

Jason hadn't asked any questions or said a word. He took one glance at me on the ground with Vic standing over me and he went crazy.

Unable to finish his insulting remarks, Vic was struck in the back of the head. Vic was used to fighting so he came up swinging.

Yna knelt over me and helped me get up. "Holy shit, Linda. Did he hit you?"

"It's okay. It was my fault. I really got him angry." My face was numb.

"Shit Linda. Are you serious?"

I had to get myself up to stop the fight. It took every ounce of strength to take a step. The fall must have injured my right leg and my hip burned like it was on fire.

By the time I heaved myself up with Yna's help, the fight had been broken up by Lucas and some other guys that happened to be walking by.

Jason shrugged his shoulders trying to get the guys who'd restrained him to let him go. When he realized the fight was truly over as Vic was being led out by James, Jason walked slowly to me and gently lifted me into his arms. He didn't say a word and didn't even look at my face; he just quietly walked us to the car.

I could hear Vic screaming at some guys who were holding on to him to let him go. I was afraid of what he'd do if he got free. Would he come after me or Jason?

I couldn't help but get emotional with the show of such tenderness after being smacked in the face so harshly.

I lowered my head into his shoulders and tried to hide my face. People had come out from the dance because they wanted to see a good fight and now they were staring at me as if I were some sort of freakoid.

My face burned not only because I was hugely embarrassed, but also because I'm sure I had one heck of a black eye forming.

Jason placed me in the passenger seat and gently put on my seatbelt.

I didn't say a word. I couldn't.

I was too worried about what he was thinking and I didn't know how to express the gratitude I was feeling.

Yna was completely silent, as was Lucas, which was a total surprise for both of them.

Jason gripped the steering wheel so hard I could see the whites of his knuckles. I wasn't sure if he was angry at me or what, but I wasn't in the mood to ask.

Lucas finally broke the silence. "Where do you want to go eat?"

Jason quickly answered his question, "I think we should go to a drive-through and we'll take it out somewhere so that you guys can eat."

Yna didn't bother to answer and neither did I, so Lucas volunteered to talk for all of us from the backseat. "We'll go by McDonald's; it's right there anyway. Then we can go to Beer Can Hill or Knotts Landing. I don't think it'll matter where as long as it's empty. I need to use the restroom so I'll get out and get the food. You guys can wait in the car."

Jason said nothing but turned in to the parking lot and let Lucas get out. He seemed to know Yna and I needed some time alone, so he stayed outside and leaned against the car.

Yna stroked my arm. "Honey, you okay? He hit you, didn't he? Is this the first time he's ever done this? Has he been hitting you?"

I didn't answer because I didn't want to tell her all that had happened. I was so humiliated about all of this.

I just shook my head and kept my mouth shut.

Yna kept stroking my arm and went for my hair. She waited for several moments for me to say something, but I was afraid I would break down completely if I said a word. I didn't trust myself.

Jason and Lucas got back in the car and offered me some fries and a burger. I shook my head on both counts.

Yna took everything and started munching away. Jason turned up the radio. Eminem was ranting about his mother and his hate for women, so I asked him to turn off the radio and we made it to Knotts Landing in complete silence.

Jack, Omar, and David were all there waiting for us. I was assuming that Lucas had called everyone from McDonald's. I wasn't sure I liked the idea, but when we parked Jack came straight to my side and helped me out of the car.

He walked me to the passenger side of his truck while the others congregated on the tailgate.

It was hard for me to walk. I hurt pretty bad and when I took a glimpse at my leg I noticed that the pretty little blue dress I had loved was completely ruined.

The dress was in shreds and what looked like oil smudged the entire right side. What was it with me and clothes? I thought about my sister's pink shirt that I made Jack throw away for the exact same reason. Both times the ruined garments weren't mine.

Breaking me out of my stupid thoughts, Jack hugged me so hard it hurt. "Don't Jack, that hurts."

Immediately he let me go and took a cautious step

back. "I won't even ask you if you're okay, but I will ask if there's something you want me to do. Shit, Linda. Want me to kick his ass? We can. You can watch if you want."

I started to shake my head as soon as he started talking about revenge. I was totally sick in the head because I still didn't want Vic hurt. I needed serious psychiatric help because I still felt like I loved him.

What the hell was wrong with me? "Don't bother. I got him real angry. I said things I shouldn't have." I held up my hand when it looked like he was going to interrupt me. "No, don't bother. I know it sounds ridiculous. Let's just not talk about it. Not now anyway. Okay? I just don't want to think right now."

Warily, Yna ambled toward us. "Lucas got some ice for your eye."

She gingerly handed it to me and I took it. I hadn't seen a mirror yet, but I was sure I totally looked like shit.

It took everything I had but I threw her a hesitant smile. Yna would take this personal like it was somehow her fault, so I had to make sure I reassured her.

The long sigh and the pitiful look in her eyes gave me a clear indication that my half-hearted smile didn't help. "Linda, how's your side? Did you break something? I can tell you can't walk."

I shook my head. "I think I'm fine. I'll have a hell of a bruise tomorrow and so will my face."

Yna turned toward the guys sitting on the back of the tailgate whispering to each other. I'm sure the conversation was all about me. "Jason wants to talk to you. He's gotta leave soon but he said he had to talk to you. That okay?"

I closed my eyes and took a deep breath. I guess I had to somehow thank him for coming to my rescue but I didn't want to thank him for hitting Vic. That wasn't the right thing to do.

I turned to Jack. "Will you give me a second? Please?"

I had to add the word please because I could tell that Jack wasn't through making himself feel better. I'm sure he, just like Yna and probably Lucas, was feeling bad for not being my hero or something ridiculous like that.

Jack and Yna walked away and I used the short time to assess my injuries. I moved my hurting right leg front to back trying to make sure nothing was broken. I probably wouldn't be able to walk at all if it were.

My hip was another story. I moved my waist to the left but jerked back suddenly when the sharp lightning pain shot through me from my hip to the back of my leg. I definitely wasn't doing that again. No way.

"Linda, I'm sorry I wasn't there sooner."

"It's okay, really. Thank—"

"Let me finish because it's eating me up." He moved closer to me but stopped when I staggered trying to take a step back. "Sorry. . . I should've been, but Lucas and I were arguing about where we were going to go eat. It was stupid but I didn't see you come out. Yna heard your scream; that's the only reason we saw you. I'm sorry."

Jason talked quickly, shaking his head and pleading with me to forgive him. I noticed he had a cut above his right eye. Compliments of Vic.

Looking down at the rocks near my foot, I tried hard to make him feel better. "It's okay. I didn't think he'd hit me."

"I take it this is the first time? He won't stop here you know. It'll only get worse. You have to report him so this'll stop and I don't live here but I'm gonna tell Lucas to watch out for you. I'll be back next weekend. I want to see you." He was rambling. He made himself take several deep breaths.

I couldn't believe he still wanted to spend time with me. He could pick any girl right now, especially one that wasn't psycho or had major relationship issues.

"After all this, you want to see me? If Vic sees us together he'll blow a gasket. That's when it'll get worse."

"I'm okay with pissing him off. He can come see me. I'll deal with it."

The machismo was starting to grate on my already frazzled nerves, but I could only nod my head. What could I say to him? *Hey listen I know you saved me back there and just got into a fight for me, but I don't feel like going out with you even though you're super hot.*

No.

I just nodded my head.

He took my hand, placed a kiss on the inside of my wrist, and brought it to his face. "I'll see you next week. I really have to go."

With that he walked to Lucas, said a few words, shot me a last pitiful look, and left.

I walked slowly to the rearview mirror on Jack's truck and I gasped.

I didn't recognize that person staring back at me.

My right eye was almost swollen completely shut, a few droplets of blood had escaped from my mouth, my hair was no longer held by the pin but falling loosely disheveled around my face, and I had a major scrape on my cheek.

I was suddenly embarrassed again. Jason hadn't cared or maybe he had and had only asked me out because of sympathy.

How was I going to go home in the morning? What would I tell my parents? Shit, Meg would soon find out. That's all I needed—her and Vic fist fighting at school.

"Are you really alright?" Lucas whispered.

I hadn't even heard him walk up to me so I jumped and a small scream escaped my lips. I shook my head again; I would never get over tonight. It would be impossible. "Really Lucas, I'm feeling better. I really want to get home. "

I walked toward everyone else sitting on the tailgate and waited for someone to say something.

No one did at first. Omar took a swig of his beer and so did David. "Do you have more beer?"

They both looked at me dumbfounded. I had been with them many times and never once had I drunk any, but today wasn't ordinary and I couldn't stand the empty feeling inside me.

Omar said nothing. He reached into the trunk of his Pinto and pulled a beer out from the cooler. I didn't care what kind it was. I had a feeling I wasn't going to like it or even taste it.

Twisting off the top, Omar handed it to me. "Cheers." He clanked his bottle to mine and I took a long swig.

My eyes watered and my face crinkled in disgust, but I chugged a majority of it.

Yna gasped. "Linda, you're gonna make yourself sick."

Jack immediately came to my rescue. "Let her. It'll probably calm her down."

"Why did Jason have to leave?" I had to know. It was a very sudden departure and he looked like he was anxious to get out of there.

"His aunt saw the fight and he had to go try to diffuse the situation," Lucas said.

"Dude, you know what diffuse means?" Omar smiled.

Instead of laughing at them I took another chug. I couldn't seem to keep my hands from shaking and I noticed it more every time I took a drink.

My friends were so awesome. Here they were trying to make me feel better, always here for me when I needed them, always trying to take care of me.

Tears rolled down my face. I wiped the tears off using my already tattered dress, but they wouldn't stop coming.

"Honey, it's okay. You can let it out. You want to talk about what happened?" Yna asked, putting her arms around me.

I could only shake my head because I couldn't trust myself to talk, but then after a few moments I couldn't hold it anymore. "He thinks I've slept with all of you. He thinks when we go out that I sleep with you. You think others think the same thing?"

Yna rubbed my arm. "People are gonna talk. He just said that to make you feel like shit. That's what he was trying to do. You want to press charges? You can."

"No. Absolutely not. How would I explain that to my dad?"

"I want another beer." I looked directly at Omar who didn't hesitate to get me another one.

I think I had three more and couldn't walk straight, not just from the beer but, also because it hurt so bad. Jack carried me to his truck and again into Yna's house. The last thing I remember is Yna washing my face with a damp towel.

My friends were great.

Dear Diary,

Vic finally hit me. I think deep down somewhere I was expecting it. I just couldn't believe it when he did it and I think he would've hit me more if he had the chance, but Jason got there and fought him.

From what I hear the fight between them was even. Both of them took slugs at each other. Vic's nose bled and Jason got his eye cut.

The fight, from what Yna told me, didn't last longer than a few seconds. I'm glad because they're both big and I'd hate to see them really go at each other. Well, I didn't see this one because I was too busy picking myself off the ground.

I decided to tell my mom that I happened to be in the middle of a fight that broke out at the dance. It explained my black eye and lucky for me she didn't notice my limping so I didn't have to explain that.

I think I have a date with Jason next weekend. I don't know what to do about that because I feel like I shouldn't jump into anything right now because I just got the shit beat out of me but Yna says that having Jason around will help with the hurt and also that maybe it'll make Vic stay away.

Vic.

I still love him. I know, I'm stupid but I do and I don't deserve my friends. He's written on my page, he's sent me messages, and every time I check my Google account, he wants to chat. He hasn't given up even after all this.

I'm starting to get a little scared. At first it was humbling and kind of neat to have him be so possessive and it made me feel like he really loved me, but now I'm just getting scared. Again I wish for a little space to crawl into and again I feel like visiting my friend in the closet because I know somehow, some way I have to face school come Monday morning.

I'm scared. I gave Vic back his gifts. I didn't want to talk to him so I gave them to James while he was talking to Julie and I guess he got the picture. I thought he'd get mad or bring them back but didn't. How can I love him? I try really hard to stop and it only makes it worse. It's like the more you can't have something or know it's bad for you, the more you want it. That's how it feels. I know it's bad to want him but I can't seem to stop. Maybe I really am crazy and maybe I really need psychological help or something. But then I move a little and the pain jerks me back to reality. I'm a rubber band. Jerked in all kinds of directions.

He seems to be getting more and more violent.

Chapter 20

Jack thought it was important to pick me up on Monday so we could arrive at school together. I didn't think Vic would do anything to me at school, but the pushing incidents had happened there and no one had done anything.

I took one last glimpse at myself in the small compact mirror I carried in my purse. No amount of make-up could cover the huge black eye I had on my right side. The scrape was a lighter shade of red, but my limp was definitely noticeable. I knew people would be asking me what happened.

"Hello, my love. Can I walk you to class and cop a feel?" At least Lucas was back to normal.

He put his arm around my shoulders and we walked into school. He did his little flip of the keys on his finger as he walked and whispered in my ear that I would forget everything if I spent just one night with him.

I was laughing at his audacity when we spotted Vic. My smile disappeared and I tensed up so much that I almost stumbled. Lucas grabbed hold of me, glanced at Vic, and signaled to the guys.

They all surrounded me which made me feel good, but I knew it was just a matter of time until he caught me alone again.

"Mrs. Balle. Can I see you for a moment?" Mrs. Hinho asked from across the hall.

I'll have to admit that I was glad to see her. The bell rang and I walked with the counselor to her smelly office.

It didn't take long for her to get to the point. "Linda, I won't pretend to know what's going on with you, but I found some references on relationships that I thought you might find interesting. I won't keep you because I know you have to get to class, but I will expect you to read this." She handed me a small stack of papers.

I read the headline, *Teenage Physical Abuse: Signs and Signals.*

I couldn't say a word. How could I with my black eye and scraped cheek staring at her in the face? Someone must have told her.

"Just tell me you'll read it and if I can do anything . . . please let me know."

I nodded but refused to say anything.

I rose from my seat and jerked back down. The sudden movement sent shivers and shards of pain down my leg. I ignored it as best I could.

She didn't say anything, simply watched me stand back up and walk out of her office.

In the hallway, I was able to take a few gasps of breath in peace. I limped slowly to my locker.

Grateful that no one was there, I took my time. My first period sucked big time because Jean and her mean friends were there.

Sure enough, as soon as I walked in the comments started.

I kept my head down and tried to hide my black eye with my long hair.

"She's probably embarrassed because he's no longer with her dumb ass." Jean's sneering voice caused me to jerk my head up. The instant she saw my face I could tell that she didn't know about it.

Her friends gasped but said nothing. I don't know where they think I got it but they quietly whispered to each other for the next thirty minutes of class. I was grateful because I could try to concentrate on the assignment and not on my aching back.

My relief was short-lived, however, because I could hear their whispers getting louder and louder.

"She's stupid. That's why he hit her."

"Maybe she likes it rough."

"She probably deserved it."

My face turned beet red and I put my head down. Maybe I did deserve it. I seemed to make him angry all the time.

"Why does she even bother?"

"I'll talk to him after class. He'll tell me everything. He always does."

"She's stupid."

I couldn't place who said what, nor did I really care. I tried telling myself that their comments didn't bother me, but of course they did. Shitty little comments like that always bother everyone. There's no escaping the pain.

"They're a bunch of jerks. Don't listen to them." Next to me, Julie grabbed my arm and squeezed reassuringly.

Giving her a half-hearted smile, I nodded. She could say that, but she didn't have any troubles. As far as I knew she didn't date anyone or even wanted to. I should be more like her. It would save me from this God-awful pain in the pit of my stomach.

Class took forever to end. When it finally did, I was the first one out. I caught sight of Lucas waiting for me at my locker and Jack was hanging back looking around. Jeesh, they looked like Texas Rangers looking out for snipers.

"Hey, losers." Just the sight of them made my heart soar.

"Hello, beautiful. Where have you been all my life? Wanna meet me behind the bleachers?"

Lucas would never change. I found comfort in that.

Getting into my locker was a cinch because Jack punched it and caused it to open without my having to fiddle with the lock.

It was a nice shortcut and it beat the hell out of my taking an extra minute to open it.

"I'll meet you at the bleachers after you do my homework," I smiled at Lucas.

"Okay, I'll do your homework but you didn't say it had to be right. You still owe me a leg rub."

"That leg rub was forfeit because of your mouth."

"You want my mouth where?"

Lucas and I continued this light banter all the way to class. From the corner of my eye, I saw people running toward some commotion near the senior lockers. Someone said it was Julie and that she had passed out. I was about to follow the crowd until we spotted Vic. I turned suddenly because I thought I heard my name.

He got right in Lucas' face. "I knew you were sleeping with him."

That was all he said. He gave us both vicious glares and simply walked away. I didn't bother to defend myself even though I really wanted to. I had to grab Jack's arm to keep him from going after him. Jack looked like he was itching for a fight: his chest heaved, his jaw was clenched and he had a look in his eyes that I'd never seen before.

I threw a sympathetic look to Lucas and Jack.

The rest of the day passed without a hitch. Julie had been wheeled away on a stretcher and rumor had it she had some eating problems or something. She was the least of my worries.

I didn't bother to go to athletics because I couldn't even walk, much less run, a few miles, so I went home early and was afraid to go anywhere else.

I had already stopped going to the store or going out to get something to eat. I even stopped going over to Yna's after school for fear that Vic would follow me there. I didn't want to involve Yna in anything more than I had to. She didn't deserve that.

* * *

The rest of the week was pretty much the same. I had to put up with Jean and her friends during first period every day, but I refused to stoop to their level and yell insults back.

The "ignore the problem and it will go away" philosophy doesn't work, but I just didn't have the guts to stand up to them. Partly because deep down I knew they were right about everything.

I saw Vic a few times in the hallway, but not once did he approach me. He leered at me like he really hated me and that was painful in itself. I didn't want him to hate me.

I can't tell you how many times I wanted to approach him and explain that I hadn't slept with anyone.

But the pain in my leg, the cell phone pictures that I still knew people were looking at, and my black eye told me it was better to give this some time.

I figured out a way to skip the football game by explaining to our sponsor, Mrs. Brad, that I had started my period and it was an especially heavy one (thank God for that). It was easier than I thought and she still let me sit on the sidelines and watch. It gave me a perfect view of the team, including Victor.

He still made my heart lurch when I saw him and he still looked over at me at least a dozen times every few minutes. I knew he still felt something for me.

I was still a little scared of him, but after a quiet week the freakiness was wearing off and I started to look forward to the weekend and seeing Jason.

After the game, Lucas, Jack and I went to our usual hangout at the Pizza Parlor on Dickinson. It was a great time because the rest of the guys showed up.

Brenda and Omar showed up together and I casually looked behind her for Lily, but she wasn't there. "Hey Omar, forget someone?"

Omar shot me a knowing look. "We can now see each other without a chaperone. I had a long and exhausting talk with her dad and since he scares the living shit out of me, we're okay now."

"You're taking a shit where?" Lucas came up behind our booth to kiss me on the neck.

I swiftly moved away from him. David was at his side and couldn't control his grin, and it was too unusual to cast aside. "What happened to you?"

Lucas punched him on the shoulder. "Loser has a real date tonight—one we can prove with a real girl this time."

David cast him a hard look. "What do you mean real?

I've told you about lots of girls."

Lucas smiled. "Yeah the nameless girls. Mysterious, elusive, and totally not there."

Before Lucas could say anything else, I stuffed a slice of pizza in his mouth. Their fighting was an ongoing occurrence, but I sure didn't want to have to listen to it tonight and ruin David's fun.

"Dude, you have a date tonight? With who?" I couldn't believe we actually had a name.

"Lily," David said in a small voice.

I struggled to keep from laughing out and pursed my lips together. Lucas, Omar, and Jack, who had just come back from talking with some friends, were different.

Their laugh was thunderous, hard, and extremely embarrassing for poor David.

"Leave him alone," I laughed.

It was great to be joking again and not having to watch my back. To say anything I wanted to, to wear whatever my heart desired, to put on make-up, to just feel free again.

I was starting to get me back.

Chapter 21

Saturday morning I woke up with excitement coursing through every part of my body. I tingled with it.

Meg came in several times to congratulate me on my date. I think she was really happy about my getting away from Vic and seeing someone else.

Not once did Meg bring up the incident with Vic, although I'm sure she'd heard of it because loads of people had. Luckily no one had approached me about any of it. Yna had kept me abreast of all the gossip since I pretty much kept to myself. I talked to the guys all the time, but I felt safe with them.

Meg even went so far as to ask Dad for permission for me to go out. She told him that we were all going out to eat together and that we wouldn't be out late.

I was floored.

She really did hate Vic and I was surprised that she hadn't taken a baseball bat to him when she found out about his hitting me.

Yna came by to pick me up early.

I still carried around a slight limp, my eye was a deep shade of purple, and the scrape on my cheek was healing nicely.

We were to meet at Jack's house.

"Yna, how are you doing with all this?" I couldn't help but feel sorry for her. She'd been dealing with my problems, yet I hadn't even really helped her with hers.

She glanced over at me and knew exactly what I was asking, but I silently hoped she wouldn't stare at me too long. She was driving really fast again, swerving through cars.

"Honey, I'm better. I take one day at a time. I can't believe it's been almost three months since he died. I know he saw other girls. I always knew that, but each time he promised it was nothing and that nothing happened or that they didn't mean anything. I was stupid but I love him."

I shook my head at her. "Randy never hit you. Look at me. Vic hit me and if I could, I'd run back to him in a heartbeat and it takes everything I have not to when I see him at school so angry with me. The look he gives me is hate and I love him. How stupid is that?"

She offered me a slight smile. "We're just a couple of fuck-ups."

I couldn't help but laugh. Yna hardly ever cussed. She was too good for that and too nice and too much of everything.

I took a deep breath. "Let's have fun tonight."

She smiled. "Okay. Let's stop at the Town and Country, get gas, and grab every chip, candy, and drink we can get our hands on. We can celebrate."

My smile widened. It was time to put all this heart-wrenching pain behind us and stop being so damn dark everyday. I felt like the clouds were suddenly lifting, like I was as light as a feather.

Finally, I was getting a chance to go out with Jason.

Yna stopped at the convenience store and we got out. We picked up loads of junk food. It was great.

Just as we were headed out she paused. "I gotta go to the restroom. I'll be right out."

She handed me the bags and I walked to her little Jetta.

I opened the door, threw the bags in the back seat, and was yanked hard by the arm.

"Linda, we need to talk."

Victor didn't give me a chance to say anything or to scream or to even cry out.

He threw me into the passenger side of his little sports car. As he shut the door and started to walk to the other side, I saw my chance to escape but hesitated for just a split second. Could we work things out? Maybe I could change him and be there for him instead of turning my back on him.

I was about to jerk the door open when he used his keys to lock me back in. Every time I tried unlocking the door, he'd push the button and thwart my escape.

He was too quick. My chance to escape went out the window as soon as he took off with tires screeching and the smell of burnt rubber.

I remembered the golden rule of abduction: fight, kick, and scream—do anything to stop the bad man from taking you and putting you in his car. My mom must have lectured this rule every time we turned on the television and another young girl or teenager was lost. Everyone knew that once you got in the car it was over. Most people didn't survive, but this was Vic. He wasn't a stranger or a killer.

I looked around waiting for an opportunity to jump out. Maybe at a stop light or stop sign. I would find some way to get out of the car.

He hit the steering wheel with both hands and when he turned to me the smell of alcohol was overwhelming. "You're mine, Linda. You will always be mine. You're probably pregnant right now and we'll be together forever."

The alcohol gave me hope. Maybe it would mellow him out and he wouldn't get so furious when I broke the news. "I'm not pregnant Vic. I'm not spending any more time with you. I have a date tonight."

As soon as I said it I saw my mistake reflected in his eyes: that soulless, vacant look came back. My head jerked back as Vic accelerated. Telling him I had a date was so stupid of me. I wanted to take it back and tell him we could go somewhere to talk, but the look he gave me made me keep my mouth shut. He was no longer with me.

He was too angry.

I braced myself for his fist.

His car veered to the left of the car in front of us. I had no idea where he was going, but obviously he was looking for something. He kept looking around parking lots.

"Where are you going Vic? Stop the car. Just let me out." I tried to sound calm.

My eyes jotted back and forth from the frantic sway of the car to his determined face.

"I told you before, Linda. If I can't have you no one can. I told you what I'd do. You don't listen."

He took a sharp right turn causing my head to thump swiftly into the window. It stung.

I forced myself to put on my seatbelt. All images of me jumping out of the car were gone. He wouldn't give me the opportunity.

"Vic, look. Let's pull over and talk about this. Yna's gonna be worried when she comes out of the store and doesn't find me there."

"You think I care what she thinks? She's part of the reason we're not together. She's one of the people who wants us apart. I won't lose you Linda."

"Do you really think it was her? What about Jean?"

Again, I knew as soon as I said it that it was the wrong thing to say.

He glared at me then shook his head. "I've already told you all about that. I know you believe me. But your friends, particularly Lucas, keep us apart."

"That's not true. They don't have anything to do with us."

"They have everything to do with us."

We were on Dickinson Street now headed west. He swerved through traffic and cars passed by in a flash. He took a few swigs out of a clear bottle. He was drinking hard liquor, not just beer. Chills went through my body.

"Where are we going?" I asked. He seemed to have an exact location in mind. He was too determined.

He gave me a fleeting look. "You'll see. We'll be together forever soon."

His statement stunned me and my eyes grew. What was he trying to do?

"You want to kill us? You're driving like a maniac."

"I'll show you maniac. I thought you understood me. I thought you were the one that would be with me no matter what. You let me down. But it's okay Linda. I'm here for you.

I've always been here for you."

His car veered into the parking lot of the car wash and jumped over the curb. Cars were lined up near the third stall. I couldn't figure out what he was trying to do and at first I thought he would go through the empty stall but he didn't. I grabbed the handle hoping to jump out as soon as he slowed down.

The guys were there already. They would help me.

He aimed straight toward Lucas's Monte Carlo. Lucas, apparently just pulling up, was still in his car.

Vic didn't even slow down.

Realization smacked me in the face and I took one last glimpse at Vic and what I saw there was evil and menacing and calculated. How could I have ever thought he was sweet? He looked like my worst nightmare, like a demon—ominous, frightening and threatening.

He wanted us all dead.

I looked outside and, as if in slow motion, I saw people with Sonic drinks in their hands, a few people dancing to the music, others looking on in surprise and then I turned toward our intended target.

Lucas' beautiful eyes clearly saw what was coming. His shaggy hair lay loosely on his face, his red shirt was crumpled, and his hand went to the window as if he could stop the car.

I put my hands up and screamed.

Then everything went blank.

Chapter 22

Dear Diary,

Vic got a really good lawyer. It's because of his dad and he seemed to think it was all an accident which is ridiculous but it's been six months.

And still I'm angry, hurt, and in shock.

I have to testify tomorrow. I don't know if I can do it. I had been in the hospital for three months and then it's taken another three to get the case to court. I think they've been waiting for me to get out and since Fort Stockton is the county seat and this is such a high profile case, it's getting into the courts real quick.

The image of Lucas right before the car smashed his face flashes like a rerun in my mind. Every time I close my eyes I see his face. Terror, disbelief, and horror—his face.

Lucas was always the happy-go-lucky guy. The one who made me laugh. The one who flirted with me. The one who had a smile on his face all the time. That image of him, along with my life, has been shattered.

I can't leave my house. My father doesn't talk to me. I think now it's worse because guilt is eating him up. My mom has been wonderful. She and Meg have been there for me but I can't bring myself to smile or to even go to school. I don't deserve anyone being nice to me.

I've spent my junior year locked up in my house and homebound. There's an ugly overweight lady that brings me my school work.

I've never struggled to do my homework but it takes everything I have to make myself do it. I just don't care anymore.

I have refused to talk to anyone. Jack and Omar have come by several times knocking on the door, tapping on my window, and blowing up my email. I have completely secluded myself. Yna came by several weeks ago and forced herself into the room. I couldn't bring myself to even look her in the face. I've talked to her a few times since, but I can't seem to hold a conversation with anyone without breaking down so I've stayed away from everyone. Meg says it's not normal, but at this point I don't know what normal is.

We're moving this weekend. I think it's the best thing for me, too, because people now know the extent of our relationship. Some people, especially Vic's sister who has made it her sole purpose in life to let everyone know, think it was all my fault.

I believe in a way they are right. I could've jumped out of that car in the beginning but I didn't.

I didn't.

I didn't.

Yesterday, I tied a sheet in that closet that now haunts my dreams. I even put it around my neck but I couldn't step off the chair. I cried for a long time. It seems like that's all I've been doing.

My mom said she was looking in to getting me to see a counselor soon. I can't imagine what they're gonna tell me that will make all this go away or make things right.

Nothing can.

Every time I close my eyes I see Lucas. He haunts me too, day and night. Because of me—because of ME he isn't here anymore.

Now, tomorrow I have to relive that night all over again in front of strangers. They get to see my face.

The bandages on my face are still there and tomorrow I will keep them there.

Lucas is smiling at me.

Brilliant and dazzling, the colors encircling me are so very vivid.

He grabs me by my arm gently. I float willingly with him to the park.

White billowy clothes flow in the soft breeze around him. He doesn't wear shoes. It's a beautiful day, clear and cool.

The wind kisses my hair and I feel it flowing in slow motion behind me. He bends down to pick a soft white rose.

I stare at his beautiful face and reach out to take the delicate rose from his hand. The thorns prick my fingers.

I drop the rose and see blood seeping slowly down my wrist.

I look to Lucas and see blood gushing down his handsome face and suddenly the white billowy fabric clings to him smothered in red and parts of his face fall in large clumps to the ground.

I woke up screaming. Meg ran into my room and shook me by the shoulders to wake me up. This was nothing new.

I've done this more times than I care to count.

It takes long calming breathes to get Lucas's bloodied face out of my mind.

My futile attempt at calmness would only work for a little while.

Meg rummaged through my closet looking for something for me to wear. Since I couldn't care less whether or not I took a shower, it had been her responsibility to arrange my clothes on my bed every morning. "We gotta go in an hour. Mom's fixing breakfast. You have to eat something and you look like shit."

Reluctantly, I got out of bed. I had to meet with the prosecution for an hour before I was to testify so we could go over all the things he was going to ask me.

I hadn't stepped one foot in the courtroom, as if I really wanted to be there or something.

Really, like I had a choice.

Being in the hospital for months puts a shitty wrinkle in any kind of visitation.

My thoughts were stupid. They had been for weeks. I'd wonder about the word shit and how anyone came up with it and why in the world the word has so many uses . . . like I said, stupid stuff.

My mom came in with a burrito from the local burrito lady. On a normal day (or six months ago), I'd selfishly grab two burritos and stuff my face, but, as usual, my stomach wouldn't cooperate. My steady weight loss was really starting to bother my mom. "Hey baby, you have to eat something."

"I will Mom. I'll eat it as soon as I get out of the shower."

Yet another excuse not to eat.

My eating habits were atrocious. I just couldn't seem to eat anything. Every time I did, I'd get a killer stomachache so I ended up making excuses when someone, mostly my mom, would try to make me eat.

I hopped into the shower and took the longest shower I could. Showers always seemed to soothe me, although I wished that a deep dark hole would swallow me up. I let the water wash down my face and back. The warm water calmed my nerves and I closed my eyes and took slow steady breaths.

I did not want to do this.

After what seemed like forever, I emerged from my shower clean and ready to face my demons.

The drive to the courthouse was the quickest ride I'd ever been on, probably because I really didn't want to be there. I talked to the prosecutor for only a few minutes and he explained to me that Vic's defense lawyer was going to be pretty tough on me because it was my word now against his.

I sat in the lobby waiting area for two hours before I was called in.

Hyperventilation was a serious threat as I walked in to the courtroom.

Wood paneling lined every section of the wall. All eyes were on me as the bailiff led me to an elevated seat near the judge.

There was no jury, the lawyer had explained, because the defense had requested something called a bench trial that gave the judge complete authority. The prosecutor mentioned something about the judge being golf buddies with Vic's dad.

Whatever it was, I had to face this.

I slowly made my procession and took my seat. I could feel Vic's eyes on me and no matter how much I told myself not to look, I couldn't help myself.

Vic didn't have one scratch on him. I think that happens a lot when people drink and drive and get into an accident. It's always the driver who lives or walks away with a minor scratch on his eye or something like that. Vic was that guy. The night of the accident he got out of the vehicle all by himself, or so I was told.

I don't remember being removed from the car and Lucas never walked anywhere again.

This thought made me straighten my back and lift my chin but I still had to tell myself over and over again not to look at Vic and not to look at the pictures that were on display on the defense table, and not to look in the direction of the audience, and definitely not to look at Lucas' mom who had attended every minute of this horribly long and drawn out process.

I had to keep taking deep breaths because I could feel the daggers of those who hated me on my back and, at the same time the warmth, love, and support emanating from my family and friends.

On television, the action is quick and fast-paced and the drama is unrealistic.

I know it's unrealistic because as I walked to the stand the courtroom was totally quiet and no one said a word. Some people even looked like they were asleep or bored out of their mind. It would be great if they were asleep.

But I could feel all their eyes on me.

Shit.

Just like in the movies I had to raise my right hand. The bailiff, who was short and stout and looked like he ate more donuts than salad, recited those infamous words: "Do you hereby swear to tell the truth, the whole truth, and nothing but the truth, so help you God?"

My *I do* was barely a whisper.

The prosecuting lawyer looked so confident with his

dark complexion, expensive suit, and salt-and-pepper hair. He led me through a series of questions leading up to the night of the crash.

The lawyer wanted to know if Vic was drinking that night or if he was agitated, why he was angry, what our conversations were like, if he ever pressed the brakes, and so many other questions.

Telling complete strangers about the night of the crash was extremely difficult.

I tried hard not to break down into a gush of tears but a glimpse of some of the pictures of the two cars caught my eye and I completely lost my train of thought.

It only took one quick glance and the photo was imprinted like a crimson stain on my mind.

The silver twisted metal didn't even resemble a car and there was blood on the ground, lots of it. I closed my eyes but still saw the pool of blood dripping from what looked like black vinyl onto the cold concrete. Death emanated from that picture and I found myself looking at it again and again.

I was so distracted by the picture that the assistant for the prosecution casually put a manila folder on top of it so that I couldn't see it.

When the defense stood up to ask me questions, I thought I was prepared for the onslaught.

I wasn't.

Not in any form or fashion. He hit me hard with the fact that I could've gotten out of the car if I wanted to. He insinuated that I had possibly grabbed hold of the steering wheel and it was a total accident that Lucas had been killed.

He asked me if I actually saw Vic take a drink of alcohol and I said yes, of course, but he wanted me to entertain the idea that maybe what was in the bottle he was drinking from was tea or a soda.

He made me sound like a lying teenager that didn't know shit.

At that point, I glanced at Vic and again the tears welled up in my throat. My hand automatically reached for the bandages on my face.

He looked gaunt, scrawny, and nothing like the wonderful, confident jock I knew. Where had everything gone wrong?

How could I still love that man?

After another grueling hour of questions, I was finally dismissed.

I felt totally defeated. I walked out with my shoulders slumped and my head down.

Meg waited for me outside of the courtroom to walk me to the car. I had no intention of staying. It was enough that I had done my part.

A hand clamped down hard on my shoulder and for a quick second, I thought it was Vic. "You bitch. It was your fault. You're the one that grabbed that steering wheel. Why couldn't you just tell them the truth?" Lilah accused.

I was too tired to respond and I had long since stopped caring what she or anyone else thought.

I sighed loud. "Go away, Lilah."

She sneered at me and lifted her finger. "He was better off with Jean. You made him crazy. You're more responsible for what happened to Lucas than Vic is and you know it."

I was about to reply but Meg got in the middle of us and pushed Lilah away. "Your family's done enough. You stay away from her or you'll answer to me. I would love for you to give me a reason."

The cops down the hall were already coming our way, sensing that something was going on.

"You need to get your head out of your ass and take a look at what your loser brother really is."

Meg grabbed my arm gently and led me down the few steps and out the door. "People are shitty and stupid. Don't let her get to you."

I didn't say anything but I knew Lilah was right. It was my fault. I'd have to live with the guilt for the rest of my life.

My life.

What was that?

Football Star Convicted of Vehicular Manslaughter

By **Nicole Koetting**
PANTHER PRESS

Fort Stockton-Pecos County Circuit Judge John Jamison is scheduled to sentence Victor Balentez,19, for the felony which carries a maximum sentence of 15 years in prison.

After a limelight trial, the judge found Balentez guilty of causing the death of 17 year-old Lucas Casadena who was killed instantly when the car driven by Balentez broadsided Casadena's car as it was parked at the local car wash.

Prosecution alleged that the accident was intentional, as told by Balentez's passenger, 17 year-old Linda Balle.

"He was drinking and he was angry and he wanted to cause bodily harm," said the prosecution.

The bench trial, in which no jury is selected, is not the norm in the small town, but the defendant's legal aide, comprised of what the town called the Wonder Team, proved that the crash was accidental. "The only witness to the crash is a jealous exgirlfriend who may have some head injuries that may cause her to distort the facts. She is not a reliable witness."

Sources close to the investigation say there were no skid marks, no sobriety tests done on the driver, and no explanation for the crash.

Sentencing is scheduled for the end of the week.

Part Two

Part Two

Chapter 23

I put the newspaper clippings back into my diary and look out the small square window. Nothing looks like it's changed. Odessa/Midland is still the same.

Fort Stockton doesn't have an airport so I'll have to find a rental and drive the hour and a half through dark and deserted roads.

This airport is very small and the handful of restaurants that line the inner walls of the building are closed for the night. The long glass windows facing the pickup and drop-off areas extend the entire side of the building. Escalators move freely.

It doesn't take long to find my bags and the rental car places sit vacant. I should have thought about that since it's three o'clock in the morning.

Maybe there's a shuttle bus to one of the hotels.

I ask an airport worker where the shuttles are and he directs me to the east side of the building.

When I reach the loading zone, I step out of the building.

The cool night air smacks me in the face. Living in California puts a damper on all other states because the weather is always so perfect, even when it rains. Being in Europe for the last few weeks with the cold and the sites was great but, regardless, I do miss Texas.

A small stout man who looks like he's about to pass out from exhaustion walks in my direction. "Would you like a ride to the Hilton?"

Before I can answer, I hear a familiar voice behind me. "Linda?"

Without turning around, I close my eyes. What a way to take me back to my troubled past.

After reading my diary on the trip home, I once again feel like I'm that same little girl that doesn't deserve anything.

I slowly turn to face him. I haven't seen him in five years. Maybe to some people five years is nothing, but to me it's a lifetime.

He looks so different. Older of course, but there are other things that have changed that others may not notice.

I notice them.

He still wears the same cowboy attire and, other than being a little slimmer and seemingly taller, he looks pretty close to the man I once knew so well. But his eyes are older somehow, wiser maybe.

"Hello, Jack."

I smile at him but I know the smile doesn't reach my eyes. My trip is not a reason for celebration.

He looks at my face as it turns a beet red. He, along with others, hasn't seen my face and the damage the crash caused. When my family drove out of town, I still had my bandages on. I force myself not to touch my face and square my shoulders and look at him head-on.

"I heard you were coming today. I just didn't know what time."

Astounded I ask, "Have you been here all day?"

His smiling response tells me that he has, in fact, been waiting all day. "Do you live here?"

If he lives near here then I won't feel so bad. He shakes his head and shifts from one foot to the other. "No, I just knew this would be hard for you, so I came to get you."

I'm floored but grateful. We haven't spoken in over five years and just like that he comes to get me from the airport. He used to call me several times each week, then month, then year before finally giving up. Even after I changed my phone number, school, and address, he still always found me. Never once did I return his phone calls.

Yet here he is.

Without saying another word he lifts my two black traveling cases and begins to walk briskly to the parking lot. I don't have a choice and I have to practically run to catch up with him.

He gets into a nice white diesel Ford truck. "What are you doing with yourself?"

I figure small talk is much safer. Anything to stay away from the real reason I'm here.

Dumping my two small suitcases into the back seat, he shrugs. "Nothing much. Just a little work here and there."

Judging from the nice truck and the casually expensive clothes, he's doing a lot more than "just a little" here and there.

·   I have nothing else to say so I keep my mouth shut. I can't judge whether or not he's happy to see me, pissed because I never called him back, or angry because I have to be here in the first place.

The highways are mostly deserted except for an occasional trucker. It feels like home.

This is Texas.

In California, the streets, particularly the highways, are always busy with weary travelers and tourists, but here, in Texas, the highways belong to the truckers.

After twenty minutes of uncomfortable silence, Jack pulls into a small convenience store. "You want something to drink? I'm getting a coffee."

I shake my head wearily. I just want to sleep. My emotions are raw after reading my diary. I hadn't read it since I closed the book five years ago and I don't know what possessed me to read it again, but I felt like I had to in order to get my thoughts straight and remember how I got here.

I can see Jack through the glass windows of the store. He looks as tired as I feel, his clothes are just a tad wrinkled, and his shaggy hair is in disarray.

Maybe a coffee is not such a bad idea. He will need the company. Fort Stockton is a good hour and a half from here. As teenagers, we used to make it in forty-five minutes. We were crazy.

With a sinking heart, I step out of the truck and head toward the store.

"Change your mind?" Jack asks.

"Yeah, I better get something to stay awake. You might need my company."

I head over to the counter and decide quickly to get one of those deliciously sugary cappuccinos, French vanilla. On impulse, I also grab a packet of powdered donuts that look like they've been there a few months.

Perfect.

Jack smirks, "That all?"

I look around wondering what other snack I can possibly grab. On my way to the counter I grab more junk food. I stop walking, suddenly feeling a little sick. The last time I grabbed things like this I was with Yna. Then my life changed.

I force myself to take another step and take a deep calming breath. I will eat this junk food and enjoy it and relax.

I have to.

I dump all my sugary treasures on the counter and grin. "I'll take more if you help me eat them."

He laughs out loud. It is a wonderful sound. "I think you have enough for five people there. Anything else?"

My hands go to my waist. "Nope. I'm good."

We happily get back on the road and I begin taking bites from every bag Jack bought.

"You're gonna make yourself sick."

Smirking with powdered sugar on my chin, I giggle. "Probably, but at least I'll be awake."

"Among other things."

We ride in silence with me eating everything in sight and him driving along taking pieces as I offer them. At least it isn't an uncomfortable silence, but it is a surprising one. He doesn't ask any questions. He doesn't even make small talk. I think he's waiting for me to open up. I can go days without talking. I've proved that over the last five years.

When we get on Imperial Highway, I notice that the weeds need cutting. They are long and crowd the road making it feel small and ominous. The highway is an undersized two lane country road that looks practically abandoned. We'll be lucky to pass three cars in the time it takes to get home.

This is the kind of road that scary movies are made of. The moon is hidden behind gray looming clouds that cause the area to look frightening.

The road tonight definitely looks like a ghost road. I begin to get a little nervous.

Ridiculous. For some reason the old town always brought out my insecurities. Maybe because I was so awkward and stupid when I was younger.

Jack nudges me softly with his hand. "You awake?"

"Yup."

"So, I see you came alone. I thought for sure you'd travel with someone."

I knew it was just a matter of time. I bet he's been aching this whole time to drill me with questions. What he really wants to know is if there's a man in my life.

I will not tell him all of the truth. No one needs to know the demons I've been dealing with or what kind of toll all this has taken on my life.

"I was gonna ask Liz, one of my colleagues, to come, but then decided she'd be better off in Europe continuing to work."

That's a complete lie. I had no intention of ever asking her to come. She has no idea what I'm doing here.

Strict professionalism is all Liz ever sees. It makes my life easy and neat to not form any attachments.

Jack doesn't need to know any of this.

A gray furry rabbit skitters across the road and causes Jack to swerve just a tad. I close my eyes and wait for the impact, but nothing comes.

Jack snickers, "You haven't changed much. I didn't hit it but I would have if I had to. Better a lost rabbit than my truck."

Jack really doesn't know me anymore but again, why bother answering? I'm only going to be here for a few days. Three tops.

"Nice truck by the way. Looks brand new."

He shrugs his massive shoulders and clicks on the bright lights. Not that it helps much; visibility has worsened because of the heavy mist that's moved in. "I bought it last year. My old truck finally died on me. I didn't have a choice. I'd have kept that last one forever, but this one's nice."

This conversation was safe, distant, and unobtrusive.

"So where are you living?" I ask.

He smiles and glances over to me. "I found a really nice house on the outskirts of town. It's not much yet, but it comes with lots of acreage and room to build."

By the whimsical smile on his face, I can tell he loves his new home. He always seemed to belong here. He was so comfortable and confident with himself that it was almost annoying. Even in high school he exuded a cool, wise confidence.

Sitting in his truck in his presence brings back all those little memories of him smiling easily with the guys and always seeming to be there in the background like a warm and comfortable blanket.

I sit back and try to breathe away the tension that has settled in my neck over the past two weeks. Jack will take care of me. I'm sure of it.

I start to doze off, but after half an hour Jack nudges me and startles me out of the comfort I was beginning to feel. "Hey, I'm falling asleep. Talk to me. Tell me where you live, what's been going on."

I blink a few times and try to figure out how I'm going to answer his question. Do I tell him that I have nothing in my life but work? That I sit at home alone and frantically grab every ounce of work my boss gives me or that no one knows me and that I don't even talk to any of my family. I could tell him all that, but what would be the point?

"I'm living in southern California. I have a small apartment. I work a lot."

"You must've flown through school. I mean, it's only been about five years."

I turn to face the window. "Yeah, I went through school pretty quickly. I worked real hard through summers and got a full time job to pay for stuff."

By the middle of my freshman year in college, I had stopped talking to my dad and I wouldn't answer even my mom's phone calls. The money had stopped coming by then and I had to struggle by myself. I found a roommate whom I saw once or twice a week and relied heavily on grants and student loans.

Jack glances at me several times trying to read between

the lines. "You talk to Meg a lot? I hardly see my two brothers."

My gaze switches from the window to my hands resting on my lap. "She lives in Kerrville. She has a little boy that I haven't met yet."

My answers are short and to the point. I think he's getting the picture because he doesn't ask any more questions but instead chooses to tell me all about his life.

"I never did get a chance to leave. My dad got sick and I kinda felt like I had to take care of my mom. I refused to work in the restaurant, so I went to work with my uncle in construction. He's getting old and the business is pretty much mine now since he doesn't have any boys."

The lights of Fort Stockton can be seen a good fifteen miles away. I always thought it was an amazing sight to see this small town out here in the middle of nowhere. The entire town can be seen from this vantage point and it makes me a little nervous. This is where it all happened. This is where I made so many mistakes.

"—he was pretty cool about things so I figure I'll give him some of the profits until I can buy it outright. He has a lot of customers who are getting used to me too and I think they're starting to trust me."

Jack continues rambling on about his newly acquired construction company. No matter how hard I try, I can't keep my eyes open.

When we roll into town, I realize he isn't taking me to a hotel. I have every intention to stay at the Atrium.

The hotel has an indoor pool we frequented when we could. Yna had a cousin who worked there and she'd let us in to swim all the time. I wanted to stay there. "You can take me to the Atrium."

His frown tells me his intentions are completely different. "Why would you stay there? Stay at my place. Extra bedroom, more space, clean sheets and all that. I'll even make you breakfast. What else could you ask for?"

All I want is to crawl into bed alone and not have to answer any more questions. "No, really. It's okay. I'll stay at the hotel. It's no big deal."

He doesn't say anything for a few minutes but he doesn't veer the truck toward the hotel.

I decide not to fight him.

"Look, Linda. It's completely ridiculous for you to stay in a hotel when you have family here and when you have me with an empty house. I don't even have a pet."

Jack's mention of my aversion to pets makes me smile. He once had this black and white mangy mutt he called Bullshit. It looked like a cross between a bulldog and a shih tzu. I absolutely hated it. All it did was sniff butts and it seemed to particularly like smelling mine. It always made me feel like I didn't wipe my ass right or something. "What happened to Bullshit?"

His dog was deeply loved by everyone except me. I just thought it smelled like its name all the time.

"Bullshit died last year." He held up his hand. "Don't say anything. I loved that damn dog."

Stifling a giggle, I get my first glimpse of the town in five years. Not much has changed: a few new restaurants, some shut down places, two or three cars I don't recognize pass us.

Memories assault me as we drive through town. We pass the gas station where Vic once pulled me over in the summer. We talked there for so long that we got honked at by someone wanting to use the gas tank. We pass my cousin Terry's house on the left where Meg and I had ridden our bikes several times when we were kids. Jack turned onto Railroad Drive where he and Lucas had dangerously played chicken among the orange construction barrels.

So many wasted memories. So much pain. So many mistakes. If only I could go back and enjoy things more or maybe just change a few minute things.

If only.

Jack lives on the south side of town so we cut right through and before I know it we're in the outskirts again.

As if reading my thoughts, Jack reaches out his hand to clasp mine. He squeezes just enough to infuse some encouraging emotions in my body. It works.

I will get through this.

Taking a deep, calming breath, I look out the window

and refuse to think about all those annoying memories my mind keeps conjuring up. "So, tell me, how long have you had this house?"

Anything to keep my mind off things.

"I bought it two years ago. I had to get out of my mom's house. I loved living there, don't get me wrong. I took care of them, but I have to have my space. Every man does."

"Yeah? And what do you need your space for?"

He threw his head back and laughed. "Leave it to you to ask a question without really asking. No I don't have anyone in my life. No I don't have a child crawling around out there. I work pretty hard, too, so I don't have time to pursue a love interest."

"So professional about it? A love interest? You sound like Omar."

Jack puts his hand on his heart. "Ouch, Linda. Omar? I guess it's better than David."

He turns onto a rough dirt road. We bump around a bit. "Sorry, the driveway is the least of my worries right now. I'm getting around to it."

When we get close enough to see his place, I can't believe my eyes. I was expecting a small busted-up house that needs new plumbing and where maybe half the restrooms don't work and you have to open the doors with a screw driver.

That is nothing like what I see before me.

This is a two-story, comfortable and cozy home with a wraparound porch and a big red door. The house looks beautiful and somehow out of place. "Wow, Jack. This is really nice."

"You were expecting a shack?"

"Well, yeah. You made it sound like it was."

He laughed. "Come on inside. We both need some sleep."

My first step off the truck is difficult. My legs are sore from sitting cramped up at the airport. My head hurts just a tad from my ponytail and my whole body aches.

Jack easily takes my two suitcases into the house and for the first time I'm happy that he's here and that I'm here. This will be much more comfortable than a hotel. I can't even remember the last time I was in a real home. My small apartment sure doesn't count and I never visit anyone.

His house is as amazing inside as it is outside. For a guy he sure knows how to decorate a house. I would have put in the necessities and that would have been it. Jack has big beautiful photographs on the walls; the kitchen is any woman's dream with its granite countertops, three ovens, gas grills, and bar. It's an open floor plan with the upstairs winding up into the far back of the house. It's completely stunning. "You lied to me. This is absolutely beautiful Jack. Very homey too."

"I'll take that last comment as a compliment." He carries the suitcase toward the back of the house behind the stairs where there are a few doors. He opens one to reveal a spacious bathroom. "You can shower here." Then opens another door to a bedroom. "Here's your bedroom."

The bedding is blue and red. There's a reading area in the left corner complete with a chaise lounge. This is definitely better than my bedroom and staring at that bed suddenly makes me so tired I can barely keep my eyes open.

"Thanks, Jack."

"If you need anything, I'm just next door."

"You don't use the upstairs?"

He smiles. "No, upstairs is what I'm still working on. I concentrated down here first."

"It's really a nice home."

He seems to falter at the doorway to glance back at me. I can't read his thoughts, but I wait for him to say something. He says nothing.

Making up his mind, he walks quickly to me and embraces me in his big arms. Caught off guard, I don't hug him back; I don't even move. I have allowed no one to touch me intimately in five years. Sensing my withdrawal he gently grabs my shoulders and his clear green eyes look into mine. "It's gonna be okay. I'll be here for you every step of the way."

I nod but say nothing. I can't. I gulp down the strangled cry that's aching to escape. I don't want to talk about anything anymore. I just want to sleep.

"If you need me I'll be next door."

Again I nod and stay completely silent. I don't even move. I could crumble at any moment and I don't want a witness.

With suddenly sad eyes, he walks quietly to the door, takes one final look at me, shakes his head, and shuts the door.

I allow one single teardrop to fall before I angrily wipe it away and get ready for bed.

As soon as my head hits the comfortable pillow, I'm gone but I'm not alone.

Vic is waiting to haunt me in my nightmares—he always is.

Chapter 24

The smell of bacon and coffee wakes me up. I lie in the enormous bed that swallows me up like a protective cocoon. I stretch lazily to postpone my departure of a comfort I haven't felt in years.

I have to find a vehicle today and, as much as I don't want to right now, check into a hotel. I can't continue to stay here with Jack. I don't want to be an inconvenience.

I reluctantly drag myself out of bed, dig through my suitcase, and jump into the shower. The shower ends up taking me at least an hour. It's one of those showers that has those streams sticking out of the walls. The steady flow pounds away on my aching limbs. It feels amazing.

Grudgingly, I dress in some comfortable jeans, a soft cotton shirt, and decide to go barefoot.

I stroll out of the room looking for the source of that fantastic smell.

Jack is busy cooking eggs and there's already a kitchen full of food. Strawberries, waffles, bacon, biscuits, and oranges litter the counter. "You expecting company?"

This worries me. Seeing someone right now, regardless of who it is, does not sound like a good morning.

His smile is bigger and brighter than yesterday's and he looks so cute with food stains on his shirt and face. "Nope. Just you and me. I didn't know what you like to eat and I woke up so early that, well, I had plenty of time to make everything."

I frown at him. "Not sleep well?"

He waves a spatula dripping with grease at me. "No, nothing like that. I'm just used to waking up early for jobs. My crew called this morning about a project we're doing on Gonzalez Road. We've been working on it for weeks."

I sit at the end of the bar and selfishly grab a cup of coffee. I cup it close to my body. Even though the oven and stove are on, there's still a chill in the air.

"You cold?" he asks.

A shiver goes through me but I smile. "Not really. Well, maybe a little. Maybe it's just me."

He walks to the thermostat, pushes a few buttons, and smiles. "Let's eat."

We sit at the end of the bar and I eat more than I've eaten in one sitting in five years. Everything tastes like home.

After several minutes of gorging myself, Jack harshly brings me back to reality. "So, what are our plans today? I figure we can take a ride, go out to eat, rent a scary movie and pig out on popcorn."

The idea sounds deliciously inviting, but I can't let myself do it. I have to get a rental car and check into a hotel. "No, I need you to give me a ride to the Hertz in town and then I can check in at a hotel. You don't have to bother with me."

Jack shakes his head slowly. "Linda, there's no way in hell I'm letting you stay at a hotel. You want a rental that's fine. I'll take you to do that, but you don't need it. I'll be there tomorrow whether you're with me or not. I'd prefer we go together."

It's my turn to shake my head. "Don't you have things to do? Isn't there something you have to get done without me getting in the way? I really don't mind staying in a hotel. I'm used to them."

He gets up and starts cleaning. "You will not stay in a hotel."

He looks just like he did years ago when he came over and roughly washed my tires. Back then it was nice because my tires never looked better, but now he looks like he's going to break something. "Here, I'll wash. You rinse."

I don't give him a chance to argue because I grab the dishrag from his hand and push him over with my hips. I guess staying here will work. I'll stay long enough to do what I came to do and then get myself as quickly as I can to the airport. "Fine. I'll stay with your ugly ass, but I still want a car."

"Okay, you got a deal, but don't comment on something

you've never seen. If you saw my ass, I'd have to give you a Kleenex just to wipe the drool from your mouth."

I laugh and shake my head. "You haven't changed, Jack."

Suddenly the smile that has lit up his face fades and he quietly looks down. "Yes, Linda I have changed."

My smile leaves me and I glance down at the white plate I'm washing. "I know."

"No, you don't know. You never answered my phone calls. Not one. The only reason you answered this one was because I called from the company's eight hundred number."

"No, I—"

He holds up a hand. "Save it. I get it. Let's clean up and take a ride."

We clean the kitchen in silence and I seriously consider the hotel again, but it really won't do any good. It will just make him angry again, plus I have to admit to being fairly comfortable. No, the reality is that I feel *extremely* comfortable here with him.

"So, where are we going?" This town's not that big so taking a ride that'll last more than ten minutes sounds a little ridiculous.

His eyes beam. "I've got to go drop something off at my mom's house and then go by the bank and I'd like to take a ride after that to Alpine."

Confused, I ask him, "Alpine? What for?"

He stops wiping the stove and looks at me. He doesn't say anything for a while but I can tell he's thinking about what he is going to say next. "Look, Linda. You and I need to talk. We have a lot to talk about."

My stare, I'm sure, is one of amazement. He isn't beating around the bush anymore.

This is going to be difficult, too difficult, and it's something I don't want to face with all that's going on right now. "I'd rather you take me to a hotel."

His sigh is loud. "You can't keep running from this. You're alone. Any fool can see it. I can't stand it anymore. I know what happened, but you don't know everything. There's so much we need to talk about that I don't even know how to start."

I watch his eyes for a long time thinking that I've never really noticed how clear and green they are. They look angry and worried and just a little nervous.

I have no intention of talking. I'll go with him to the rental car place and sneak away. I'll see him tomorrow for a little while. He'll be angry, but I'll get myself straight to the airport and I won't have to answer any questions.

"Fine, let's go." I put the damp rag on the counter, head straight to my bedroom, stuff tomorrow's dress into my purse, put my tennis shoes on, and we're out the door in less than five minutes.

He opens the truck door for me and I hop right in. He goes around to his side and I watch him. He's so muscularly built. Odd that I don't remember that. He really does have a nice butt.

"I've got to go by my mom's house to check on her. She's not been feeling well and I told you my brothers are out of town, so it's pretty much been up to me."

I simply nod. Seeing his mother again will be fine. I don't mind that, but I would rather not see anyone else.

It takes ten minutes to get to her house. She lives clear on the other side of town. Jack takes the long way and goes around town through the outskirts and feeder roads. I don't know why he does it, but he seems in no hurry.

His parent's house is no different from what I remember. A smile lights up his face. "Come on. She'll want to see you."

I move my hair in front of my face and get out of the car. We find his mother sitting comfortably in the living room watching her soap operas. She's definitely older than I remember, and a little heavier, but the warm smile on her face is inviting and knowing.

"Linda, how good it is to see you, *Mija*." She uses the Spanish word for daughter that I haven't heard in a long time. Her English is still a struggle, but she looks genuinely happy to see me.

A pang shoots through me and pierces my heart. I haven't given myself time to miss my own mother. Jack's mom seems so comfortable in her own skin, so calm. All I want to do is curl up like a baby and lose myself in her soothing arms. "Hello, Mrs. Santiago. It's really nice to see you."

She takes both of my hands in hers and holds them while looking into my eyes. Her hair hangs loosely to her shoulders and she smells like vanilla. "You've always had the most beautiful blue eyes I've ever seen."

My hand shoots straight to my hair to cover my face. It is a motion that has become second nature to me.

Meg pointed it out years ago in an effort to stop me from doing it. It worked for about five minutes and the disappointment and frustration only made things worse.

Mrs. Santiago grabs my hand away from my long hair and brings it calmly to her heart. "You do not need to hide. You have done nothing to shame yourself. Beauty is in your heart and you are beautiful."

Too surprised for words, tears threatened to spill down my face. I blink rapidly to try and keep them from coming down but two unbidden tears fall freely. My not expecting this is an understatement.

I angrily wipe them away. Glancing to Jack to see if he's been listening, I find myself alone with his mother. He isn't even in the room. Maybe it was his intention all along to get me in here to face his mother.

"Uhmmm . . . where is Mr. Santiago?"

I have to try to change the subject. I know I'm going to face the many people in town who can say things that will tear me up. I knew the tumultuous emotions would veer their ugly heads as soon as I stepped one foot in this town. It is why I have avoided it for so long and would have continued to avoid it had I not *had* to come.

"He went to the store or something. He's always got errands to run for the restaurant. You know men, they feel useless if they're not driving everyone around them crazy."

With medications in hand, Jack strolls in to save me from her knowing and wise eyes. "Come on Linda. We gotta go."

He hands her the medicine with specific instructions as well as some reprimands about junk food and cake. She throws me a wink and we head for the door.

"Linda?"

I thought I had gotten away without her telling me more, but the old woman is not done. When I walk back to her she grabs my hand and places it on my heart. "You have to love yourself before you can love someone else. I hope you can come back soon. *We've* all missed you."

Her eyes move toward Jack several times.

Confused, I only nod which makes her smile widen.

Shaking my head as I try to figure out what she is trying to tell me, we leave Jack's house.

He doesn't ask any questions about my conversation with his mother. He obviously trusts her judgments and concerns.

Our next errand takes us to Railroad Drive where his construction crew is hard at work. He asks me if I want to look around, but I'm already shaking my head. Seeing people I know is not something I want to do.

Jack walks confidently throughout the site instructing and answering the questions of men much older. Trust and assurance are in every stance and nod of his men. They grin and easily joke with him. He is obviously well liked and respected.

His lopsided grin when he hops back into the truck assures me that he absolutely loves what he does. "Ready?"

I nod.

I'm in awe. Where did this man come from? He'd always been easygoing and solid, but this confidence, self-assurance, and coolness is amazing to see. Jealousy is my first thought but it's quickly smothered by acceptance. Some people's lives just work out. Others, like mine, just plain suck.

* * *

Jack's errands take us another hour to complete and every time we stop I'm floored by the admiration this town has for him. He is an all-around great guy.

Finally, we head to his last stop. I didn't ask him where we're going.

No doubt, it's another place that will sing his praises.

We pass Cemetery Road, where we went that night so long ago to knock on those mausoleums when Lucas was angry at me because of Vic. He hadn't taken long to get over things, as usual. That's the way he was. He'd get angry with me for a few minutes and then he'd be the one trying to make me laugh or feel better because he felt bad for making *me* feel bad.

Then we pass the park where Vic and I really started to talk. He had taken me out on a ride one night and we had talked for a long time. I thought then that he was different with his easy smile and cool confidence.

After the park is the VFW Hall where Vic and I had co-incidently attended a dance. We had talked and he had opened doors for me and made me feel so special hanging on every word I said. He had looked so cool and confident around his older friends and showed me so much attention. His easy smile, easy stance, and knowing looks hinted that we shared some intimate secret; he had looked at me like I hung the moon.

This town holds so many memories, some good and some I'm embarrassed about. The rumors told. The ugly accusations. They are all still here wrapped up in this small town.

When we pass the old hospital, I realize that we are headed out of town. "What are you doing? I thought I was getting a car."

His smirks raise my ire. "You honestly think I'm stupid?"

He holds up his hand the second I open my mouth. "Don't answer that. I know you. You want me to get you a rental so you can go to a hotel and you don't have to face me so we don't have to talk."

He continues to steal glances at me for a long time. "Look, I'll talk, you listen. Okay?"

My eyes are wide and all I can do is nod.

His sigh is louder than the hum of the truck, but he dives right in. "When Victor jumped that curb speeding toward Lucas's car, I saw it like it was in slow motion, but I know it must have been only a few seconds."

I remembered having that same disconnected feeling like floating. "Don't say anything. Don't you think I've relived that night more than anyone? This is only to make you feel better, but this doesn't make me feel anything but more pain."

Jack quietly steers the truck onto the side of the road and takes my hands. "This has to be done for both of us. I've been waiting for this for a long time. Do you think you're the only one that has guilt? I knew how Victor was getting. I knew he tried running Lucas off the road and I didn't do anything."

My confused look must give away the fact that I have no idea what he's talking about.

"See, you don't know because I didn't do anything about it and I never told you. Maybe if I had—"

I shake my head the moment he starts talking about guilt. He doesn't know what guilt was. "You can't blame yourself. It's all my fault."

He quietly shakes his head, takes a deep breath, and continues on as if I haven't tried to stop him from talking. "I saw his car coming. I saw the whole thing. I saw Lucas put his hands on the glass as if to stop the car. I saw your hands raised and I heard you scream at Victor to stop."

Tears begin to escape steadily like rain down my face. I can see it like it was yesterday. I don't know how much of this I can bear.

"I was the first one there. I thought you were dead; there was blood everywhere as if something had exploded." He puts his head back against the headrest. "I couldn't get to you and I couldn't get to Lucas. Your door was wedged in and it wouldn't open and you were losing so much blood."

He turns back on the road again and after awhile he continues. "I knew Lucas was dead the moment I saw him. He was—"

He stops talking for a few miles, I guess trying to get back his composure. I don't bother looking at him. I know he's struggling with things just like I am and for the first time in the last five years I find someone who's been hurting just like I've been.

Once we pass Marathon and turn west toward Alpine the mountainous terrain becomes like no other. The landscape is beautiful with dark shadows of mountains in the distance. It's just like Fort Stockton but with cooler temperatures throughout the year because of its elevation.

It's a beautiful area and I seriously considered attending college here. Sul Ross University is a small college, but one I was willing to attend for financial reasons. Who'd ever guess that I'd end up going across the country to get away? Even that wasn't far enough sometimes.

"Victor pushed Lucas into a ditch a week before the accident. I didn't want to tell you because I wanted you to leave him on your own. I wanted you to see for yourself what he was. Lucas wanted to tell you and we argued several times with the guys but I wouldn't budge and they just let me have my way. Did you know he unscrewed the lug nuts on David's truck? When David made his first stop his wheels just kept on going. "

I turn to look out the window as soon as he starts to talk but when he mentions the tires on David's truck my head snaps back to him. "What do you mean?"

Jack looks a little strained when he answers, as if he's saying something he shouldn't be saying. "I wanted to tell you, Linda, but I just thought I was doing the right thing. That's not all I didn't tell you."

I don't want to hear anymore and I try to tune him out but I just can't do it.

"Victor was always messing with us. He never did anything to me and I'm not so sure why, but that was one of the reasons I never approached him about any of it. Plus, we didn't have any solid proof."

Jack pulls over at the local Dairy Queen and doesn't even bother asking me what I want. When he pulls up to the intercom, he orders some food and drinks. Everything he orders is exactly what I would have ordered.

He remembers me.

Ignoring that fact, I quietly eat my food even though I'm far from hungry. I take enough bites to keep Jack off my back and wait for him to keep going with his revelations.

Maybe some of this knowledge would have made a difference in everything. Maybe none of this would have happened and Lucas would still be here and Vic wouldn't be sitting in prison right now if they had told me the truth.

Anger shoots through my body hard and strong. Telling me all this isn't making me feel better. It's pointless. "Why didn't you tell me all this?"

The edge in my voice is obvious even to me and I don't care. Jacks seemed to know the question is coming because his answer comes quickly, too quickly. "I thought I was doing the right thing."

I snatch my bag of food and hop angrily out of the truck, almost spraining my ankle in the process.

"Shit," I mutter.

I don't even bother looking back but my quick exit and the throbbing pain in my ankle reminds me of a distant memory.

One time during the summer before we began dating, Vic happened to be driving his father's work van by the swimming pool. He saw Yna and me walking and offered to give us a ride home.

The truck was one of those white utility trucks that are empty shells for storage. He took Yna home first even though I lived closer to the pool.

On the ride to my house, he asked me to go to the back and grab a drink from a cooler. As thirsty as I was, I never once thought he might have an ulterior motive.

Crouched and lowered, I hobbled to the back as the van drove along. As soon as I reached the cooler, Victor hit the gas and swerved along the road with me struggling to find something to hold on to in the back. When I looked back at him it confused me but then it pissed me off enough to yell and cuss as I clumsily clambered along.

When we got to my house, I jumped out of his van and I clumsily fell and twisted my ankle.

When I turned to look at him, his face shook as he tried to subdue his laughter.

I couldn't help but smile back because it really was funny with me bouncing around with nothing to hold on to.

Looking back now, I can see a sadistic side of his humor that I hadn't even realized or let myself realize. Makes me wonder what else I missed.

There were signs. I know that.

Victor telling me I couldn't wear certain things because it drove him crazy with jealousy. Vic forbidding me to talk to my friends. Vic possessively putting his arm around me in the hallways whenever another guy passed by, Vic asking me not to wear so much make-up and me feeling like I had to do things I didn't want to do only because I thought I'd lose him. Vic making me feel like it was a privilege being with him, Vic grabbing my arm forcefully at the Rat Hole, Vic pushing me against the locker, the sex, and the list goes on and on.

It hadn't mattered what Vic had done. I loved him regardless because I was stupid enough to think that I was different, that I'd be the one to change him, and he'd love me and everyone would see. I had talked myself out of breaking up with him even after I got that phone call from Jean.

Even after I saw Jean's smirking face and that little person in my head had screamed a warning at me, all I had done was ignore it.

I somehow blamed Vic for my problems at home. He was the reason I had walked in so late with a blood stain on my skirt and my hair in disarray. He was the reason that I had moved away and spent my senior year at Permian High School with a bunch of strangers instead of at home surrounded by all my friends and family.

I chunk my trash in the bin outside the restaurant and glance back at Jack. He's watching me. I see, even from this distance, the intensity of his gaze.

Instead of walking back to the truck, I decide to go into the Dairy Queen and use the restroom.

The stalls are empty so I stand in front of the mirror looking at my reflection. I don't know her. She's a stranger.

Most times I stay away from mirrors because they're too hard to take. I can see my unsightly white scar more prominently in this fluorescent lighting. My dark hair hangs loose, flat, and unattractively against the light pallor of my face. There used to be a time when I liked the stark contrast between my hair and my face. Now it just makes my scar look more notice-able.

It sucks.

Lucas would still be here had it not been for me because I brought Victor into his life.

This thought brings me back to Jack. Even if I had known all those little things about Victor that Jack knew, I don't think I would have believed him.

They had no solid proof. I would've made excuses for him or worse, Vic would have made an excuse and I would have believed him over them.

The guilt Jack has carried around with him for the last five years is unfounded. This is still my fault. No guilt has been lifted.

Telling Jack he's off the hook is something I have to do, but in doing that I have to put myself out there for him to un-derstand that it all lies on my shoulders. I have to make him understand that I wouldn't have believed him and would have called him a liar because I thought Victor loved me.

But he didn't. Never did.

Maybe in his own way. Maybe.

I think he saw me, sees me still, as a pawn.

Over the years, that realization has been the hardest to take. How could I have fallen so desperately, blindingly in love with Victor? Was I desperate?

No, I wasn't. I was happy and I thought I was special because he was interested in me.

I blow my nose and hide my face when two young teen-agers bounce into the restroom. They chatter loudly about some guys and some horrible girl that looks like a skank.

I quietly leave feeling a little hint of jealousy for their carefree gossip.

Jack is waiting outside leaning casually against his truck. He is striking and handsome and he gives me a nervous smile that tries to ascertain my mood.

I smile at him, now determined to make him feel better.

He opens the truck door for me and holds my hand as I get in. "You ready?"

When he starts the truck I smile. "All this way for Dairy Queen?"

"No, all this way to confine you." He looks pointedly at me and we drive off.

This small town has all those wonderful little general stores where you can find pretty much anything you want. There are expensive stores and cheap ones. Clothing, Mexican pottery, small hole-in-the-wall restaurants, and jewelry stores litter both sides of the street. Jack drives around for a while until we find a store that offers metal arts, ceramics, and handmade wrought iron décor for houses.

I've always loved those types of stores, so when I spot one, I all but break my neck looking back at it. Jack takes the hint, makes a u-turn, and heads back there.

I get out as soon as he comes to a stop and rush around the store. I haven't seen a store like this in years. I savor its merchandise and touch everything I can get my hands on.

"You want that?"

I'm holding a ceramic sun with a face and flames edging around the sides. It's very pretty but I have nowhere to put it in my stark apartment. "No, I just like it."

"You think it'd go good in the house?" Jack picks it up and examines it.

I sigh, knowing it would be perfect for his porch. "Yes. It would look great out back."

He smirks. "I know exactly where you're talking about. I'll get it." He looks around the store. "See anything else?"

Together we shop for more than an hour walking throughout the streets and from one store to another. We stop at an old-time general store that carries every candy you can think of, especially those candies that are no longer available in most places. Jack buys some ice cream for us and we sit on a bench outside the store to enjoy it.

Things always seem so simple in small towns like this. People pass by and smile or say hello or tip their cowboy hats at us. It's a friendly place.

We stroll along further up the street and find a wonderful little place that sells fruit cups. Watermelon, coconut, mango, melon, and pineapple fills the plastic cups and permeate the air with fresh citric smells. "Smells awesome."

"You want some?" Jack asks again. This time I let him buy some because it will be great later when the sun starts to make its descent.

"Yes, I do, but I want more than one cup."

His laughter fills me with the first spark of joy today. "Whatever you want Linda. I'll get it for you."

His statement seems loaded to me. Confusion fills me and I have to stop walking and take a look at him. His gaze is steady and strong as he lets me look at him. He seems ready.

For what, I'm not sure, but he is unwavering. His clear green eyes dare me to ask, but I'm not sure I want to. The moment passes as an old man bumps into him. The excuses are quick but whatever has passed between us is gone.

"You ready? Let's go home and watch that movie."

He comfortably holds my hand and we walk back quietly to his truck. I find that I like holding his hand. His hands are rough and coarse with calluses, but to me they cry comfort and protection. It has been a wonderful day.

We make our way back to Fort Stockton and get to his house just as rain starts to pound on the roof. Laughing at our sprint inside, he pushes the button to listen to his messages.

The smile and the warm fuzzy sensations I've been feeling are extinguished by the rough, raspy voice of a man.

"—parole hearing has been postponed until Tuesday morning."

An entire week away.

Chapter 25

The message is clear even if I don't want to hear it. I have come to this town I love so much to testify, once again, against Vic.

Lucas' family, along with Jack, has asked me to make an impact statement.

When I was first told about it, I flat out refused. Coming back is a struggle. Coming back *and* testifying is a nightmare.

My nerves for the last two weeks have been shattered and I'm teetering on the edge of insanity.

Now I have to postpone this horrible situation for another week. I have things to do. I have to escape.

I had no intention of staying here longer than two days. Now I'll have to call Liz and give her the bad news.

Jack and I don't even talk about it. He walks away quietly and I go to my bedroom to hide.

Looking at my watch, I know Liz is probably up to her elbows in reports and promotions. I pick up my cell and hope that for once luck is on my side.

It is.

She doesn't answer the phone. I leave a message letting her know that I will not be leaving as scheduled and give her a lengthy list of items she has to postpone or reschedule.

It can be done, but the realization that I'll have to stay with Jack for a week doesn't hit me until I hang up the phone. Staying at a hotel doesn't seem appealing to me, but neither does inconveniencing Jack.

I make up my mind to get a hotel regardless of what Jack says. I can't hide in my room forever, so I wash my face, slip into some pajamas and go in search of Jack.

He's not in the living room or kitchen and a check of the

restroom finds nothing. Finally, I go out to the back patio. He's sitting there on his porch swing quietly looking out into the distance. When he sees me, he pats the seat next to him.

Quietly I sit next to him. After a while I look up at him and he gives me a reassuring smile. He moves a lock of hair out of my eyes and trails his finger down my scar.

"I have to stay—"

He moves his finger to cover my mouth. "Shhhh."

He knows me. He knows I'm about to offer to go to a hotel. Already, I know he will move mountains to make sure I stay with him. It's comforting, but it makes me nervous.

I don't know why.

I take his fingers in my hands. "I want you to know that even if you told me about all those horrible things Victor did, I don't think I would have believed you. I would have made up an excuse or stupidly believed whatever bullshit excuse he would have told me. None of this is your fault."

I want him to believe me. I want to assuage the guilt he is feeling. Take it away and destroy it.

"You can't take this all on yourself and you've never once blamed anything on Victor. This is his fault. No one else's."

I blink a few times in confusion.

Have I been doing that?

Internally I think I do blame Vic, but most of the blame is on myself. "I should've done things differently. I should never have gotten into that car."

"Linda, you didn't have a choice. And don't tell me you believe that lawyer when he said you had time to get out. You had no idea what Vic was going to do."

"No, but if I had gotten out, then maybe—"

"Maybe nothing Linda. You had no control over what he did. He intentionally drove that car into Lucas' car. He wanted you dead. Do you still love him?"

I take my time answering because I don't want to hurt him but I also don't want to lie to him. "Yes, I think I do. I love what he was before he got so aggressive and jealous."

He shakes his head. "No, Linda you love the idea of him. There's a difference."

It's my turn to shake my head, but in confusion. Could that be it?

I have to think about that one. "Maybe. I don't know anymore, but I do know that he haunts me. Most times it's nightmares, but other times it's the nice things he used to do for me. The way he smiled or held my hand."

"Linda, you've never had another boyfriend. You only know him. Have you ever given another guy a chance? Don't answer that. I know you haven't. You may not answer your phone, but other people do."

His words sting.

He has been keeping tabs on me and if he knows I have no love interests, then maybe he knows how I spend nights alone without family or friends. I think I should feel humiliation, but I don't. I'm glad he knows. It beats my having to tell him or, worse, lie to him.

We sway to the songs of the crickets in silence, each deep in our own thoughts.

The nights in Fort Stockton are surreal. They are wonderful and every night when I was away and the sun would go down, I'd think of them.

Being here and smelling this clean, fresh smell after the rain is amazing. I take a deep breath and fill my lungs with the clean air. "I missed these nights."

"Yeah, I moved away for a few years before I bought the house and before Mom got sick, and that was one of the things I missed the most."

Quizzically I look at him. "I didn't know you went off to college."

He smirked. "Yes, Linda. I got my degree and then came back. Don't get me wrong. I know you might think I'm stuck, but it's my choice to be here. This is where I belong."

A twinge of pain hits me from nowhere and my heart sinks. I don't know why, but it's disturbing to know that he'll be staying here no matter what.

"You ready for that movie?"

"Yes," I answer.

I move to the living room while he changes into something more comfortable and makes popcorn for us. "Want just butter or movie-style butter?"

Trying to be in good spirits I say, "Movie-style butter."

"That's my girl."

We sit comfortably on his oversized couch and he puts his arm around my shoulders. I dig my head into him and enjoy the musky clean smell of his cologne.

"In case you're wondering, I've called the leader of my crew and let him know I won't be coming in for the rest of the week."

Shaking my head, I respond, "Don't do that. I don't want to be an inconvenience."

"Stop it. I want to spend time with you while you're here. It'll be fun to take a few days off and take a little bit of a vacation."

It would be nice to be carefree for a little while, but how carefree would we be with my testimony hanging over our heads?

Regardless of how I choose to spend it, I have to stay here another week. I've given my word, so the alternative is my spending time alone in a hotel.

Jack.

I would rather spend time with Jack. He can help take my mind off things.

"Okay, we'll do something different everyday."

"Deal." He shakes my hand.

We watch a B horror movie where the actors are completely unrealistic and the plot is confusing. We have to laugh ten minutes into the movie and decide that the hour shouldn't be wasted on the rest of it.

"So what do you want to do?" Jack asks.

"I don't know. I haven't had this much time to spare in a long time."

"Well, let's see. We can go for a ride, sit outside, play a game, talk, I don't know."

Laughing at him, I answer. "We're pathetic. We have nothing. How about a card game?"

He smirks. "You mean like strip poker?"

With a giggle, I softly punch him in the shoulder. "Like poker, high stakes."

"High stakes, like strip poker? A bra, underwear. Maybe some socks. That sounds pretty high stakes to me."

"No, I mean money. Real money."

We sit at the bar in the kitchen and play poker. After half an hour Jack offers something to drink. I gladly accept soda.

We start to laugh at stupid things and start to listen to music. Jack was always the one I used to look for at dances because he knew what he was doing. This is no different.

He asks me to dance and we spend the next half hour shaking our butts. A slow dance comes on the radio and we don't skip a beat.

We sway to the music and I close my eyes to enjoy the dance. Feeling more than comfortable in his arms, I lose myself. He makes me feel small and his tall stature and big arms protectively soothe me even further.

He starts to rub my back and stroke my hair. I find myself doing the same thing. The feel of him has rattled my senses and lowered my defenses. I let the emotions roll and leave my worries behind.

I look up into his green eyes and the intensity is there again. It's a wonder I never noticed the small mole near his lips. I stare fixated on that spot and suddenly he bends down and kisses me.

It's a slow warm kiss, full of promis and hope. He tastes of soda, but it's not a foul taste. It's a good taste. I can't get enough. I move my body toward his and grasp the back of his head. I want him closer.

He gently stops the kiss to look into my eyes. "I love you, Linda. I always have."

His words shock me.

I never would have known. Not in all the time he's spent by my side. Where did this come from?

I can't say anything. I don't know what to say. I'm not ready for any of this.

I get up on my toes and try to kiss him again, but he doesn't let me.

Disappointment is clear on his face, but I will not attempt to give something when I know I have nothing to give.

Whatever it was died with Lucas or resides with Vic.

He takes both my hands in his and kisses them. "Good night, Linda."

He guides me to my bed and tucks me in like I'm a little child.

Chapter 26

The next morning hurts. My head aches and I feel like shit. Maybe it's the change in weather for me but Jack, on the other hand, looks like he could run a mile. He hasn't been on an emotional rollercoaster and he's in good spirits. "Good morning, sunshine. Want to go get breakfast?"

I don't want anything but coffee, so I shake my head and put my hands on my head.

"Come on. It'll make you feel better."

I nod and turn around to amble toward the bath to take a long shower. When I emerge clean and hungry he's there waiting in the living room, keys in hand. "Took you a long time. I'm hungry."

"It's your fault. Why would you make such a luxurious shower if you don't want people to spend an hour in it?"

He smiled. "Do you really like it? People thought I was crazy for putting that in, but I remembered how you liked your showers."

The implications of that statement confuse me until I remember the kiss and his words. I quickly look away and he laughs. "Come on, beautiful. Let's go."

He takes me to one of those taco places that looks like a small travel trailer. He buys me something called a hippo; it's huge but tastes like heaven.

We sit on his tailgate beside the trailer and enjoy our breakfast.

"So, what are we doing today?"

He wipes his mouth with a handkerchief. "Sky's the limit. What do you want to do?"

I volunteer a suggestion to go to the natural spring pool

not far from town where we can swim and enjoy the day. When I suggest it, he smiles and we get back in the truck.

In less than an hour, we're packed up and ready to go. It's another wonderful day. We swim for a few hours, playing and splashing around in the deep clear pool. He makes us burgers on the grill and we eat. We swim a little more, get a little more sun, lie around, and generally do absolutely nothing.

The wonder of that pool is amazing. It's more than 40 feet deep and I've heard that there are caves at the bottom to explore, but when Jack mentions us diving, I laugh. I know nothing about that.

The rest of the week is the same. We travel each day to another place. We make it out to the Marfa Lights Festival, go and take a tour of a winery, hike through Kokernut Park near Alpine, and even make a trip to Big Bend.

It's a wonderful time full of fun and laughter.

On our drive back Friday from Big Bend, I sit next to him in the truck with every intention of falling asleep on his shoulder. The hike we took was an exhausting, yet fulfilling, one. The trek down the side of the cavern was exhausting, not to mention my having to haul myself back up. Jack seemed to take it all in stride and never complained one bit. He's in much better shape than I am.

"You tired?" I ask.

He's been driving around all week and never once whined about it. It's nice to be driven around and not have to worry about anything.

"I'm a little tired. Talk to me."

He drives with one hand and holds my hand with his other. "Tell me about your life in California."

There's really nothing to tell about except maybe work, so I rack my brain trying to find something interesting.

I get nothing.

"You're thinking about what to tell me or are you thinking about how much of the truth to tell me?"

Sometimes his truthful insights about me are irritating. Why does he have to know me so well?

"I don't do much; I work a lot. I lead a boring life."

He smiles. "I doubt that. You're busy with work, you have to entertain clients and make speeches and all that."

"Well, to tell you the truth, Liz does most of that kind of work. She's pretty and a people person. I do all the hard work and she does the glamour."

He is silent for a little while and then asks, "Do you think you're not pretty?"

Blinking several times at him, I wonder where he's going with this. "I don't think like that."

"Sure you do. You just don't want to tell me. Do you think you're pretty?"

I think for another few minutes and judge my words carefully. "I think that I have some favorable attributes."

"What the hell does that mean?"

"Well, I think some things are pretty, like my hair."

"I meant your face and you know it."

I look away towards the horizon. Of course I think I'm hideous with this scar that swallows half my face. Who wouldn't? It's enough that people stare at me or, worse, look at me with pity.

Jack squeezes my hand. "Linda, you are a knockout. I can't believe how beautiful you are. When I first saw you at the airport with your regal walk . . . you took my breath away. It kind of made me angry and took me by surprise."

I remember how he had stalked off toward his truck and all I could do was practically run after him. "Why did that upset you?"

I don't think I am the least bit beautiful.

"You wear next to no make-up, you have piercing blue eyes, and your lips . . . you have to know you drive men crazy."

At that, a smile tugs at the corners of my mouth. If he only knew, I haven't been asked out in a very long time.

"You think I'm lying to you."

"I think you remember the Linda I used to be. I'm not her anymore. She died a long time ago."

"No, she's just forgotten how to live that's all."

I look into his eyes and notice that he isn't kidding anymore. My heart leaps.

I haven't experienced this feeling in ages. I have to force myself to look away. Jack is getting dangerous.

"You walk around like people stink."

A giggle escapes. "What?"

He smirks and I laugh harder. "You know, you walk around like you're mad at everyone. Like they better not talk to you or you'll shank them."

"Shank them?"

"Yes, I did time a few years back."

Surprised and unbelieving, I look to his face to see if he's lying. "You're lying. Your mother would kill you. Or shank you."

His head drops back a little and he laughs. It's a heart-felt, wholesome laugh and my heart does another somersault. It's an amazing feeling.

"Yeah, I'm lying. She'd kill me. She'd visit me every day, but she'd kill me."

Jack turns to face me and notices me looking at his lips. They're full and pretty and extremely kissable. His smile leaves his face and he veers toward the side of the road. As soon as he stops the truck I pounce on him.

I force myself to savor the moment, the feeling, the emotions. He cups my face with both his hands and tenderly kisses my lips.

After a few minutes, his kisses deepen and I feel his tongue lick mine with more ferocity. Jack pulls me toward him and I melt into his arms. He caresses my back, my hair, and then slowly, carefully he goes to my breasts.

Another shock of emotion.

How can this be with Jack? Where did our relationship change?

The emotions are raw and his caresses deepen. I let the feelings he's awakening caress my heart and mind. I lay back and enjoy his touch, his smell, his taste. I part my lips and a low moan escapes me as he blazes a trail across my neck and shoulder.

Unzipping my pants, his hands delve deeper.

Shock courses through my body.

A loud honk startles us out of our frenzy. We both jump and then laugh when we notice the semi-truck that's just passed us. I look to see where we are and notice that Jack hasn't even made it to the side of the road. He stopped a little to the right so that cars would have to go on the other side of on-coming traffic to pass us.

Jack notices too and we laugh. The spell is broken, but my lips feel swollen from his kisses and I can still feel the burning passion of his hands on my body.

We travel home in comfortable silence and somewhere along the way I fall asleep.

Jack carries me to my bed and I wake just enough to feel him press a kiss on my forehead.

I move further into the blankets and close my eyes.

* * *

When I wake up, the first thing I notice is Jack lying next to me. His face is relaxed in sleep and his lips are slightly open. I can feel his steady breath on my cheek.

I look to the clock just above the bed and take in the fact that it's early in the morning. The sun is slowly making its appearance.

I watch Jack sleeping for a while and remember our kiss from the night before.

His eyebrows are small and regal, his lips are full, and he has that mole near his mouth. His hand is resting comfortably on my side. I have to force myself not to caress his face or move his hair out of his face.

Every morning since I've arrived he's been in charge of breakfast. I get up to do my share. I reluctantly take the shortest shower since coming here and head for the kitchen while trying not to make any noise.

I turn the radio volume down and am humming to the music when I notice Jack watching me. "How long have you been there?"

His smile is slow and steady. "Long enough."

A warm sensation touches my cheeks and I have to turn

away. His gaze is too intense, too intimate.

I clear my throat. "I made pancakes, bacon, and eggs."

Chuckling behind me he takes a seat at the bar. "I had pancakes?"

We haven't gone to the store all week because we've been out and about, but I have managed to scrounge up enough ingredients for the pancakes and several small to-go syrup containers from his fridge. "They're from scratch and don't say anything."

In all the time he's known me, which is an awfully long time, he's never seen me cook.

"I didn't know you could cook."

I smile knowingly. "I can't, really, but I've gotten better."

We eat in silence while I watch him swallow down the food. The scrambled eggs are a little too salty and the pancakes are lumpy, but he says nothing and empties his plate.

He pats his stomach. "That was good. What are our plans today?"

The obvious lie is sweet.

I can't think of anything else to do today so I offer, "How about sitting around the house and vegging out?"

He shakes his head. "Gotta go see Mom and there's somewhere I want to take you tonight, but before you tell me no, I want you to really really think about it."

Worry obviously fills my face because he states, "No, it's nothing bad, but I know you'll say no at first, so I want you to think about it."

Frustrated, I put my hand on my hip. "Jack, just tell me."

He groans real loud and dives in. "There's a dance tonight and I really want to go. It's a Spanish dance like the ones we used to go to. I have tickets and I've been waiting for this band to come to town for a year."

When he tells me what band it is a thrill shoots through me. I've never seen them in concert, but I grew up listening to their music.

The idea is tempting, but I don't know if I'm strong enough to face the curious stares and frowns. Some people in this town hate me. "I don't think it's a good idea for me to go out."

"I knew you'd say that, so I've invited David and Omar and some of my family will be there."

Astonished, I can't help but ask. "Omar and David live here?"

He shakes his head. "No, David lives in Andrews and Omar lives in Midland, but they both have family still here and come down all the time. They already know you're here. Lots of people do."

My sigh is deep, long, and loud. "I guess it's inevitable, but I'm not sure I want to go."

He stands up and moves slowly to me. "Linda, you'll be safe with me. I'll take care of you. I promise. It will be fun. We'll dance the night away and I won't leave you alone for a second."

I have to consider the alternative. I stay home and Jack will stay with me. He's been waiting for this for a year and I know he won't go without me. I know that.

Seeing Omar and David again will be nice. I used to have the most fun when I was around all of them, but Lucas won't be there. There will be something missing.

People will stare.

Most of my classmates haven't seen me since the trial and the others who didn't attend haven't seen me since my last day at school. It's been a long time.

I've been hiding for so long that I don't know what else to do.

Jack bends down to kiss me and I lose myself in his arms again. This is a different kiss, one full of reassurance and love.

Love.

From Jack.

He releases me gently. "You ready to go see Mom?"

My sigh is loud again. "Yes."

He laughs. "I know how my mom is. She's not shy with words, that's for sure. You'll get used to her again."

I stop him by grabbing his hand. "Jack. We'll go to the dance, but I want you to promise me you won't leave me. Also, I don't have anything to wear. I've been wearing the same thing over and over. I need to buy something."

He squeezes my hand. "Done. I'm sorry I hadn't thought of your clothes situation. You changing your underwear?"

I push him away laughing.

"What? I have to ask. Cleanliness is important to me you know. If you're not sure, I can check them for you. I'll just take a whiff," he says.

I walk away to get my shoes. "You're ridiculous and gross. I don't stink and I brought lots of underwear. I always do."

To my back he shouts, "Yeah? Let me see."

* * *

He's waiting for me in the truck when I emerge ready for some shopping and his mother.

We stop at a little boutique on Main Street that has the cutest clothes and I soon find something simple to wear. I'm about to pay when Jack interrupts me. "You're not gonna try it on?"

I shrug. "Nope, I know my size."

He shakes his head. "Not good enough. You have to try it on so I can see."

"Why? I already know it fits."

He smiles gently and picks up my outfit. "I'm not gonna look at it but I can bet I can describe it. It's boring and dull and looks like something my mom would wear and you don't want to attract any attention so you're just gonna get the ugliest thing you can find even though not much in this place is ugly."

I hate that he knows me so well. "It's not ugly, it's just simple. There's a difference."

He puts the outfit back on the rack and lets the kind old woman behind the counter know that we're not finished yet.

He picks out three outfits that I wouldn't dare wear. I'm already shaking my head. "No, Jack. I'll look like a skank."

His only reply is to hand me the outfits and guide me to the dressing room. My first instinct is to sit on the little stool situated near the mirror in my stall and wait, but then I wonder what it is that he picked out. I see shiny stuff on the front of one of the shirts.

Sighing as loud as I can so he can hear me, I try on the first outfit. It's elegant and classy with a bare back and it ties at the neck. The pants are long but form fitting. It works on my body and I frown. How can a guy know how to dress a woman?

I step out and he whistles. "Nice, but not quite. What do you think?"

I look down at my pants and then the mirror. "No, I don't like the pants."

I step back in and try on the next outfit. Same thing. We both don't like it.

Again I sigh. "I hear you," Jack says just beyond the curtain. "I can help you change if you want."

I shake my head even though he can't see it and wonder what the old woman is thinking. I dress quickly before he can come in; I wouldn't put it past him.

This dress is pretty. Again, the bare back and slim waist. It's a beautiful dress that's not too dressy and looks classy. I would never have picked it out for myself. When I emerge, Jack says nothing for a long time.

"You are beautiful." The look in his eyes tells me that he really means it and a flush creeps up my cheeks.

"Okay, I'll take this one."

He doesn't let me pay for my dress or anything else I pick out.

We make it to his mother's house in silence. The little butterflies creeping into my stomach are starting to get agitated the more I think about seeing people that I haven't seen in five years.

His mother is, thankfully, asleep when we arrive so we set about to clean her house a little by washing her dishes, doing some laundry, and taking out the trash. I find the tasks comforting.

By the time we're done, it's past lunch time so we head over to a drive-thru and grab some burgers.

Suddenly I want to take a jog. The idea fills me with joy. I haven't run in so long that I'll probably die. I work out at the gym a few times a week, so I am in shape, but running is a totally different form of exercise.

When we reach his house, I tell him I'll be back. He seems to be happy with my choice. "Sure, take your cell phone."

I grab my phone and notice for the first time in five days that I have fifteen messages. No doubt Liz is trying unsuccessfully to contact me.

I'll call her back later.

I stretch near Jack's fence and head out away from town. My stride lengthens as I relax and begin to enjoy my run. It's wonderful. The air is cool and the clouds provide cover from the sun. I follow along the highway and stay clear of the road. With the speed limit above sixty, cars and trucks travel fast.

My semi-vacation with Jack has been more enjoyable than I could ever have hoped for. Had Jack not been here to fill my days, I probably would have been holed up in a hotel for the last few days. It really would have sucked.

Jack.

What am I doing? I feel so comfortable with him, so loved. It's an amazing feeling and it will all be over soon. This will be a distant dream.

I'll go back home and he'll go to work.

It will be another five years or more until I see him again. By then, he'll be married with children enjoying his life in that beautiful house in this wonderful town.

He'll be content and I'll be alone.

It's easy to let my guard down with Jack. He knows me. The real me.

And I'll have to leave soon. It hurts my heart more than I can fathom.

I increase my stride in anger. If it weren't for Jack, I'd still be oblivious to my despair.

I have been lonely, sad, and depressed. I haven't allowed myself to feel any kind of emotion and I was content. Far from happy, yes, but content.

Now, how am I supposed to leave here and not feel Jack's comforting embrace? This week has been charged with emotion. It's as if we've used up every emotion I can think of in the past week. It's been exhausting yet exhilarating and eye-opening and wonderful.

And it will all soon end.

I feel the first drops of rain fall on my nose. I angrily brush them away and pick up my pace.

Jack has never even mentioned having a relationship with me or anything remotely close to that. He's probably waiting for me to leave next week so he can have his life back. I've got to stay strong and let Jack off easy.

The rain suddenly begins to pour as if someone up in heaven has opened up a valve.

I am going to get drenched.

The town is farther away than I thought. I'll never make it home in time. I shrug to myself. A little rain's never hurt anyone.

I take off in a steady pace and run breathlessly back towards Jack's house. Just when I think the rain can't come down any harder, it does and the wind picks up so that the rain's not coming from just the sky anymore.

Horizontal rain is the only way I can describe it and when it hits the mud and rocks, it is all I can do not to scream out in pain.

I hear several honks and see Jack, my knight in shining armor, ahead of me and getting out of the truck with an umbrella in hand.

He hugs me close and guides me to the truck. When he gets in on his side, he too is drenched. "Are you crazy? Did you not see it coming?"

Concern and anger cloud his face. I'm amazed. I've never seen him angry.

"I didn't see it coming and when it started to come down it was too late. Are you mad?"

He sighs, "No, sorry. Just worried. And—"

He says nothing for several minutes as we make our way back to his house but suddenly he looks at me intensely. "I got in a fight with Vic the night of the accident. It was just before he found you at the store. It was my fault he was so angry."

Chapter 27

Sometimes people share information with you that you wish they hadn't.

This is one of those times.

I sit in silent confusion all the way back to his house. He says nothing else. He hasn't dared. I'm so angry.

There are a million questions jumbling up my thoughts. What could he have told Vic to make him so angry? Was Vic already angry or did Jack make him angry?

This shower feels great against my skin. I dip my head into the stream of water and breathe through my mouth. The water soothes me.

The implication of his confession strikes me like a stake through my heart. All this time, I thought it was my fault when, all along, it could have been Jack's.

As soon as the thought enters my mind, I dismiss it. Jack is not to blame, even if he had fought with Vic. I got into that car. Vic had a relationship with me.

I turn to let the streams hit my lower back.

Now I know why Jack had been waiting for me at the airport, why he's dropped everything to be with me this week, why he's been so kind, why he's paid so much attention to me.

Guilt.

It's guilt, plain and simple.

Do the attorneys know? Surely they do. They have to. Jack would not have withheld information so vital.

But to wait all these years to tell me today, right now. There is no point to it. It's his own guilt he wants to assuage more than actually wanting to tell me.

Anger courses through me and I have to take deep calming breaths. I should walk out of here now and just get a hotel.

"I know what you're thinking."

Startled, I let out a strangled gasp and cover myself with my arms.

"Don't worry, I can't see you but you can hear me," Jack says quietly.

Putting my head under a stream, I wait for him to lie to me some more.

"You're thinking that you want to go get a hotel. You're angry with me. You're wondering what Vic and I fought about. You're wondering why I didn't tell you before."

Jack waits for me to answer. When I don't, he sighs a little and continues.

"That night he hit you, I wasn't there for you. When he slammed you into the lockers, I wasn't there for you. When he sent out those pictures, I wasn't there for you."

Shame and humiliation fill me. I have to close my eyes.

"I wasn't there for you—ever. When Lucas told me about Victor hitting you, I had to approach him. I didn't see him until that night. He was leaving his dad's dealership and I had just left work. He stopped at the store and I got out. He was so cocky and shitty. He called you a few names, we argued, he took a swing at me, and we fought. Some workers from the store stopped the fight. I told him I'd kill him if he ever laid a hand on you again. He threw some money out of his pocket and told me you weren't worth even that. I thought he'd leave you alone. I saw him go into that store and buy liquor. Didn't even get carded. They never carded Mr. Money."

I close my eyes again and remember the smell of alcohol and Victor's angry eyes.

"I got so mad I started to go after him but—he always got what he wanted. Even from his parents. Always. People just didn't tell him no." That thought did nothing to fuel my anger but brought only sadness to my heart.

What would happen to me if I was never told no?

I read a book once about a rich kid that stabbed another kid in the park. When his girlfriend tried to defend what he'd done she said it was because he was never told no. I remember thinking what a cop-out that was, but now, I'm not so sure. That fits Vic so completely.

I can't let Jack take all the blame and I can't let him think it's his fault because it isn't. Something else would've set Vic off, maybe seeing me with Jason or seeing me talk to someone else. Any of those things would have set him off.

I turn the water off and ask Jack for a towel. "This isn't your fault. None of this is."

Jack hands me a towel when I open the door slightly.

The glass door is clear with no hazy film. I know he's caught a glimpse of skin, but he's too polite to get a good look so I let it pass.

I take a deep breath and ask him the question I've been dreading since I got his phone call weeks ago. "Do you think it's my fault?"

His answer comes too quickly. "No. You did nothing wrong. This isn't about who has the most fault, Linda. The fault lies solely on Vic."

I wrap the towel around my body and step out of the shower.

Jack's pleading eyes and somber expression make me want to melt into his arms and take the pain away, but I can't. He's only here because of guilt.

My eyebrows furrow and I press my lips together. "I don't think it's a good idea to go out tonight. I think you should go out on your own. I'd really like to work tonight; I haven't done anything all week and I'm gonna be swamped when I get back. Besides, I'm a little tired and I'd like to just stay in and relax."

He takes one step toward me. "If you don't go, I don't go. It's that simple."

I clench my fists and stare at him. "Why? It's not like you really want to be here with me. I'd rather be alone."

Jack squints his eyes. "Is that what you think?"

My only reply is to stare at him. I should've stayed at a hotel. I should've refused his help the second I saw him at the airport. I need to keep things simple.

I must keep to myself.

"Go with me. It'll be fun. We'll be okay, you'll see."

I nod and he walks out the door. Vic said those very same words right before he tore my heart out and ruined my life.

I will not be that stupid little girl again who believes everything a guy says or, worse, a dumb-ass female who's only goal in life is to please some two-timing idiot she calls her boy-friend.

I go to my room, pack my belongings, and dress for the dance. I might as well go and try to have a good time. This will probably be the last time I ever step foot in this town. I can't imagine myself coming back to all this.

The dress Jack picked out still makes me feel uncomfort-able, but I'm wearing it anyway. I might as well.

I take my time doing my hair and decide leave it down. The soft curls and waves will cover some of the bare back of the dress. My make-up is scarce but natural. I will not look like a tramp.

When I finally emerge from my bedroom, Jack is pa-tiently waiting for me while he watches a college football game.

He glances at me but then does one of those double takes you see on television where the girl has a miraculous make-over and she suddenly looks like a completely different person.

I guess I have been letting my appearance go with pony-tails, t-shirts, and jeans.

"Wow, Linda. You clean up real nice."

I give him a lopsided grin. "Call me Princess Linda."

He walks deliberately to me and kisses me. He breaks it off after several intense minutes and holds out his elbow. "Prin-cess Linda, your chariot awaits."

I laugh. "You sound like Omar."

Jack's deep laughter makes my stomach somersault. Strange that I feel like this with Jack.

"Omar is no longer in the ancient era. He joined the real world after Lucas died."

The smile quickly leaves my face, but Jack grabs my hand and leads me to the truck. "Don't, Linda. We have to learn to talk about this without it breaking us. You have to learn to live."

When I start to shake my head and speak, he puts his two fingers gently onto my lips. "Linda. You deserve to be happy."

He cups my face in his hands. "Do you understand that? You deserve to be happy. Lucas would have wanted you to live. He would have wanted you to move on. He loved you. You know that. He wanted to protect you. He always did."

Big fat tears well up in my eyes but I can't say a word.

"Shit Linda. It seems like everything's so serious all the time. Let's let loose tonight. Let's have some fun. No more tears, not for the night."

My sigh is loud, but I nod my head. He is right. I will force myself to let loose.

* * *

We get to the Civic Center in no time. It doesn't look any different. The crème walls are still a little dingy, there is a hint of green on the entrance walls, the cement dance floor is still there, and the spot where Vic hit me is still located directly to the right of the door.

I will loosen up.

"You ready to get exhausted, Ms. Balle?" Jack asks as soon as we enter the building.

I smile.

Not until I hear those familiar Spanish tunes do I realize how much I have missed these dances. It used to be the only time I felt completely free and happy.

I grab Jack's hand and lead him to the dance floor. We dance through ten songs before he puts a hand on his sweaty forehead and begs for mercy. "You trying to kill me? Let's get something to drink."

He leads me to get a drink when someone suddenly whispers in my ear. "Linda, you hot babe! Where have you been?"

It's David.

Omar stands behind him with a quirky smile.

They look older. Other than the receding hair line creeping up on David's head, they look much like they did five years ago.

My smile widens; it's so good to see them. "Wow, hey you guys!"

They each take turns hugging me and asking very general questions. I find out that David is living in Andrews and works as a mechanic. He lives alone and dates so many girls that I lose count after ten. His so-called exploits are bigger, grosser, and much more outlandish.

Some things never change.

Omar works in Midland operating heavy machinery. He gets loads of days off and lives with Bambi, some bombshell blonde he brought along. He's attending school, but has no idea what he wants to be. His charm and David's lies are a welcome change to my mundane and lonely life.

Our easy camaraderie is easy to fall back on. They treat me like I haven't just taken a five year leave of absence.

I dance with David (who steps on my feet so much that it's my turn to beg for mercy) and his sheepish grin tells me that he knows that his dancing sucks.

Omar was never one to dance and tonight is no different. He stands, smiling next to Bambi who seems to idolize him. She seems a little lost with most of the conversation and by the look of things; Omar enjoys it more than I can fathom.

Jack grins knowingly at me. "You know Omar—he doesn't care as long as she's willing."

I stifle my laugh and coerce Jack to dance with me again.

After another two dances, it's me who begs for a break. I've been drinking water steadily since we'd arrived and I've got to make a pit stop.

I turn to the front of the building where the restrooms are located.

Before I can open the door to enter, a hard push crashes me into the side of the wall. It's all I can do to keep the door from slamming into my face.

"You bitch. What the hell are *you* doing here? You have some nerve to show your fucked-up face in public."

It is Lilah, Vic's sister, standing with Jean smugly behind her. I knew this would happen eventually. Me showing my face here for the first time is inevitably going to cause anger, but I'm completely unprepared for this assault.

Lilah looks like she's eaten everything in sight for the last five years and Jean looks just the opposite. They both wear what can only be described as old prom dresses and too much make-up.

A pity, but I say nothing.

Lilah pushes me again. "You have nothing to say? You're here dancing as if Vic's not sitting in prison because of you. You were so jealous of Jean that you had to make up shit about my brother."

She steps closer to me getting in my face.

I finally find my voice. "Who the hell do you think you are? You weren't in the car the night your *drunk* brother decided to ram his car into Lucas. You can make excuses but I know the truth."

She doesn't back down. "You don't know shit. You're a shitty person and a lying bitch."

"You can call me whatever you want. He did it on purpose."

"At least that ugly scar on your face is an improvement."

"Maybe, but I'm not in denial." I look to Jean. "And I'm not still waiting for Vic to grow up and take responsibility for his actions."

Lilah pushes me against the wall again.

I've had enough.

I've finally had enough.

I have to stand up for myself.

I push her back with all of my might and she falls backward, stumbling into Jean. "You stay the fuck away from me. You want to hit me like your brother did? You and your family will not do shit to me again."

Lilah's eyes narrow and she starts to come at me again when Jack suddenly stands in front of me. "Lilah, if you worried about your husband and who he's fucking now, maybe you wouldn't have time to worry about others. "

Taken aback, Lilah starts to yell at him, but Jack doesn't

let her. "Leave, Lilah or I'll call Jake over there to escort you out again. It wouldn't be his first time."

Lilah nervously glances at the rent-a-cop who's been warily watching and gives me one last hateful glare before stomping away with her rolls bouncing slowly under the taffeta hot pink dress.

Jean stays put. She is looking at me as if taking in my face. I find Omar and David suddenly standing next to me. They give me the extra strength and courage I need to face her.

I know Jean's looking at my scar. "What? You want to take more shots at me? I'm ready; I'm not the same scared little girl anymore."

As soon as I say those words, I realize they're true. I will never be that scared, stupid girl that keeps her mouth shut while people make fun of her.

Jean walks slowly to me and I stand a little straighter, ready to stand up for myself.

Jean's eyes water and she looks down to the ground several times before she whispers, "I'm sorry for all that I ever said to you. It could've been me in that car. He was obsessive and controlling. I was stupid for the things I did. I hope that one day you can forgive me. I know what he was like. What he *is* like."

And without giving me a chance to respond, she walks quickly to the exit and leaves.

My mouth is open and I can't seem to form any words.

Jack grabs my hand and starts to lead me back to the entrance to the restroom. "I don't even think you got a chance to go, did you?"

A weight has been lifted and I feel like I can dance all night long. I smile when I look up at Jack and walk quickly to the restroom.

I enter the restroom and flashes of memory assault my mind: Victor standing next to me so that I can't dance with anyone else, Yna trying to help me get out safely, Jason standing up for me outside, the old women arguing about some woman hitting on their husbands, and the pain as my face connected with Victor's fist.

Unlike before, there is no one in the stalls. The mirrors,

which I usually ignore, are aligned against one wall so I walk slowly to one and gaze at my face.

Yes, the scar is there. Yes, my eyes are blue. Yes, the woman looking back at me in the mirror doesn't look so desolate and alone.

Somehow, somewhere, I find I can smile.

I will survive this too. I've survived the crash, the horror, the fear, and now I will survive the parole hearing.

A young girl walks in and shoots me a weird look after she sees me smiling at myself into the mirror.

I don't care. I smile, shrug my shoulders, and walk swiftly out the door to find Jack.

Chapter 28

I lie in bed the next morning after an emotionally charged day.

Jack and I danced until the place closed down and then we went to eat at IHOP. I didn't stop laughing until the food came and then I realized I was famished. I ate everything in sight and even a little of Jack's food. Bambi refused to eat anything in front of Omar.

She confided in me several times through the night to share insights on the latest fashion or the cute jail-bait waiter that looked like he couldn't be older than sixteen. Her insights reminded me why I had become so close to the guys in the first place. It took everything I had to follow along with her babble and, after awhile, I just gave up trying and flat out ignored her.

David enlightened us some more on his exploits. According to him, he had five girlfriends he hoped would never learn about each other, and he'd been doing it for so long that he had gotten pretty good at it.

I didn't care about the lies. It was nice to hear his bullshit again and it was mysteriously comforting.

Jack watched me like a hawk. Several times, I caught him looking at me and I couldn't hold his persistent and knowing look. It was as if he knew me better than anyone else. He would smile at me, but his looks ran more along the lines of self indulgence than friendly camaraderie.

I'm so exhausted this morning but I feel good. Seeing Omar and David was bittersweet. I promised them both I'd stay in touch.

Jack and I shared a quick but emotional kiss before I excused myself. Maybe he thought the night would turn out differently, but the complications and implications would hurt more in the long run.

It's better this way.

I have to prepare myself for leaving and my getting closer to Jack at this point will only do damage to both of us. I see Jack and I know he cares about me, but I also know that my life is not here and him moving to California would be wrong.

His parents, his business, and his life are all here in Fort Stockton. He could never be happy anywhere else. I could never do that to him and we all know that long distance relationships don't work.

Not that my doorstep or cell phone are breaking down with calls or visitors, but still, Jack needs a clean break and I don't need anything else.

Taking out my diary again, I open it to the last entry. I try not to read it, but the words of anguish are too sad to ignore.

My eyes well up with tears as I read my thoughts and the raw emotions that seem to jump out of the page.

I can't stand it anymore, so I chunk the diary towards my bedside and a small newspaper article slips out.

As I read it the words begin to blur with more unshed tears. I let them fall.

This is why I'm here. This is why I had to come back. This is why it's unfair and unjust.

I can't help myself. I have to read it again.

Outrage in the Fort Stockton District Court

By Nicole Koetting
PANTHER PRESS
Fort Stockton-Pecos County Circuit Judge John Jamison
sentenced Victor Balentez 19, to 8 years in prison for the
death of 17 year old, Lucas Casadena. With a maximum sentence of 15 years in prison, the short prison sentence caused a
vocal outrage in the courts. The gavel rang out several times
to restore order.

Lucas Casadena was killed instantly when the sports car driv-
en by Balentez broadsided Casadena's car as it was parked at
the local car wash.

Prosecution alleged that the accident was intentional as told
by Balentez's passenger, 17 year-old, Linda Balle.

"This is a sad day for our town. We expected justice and we
got cheated. He should be spending more time in jail for
murdering that young boy. The family is outraged and I don't
blame them," said the prosecution.

Balentez will serve his time in Fort Stockton so that he can
be close to home.

When asked about the family outrage, the defense had a lot to
say. "We are satisfied with the judge's decision. There are no
winners here today. This was an accident and my client will
have to live with that. He is a good person."

Casadena's family refused to comment.

Disbelief.

How could they give him so little time in prison? Reading the newspaper articles always made me feel dirty, as if I had made everything up and I was a silly little teenager trying to get back at an ex-boyfriend. They sentenced him to eight years but he only surved five.

It's because of Vic that I am here today. Because of him I will never look the same or feel the same or be free. He's the reason that Lucas is gone.

Lucas.

Lucas leaning over to whisper some naughty comment into my ear. Lucas kidding around trying to make me laugh. I can still see him at my locker waiting for me.

And I can still see him with his hands on the window right before he died.

He looked right at me. He didn't look at Victor or at the car, but at me. Right into my eyes.

I saw the terror.

I suddenly let it all go. I gasp and snort and cry for the five years that I've lost. I cry because my father and I don't talk and I cry because I don't answer any of my mother's or Meg's phone calls. I sob away the anger and pain I've had.

Maybe I should be crying more for Lucas and my screwed up family life, but I'm not. I'm crying for me.

The me that cried for days when it happened. The me that used to be so carefree, when simple things like dancing made me happy. The me I lost.

The me that looked to the closet and wished I had the courage to end it all. The me that had to suffer through counselor after counselor, plastic surgery after plastic surgery.

The anguish is hard to bear even after all this time.

I feel comforting arms wrap around my waist. Strong arms cup my face and caress my hair and back.

Jack whispers encouraging words into my hair as I let the tears fall. My tears soak the pillow.

"Let it all out, Linda. It's good for you. You try so hard to show a tough front but sometimes it's good to let it go."

I look into his eyes and notice a tear that trickles down

his face. It is only one tear, but his hurt and pain is evident.

Jack lifts me up into his sturdy arms and pulls back the covers on the bed. He takes the towel wrapped around my head and throws it toward the restroom.

I can't stop crying.

Once when I was little, I got hurt at school. I was running around the small track behind the school when I tripped and fell. I tore my jeans and blood trickled down my leg. The nurse called my mother and it wasn't until she showed up at the door that I let the tears go.

It's the presence of comfort that sometimes makes the crying worse.

Jack's arms of reassurance serve that purpose and the tears go unchecked for a long time.

Somehow, in between the snorts and sniffs, with him lying behind me caressing my back and the constant rhythm of rain falling outside, I fall asleep in his arms.

Chapter 29

O n Sunday, I wake to the now familiar smell of bacon and potatoes. Only today there is another smell and another voice.

The smell of tortillas.

A smell I haven't experienced in years. Not since I left my parent's house and never looked back.

I can hear some low voices and mumbles as if they are trying to talk quietly without waking me up.

I creep silently to open the door as slowly as I can to take a peek and find out who's cooking and who's here.

I can't see anything.

It has to be his mother or maybe a girlfriend or something. The voice sounds too young; it has to be a friend of Jack's.

I know this is a possibility.

It is one of the reasons I haven't let myself wish for anything more with Jack, but now, with evidence right here, I can't help but feel a pang of hurt.

No, not just hurt. Real pain.

Like I want to cry all over again. What a loser I've become.

I grab a change of clothes and quickly slip them on hoping to find out once and for all who is out there. I never was the type of person to wait for punishment or wait for my turn. I always want to get things over with.

I open the door slowly and brace myself for a beautiful bombshell like Bambi (with brains, because Jack would never look past the fact that there is nothing in the empty space between her ears) to be sitting next to Jack.

"Hey Linda!"

Instead Liz, my wonderful assistant that I've been ignoring for the last week, is standing in the kitchen. She looks fresh in her white linen outfit and her perfectly-styled dark auburn wavy hair.

I smile guiltily and glance around. Never have I seen Liz lift a finger to cook anything so I know the smell of tortillas is not coming from anything she's made.

Jack's mom gives my backside a pat as she passes by. She smiles at me deliberately which causes a horrendous red blush to crawl into my cheeks.

I wonder if she came in and found Jack in my bed. As if reading my thoughts, Jack chuckles.

I meet his gaze and he winks at me. My stomach does that sweet somersault thing again.

I sigh a little (because it's not something that can be helped) and sit down at the bar to join Liz. "Okay, Liz. Let me have it."

She doesn't even answer me; she's too busy following Jack's every move and when he walks toward the sink and puts his back to her, so her gaze drops straight to his backside. I can't stand it any longer.

I give her a push.

I mean only to push her a little, but I almost unseat her instead. I don't care; her ogling is a little annoying.

Her smirk tells me she knows exactly why I pushed her. "Well, Linda. You missed some very boring and unimportant meetings, but there are a few things I need your John Hancock on and several other things I need okayed."

Reality sucks sometimes.

Back home, I work long hard hours and I hardly ever give myself a chance to sit and do nothing. Most nights I fall asleep with spreadsheets thrown across the bed and my mornings and days are full and jam-packed with meeting after meeting.

Most nights I'll make it into my apartment way past five o'clock and throw myself on my bed in exhaustion. Jack has given me this opportunity to see what it is I've been missing.

Life.

I've missed my fun college years, afraid to catch a guy's interest. I've missed Meg's baby being born, my mom's surgery, my graduation, the beautiful sites in Rome, and Jack.

I frown at Liz, realizing something. "When did you get here? And why are you here?"

Not thwarted in the least by my abrupt and impolite questions, Liz explains with a wave of her hand. "Oh, Jack answered your phone and told me that you had to stay here a little longer. He opened up his home to me and I didn't say no."

My scrutinizing gaze darts back to Jack (who doesn't even turn around) so that I can glare at him. "I didn't know you were coming."

Another wave of her hand. "Jack said he'd take care of it. He even had some guy named David pick me up."

She stops talking just long enough to grab a tortilla off the top of the hot stack and tear off a piece. "He's hot by the way, probably has them lined up. He asked me out tonight and I had to say yes. Had I known Fort Stockton had all these cute Texas hunks walking around unattached, I'd have been down here long ago."

She smacks her lips together and gives Jack's mom more compliments than the law allows. Jack's mom is eating it up.

I look at Jack who's unsuccessfully trying to suppress a laugh.

We must be thinking the same thing. Maybe David hasn't been lying all this time and he does have loads of girl-friends.

Maybe the sky is really red and we just call it blue. Maybe Liz can handle a long distance relationship and maybe, just maybe, I get to keep Jack.

Impossible.

Jack walks over to me and kisses me lightly on the forehead. "How'd you sleep?"

He knows that I cried myself to sleep. He was there.

"Fine," I say, ignoring his gaze.

"I slept very, very comfortably by the way. If you wanted to know or were just . . . curious or something."

I frown at him and try to gauge what it is he's trying to

tell me when I shift my gaze and look into Liz's cool blue stare of astonishment.

I can only nod my head.

If implying a relationship is Jack's intent, he accomplished that long before I got out of bed.

"So, what are our plans today?" Jack asks me.

I purse my lips together and wonder what we should do. I'm too tired to go out and do anything. "How about we rent a movie or something."

He's already nodding his head and looking at me intently. "I was thinking the same thing. I'll go get a movie and we can barbecue. Sounds like a plan, and, if you want, we can invite David."

"That'll be cool. He did ask me out though, so if we leave for a little while after we eat, don't wait up," Liz says smiling sheepishly.

Leave it to Liz to find someone the moment she sets foot in Fort Stockton.

Every time we go anywhere, she has some hot date or a previous engagement. It never fails to amaze me how she can be so carefree. We are such opposites.

We sit down to a delicious breakfast. While Jack and Liz constantly make fun of each other and Liz compliments every bite she takes, the smile on my face never fades but seems to grow bigger with every bite.

Jack's mom doesn't give me any lectures about my character, but she does make several pointed comments about the sleeping arrangements. "If you're sleeping in the extra bedroom, then you haven't seen the beautiful lamp in his bedroom that I bought for him in Mexico last month."

Not quite a question, but still fishing for information. "No ma'am, I haven't seen that lamp yet."

In all honesty, I have been sleeping in my bedroom. He just hasn't been sleeping in his.

With smiles and chuckles, Jack easily tolerates his mother's pointed comments.

We wash the dishes and clean up our mess together.

It's the best breakfast I've had in as long as I can remember.

Jack's mother leaves shortly after giving me a hug and asking me some questions about getting together next week.

I won't be here next week, but I don't want to tell her that, so I thwart the questions with comments about her cooking. She smiles warmly and shuts me up quickly by making a smart remark about my having to feed her son with good food from now on.

Jack laughs as Liz gives us a quizzical look, knowing there's more to that statement than she realizes.

Walking into the living room, Liz takes out her computer while making as much noise as possible. This is her signal that we have work to do.

Jack hugs me from behind and whispers in my ear sending a chill up my spine. "What do you want for dinner, Ms. Balli?"

I smile. "We're in Texas, so t-bone steak, coleslaw, mashed potatoes, corn-on-the-cob, and Chappell Hill sausage."

It's like my last dinner before execution.

He laughs because he knows that's a lot of food. "Your wish is my command, beautiful."

After Jack leaves for the store, Liz and I sit comfortably in the den and spread the work out on the floor and coffee table. I prop up my feet and set to work.

Liz sighs every few minutes but continues to work while saying nothing. After about the fifteenth sigh, I have had enough. "Okay, what is wrong with you?"

Exasperated, she gets up and starts to pace. "What is wrong with *me*? For the last two years I've watched you walk around like some kind of robot, angry and hurt and . . . I don't know. Lifeless."

She stops to stare at me, her blue eyes huge. "Look at you. Your face has a faint sunburn, your eyes are . . . I don't know, alive. You look absolutely wonderful and that guy. That super-hunk looks at you like he'd like to eat you up."

Liz holds my gaze. So what if I feel different than the last time I saw her? This isn't going to last. It can't. I'll be gone tomorrow afternoon after my court appearance. "What is your point?"

"My point?" Liz asks frustrated. "My point is that you have something here Linda. I've watched you push away everyone everywhere we go. Guys ask you out and you act like they have some disease that's contagious. You look at Jack differently. What are you gonna do?"

"I'm not—"

I don't even get out any kind of denial. She holds out her hands. "No, don't deny that there's something going on between you two. Any fool can see it and I'm no fool."

I sigh. "It doesn't matter anyway. Tomorrow I make my statement and I go home. It's that simple, so, yeah, I can't deny something's going on here, but seriously? There's nothing I can do about it."

Liz puts her pen in her mouth. "I don't know what is so important that you had to come back here or what statement you're talking about, but first I want to talk about super-hunk."

I say nothing. I can't because I've never shared any kind of confidences with Liz. Sure, we talk about her love life, her taste in guys, her ideas of fashion, her family, but none of our conversations have ever been about my life.

Ever.

I guess she just always knew that I didn't want to talk about things and she was happy to talk about herself.

For once, she is having the rare opportunity to delve into my life.

"Most of your work is done on the computer. Most weeks you work from your apartment and don't bother coming in to the office because I do most of that end. You could so live here and still work. It can be done."

I start to shake my head as soon as she starts talking. "No Liz, I'd lose my job and what would I do here? It's not possible, besides on those days that I'm not in my apartment, I'm in the office."

She takes my hands in hers and sits next to me on the comfortable couch. "Sweetie, does it really really matter? You've found someone. From the looks of things you found him a long time ago but you just didn't know it. Take the plunge. Live a little."

I can't do it. I can't just up and stay here. Sure my family is still here. I have aunts and cousins that are here (and luckily I hadn't seen any of them), but I stopped talking to them long ago. Meg is four hours away; my mother and father are settled only two hours away in Comfort. I have friends here.

I just can't do it.

Besides, Jack hasn't even shown any kind of interest in having me stay and not once has he mentioned the future.

Jack walks in with a armful of bags and his presence puts a stop to our conversation. Liz looks perturbed but I am happy to stop talking. I don't want to talk to her about Jack when I'm not sure how he feels about me.

We help him get the rest of the groceries and I see that he's bought more than we could eat in two weeks. "Who's coming over?"

He glances at me and throws me a smile that warms my heart. "I invited Omar and David. Then me, you, and Liz and whoever Omar decides to bring with him. You know how he is."

Yeah, I know how Omar is and I won't be the least bit surprised if he brings Bambi again, although I hope he doesn't for Bambi's sake. Liz isn't a quiet-keep-it-to-yourself kind of girl.

Jack puts things away and asks me if he can talk to me in private for a second.

Frowning, I follow Jack to the back patio. Liz winks at me and pretends to make-out with her arms. I roll my eyes at her because she looks ridiculous. As soon as I step across the French doors, he pulls me into his arms. The kiss is searing and I feel it all the way down to my toes. I revel in it.

The kiss is beautiful, ravishing, and promising.

After several breathless minutes, he pushes me back slightly and looks at me. "You are beautiful. Let's have a good time today."

I try to read his expression and his manner but I can't. The statement is loaded with what I think is a goodbye. Let's enjoy today because we won't have a tomorrow. I look down and try to gain my composure.

When I look up at him again, I hold his gaze. "Yes, let's have a good time today."

I walk quietly away and get ready to work all afternoon with Liz. I can feel his eyes burning a hole in my back. I'll never understand men. He wants to kiss me that way and then send me off in the next instance.

So confusing.

Jack works in the kitchen and Liz and I work hard for the next several hours. It's somewhat relaxing to get back into things. I am able to lose myself in my research and ignore everything else—for about ten minutes.

Liz continues to smack her mouth or sigh and Jack's humming and overall good cheer grate on my nerves. I should be happy for him. He will not have to deal with me for much longer and when we get back to California Liz will go back to talking only about herself.

Listening to Jack doesn't make me feel anything except regret and anger.

I can't really be angry at him though because I'm the one that pulls away most times, but I do it because I want to protect both of us. It'll only be harder on Tuesday when I leave.

I could live in California and come home on weekends every few months, but somehow I know it won't be enough for either of us.

"Earth to Linda, hello?"

Lost in thought, I didn't hear Liz asking me a question about some paperwork. She points her thin long-nailed finger the laptop computer screen where she's found that pesky document she'd been looking for. "Here it is Linda. I told you the research was sound. I think it'll work."

And so it goes for the next few hours. I pay absolutely no attention to Liz but focus on watching Jack work in the kitchen, do laundry, sweep the patio, change a light bulb, change my sheets, and then he really does me in when he takes off his shirt to climb the stairs and work in one of the upstairs bedrooms.

I watch him as he goes up the stairs with my mouth

open. Liz gently reaches over and closes my mouth with her hand. "Baby, you got it bad."

"Shut up." It's all I can say because, really, I can't deny that watching him work without a shirt on has done something to me.

She smiles. "I can't believe I'm finally seeing you in love. This is awesome."

She bounces up and down like a lunatic. I remind her that it doesn't matter, but she isn't thwarted from her apparent excitement and after a while it gets contagious.

I laugh with her and for the first time in our relationship, I make jokes and talk about all those crazy naughty wonderful things I could do to Jack to drive him crazy.

"Had I known Liz was going to make such a positive change in you, Linda, I'd have gotten her on a plane a long time ago," Jack says as he leans over the railing.

I don't know how much he heard, but already my cheeks are burning.

Liz starts to laugh. "I don't mind trying anything once, Linda," Jack says and walks away laughing.

Shit.

He's heard everything I said, but suddenly I don't care and I'm happy.

Chapter 30

Omar and some chick arrive shortly after to mark the end of our work session. When I look at our work, I realize that we have actually gotten quite a bit done regardless of my momentary lapses in reality.

Omar walks up to Liz ogling her every step of the way. He introduces the show-piece clinging to his arm but I fail to catch her name. I can only think of one word for her— Aphrodite. It fits her and I can think of nothing else when I look into her cool blue eyes. She speaks in a whiney voice and it is all I can do to stifle my laugh.

Typical Omar.

At least this one seems to have some brains because she doesn't bore us with her latest fashion find or the size of her closet, but instead bores us with the weather patterns of the week.

It's a small step up for Omar, but at least it's a step up.

"Jack! Omar's here." I yell as I walk up the stairs looking for him but he doesn't allow me to get one foot past the second step. He comes out practically running and ushers me back down the stairs. My eyes narrow quizzically at him but he ignores my look.

"Hey, Omar! How you doing?" Jack greets him with a handshake.

I notice Aphrodite hungrily ogling Jack like he's some kind of delicious dessert and I have to bite my lip and squeeze my fists not to yell or beat the living shit out of her.

Jack lights up the grill and we all sit on the patio. The ambience is definitely working tonight.

The dark red cherry-wood seats surround a large wooden coffee table. The tiki lights and candles burn lazily on the tables that are situated along the house wall.

David comes in through the back of the house with a bouquet of flowers in his hands. With his soft yellow buttoned shirt, jeans, and boots, he looks good.

He walks straight to Liz and hands her the bouquets. Who would have thought David had it in him? Amazing.

I look around and notice that we're all paired up into couples.

I steal a glance at Jack. He's looking at me across the furniture, so I get up from my seat to walk toward him. I see the calm ease in his cooking, the comfortable way he holds the silver spatula, and even how easily he leans on one foot. He is comfortable with himself. I wish I could have just a little of that natural self-confidence he seems to exude.

I stand in front of him, look into his clear green eyes, and beg him with my eyes to kiss me. His head tilts a little to the right but he doesn't move toward my lips.

He's showered and his hair is still wet and he smells like toothpaste and cologne. His purple sweater makes his eyes stand out and his jeans hug his butt in all the right places. I clear my throat and go to the sink to wash my hands instead. "Jack this sink out here is really cool."

The grill is built around rock and cement and comes complete with a stainless steel sink, burner units, drawers, side burners, and a food prep area. "You must use it a lot."

He runs his hands along the rock. "Me and Dad made it last year before he started getting sick and I haven't used it but once last year. I had my family over to see the parts of the house I've rebuilt."

I haven't had the opportunity to see his dad and a feeling of sadness enters my heart. Just another thing to remind me that my time here is limited. "I like it. I can't believe that you made this. Then again, I guess I'm not too surprised: the house looks great. All of it."

Jack smiles at me and grabs me around the waist. "It means a lot that you like it."

We hear some laughter and a scream from Aphrodite as she sees a black vinegaroon under one of the seats. It's an evil-looking little insect that resembles a scorpion. I haven't seen one in a long time and thinking about the feel it would make walking up and down my arm makes me shiver. I look at Jack and see his concern for Aphrodite. My eyes narrow. "She's pretty."

He looks at Aphrodite as she skips around before jumping up on top of the furniture and then he turns his attention to me. "She has nice green eyes, but I prefer blue. She has pretty brown hair, but I'm swayed by my beautiful brunette. She has an okay body, but I prefer my athlete."

Beaming at him, I find myself speechless. He bends down to kiss me. I lose myself in it. His tongue slides between my teeth delving deeper. I even wrap my hands around his neck and pull him closer to me not feeling like it's enough.

"You're gonna burn the meat." Omar smirks at us.

I pull away but not before he plants another sweet soft kiss on my forehead. "Later."

A chill goes up my spine.

"Heeeelllllooooooo!"

My head jerks around. I know that voice. I could recognize it in any crowded room.

Running into the house to find the source, I catch a glimpse of curly black hair bobbing up and down as she turns to shut the door. I hear a laugh that sings to my heart when she trips on the rug beside the sofa.

I slow down, desperate to soak up every ounce of her appearance and see her lithe body, the black pants and black shirt she's wearing that are so typical for her.

Yna turns away from the closed door and, as if in slow motion, her smile fades reading my thoughts and my fears in a single second. Tears well up in her eyes and she is throwing her arms up to me as we both move quickly to each other.

Somehow, I know Jack is responsible for this. He has brought me Yna when he knows I will need her the most. She holds me in her arms and I let the tears fall freely.

After months of trying to contact me by email, phone, and my family, she had given up just like Jack.

I haven't talked to her since our family moved away. At first it was because I didn't want to face the memories she invoked or see the extreme pity that passed through her eyes every time she looked at me. After a while, it was because I had ignored her for so long that I was embarrassed. After months of trying, she had given up on me. I couldn't blame her. I had given up on myself.

I've always felt I had let her down.

I've felt like I wasn't a good friend to her because I had gotten into that car when I knew that I should've stayed with her.

I should have been there for her when Randy died and I wasn't; not once do I feel I have been there for her.

Jack is giving me an opportunity to make things right.

She steps back to take a look at me with tears leaking openly down her face. "Sweetie, you look beautiful."

This simple comment makes me chuckle. She is not a good liar. I know what I must look like after the self-deprivation I've suffered through the last five years.

She squeezes my hands. "We have too much to talk about. Where have you been? How are you? What is happening in your life? I want to know everything."

Yna has come back into my life.

Jack laughs from the doorway at our tears. "Women are crazy sometimes."

I turn to look at Jack and wonder what other surprises he has under his sleeve. He shrugs but smiles, knowing he's made me happy.

Yna and I are inseparable. She holds my hand and we talk about everything we've missed over the last few years. The gossip is sweet and wonderful because, for once, it doesn't have anything to do with me.

I learn that Yna lives in Dallas with her fiancé and she owns a dance studio and a restaurant.

I give her a quizzical look at this interesting news, and she snorts. "I know, what a combination. We're always on the road going from one business to the other, but it just sort of happened and I like it. My fiancé handles most of the restaurant business ... oh, Linda. You would love him. I can't wait for you to meet him. When will you be back in town again?"

I glance nervously at Jack. "I'm not sure."

"We'll go out to dinner and drinks tomorrow. It'll be so much fun."

My first instinct is to say no, but then I remind myself that I have to let things go and go with it. "I think it'll be fun."

Excitement rushes through my veins. It's been too long since I have allowed myself to feel eager about anything.

Jack's juicy steaks are done in no time. We sit outside and enjoy the night, the friends, and the food.

The smell of a distant rain fills the air and there's a slight chill in the air. I wrap my arms around myself, a move that catches Jack's eagle-eye attention. "I'll build a fire."

He lights the ceramic fire pit and the heat rises quickly to make the chill leave my body.

With the food and the camaraderie surrounding me like a comfortable blanket, I sit back and relax, scooting closer to Jack to cuddle.

Liz leaves with David soon after dinner, but Omar and Aphrodite opt to stay behind and play board games with me, Yna and Jack. "That's when we know we're getting old. Sunday night and Pictionary," Omar says smiling at me.

"I've offered strip poker but Linda won't go for it," Jack says.

"Shit, Omar. You're getting old. I just like playing this game," I laugh and ignore Jack.

"I'll show you old."

I giggle because it's fun. "Or you'll show me the Oxford English Dictionary?"

Jack and Yna laugh, but Aphrodite is oblivious. "What did I miss?"

Omar gives me a lopsided grin. "I thought the way to a woman's heart was through my intellect when I was in high school, but I was wrong, my dear; it has nothing to do with intellect." His eyebrows go up and down.

"So, you're saying that the way to a woman's heart is through your checkbook?" I ask feigning innocence.

Our banter and teasing continue throughout the rest of the night.

We play Pictionary, the wrong way, cheating wherever we can.

It's great.

We then play poker (and not strip poker, like the guys want to), but real high-stakes poker with money. I win the big pot of money, which feels good even though I have a feeling Jack let me win.

As I step into the cold air at the front of the house while walking Omar and his trophy out, I can't help but feel like this is all too good to stick. Like the life I have experienced here is too good to be true and I realize that I've been waiting for something bad to happen to me ever since I stepped off of that plane. It seems that when everything's going right and calm and good—then God throws you a screwball.

After the accident, everyone told me that God wouldn't give me more than I could handle. I never quite understood why God would intentionally give me heartache, misery, and solitude. In my mind, it wasn't God that gave me all those evil things; it was a guy.

Omar walks Aphrodite to his car by the small of her back. They have opted to spend the night at Omar's brother's house even though we offered them the couch.

I wrap my arms around myself as the wind whistles through the trees. It's a cold night without the fire near. Omar's little car passes through the gate and out of sight in no time.

Crickets sing their music. The clean air gently breezes through my hair and the quiet calmness of the town comforts me. The tranquil feeling makes me lean my head back against the porch. This is the life.

"Come on, let's get you inside," Jack says, pulling me close.

Yna had a long day and waved a weary goodnight minutes ago when Jack offered her his bedroom. I thought she'd sleep with me, but by the looks of Yna's tired eyes and crumpled hair, she didn't care where she slept as long as there was a bed.

Jack and I stand alone in the middle of the kitchen. We're finally alone but I'm too exhausted to think of anything but sleep. "I'm really tired."

He begins to cleanup the kitchen. "Go on in and get some sleep. I'll finish up here."

Guiltily glancing around the mess, I ask, "You sure?"

"Yeah, you have a big day tomorrow with Yna. No doubt she's gonna make use of every second." He smiles and gives me a reassuring hug that gives me a great whiff of his clean smell before he pushes me gently toward the bedroom. "Go on, really."

I'm too exhausted to shower. I throw myself on the bed and I'm out before my head hits the pillow.

Chapter 31

Yna is a veritable whirlwind of energy. She has gone for a run, prepared breakfast, showered, and changed clothes before I even wake up. I've gotten so used to things here that I no longer wake up searching my surroundings.

I guess people call it comfort, but I'm just going to ignore it. I will not dwell on the fact that this isn't going to last.

Yna's flipping pancakes up in the air like a pro. "Wow, when did you learn to cook?" Yna has never cooked in her life, nor has she ever wanted to get her hands dirty.

She grins. "Freddy taught me. He loves to cook and for a while the only way to get close to him was to cook with him. I found out that I actually like it."

"Who'd have thunk it?" I shake my head.

"Not me. That's for sure. So, what are we doing today? I have it all planned out tonight but I got nothing for the day."

I purse my lips together thinking about the kind of activities she'd like to do, which in this small town isn't much. "How about going shopping?"

I hate to shop but for Yna I think I can stand it.

"Okay, but I have to make time to see my family. They'll kill me if I don't."

Liz is still asleep on the couch. When I go to shake her, she groans and pulls the blanket over her head.

Realizing that Liz took the couch, I have to wonder where Jack slept last night. I know he didn't sleep with me.

After several more attempts at getting Liz up, I give up. I'm able to rouse her enough to find out she's meeting David later tonight for dinner, so she's not in for our girls' night out.

Jack comes into the kitchen, grabs some bacon and puts

his boots on, ready to go to work.

He doesn't even look in my direction, which makes me think he's taken the first chance he can to get me out of his hair and get back to work. His long-sleeved red and white lined shirt is unbuttoned and he looks a little tired. Probably exhausted at having company for two weeks.

I feel terrible suddenly.

"Gotta go to work for a little while, but how 'bout you beautiful young ladies meet me for lunch?" Jack asks not even looking at me.

He's out the door without waiting for an answer or kissing me goodbye. My heart sinks and I feel a little disconnected.

* * *

Funny how different Yna and I are. Her idea of a good time is hanging out at one store for an hour and then hanging out at different store for another hour.

After our third store, I don't think I can stand it anymore. "Okay, we've got to meet Jack. Where are we eating?"

Jack has been on my mind all day and I have wracked my brain trying to figure out if there is something I missed last night.

Have I done something wrong? Is there some remark I made to make him angry? I just can't put my finger on it no matter how much I try and it is driving me crazy. I want lunch time to hurry up, but as is usually the case with me, time slows down to a weak crawl when I want it to go faster.

Yna's cell phone sings a song I don't recognize, something that doesn't surprise me because I don't listen to music much. I haven't gone out dancing since the night I was here at the Civic Center.

I am totally boring.

"We can eat anywhere that's convenient for you," Yna says into the phone. She's got three bags hanging on her arm while I have nothing.

She turns to me. "You want pizza?"

"Sure."

Walking away from me Yna picks up shirts and blouses as she talks animatedly with Jack. A hint of jealousy enters my veins.

She flips her pink bedazzled little cell phone closed, turns to me, and holds up a strapless green top. "This will look awesome on you sweetheart. I think you need to buy something."

"No, I don't."

Her eyes narrow. "What's going on with you? I've been telling you all morning about myself, it's your turn."

I purse my lips together. I have to figure out what to tell her without really telling her the truth. It's bad enough that I already get pity from Jack. I don't want pity from Yna. I want to be carefree and I don't want to think about my boring life or why I'm here or what's going to happen when I reach my lonely apartment. "I live alone in California. I've got a great job at a marketing agency. I don't have a significant other. I've traveled a little for work . . . there's really not much to tell."

"Do you go out?"

"What do you mean go out? I have a job. I go there. Sometimes I go out to eat." I don't tell her those lunches are meetings.

"I mean do you go out out. Like in dates, girls' night out, dancing?"

I pick up a pink shirt that looks eerily like the one I messed up the night I got in a fight with Jean and I sigh. "Well, I guess I go out every now and then. I guess."

She studies me for a few seconds while I pretend to ignore her. Her eyes narrow, her lips purse, and I swear I can see a little puffs of smoke coming out of her ears from the corner of my eye. "You do absolutely nothing don't you? You probably sit at home and throw yourself into your job."

Frustration fills me. I had a great life before I came here, or that's what I thought anyway. "What's wrong with throwing myself into work? I've done well for myself. I'm completely self-sufficient; I don't ask anyone for money and I'm content with where I am."

She takes a long look at me. "Really."

It's not a question. To her it's a statement. She continues to look at me, trying, I guess, to find the right words.

"What? Why are you looking at me like that? I'm fine."

Yna walks away with her head down, lost in thought.

She pays for the green shirt she has in her hands, shoves it at me, and dares me with her eyes not take it. "I saw you looking at it. It's cute. You should buy yourself something every two weeks. Sort of like a reward for surviving."

She stops suddenly and gives me another measuring look as soon as we exit the store. "Look, I know we're meeting Jack in an hour and all that, but we need to talk. No, strike that before you say anything. I need to talk. You can listen or talk or whatever you want to do. But I think I have the right to talk about things. It's time."

I say absolutely nothing. My blank stare must have jarred something in her. "Look, you can look at me like that if you want to but it's time, sweetie. It's just time."

She dumps her bags into the back seat and drives us to the park.

The park is great. You can enter it on only one side, it has a great walking/running path, and the large trees are scattered throughout make it a great place to park and talk.

Shit. Here we go again.

Yna turns off the car, gets out, and sits patiently on a bench under a tree. It's a little cold out, but nothing we'll need a jacket for. I hesitate getting out, but I know I have to. I have to face another barrage of questions.

As soon as I sit down she starts talking, "That accident didn't ruin just your life. I don't know of a person in this town it didn't affect. Well, the people that count anyway. It was horrible when I found out. I walked out of the store and you were gone. Ten minutes later there were ambulances everywhere. I knew in my heart you were in whatever was going on. When I got to the car wash, I got out, Jack was there, and he wouldn't let me get close. He just kept telling me to let the people work. Let the people work."

She stands up and walks a few steps before she turns to look at me. "He looked horrible. He looked like he was in shock. He put his head in his hands every few seconds. Then Meg got there because, well, it's a small town and people are gonna get on a phone and start texting everyone. It was a nightmare to watch her freak out. It was like Randy all over again. I thought God was going to take another person I loved. I got so angry at God. I blamed him for everything. I don't blame him anymore but, I did. I really did."

She waves her hand. "Anyway, when you were in the hospital I went almost every day and then you got out and you didn't want anyone near you. I knew it was because you were hurt and scared but then I got mad at you. I was angry at you for a long time. For not being there for me when Randy passed, for getting in the car with Vic, for not seeing what he was . . . then again, who could have guessed what he'd do? Certainly not me. I never knew he was that violent, Linda. Did you know that?"

She glares at me waiting for a reply. "I deserve answers Linda. I've earned them."

I look down at my hands that have been gripping the bench so hard they're turning white. I know she deserves answers. I owe her. Jack has given me the opportunity to make things right. "He did lots of things to me. It wasn't the first time I was scared of him. He was drinking. He was mad at Jack and when I told him I didn't want him anymore—he just snapped. No one had ever told him no."

I tell her about the first time we had sex, about how he always made me tell him where I was going to be, how he changed how I dressed, the make-up, how jealous he was, and how much I did for him because I thought he loved me. I let it all out. Every time I tell her something new, she cries harder but I don't give her a break.

I tell her about my remaining year at high school and how I stopped going out, stopped talking to my family, went into seclusion, the many grueling surgeries I endured. I even tell her about how boring my life is.

She takes it all in, interrupting only a few times. She looks into the distance and nods, shakes her head, or buries her head in her hands saying over and over again, "I didn't know."

It feels good to let it out and confide in her. It's a nice change to be able to let someone else in.

She dries her eyes after a long while and smiles at me. "Thanks. I think we needed that. Let's go eat."

I have to laugh at her. After all the crying she does, she still wants to stuff her face. "Yeah, let's go meet Jack."

We meet Jack at the Pizza Parlor—the same one where Lucas and David met me a lifetime ago. Jack doesn't look at me much and carries the conversation mostly with Yna.

I try to engage him in conversation, but he doesn't acknowledge me. I begin to get the picture that maybe he's in love with Yna or something and I just didn't know it.

Jack leaves after only thirty minutes, saying he has a ton of work to do and he won't be home until late. Again, he doesn't look at me and leaves without a word.

Yna sees or mentions nothing about his behavior but grabs my hand on the way out and brings me closer to her. "I have a surprise for you. I think after all we've talked about, this is going to be just what you need."

Frowning at her, I ask, "What are you talking about? I don't want to see anyone else. I don't think I can handle it."

She smirks at me. "You'll like this one."

We end up going to her family's house. They're a close knit family who seem genuinely happy to see her. I can't even imagine what kind of reception I would get if I walked into my family's house. They'd probably kick me out.

As we're leaving her aunt's house in the outskirts of town, Yna gets a phone call. Her smile gets bigger and her eyes light up.

"Your surprise is here. We're going over to Jack's house."

Going back to Jack's house is a great idea. I can rest, hide in my bedroom or take a nap.

Yna's Kool-Aid smile only gets bigger the closer we get to Jack's house. I think maybe Jack has something to do with this somehow. Maybe he bought me something or made me something and he's just acting distant to throw me off.

I don't recognize the maroon Chevy truck outside Jack's house. I figure it's one of Jack's workers.

A slim, tall silhouette appears on the large porch. I don't recognize the figure and even when he steps out of the shadows his face seems strangely familiar, but not enough to spark a definite name.

"Hey handsome." Yna smiles and goes to hug him.

He smiles.

Dimples.

I know those dimples.

"Hey Linda."

Jason smiles at me and my stomach drops. He is now beyond good-looking. His soft wavy hair falls over his eyes just enough to make him look sexy. He's taller, more muscular, and his face is clear of all blemishes.

I grab my hair to put it in front of my face. This perfect hunk can't possibly be my gift. I look to Yna and her smile gives me the answer. He is definitely my gift.

I give him a weak smile, and find that I have absolutely nothing to say. Does he blame me for Lucas? He is, after all, his cousin. Maybe his family hates me.

I never did talk to Lucas' mother or his family. I just left everything behind me. Not once since I've been here have I thought about visiting them. To be honest, I had no intention of seeing anyone. I came to do a job and that was it.

They are both looking at me. I realize that they're waiting for me to say something. "Hi, Jason."

It's all I have. I had no idea Yna was going to do this and I find I'm completely taken aback and totally unprepared.

Jason's taller than I remember, much taller. He drops his head when he enters Jack's house to avoid the top of the door. He seems to have been here many times before because he nonchalantly opens the fridge and grabs a soda.

He motions for us to sit at the bar with him and I numbly move to sit, thankful that I don't have to rely on my wobbly legs anymore for support.

"So, Yna tells me you're in marketing."

This is a statement and not really a question, so I simply nod.

"Hey, you want something? I just grabbed something

for myself. I wasn't thinking."

He gives me a pointed stare that seems to sear through me. I don't know what's wrong with me. I feel like that stupid little girl all over again. Clearing my throat I answer him. "I'll take some water."

"Me, too," Yna says still smiling broadly.

Jason grabs the drinks from the fridge and I have to wonder how it is that he feels so comfortable here.

After a few seconds of complete awkward silence in which we're just staring at each other, Yna breaks in and this time it's her turn to clear her throat. "You ready to go?"

My eyes narrow. "Where are you going?"

Yna smiles. "Not me, sweetheart. You two. Jason's taking you out for a walk and dinner tonight. I set it all up."

Fear shoots through me. I don't even know this guy and I'm expected to be alone with him for the next few hours. I'll be catatonic by the end of the night if things continue the way they are going right now.

Jason smiles warmly at me and suddenly my fear dissipates. Jason was the one who saved me that night at the Civic Center. He's the one I was looking forward to seeing the night of the accident. "Where are we going?"

Jason grabs his keys and opens the door for me. "My family is having a barbecue today. I figure we can go there. Then maybe go to a movie or something."

I stop in my tracks. I don't want to see his family. They hate me, they'll want to bring up Lucas, they'll want me to explain to them why Lucas was killed when I wasn't. I'm already shaking my head before he finishes talking. "No, Jason. I can't possibly go there. They hate me."

I say the words out loud without even thinking about them. The instant I say the words, I regret it because the look in his eyes is that of pain, sorrow, and horrible pity.

"Let's just go. You'll be fine. You'll see."

I turn to Yna who smiles encouragingly at me, throws me a thumbs up, and waves.

I can't help but feel anger. I know her heart's in the right place and I know she thinks she's doing the right thing, but honestly I just want to crawl in a hole and die.

With no other choice left, I walk out of Jack's house and step into Jason's truck.

We ride in silence for what seems like forever. My hands are sweaty and I'm holding them tightly on my lap. I feel underdressed, gawky, and disillusioned.

"We don't have to go to my family's house if it makes you nervous, but they don't hate you. Not by a long shot."

I say nothing because I don't want to call him a liar to his face. He's trying to make me feel better, I know that, but it only serves to make me feel worse.

He puts his hand on my lap. "Look, how about we go to a movie. The drive to Odessa will give us a chance to catch up on things."

I stare down at his hand. I don't say anything and I can't answer because heat radiates from his hand and into my body, suffocating me.

He looks to me and then to his hand and slowly removes it. "Sorry."

Saying nothing, we leave Fort Stockton and head north to Odessa. It's a good hour and a half drive through lonely roads. The seclusion of the town is both amazing and scary. The closest large city is Odessa and that's not saying much but the drive, as usual, takes me back to the old times when Omar and David would race each other to Odessa.

We'd all hop in two cars and go to a movie or hit the mall. Omar once made it in forty-five minutes, or so he said, and every time we'd climb into a car heading north we'd try to beat that time.

We were so reckless and carefree. Never once did I imagine anything happening to any of us.

Jason takes his time, leans back and starts asking me questions. "So, where did you go to school? Where are you living in California? And what have you been up to?"

He smiles, knowing he's asked me several questions at once. I answer all of his questions with as few words as possible and with absolutely no enthusiasm. I've already established that my life sucks and I'm a complete bore.

I think back at the first time I met him. How I thought I was acting mysterious and how I actually felt a magnetic attraction to him.

I glance over at him and his smile widens, those cute dimples form, and he looks to be trying real hard to keep up the conversation.

But then he drops a bomb. "Have you ever wondered what would have happened to us had we gone out on that date? I wonder sometimes . . . well, to be honest lots of times. It would have been nice to have gotten to know you. To see you pissed off at me, to see how great of an arguer you are. I've always felt like you were the one that got away."

Startled at his admission, I'm at a loss for what to say again. I shake my head. If I am completely honest, I'll tell him that he hasn't really crossed my mind much. Sure, I think about how he took mine and Vic's relationship at the beginning or whether or not he blamed me for Lucas, but never anything past that. Jack has completely taken all of my time while I've been here so, no, I really haven't thought of him much. "Sure, I think about it sometimes."

Which isn't a complete lie, but close. He smiles again and I do get a weak flutter in the pit of my stomach. I smile back and I guess he takes that as some kind of waiver because he puts his hand back on my lap.

I do nothing, but I decide to shift things back to him. "So what have you been doing with your life?"

He hesitates. "Well, not much. Not like you. I didn't go off to a big city or anything like that, but I did go to college for all of a semester. I didn't do well, though, so I came back and now I work at the plant near my house. I come to Stockton pretty regular. I see Jack most times. We've become pretty good friends."

He looks over at me again. "I called him last night pretty late. Told him I was gonna take you out tonight because Yna had asked me to. He sounded a little angry at me after that; maybe I caught him at a bad time or something."

I knew Jack was angry. He hadn't talked to me much today, but I didn't say anything. "So, you're taking me out because Yna asked you to?"

I feel a little angry for that one.

"No, I ask about you all the time. I always have. Jack usually told me he didn't talk to you much, but well, you're staying at his house so . . ."

"Jack and I haven't spoken in years. It was nice to see him again though."

"Yeah, Jack's a great guy. He's liked by everyone, but no one will cross him. He can be mean."

I smile. "Yeah, he can."

"Anyway, I haven't been out on a date in a very long time. I spend a lot of time with my family. I guess you could say I'm pretty boring, but I like it."

I laugh for the first time since I've seen him. "You are not boring. Me. I am boring. I do nothing after work and I certainly don't date. At least you can remember the last time you dated. I can't even remember dating."

He throws his head back and laughs. "See, already something in common. Let's be completely boring together tonight."

After that, I actually end up having a good time. We watch some ridiculous movie about zombies, eat at a nice steakhouse because I can't get steak like that in California, and then we go for a walk in the mall.

No pressure, no more questions. He slips his hand into mine as we walk and, at first, it feels a little awkward, but then I try to let myself have fun and he doesn't push me.

On our way back home a little before midnight, he tries to kiss me. I have to draw the line somewhere. While I've had a great time, I just don't see it anymore. Not like I used to.

I step away from him and give him a weak apology. "Sorry, I just can't right now."

He holds my chin gently and kisses me on the forehead. "It's okay. I've really enjoyed myself. We should have done this years ago."

I climb into his truck and wonder again if I would have fallen in love with him years ago. He is absolutely gorgeous, his manners are impeccable, and he has handled me with kid gloves all night. What is wrong with me?

"Do you think we could see each other again tomorrow? I would like to take you out somewhere else."

Jack's image suddenly appears before me. I just can't do it. I gaze at Jason and I can't stand it. All I want is to be with Jack at this moment. I have completely lost my mind. "I'm leaving tomorrow. I don't know when I'll be back."

I throw him a thin smile. It's been nice. Yna was right. I did need this. I needed to know that I could go out and date again and that I wouldn't crumble and I'm not scared anymore.

He says nothing the remainder of the drive home but he does slip his hands into mine. He doesn't bring up Lucas or the accident. I guess those things are too painful for him or maybe he feels like it'll be too hard for me.

When we get to Jack's house, he walks me to front door. "Linda, you are beautiful. You take my breath away. I'll see you tomorrow. At least think about it and if you change your mind, I would love it."

He picks up my hand and places a gentle kiss on my wrist. I feel nothing. Jack did that not too long ago and it was all I could do to keep standing.

I nod because I don't trust myself to say anything else. I could've told him absolutely not, which is what I am feeling, but I don't want to hurt him.

When I walk into the house, Jack is waiting in the dark for me on the sofa.

Chapter 32

I slowly move toward the bathroom to shower. I know I'm going to take forever under those hot steaming jets. Out of the corner of my eye, I see the kitchen's a wreck. He must have had a party or something without me.

Since Jack hasn't talked to me all day I decide to ignore him.

"It's past midnight."

My eyes narrow. "Are you my father?"

Suddenly, I'm angry at him because he's been ignoring me and because every time I looked into Jason's eyes I saw Jack.

"Where did you go?"

His voice thunders through my body.

Fear, dread, and anger course through my body.

I ignore him and walk into my bedroom. I don't see Yna, so I can only assume she's sleeping in Jack's bed again.

"Where did you go? Did you kiss him?" He runs his hands through his dark brown hair and then they're at his side, his eyes accusing me. Flashes of Vic enter my mind.

"Do you care? No, you don't. You ignore me all day. Why do you want to know?"

"I do care. How can you say I don't?"

"Because you ignored me all day."

"You had a date with Jason."

"I didn't know. Yna set it up."

"You didn't set it up?"

"Of course not. How could I? When could I? That's ridiculous. Is that what you think?"

I don't even let him answer. I grab my clothes and jump in the shower, half expecting him to grab me forcefully and push me against a wall.

Men are infuriating. One minute he's smiling, then he's ignoring me, and now he's accusing me.

"I'm sorry. I thought you wanted to go back to him."

Jack's appearance in the restroom doesn't startle me this time. Next time I need to seriously consider locking the door.

The steaming water isn't hot enough so I make it hotter, almost scalding. I put my head under and continue to ignore him.

"I missed you today."

I close my eyes. It feels good to be missed by him. It all makes sense now. He hated me going out on a date, so he got angry and ignored me.

"Why didn't you just ask me then, instead of me having to wonder why you were suddenly so angry with me?"

He throws a towel over the shower door. "Because I'm a man."

I smile. Exactly. He's a man.

I step out of the shower covered by my towel and take a good look at him. His green eyes are looking at me closely. I realize that he's always looking at me like that—like he wants to throw off the towel, pull me to him, and lose himself in me. A shiver goes up my spine.

Jack pulls me to him and I can smell his scent. I take a deep breath trying to breathe as much of it in as possible. He drops his head and kisses me slowly. He has never yelled, pushed me, or hit me. I can never see him laying a hand on me. It's a different kind of love: passionate, intense, and adoring.

Abruptly, he releases me. "You have a long day tomorrow. Get some sleep."

He walks out without another word.

Tomorrow.

All day, all week, I've been trying to ignore what will happen tomorrow.

I'll have to face Vic.

I will have to see him. I'll have to look into his dark eyes and remember what he's done; remember the ragged emotions he used to invoke so easily.

What will he look like now? Will I still feel that magnetic

pull toward him like I used to? I close my eyes and see his face. He is looking at me intently in front of his house. Smiling at me outside of the Pizza Parlor. He's arguing with Lucas at the Rat Hole. He's asking me if I need a ride home after my marathon run. His eyes glare at me wickedly just before he hits me.

The evil I saw right before he crashed his car.

I see it all in my mind and I can't seem to escape the memories. They will be with me forever, everyday, second after second. He has branded himself to me for life and in a sense I have become a great big part of his.

I wonder if he thinks of me, of what we could have become, of how things could have been so very different.

I have to be strong. Victor is my demon. I have to face my demon. He haunts me.

I take a deep breath. I will survive. Jack has made me live again. I will never go back to what I was—an empty, lifeless shell.

Jack.

He has been my lifeline.

I shake my head to clear my thoughts, step into my bedroom, and change into one of the huge oversized t-shirts I got from Jack's dresser.

I find the kitchen clean when I come out, but Jack is nowhere in sight. I'm guessing he is asleep in his bed. I feel a little bit of disappointment but shrug it off because I know it's for the best.

I lie on my bed looking outside. I love this town. I always have. This is my home and I've missed the smells, the sights, and the people.

I will leave soon, and regret and longing fills me.

"Would you like me to leave the hallway light on?" Jack asks me from the door. He has checkered pajama bottoms and no shirt. His muscles flex even as he stands there motionless.

I only shake my head.

Instead of walking back to the couch, he turns the lights off and climbs into bed with me. My heart skips a beat and immediately I feel the heat emanating from his body but this time, I welcome it.

"Did you have a party? I saw lots of dishes."

He chuckles. "No, Liz tried to cook. It was a disaster until Yna jumped in and then they started to argue. Thanks, by the way, for leaving me with that."

I smirk. "Did they really fight?"

"Yeah, but they both enjoyed it. David did too. He kept telling me that maybe they'd fight with water."

"Water?"

He gives me a lopsided grin. "You know, he thought we could have a wet t-shirt contest. It's okay, but Liz took off again with him and Yna's in bed already. That left me with the kitchen."

I feel a little guilty, but not much. "Sorry."

"Don't worry, it was fun."

He turns me around slightly so that my back is turned to him and hugs me from behind. "Goodnight, my love."

It is the closest admission to love I've gotten in a while but I don't allow myself to hope.

I put my head down and try to melt into him, enjoying the feel of his strong arms around me.

Sooner than I expect, he is asleep. His rhythmic breathing is soothing but I cannot sleep. I have something I need to do before I can sleep.

Careful not to wake him, I slip out of the bed. I sit at the small side table in the room, curl my legs under myself and start to write. I watch him sleep and he gives me strength.

Chapter 33

The morning is hectic. Jack has let me sleep in so I'm running around trying to stay busy as I get ready to go to the courthouse. I have been dreading this day since I got Jack's phone call.

Liz has many questions about today's events, but I ignore her and pretend to be too busy to answer any questions. Jack finally soothes her by explaining a few details, but I choose to tune them out.

I walk into the bathroom to put on a little make-up. My eyes are red and look bloodshot and scared.

Already.

I haven't even seen him or started this insane event, yet here I am already looking like a scared puppy.

Before I can think, we are in Jack's truck. David shows up as we're backing out and hops in the backseat with Liz. He says nothing but I hear shuffling in the back and know they are sitting close together whispering.

Jack grabs my hand and squeezes. "I will be with you every step of the way."

I know he means well but he can't be there every step. I alone have to walk up to the font and speak. I alone have to face my demon.

I nod solemnly but remain silent.

The courthouse parking lot is packed. After ten minutes, Jack finally finds a parking spot. I'm shaking by then and I can't seem to control my voice. "There's a lot of people here."

My voice shakes. Jack takes my arm and guides me into the building.

Parole hearings, from what I have learned on the internet, are typically pretty boring because there are usually only a few people there. Today, though, people are interested in the proceedings because of Victor and his family's notoriety in the town.

Going through security checkpoints at a prison is nerve-wracking. It's uncomfortable when the guards look at you like you're hiding something.

When we walk in to the conference room, there's a panel of stuffy looking people; two males and one female write hurriedly on a notepad.

Victor isn't here yet, but his family is. His mom and dad sit in the front row and Lilah sits behind them with other people I don't recognize.

Lucas' family is on the other side and Jason sits holding Lucas' mother's hand. He smiles at me encouragingly when we pass. Jack and I sit together in the front row.

"You okay?" Jack asks me when we sit down. My legs are shaking, my heart is beating fast, and my hands are cold. "Yeah, I'm fine."

Suddenly there's a hush that moves across the room. I turn away from Jack and stare at Victor's face. He looks older, leaner, and more built. He has a barbed wire tattoo that crawls across his neck like a vine.

My heart skips a beat. I want to cry. I want to run away. I feel myself suffocating. His eyes find mine and he stops walking. Our eyes meet. I can't breathe.

I shake my head. Things could've been so different.

Vic smiles at me a little and I can't believe it. Why would he smile at me? Does he not realize what I'm doing here?

The proceedings begin quickly with a description of Vic's life for the last five years. How he's been a model inmate, how he's taken college courses, how he's found God, how he's helped others and completed hours upon hours of community work.

I feel Vic looking at me. A shiver like electricity runs through my body. I feel naked.

Suddenly it's my turn. I'm called up to speak and at first I don't think I can do it. Yna and Liz put comforting arms on me, but it's Jack's strong grip that gives me the strength to slowly walk up to the podium to speak.

From my jacket pocket, I pull out a hand-written a piece of paper.

I take a deep breath and recite the letter I wrote last night as I watched Jack sleep.

For five years I've been trying to figure out what it was that I'd say when this time came.

Not once could I bring myself to write a single word down.

Last night I was forced, again, to relive that fateful night that has changed not only my life, but also the lives of those around me, and around Lucas, and, yes, even around Victor.

I take another deep breath and forge ahead.

I loved Victor. Part of me will always love him, the idea of him. He was my first in so many ways that I'll never be able to forget him. He haunts my dreams, my thoughts, and my days. It was my fault that I didn't get out of the car that night. It was me who didn't get out when I could.

I smelled the alcohol on his breath. I saw him take big drinks. I saw the anger in his eyes.

And I felt the fear, the terror, and the desolation.

I knew then and I know now that there was nothing I could have done to stop him once we were on the road. He made a conscious decision to strike Lucas with his car.

I felt and I still feel that his intentions were to not only kill Lucas, but to also kill us both.

I don't know why we survived and I don't know how, but someone up there thought we needed to live.

I've spent the last five years hiding. I have been in prison right along with Victor. I've been estranged from the people I love and I've been dealing with that one night every day of my life.

Every time I look in the mirror, I'm reminded of that night. I can never forget.

But we were the lucky ones.

I finally look to Victor and tears blur my vision and this time I welcome them because I do love him and I know, even now, looking at him sitting there, I know that he still loves me.

Things could have turned out differently. Victor, you could have had a wonderful life full of hopes and dreams and you still can. I still can.

But Lucas can't. He will never be able to kiss a girl or get married or have children. His mother will never be able to see her grandchildren or see the white wisps of grey touch his hair with age—because you decided to ram his car.

You and I and God know the truth.

I know now what kind of a person he really is.

He is overbearing and wants everything to go his way. He is mean, unfaithful, and he treated me like property instead of like a girlfriend.

What would have happened if I had been killed or someone else had been murdered?

He wants everything for himself. He found me weak at a time when I was already self-conscious and naive.

I allowed him to do this to me. I let this happen. I never realized what was happening to myself until seconds before his car rammed into Lucas' car.

I will have to live with that guilt, but he will have to live in jail.

I turn to look him in the eye and this time I don't flinch or look away. I meet his gaze head-on.

People have to know what kind of a monster he is.

He will do it again, his family blames everyone but him—and they will allow him to kill or hurt someone else.

I take a deep breath and forge ahead knowing that my next few sentences will hurt him and possibly cause him to stay in prison longer.

Victor purposefully and deliberately jumped the curb with every intention of doing bodily harm. He was drinking and angry, but he knew exactly what he was doing.

I am guilty of not seeing Victor for what he really is—heartless.

Victor took Lucas' life because he felt threatened by him.

Lucas was a wonderful person who didn't deserve this. I didn't deserve this.

No one did.

I look back to the panel.

No one does.

You cannot, in good conscience, allow a man like Victor Balentez to get out of prison after just five short years. It is unfair to the memory of Lucas and his family to let him out after only five short years.

Is Lucas' life worth so little?

Victor has not taken responsibility for his own actions; instead he chooses to place blame on others.

My face is scarred for the rest of my life, but I am alive.

Victor sits in prison, but at least he is alive.

Lucas died knowing that a car was headed his way. I saw his face. The terror and fear is embedded in my heart.

I implore you to send Victor a message. Do not let someone who takes no responsibility for his actions out of jail. He must learn from this. He must be held responsible.

He must stay in jail.

I can't believe I did it.

I am able, after all these years, to face my demon.

I take my seat next to Jack and he puts a comforting arm around me and gives my arm a heartfelt squeeze.

The only sound after I finish is the panel scribbling notes on their yellow notepads. Lucas' mother weeps quietly behind me.

I look to Victor to see what he thinks about my letter and I see him glaring at me. Anger radiates from him and I see neither love nor supplication, only hatred.

The hatred is so real that I can almost feel it suffocating me. A chill creeps through my body and goes deep into my bones and I reach to Jack's hand for comfort.

Vic sees my movement and I see his jaw clench and his fists squeeze so hard that I can see the whites of his knuckles.

Jack sees him and pulls me closer to his body protecting me, kissing my forehead. He trails a comforting kiss on my temple, on my scar, and then moves toward my ear. He starts to whisper something, but I can't look away from Vic for he is watching me intently. I have seen that look before. Anger, rage, abhorrence, and disgust cloud his features making him look gaunt and more menacing.

As soon as Jack puts his mouth to my ear, Vic is out of his seat and hurling himself toward us. Fear shoots through me and disbelief causes my body to freeze. After all these years, Vic still can't stand seeing me with someone. Doubt clouds my mind; maybe he hates me for what I've just done.

Whatever the case, he is not able to get to me. I see him pushing people, desperate to get his hands on me. Bailiffs, his lawyer, Lilah, and even his father struggle to stop him, but he is able to get close enough that I hear his threat. "You will always be mine."

My body starts to tremble and I am shaking my head. Jack and a prison guard are between us now and before I can do anything, Jack punches Vic violently sending his head backward so that his head hits the table. Lilah screams something at me, but I don't hear what she says.

I turn and walk rigidly away. I can handle no more of

this. I have done what I was supposed to do and I am finished.

Vic has probably sealed his own fate by what he has just done to me.

I walk through the double doors and try to catch my breath. Escape and my little apartment call to me. I want to be alone. I want to go hide. I have to go hide for both my sanity and my fear. I packed this morning, gathered all of my things so I know that all I need is to get to Jack's and pick those things up and I can be out of here in less than ten minutes.

I scan the parking lot looking for a means to escape. "Linda? You okay?"

I turn, recognizing that voice in an instant even though I only just remembered it last night.

Jason has his hand on my shoulder. I just want to get away from here.

"Can you take me to Jack's house?"

He smiles at me. "Sure."

He guides me to his truck and we ride in silence.

When he turns into Jack's property gate, Jason turns to me. "I couldn't stand it in there listening to all that crap about how great he is now. He killed Lucas."

I can't trust myself to talk. He obviously wasn't there when Vic bounded over the table with so much hatred in his eyes trying to hurt me.

"I'll come by later and talk if that's okay. I know you're not in too much of a mood right now, but I'd like to talk."

I can only nod.

Goodbyes are hard so I'll spare Jack and myself the anger, finger-pointing, and the hurt. I grab my bags and look around quickly for anything I may have missed. My phone is in the kitchen with my computer. I turn to get them and run right into Jack standing in the doorway.

"Linda, I need to talk to you." His eyes are steel, his lips are tight, his jaw is clenched, and I can almost hear his teeth grinding.

He is obviously furious about my leaving without him. A goodbye can obviously not be avoided.

I smile at Yna who's standing right behind him, but the

smile doesn't touch my eyes.

I let Jack in before I shut the door. "Can you give me a ride to the airport?"

We can say our goodbyes in the truck on the way. It'll be easier with him occupied.

"No."

Whipping my head up to look at him, I am astonished. Never has he told me no. Not once.

He locks the door behind him and blocks my get away. "We need to talk. Right now."

I shake my head. "That's what we've been doing for the past week. We can talk in the truck."

"You will not run away. Not this time."

"I'm not running anymore. I stopped running the second I got off that plane."

"You're running to get away from me. You're running to get away from this town even though I know you love it here. And you're running away from us."

"There is no us. I live somewhere else. My job is somewhere else. This . . . us . . . can't work," I say with a sweep of my hand.

He takes a step toward me, his lips pursed. "You and I are just getting started. Finally. We are happening. We will have a life together. You can't deny the feelings we share."

"Sometimes love isn't enough. I know that now."

"Are you talking about us or about Victor? Victor wasn't in it for love. He was in it for possession, power. It was never about love."

Tears well up in my eyes. Shit, all I do here is cry. More reason why I have to get the hell out. "I see now that you are right, but I loved him. It didn't matter."

He steps closer to me and cups my face in his hands. "Do you love me? Tell me you love me. Or am I wrong? Tell me to my face that you don't love me. Because if you don't love me I will take you to that airport and I promise not to ever contact you again."

My eyes widen. What would my life be like without him? Now that I've felt his tender touch, his strong arms, and those luscious lips against mine.

He has been there from the beginning.

My eyes widen more.

Realization.

He has been there *since* the beginning.

Introducing me to the guys, coming over mad as hell at Lucas for what he put me through, finding me out on those country roads to invite me to a party, taking care of me, always there understanding. Unconditionally, even when I really screwed up. He has always been there.

He loves me. He really loves me.

I look into his green eyes and I see comfort, love, tenderness, consolation, and, thankfully, protection.

I love this man. I could never bear to be away from him again. I would be miserable. "I love you."

With those simple words, he loses his composure. He crushes me against himself repeating over and over again those words I thought he'd never say. "I love you. I love you."

He throws me on the bed. The hunger is evident in his touch and the fervor of his mouth. I meet him touch for touch desperately trying to bring him closer but not being able to. I feel his touch soften just enough to become bitterly tender. His eyes are filled with so much emotion that a tear escapes. I wipe it away, feeling my own start to fall. "Why are you upset?"

He traces my scar and I find I am not ashamed and I do not cringe away. "Because I have loved you for so long that I can't believe I finally have you. You have always been there in my eyes. I have watched you grow up, fall in love, be destroyed. I have loved you through it all."

Disbelief fills me, but I can see it now clearly. Blind. I have been blind. Getting up reluctantly from the bed, he asks, "Can I show you something?"

He leads me out of the room before I can respond and we're walking up the stairs. I have never seen this part of the house. He always said it was a mess, but it's not. Plush tan carpet covers the floor, there is a sitting area at the top of the stairs, and five doors, all of them closed. We pass all but the last one. He looks to me then and smiles. "This one is yours."

When he opens the door, I find myself speechless. The room is decorated in wrought iron décor and the sun we bought together in Alpine sits above the bay window near the oversized mahogany desk. A black laptop, printer and telephone sit atop the desk, waiting for me to start work. The view through the bay window is beautiful. I can see for miles. "When did you do this?"

"I've been making this house for you for a long time. Hoping one day you'd come live with me. Could you leave the city life?"

I think of my bland apartment and the hateful sounds of the city. The rush, the taxis, and all those screaming loud people next door and outside. "Yes, I could leave the city."

"There's a nursery next door. Three of them up here,"

My heart skips a beat. I turn to look at him both astonished and speechless. This is Jack and I love him. I smile. "Okay."

Suddenly, I know what I want to do. "I've got something to do."

Jack looks at me quizzically but says nothing. I run downstairs and grab my phone.

My first call is to my mom who is more than happy to hear from me. The conflict with my father will have to be solved in person. I will make sure of it.

The second call I make is to my sister Meg. I suddenly want to see my nephew more than anything and I promise to visit her sometime in the next few weeks.

After thirty minutes, Jack comes looking for me. "What are you doing, beautiful?"

And for the first time I feel beautiful. I feel alive and happy and content and excited for my life ahead.

Victor will always be in my thoughts. I don't see myself ever releasing the past, but I can accept it and come to terms with it. Jack will be here to help me when the time comes that Victor is released. We'll handle it together. My family, my friends, and Jack; we'll do it together.

I beam at Jack and throw myself in his arms. "I'm finally getting me back."

According to national statistics, one out of three teenage girls is abused, either physically or emotionally, by a boyfriend.

Just because you can't see the bruises, black eyes, or swollen lips doesn't mean that abuse is not present. Learning to identify a positive relationship can become difficult as the person being abused looks within for the reasons or excuses to justify the abuse.

A gripping, gritty, and realistic portrayal of teenage life in our high schools today.

For More Information on Physical and Emotional Abuse, Please Visit www.Grelibooks.com

Acknowledgments

Again I am astonished at the complete and unwavering support of my editor, Stacy Kinney, who has been a savior when things didn't always turn out like I wanted it to.

Also Raul Villesca, my web and cover designer, who is always ready to answer any of my questions day or night and who has worked so hard on all projects.

My family who has supported me, even though I stay up into the wee hours of the night trying to get things just right.

Maryissa Gonzales and Leslie Poole for reading my manuscript and giving me honest and sometimes brutal criticism.

Freeport Intermediate staff for allowing my books to grace their bookshelves at home and in their classrooms.

I thank you all.

And of course, I thank God for giving me the strength, fortitude, and opportunity to accomplish my dream.

The Truth about ME

MG VILLESCA

Turn the page for a preview of the next book in

The Me Series
By MG Villesca

The Truth About ME

I hate looking in the mirror.

I don't know who she is. Sometimes I don't think I've ever known. She's some girl who doesn't know what she's doing half the time, who's afraid to ask questions, who has no one to turn to, who has nothing to live for. That's who she really is now.

Who I've become.

Once, I was a girl that was sure of herself. Who took life by the horns and steered it in whatever direction I wanted.

I used to be outgoing and the loudest one at the party. A few months ago, when Victor Balentez, the superhunk, had his party, I was the center of attention and I didn't go home until the sun came up. Some of my "friends" begged me not to go home.

I was *that* girl people gravitated to. I could make a monk laugh at a funeral. I could make any number of my friends smile with a simple look.

I was careless yet methodical. I took chances all the time, like when I knew Steve and I were going to get caught stealing the answers off Mr. Farks desk, but we did it anyway.

Most times, though, I wouldn't get caught when Steve and I took things. I'd align every detail of our pilfering trip to ensure the most success with the least risk.

I was awesome to have around.

Now, I have this tube stuck in my arm and all I want to do is yank it out.

My mom came in earlier today from work wearing her correction officer uniform. She didn't even look like she wanted to see me. Her accusing eyes never left me. The counselors said I had to stay until my lab work was complete but, seriously, who cares? I sure don't.

At least here I get three square meals a day (not a chance that I'll eat them, but it's nice to know they're there) and I don't have to listen to Carl beat up my mom when he's had too much to drink. People stare at my mom like she's some kind of fungus.

I'll admit to looking at her like that too, but for reasons completely different than her looking like a butch alien freak in her gray and navy blue beautiful attire.

Here at least I'll have some relative peace and quiet.

The nurse comes in and tells me to rest and lie down but I told her she was absolutely crazy. Who can rest at a hospital?

It should be an oxymoron. Rest/Hospital.

No.

More like—let me wake you up every thirty minutes so I can give you something so you can sleep.

How about just leave me the hell alone so I can get my beauty sleep.

Beauty.

That's a relative term. No one really knows what true beauty is because that's an opinion. People lie and say it's from the inside that counts but it's not true. No one wants to get to know you when you're ugly except other ugly people. So really, the outside counts more than people are willing to admit.

Not me, though.

I'll admit that beauty comes from the outside first. Then depending on what you look like, people will try to get to know you but not before.

No one's come to visit me. Steve called an hour ago but he sounded distant like he didn't know what to say. Everyone else has chosen to stay away and pretend that what happened didn't really happen.

We all know the truth though. Sooner or later they'll join me here as well. It's just a matter of time.

"You ready to go Ms. Rivas?" Nell, my therapist, asks.

I roll my eyes at her because she and I know that it's a waste of time. She's a waste of time.

She refuses to call me by my name.

I don't need her.

I don't need anybody.

"Come on. You're session is only an hour long. You'll survive. I'll help you from the hospital bed. It's only across the hall."

My sigh is loud, obnoxious, and hateful. "Just call me Julie."